Madame Cristobel's Secret

by

Sharon Sobel

Dedication

Dedicated, with Much Love, to the Newest Star in Our
Family Constellation
Ione Elena Nellis
with the Hope That You Will Always Shine with Joy
and Wonder

Chapter 1

Abruptly stopping on the crowded curb, Francesca was nearly struck down by a carriage racing down King Street. Distracted pedestrians, momentarily blinded by the swirl of dust and dirt on this late winter day, bumped into her unmoving form, knocking her into the roadway. While mumbling curt apologies or expressions of irritation, they nevertheless continued to stream around her, like a torrent of water diverted by a solid impediment in a riverbed.

But these things she scarcely noticed, for she sensed that something was terribly wrong. Her small shop, on the opposite corner, was not as she left it the evening before, when she closed the draperies so the bright sun of the next morning would not fade the precious books displayed in the window. That small display was now askew, and the draperies parted. The neatly lettered "Closed" sign on the door hung on its end, so it wasn't altogether clear if one should try the door latch or not, enter or turn away to continue on to another shop. Francesca was sorely tempted to do the latter, but she really had no choice. It was her shop, after all.

She took a determined step forward, caught her toe in a cracked cobblestone, and tripped into the stream of morning merchants, customers, and men of affairs. But they swept her along the modest façade of FW

Wadsworth, Bookseller and Antiquarian, where they unceremoniously abandoned her to her own business as they surged along.

A trick of the light startled her, for it looked as if a strange woman stared at her from the window. But that wan and slightly mussed creature was herself. She struggled a bit with the lock—though that was nothing unusual—and took a deep breath before entering what had always been her quiet sanctuary along one of the busiest streets in London.

The sight of her ransacked shop knocked her to her knees. She staggered for a moment before reaching blindly for a chair, missed, and dropped to the floor. The disarray that greeted her was no mere mischief of an idle intruder; here was a violation of the most malicious sort.

Precious books were strewn on the floor and across the broad wooden countertops; glassware and lamps had been thrust aside so that maps and old prints could be unfurled upon a mahogany table. A box that had contained a sea captain's ivory pipes was upturned and its contents on the floor. The metal door to a birdcage was left open, and its stuffed inhabitant pitifully plucked of its colorful plumage.

And for what? Francesca pulled herself up, realizing she might never know what the intruder sought or if anything went missing. It would take her days to put everything to rights, and months before she might search for something in its old, familiar place, and find it missing. Hers was a shop of unique treasures, where a customer came in looking for something most specific and left with a rare find, absolutely unexpected. The same might be said of herself, for it was her father who had amassed this eclectic collection, and she could not say for certain what was hidden on the back of a shelf or remained in a dusty box in the attic. Only yesterday, Mr. Dickens' son had come by, and avowed that there was nothing like an old curiosity shop to spur on the imagination. He'd probably learned that at his father's knee.

As one, the melodic chimes of twenty-seven clocks filled the air, perfectly on schedule. Francesca dutifully wound them up each evening before closing, as had been her father's practice, so they would greet her in the morning. Her regular customers might stop by, just upon the shop's opening, to listen to the brief concert, and possibly buy something they had contemplated on a previous visit. Mr. Dickens, who always had something to say, had solemnly noted that there was nothing like the bells of so many clocks to remind one of the urgent passing of time. Just now, they seemed like a death knell, though for what, exactly, she could not say.

"Francesca, I am just back from the docks and there is a shipment, recently arrived…" The familiar voice behind her hesitated and then softly continued. "…from China. What happened here? The rats get in?"

"Just one rat, I fear," she said, turning to face her neighbor. "Good morning, Will. Though I'm not sure there's anything good in it."

"When? How?" William Picardy, purveyor of fine cheeses and marmalades, for once had nothing sensible to say. "Who?"

"I have only just opened the shop, but I doubt I'll ever have those answers. Perhaps someone most desperately wanted a new edition of *Rob Roy*, or needed a map to find the best route to the coast."

"Perhaps the blighter needed some fine silver to finance his trip to America after he reached the coast," Will grumbled, and bent down to retrieve a book from the floor.

"The silver. Of course." Francesca suddenly dropped the ivory pipe she held and ran to the back of the shop where beautiful silver and gold pieces were kept under lock and key. The lock was secure, the glass unbroken. Whatever the intruder sought, it was not anything easily pawned. "No, he didn't find it."

"What do you think he did find?" Will asked, sorting through the row of books he now balanced along his left arm.

"I can ask myself the same question. I am not quite sure. It is not as easy for me in my own shop as it is for you, in yours. I daresay you would know in a moment if someone walked off with the cheddar."

"And I would be able to track his scent through the streets of London." Will sniffed as he laughed. And then, more seriously, "You need a witness, someone who saw it all."

"It is too bad, then, that I haven't encouraged squatters. If only someone sleeping under the table was awakened by our thief," she said tartly.

"Still, a witness is a good thing," Will insisted.

Francesca glanced up and met the gaze of Madame Cristobel, a rare and exquisite automaton fashioned in the workshop of the master clockmaker Mollinger more than a century ago. The automaton was the only witness to the crime; her unblinking eyes saw everything that passed in the shop. A small wooden lady, she sat at her miniature drawing desk, in her faded velvet gown, her hand poised over tiny sheets of paper upon which she once wrote pithy little commentaries. But her mechanical works were long broken, so if she had observed anything last night, she was no longer capable of revealing it. Though beautiful to behold, she was now little better than a violin without strings, a clock that couldn't tell time.

"Francesca?" Will prompted her to return to more immediate concerns.

"Do you not have to open your own shop, Will?" she asked, idly. Her thoughts were elsewhere.

"Yes, yes, there is that," he said impatiently. "But there is something odd about these books."

"That no one is interested in them, except for you? Please help yourself to them and put that fine education of yours to good use."

"Well, there's nothing odd about that. A man can choose to do something tasteful with his life other than study law or religion."

" 'Tasteful' is certainly the right word," Francesca murmured.

Will studied the collection along his left arm and inserted another volume between two others. "All of these books were written by someone whose name begins with *B*."

"Perhaps the thief made off with his favorite books by Lord Byron." She sighed.

"Then he missed a few. Here's one, and yet another."

"Then there is our first clue. Is that what the Metropolitan Police call that? A clue?"

"Yes, I rather think they do. And this may be more of a puzzle than you might first think." Will looked around the shop, at the rows of cluttered shelving. "Do you organize the books alphabetically?"

Now her good friend seemed to suggest this mess was her own fault.

"I try to, I really do. But I scarcely have the time, while I'm alone in the shop. My father won't be back for months." She wished she had a better excuse. "No, they would not have been in alphabetical order," she admitted.

"Then your thief sought these books out. He was looking for something most particular."

Will was right, of course. Such books would not have haphazardly fallen off the shelves in correct order. Francesca glanced back at Madame Cristobel whose pale blue eyes looked as knowing and complacent as ever.

"Byron it was, then," Francesca said lightly. "The mystery is solved. I shall endeavor to organize my inventory so selections can be easily found in the future, preventing a book thief from getting frustrated and making such a mess."

Will shook his head, clearly bothered. "Perhaps he wasn't looking for a book."

Francesca slapped her hand down on the counter in a gesture of frustration, finally engaging Will's complete attention. He looked at her in confusion.

"Will, did you not just prove to me that he was very specifically looking for a book?"

"A certain type of book, certainly. But then why bother with the maps or the pottery or that poor little bird in the cage. I hope the fellow was already dead, by the way."

"If you mean the bird, he was already dead before Anne Boleyn met her fate."

"My, that's a rather unpleasant reference coming from a sweet young thing such as yourself."

"I'm in the mood to be rather unpleasant this morning," Francesca said, and kicked an old painted milk can. "Neither am I a sweet young thing."

Will gently slid the books down his arm so they stood upright on the counter. He flexed his arm, which must have gotten stiff under the weight of the volumes.

"That is the truth of it, my darling Miss Wadsworth. Your friends know you're quite worldly, your business associates know you can be as tough as any man, but the casual acquaintance—a new customer, perhaps—would see you as an innocent, a young lady minding her father's shop. It makes me think you would be an excellent opponent at cards."

"I cannot abide cards," Francesca said. "And why would it matter to anyone if I am sweet or bitter?"

"It might matter, one day, to the man you wish to marry."

Francesca started to protest, when Will put up his hand, stopping her mid oath. "And it might matter to someone who intends to do you harm. Someone was here, looking for trouble. He might be back when you are here quite alone. You cannot rely upon your estimable wit to scare him off."

"What should I do, then? Keep a pistol in the drawer with the cameo brooches?" Francesca managed a practiced sarcastic tone, but in truth, the thought had already occurred to her.

"Would you be willing to use it?" Will asked sensibly. "I imagine you would be about as effective as…" He glanced about the shop. "That doll that sits up there on the shelf."

"That is Madame Cristobel, and she is no doll. She is quite old and infirm, so kindly treat her with respect."

"Madame Cristobel," Will said solemnly and bowed in her direction. "No, I have a better idea. I suggest you hire a man as your assistant."

"Surely you are not offering yourself?"

"Surely I am not. I am perfectly happy with my bramble marmalades and quince preserves."

She was not surprised by his answer. "You think I should hire a bodyguard, then."

"Nothing so drastic. Perhaps hire someone to organize this mess, sort through the books, sell off some of the old silks to the ragman. It doesn't matter what he does, so long as you are not alone in the store."

She nodded, thinking it over. It wasn't a half bad idea, though she wasn't sure she wanted to share this intimate space with a stranger. She did not reside here, of course, for she retained a small coterie of loyal servants in her parents' modest but elegant town house. But she had already given some thought to setting up a small office in the attic flat at the top of the stairs, where she might research the provenance of merchandise for which no history was thus far available. Since such work could only be accomplished while the shop was closed, she thought she might spend occasional evenings on site, and even use the little kitchen to cook modest meals for herself.

But if she had someone to mind the wares and deal with her customers, she could spend her daylight hours upstairs doing what interested her more than dusting the shelves, and perhaps even write a bit about the things she discovered. The prospect was elysian, even if it meant giving up some degree of privacy.

"I shall consider it," she said, noncommittally.

"I have considered hiring someone as well, for business has been brisk. And yet, my finances are always tight. Perhaps, if I manage to find someone to work with me in the mornings, you can hire him for the rest of the day? If I remind him to scrub his hands of the smell of cheese?"

Francesca smiled for the first time this morning. This prospect was getting better and better.

"I most certainly shall consider it," she amended.

****

Mr. Nathaniel Endicott dodged between two carriages on King Street, perfectly pleased that his long-ago days on the playing fields at Eton served some practical purpose. He apologized to a well-dressed man who was startled when he jumped onto the curb, avoiding a filthy puddle, and just about avoiding him.

"You managed that quite well and are surely accustomed to our London traffic," the man said, smiling. "And yet I see you are holding a map of the city."

Nathaniel glanced down, having forgotten that the wrinkled paper he held was a veritable announcement of his arrival as a newcomer to these busy streets. "I have not been here for many years, though managed to practice my skills in other cities, other countries."

"You might have, indeed. But I doubt the vehicles were driven by the residents of insane asylums. One might think that the horsemen of London particularly aim to run down anyone daring to cross the street." The man frowned as he brushed some imaginary dust off his dark jacket. "It is a battlefield."

"I hope I am up to the challenge, then, as I may

sojourn here for some weeks."

"Best of luck to you, sir," the man said, and then scowled as a carriage splashed through a puddle. "Do you require some assistance in finding your destination?"

"Thank you, but I believe I am quite near. I am looking for an antiquarian shop in this vicinity. I have the direction right here..." He held up the small hand-written map and tried to orient himself.

"No matter with that scrap of paper," his companion said cheerfully. "It could only be FW Wadsworth you seek, for the shop is a landmark on King Street. It is just yonder, past the cheesemonger. In fact, it is more likely that you will lose yourself once you're in the shop, for there are wonders to behold there. Not the least of which is FW Wadsworth. You may wish to purchase something in the cheese shop before you go on, just to sustain yourself."

"You have been most helpful, sir," said Nathaniel. "I was advised not to expect this from the citizens of London."

"But then, if we knew what to expect every time we set forth on a journey, there would be no point in visiting." The man tipped his hat and went on his way.

Nathaniel looked after him, wondering how a stranger could possibly know that he truly did not know what to expect here in London, and if his visit would prove a fool's errand. But his advice seemed sound, and Nathaniel had not eaten in several hours, and he would undoubtedly require some sustenance.

****

Will was right, but then, he usually was. Francesca had known him since they were children and certainly well enough to appreciate that he was too well educated to have ever aspired to be a cheesemonger and purveyor of sweet condiments. And yet, despite his parents' protestations, it suited him. He was uncommonly good-natured with his customers, some of whom were demanding enough to frustrate the most amiable soul. He cared about his merchandise, traveling regularly to farms in Holland and Belgium to purchase delicacies and relying on home kitchens in the English countryside for the splendid array of preserves and marmalade that lined the shelves of his shop. In this, he supported the livelihood of many women and their families.

And he was creative, presenting his merchandise in the most attractive displays, guaranteed to entice even the most resistant of customers into the shop.

Francesca wished she had even a small part of such talent. But she had come into her trade by necessity, inasmuch as it was the best offer she had by the time she reached her twenty-fifth birthday, and by good fortune, for this was her legacy. Her father, Frank Wadsworth was very much alive, but retired from the business he inherited from his father, and his father before him. Francesca's brother was off at sea for several years at a time, and so infrequently was he on solid earth that he continued to sway with imaginary waves even when standing in Piccadilly Circus. Her sister Maribel made a sea journey only once, vowed never to do so again, and remained with her American husband and children in Philadelphia. She was industrious in her way, as Francesca was in hers; even now, Maribel was quite busy with the ladies' auxiliary of the Philadelphia Centennial Exhibition and sent

Francesca newspaper articles in which her contributions were duly noted and praised.

And so, while some women were pillars of their community, or lived under the protection of a husband, or inherited diamonds or great wealth, Francesca inherited a narrow and dusty shop, and a collection of treasures. Or junk, depending on your point of view.

She looked around her, at the merchandise strewn around the shop, at the broken china and torn pages of her business ledger. This was her legacy.

Just now, she was sorely tempted to just walk away and take up home sewing or something of that sort and make her uneventful journey through life in a more sedentary way. Perhaps she could sell flowers and stand outside the theaters with her perfumed wares. Perhaps she would domesticate a feral street cat and teach her tricks with a little red ball.

Francesca rubbed her forehead until her hair came undone from its pinnings. Her present distraught state was in complete disproportion to her circumstances; she was now twenty-six years old, for heaven's sake. She did not live during the reigns of the Georges or in some wretched place on the other side of the ocean. She was an Englishwoman, and Victoria was her queen.

Francesca tucked her loosened hair behind her ear and reached for her apron. Perhaps she should just clean up the mess and get on with it.

And so she did, and so she was several hours later when Lord Anthony Maitland came into her shop.

Francesca had dusted and swept up shards of broken glass and decided to put some delicate merchandise safely away on a high shelf. Once there, standing on a stool, she came face-to-face with the rather exotic face of her old companion, Madame Cristobel, who looked rather forlorn.

"Having a tough day, my darling?" Francesca asked. She blew a layer of dust off the breast of the minute automaton. "Believe me, you don't know the half of it."

Madame Cristobel sat wordlessly at her sturdy desk, the hand that once held a pen slightly aloft.

"Would you could still write your letters. You'd make a fine companion, if one doesn't mind a certain repetition of thought." Francesca pressed down on the tiny wooden hand, but it was stuck in place, fated to forever be in a state of anticipation. "But then, I suppose that would not make you so very different from Mrs. D'Oyley, whose only subject of conversation is the cleverness of her son, the splendid Richard."

"Who is this splendid Richard? I shall challenge him at once," came a voice from between the bookcases.

"Lord Anthony, is that you?" Francesca called out, steadying herself against a wobbly cabinet. "I did not hear you come in."

He emerged from the tunnel of stacked old volumes, looking as elegant and polished as always, in sharp contrast to everything around him. Francesca, not for the first time, wondered if he had a team of valets working on him throughout the day. Or perhaps just one exhausted servant.

"Is that you up there, my dear Miss Wadsworth? I can scarcely see you through this dust storm. What on earth are you doing?" He raised his gloved hand to help her step down from the stool. "And to whom are you speaking?"

Francesca laughed a bit sheepishly as he released her, and she smoothed her hair back. She looked a wretched mess and felt it all the more keenly in his presence.

"There is no one else here, Lord Anthony, and my only companion is Madame Cristobel." She paused and shook her head. "But there was someone else here last night, and perhaps finding no one to entertain him, decided to wreck the place. I have been busy this morning trying to make some sense of it all. He must have been looking for something, but I am not aware that anything is missing."

Lord Anthony looked confused, but perhaps nothing in his experience allowed him to imagine such a violation. "How do you know it was a man?"

Francesca was surprised, for she did not think this would be the cause of his consternation. "I do not know, but it does not look like the act of a woman."

"Then who is this Madame Cristobel, for she sounds suspicious to me," he said, glancing around.

Francesca laughed out loud, and she realized it was the first time in many hours she had been tempted to do so. Her facial muscles felt strained. "She is the wooden lady, up on the shelf," she said, pointing. "A long-time resident of FW Wadsworth. She has been here so long, I ought to charge her rent."

"Madame Cristobel," he repeated thoughtfully. "I don't believe we've met."

"Would you like a formal introduction?" Francesca asked gleefully. Lord Anthony could not have guessed how much pleasure this little charade was giving her, for it was a relief from all her present cares. She turned back to the stool.

"Allow me, Miss Wadsworth," he said, surprising her. It was not so much that he was gallant—for she expected no less of him—but rather that he would risk getting dust and goodness-knows-what-else on his jacket. He edged past her to step up, his arms outstretched as if he were receiving grace. "She's a lovely little mannequin, for all that she has a bit of dry rot on her cheek."

Francesca gestured for him to place Madame Cristobel, desk and pedestal, on the counter, where they studied her for several moments.

"She isn't a mannequin, Lord Anthony. She is an automaton."

"I am not certain I know the difference, though it sounds much more sophisticated."

"Truly, it is. And of course you have seen some manner of automatons before, in the form of those little birds that pop out of Black Forest clocks on the hour, or dancing figures on music boxes."

"Does Madame Cristobel dance, then?" Lord Anthony asked, and picked up her skirt to glimpse her knobby wooden legs.

Francesca playfully slapped his hand. "Silly man. She doesn't dance, or chirp like a cricket. Once upon a time, she moved her writer's hand to craft little messages and illustrations. I am told they were very cunning. But for many years, poor Madame Cristobel has not done very much but stare at my customers."

"She must know a good many secrets, then," he said thoughtfully.

"Of course. And such secrets are safe with her, for she will never reveal them."

"And yet you were asking her about something,"

he murmured.

"Yes, I was. Perhaps I am lonely and lack for good conversation," Francesca said, realizing how true it was.

"I had not realized how very much alone you are. Perhaps we might go to the theater someday," he offered. "Or stroll through Kensington Park."

"Perhaps," she echoed, realizing that he thought her somewhat pathetic, like a charity case. But he had offered such vague invitations before, and they never came to anything. She was not immune to his attractions, but she suspected his mother would be immune to any of hers, such as they were. Lady Margaret Maitland was known throughout society as a bit of a Valkyrie, with little patience for any single young lady who was not directly related to the queen herself.

Francesca was not even directly related to the person who cleaned up after the queen's puppy.

"Or you might get a dog."

She looked at him in surprise, wondering how he knew her thoughts.

"You needn't be so amazed, my dear. It is not as if I suggested you adopt an elephant. A little dog would be a very fine thing, a big dog even better. He would protect you, guard the shop, be forever loyal. In fact, a good dog is infinitely preferable to a man."

Francesca laughed again. "You have a sad opinion of your sex, Lord Anthony. Do you not think there is a single gentleman in all of London, who would satisfy?"

He laughed along with her. "Aye, there's the rub. He would have to be a single gentleman, would he not?"

"That is not the way I meant it, and you know it." She wagged her finger at him.

Lord Anthony caught her hand and kissed it. She started to pull away, but his clasp remained firm.

"I wish I were that man," he said.

Francesca realized, under other circumstances, this might have been a proposal of some sort, and that he had given her a cue to answer him, to proclaim that he was, indeed, the man she needed and wanted. But she knew he was not, for all that he made her laugh. If such a man existed she had not yet met him, and she had met a good many men in her twenty-six years.

The light jingle of bells at the door announced that they had company, and Francesca finally pulled away, though Lord Anthony remained at her shoulder as she walked to the front of the shop.

A tall, lean man stood there, in a shower of dust motes that danced around him.

"May I help, you, sir?" Francesca asked, as she always did. "Is this your first visit to FW Wadsworth?"

"Bookseller and Antiquarian." He finished the sentence for her. His voice was deep with a slight gravelly edge to it, as if he was not accustomed to speaking very much. He cleared his throat. "It is my first visit to your establishment, and I have not been to London in some years."

"It gives me pleasure to welcome you to both. I have lived in London, and in this shop, all of my life."

"Am I speaking to Mrs. Wadsworth, then?"

"You are speaking to Miss Wadsworth, sir. How may I help you?" she repeated.

He glanced over her shoulder and she was reminded that Lord Anthony was still there. But it was not her place to introduce them. This was her place of business, not an evening soiree.

"Tony? Well, I never. What brings you here? I would not have thought that books would have much interest for you." The stranger spoke with an easy familiarity, though clearly, and not happily, surprised.

Why, what was this?

Lord Anthony spoke up at once, as if he waited for this stranger to come through the door. "There are things here besides books, and I find much to interest me," he said, his cheerful manner now turned to ice. "I happen to be regular customer of this establishment, as well as a loyal friend to Miss Wadsworth."

Francesca thought his choice of words were directed to her. But the newcomer seemed to think they were a challenge to him, for he stood straighter and proffered his gloved hand.

"I am Mr. Nathaniel Endicott of Watch Hill in Cornwall, Miss Wadsworth," he said.

"It is the estate of the Earl D'Arcques," Lord Anthony murmured.

"It is. At least, so it was when I left it over a week ago," Mr. Endicott said.

There was some tension here Francesca could not understand, for the two men seemed to be circling around some issue, as well as herself.

"That is a most peculiar way of putting it, Mr. Endicott," she said, reminding them that she still stood between them.

Mr. Endicott turned his dark brown eyes upon her. The creases at their corners suggested he was a man who liked to laugh, but rarely had she encountered such a solemn demeanor in anyone.

"It is not so very peculiar, Miss Wadsworth. The Earl D'Arcques is a very elderly man, whose health changes as readily as the sky over his windblown estate."

"Are you a relation?" she asked.

"Perhaps one who imagines he is the heir?" Lord Anthony asked impertinently. Francesca gave him a warning glance.

"I live on the estate," Mr. Endicott said simply. "Still."

And then they seemed to be at an impasse. Francesca reflected that it was no wonder that there seemed to be so few appealing men in London, if the briefest introduction could somehow set two of them at loggerheads with each other in a matter of minutes. They were ridiculous, really.

"How can I help you?" Francesca asked for the third time. "I have only just reorganized my bookshelves, and I have several copies of *Martin Chuzzlewit.* Mr. Dickens signed them himself. There's one copy of *The Domestic Manners of the Americans*, by Mrs. Trollope, who was a favorite of the Prince. I also have several shelves devoted to books in French and German."

"There are several excellent ship models, and a longtime resident of the shop, whom I have only just met. Her name is Madame Cristobel," Lord Anthony, sounding like a shopkeeper. His mother would have been appalled to hear him.

Mr. Endicott looked curiously at him before shifting his gaze. "Madame Cristobel? As in the poem?"

Francesca considered herself a good judge of

character, as well as of the type of merchandise in which that character might be interested. But she was utterly at a loss here. She thought Mr. Endicott a bookish fellow, and yet he was interested in a broken automaton. On the other hand, perhaps he did not realize that yet.

"She is a lady, which is not what Coleridge intended, and was created in foreign parts. In Trieste, I believe," she explained. "She is an automaton. Or was."

"Sort of like the earl, you see," said Lord Anthony. "Either he is still an earl, or he is dead and is not."

"Ridiculous" was certainly the right word for this conversation. But it was to get even worse.

"Are you employed here, Tony?" Mr. Endicott asked, more nasty than curious.

Lord Anthony took it precisely as Mr. Endicott surely intended.

"I do not require or seek employment, as well you know," Lord Anthony said loftily.

Mr. Endicott walked past him to the table where Madame Cristobel sat at her desk, her hand still in the air. Francesca imagined the automaton gestured to Mr. Endicott, encouraging him to come closer. He did, bending to gaze directly at her face, spending several moments in thoughtful contemplation.

"I do," he said succinctly.

Even so, Francesca was not certain she heard him correctly. "You seek employment?" she asked.

Lord Anthony made a sound of derision.

Mr. Endicott turned from Madame Cristobel and faced them both, with the same determination with which a man might face a firing squad.

"I do. I have just come from the cheesemonger,

down the street."

"So, you have not come here to buy, but to sell," Lord Anthony said. "The fellow did not hire you?"

Francesca put up her hand. "Lord Anthony, did you not mention that you intended to go there yourself, as you are in need of sweet marmalade?" He had not mentioned anything of the sort, but he got the message.

"If you are certain that you do not require my services here," he said, looking at Mr. Endicott while he spoke.

"I am certain I am quite safe with Mr. Endicott, for you can vouch for him, yourself. Can you not?" said Francesca. He did not answer. "And if I have any concerns, I can always rely on my very large dog in the back room, could I not?"

"Yes, he is a real brute, with dangerously sharp teeth. Have a care, Nathaniel, for I recall you don't care much for dogs," said Lord Anthony, clearly enunciating each word. "I will be off, then. But I will be back."

"I enjoy the company of dogs," Mr. Endicott said. "They are often to be trusted more than men."

"Lord Anthony, I look forward to your next visit," said Francesca quickly. "And do send my best regards to your mother."

Lord Anthony scowled at her words and then walked so slowly to the front door, Francesca could have written a novel in the time it took him to do so.

"Does he still reside with the Paragon of Pride?" Mr. Endicott asked. "She certainly was remiss in teaching him manners."

Francesca laughed. "Well, Lady Margaret Maitland is not known for her own manners."

He did not seem to find that funny.

"Do you really seek employment, Mr. Endicott?" she asked, though if he did, why would he insult a man who could very well be her betrothed or close relation?

"You can trust me on that, Miss Wadsworth. A man who has modest means and is wishing to reside in London must make his own way."

"Do you have a place to live?"

"I presently rent rooms on High Street that are not as fine as advertised. They will do for now, but I have no long-term commitment to the landlady." He looked around, and Francesca thought she finally saw the slightest glimmer of a smile on his lips. "Were you going to ask if I wanted to rent the back room? And live with the dog?"

"What dog?" Francesca asked, caught off guard by that smile.

"The very large one with the brutish teeth. Or was that an invention purely for my benefit?"

"I would not say it was for your benefit, Mr. Endicott, but do sit down. We seem to understand each other perfectly."

There was a small table between the bookcases, where customers might sit and read the books they considered purchasing and where Francesca often sat and did her work. She was again reminded of the prospect of a private office, upstairs. Glancing at the breadth of Mr. Endicott's shoulders and his capable-looking hands, she decided he might be quite capable of protecting her and her merchandise. He carefully selected a sturdy chair from among the somewhat rickety collection, then settled in as if assessing its comfort. Or possibly daring it to collapse under him.

"Mr. Picardy told me there was a robbery here last

night," he finally said.

"He may not be entirely accurate, for it cannot be a robbery if nothing was stolen. I am still trying to ascertain what damage I suffered, and if any merchandise has been lost. I did not acquire most of the items you see here, and my father kept indifferent records. I rather hoped to change that." She sighed, thinking of the enormity of the task. "I just haven't done so yet."

"What is it you require in a man?" He paused as her eyes widened. "Of work, of course."

"Of course. I have not yet thought about it very much, but Will Picardy seemed to think it a good idea. I believe I wish for an assistant to better organize the shop, and in doing so, create a comprehensive inventory. That way I will be better prepared if something like this happens again. Also, I have also given some thought to researching the history of some of the treasures we own, and having an assistant would allow me the time to do so." She thought about her other needs. For the shop, of course. "Someone who is able to fix things would be very helpful, as well. As you lived on a great estate, perhaps that was part of your responsibilities?"

She blushed, thinking she was no better than Lord Anthony. Why should she make any assumptions? He did not look like someone who sawed wood or mended fences.

"It is not a very great estate, but is a lovely one, situated on a cliff above the bay. For many years, the most likely job for a fellow at Watch Hill was to warn the inhabitants of an impending invasion. But those times are past, thank goodness." Mr. Endicott idly reached for a book and fingered its pages. "My father is the earl's secretary, as was his father, and as I will undoubtedly be, some day."

"Then you are a man attentive to details," Francesca said, thinking that this would be an excellent credential for whomever she hired.

"I am, indeed. And yet, even with my present expectations, I trained in Trieste for some years as a watchmaker. My great-grandfather lived there many years ago."

"Then it is no wonder you live at Watch Hill."

He looked at her as if this were the first time he caught the allusion, as perhaps it was.

"Yes, I suppose so," he said thoughtfully.

"There are watches and other things for you to fix here," Francesca said cheerfully, glancing at the silent Madame Cristobel. "Perhaps we can advertise your services as a watchmaker and bring in more customers."

"Your requirements for this position already suggest I will have more than enough to do. Is there anything else I should know about in that regard?"

Francesca looked away from Madame Cristobel and studied him, liking what she saw. His face was handsomely expressive, and he sounded intelligent and sincere. First impressions were no prediction of reality, and yet she felt she would like to have him here with her, sharing the work of each day. But what if he finished the organization and inventory in a matter of weeks? Had he not said he was only visiting London? She felt compelled to let him know that their relationship might be longer in duration.

"Mr. Picardy is a good friend to me and often

worries about my safety. It was he who suggested that a man about the shop might discourage intruders. I suppose the same might be said of nuisance customers."

"That they would also discourage intruders?"

She laughed, something she did so rarely while at business. "That a man who worked for me might discourage them, Mr. Endicott." She added "wit" to the man's already estimable qualities.

"But then, you have Lord Anthony to do that. I am sure very little escapes his gaze."

Francesca blushed. "He is seldom here, Mr. Endicott. And he certainly wasn't in the shop when the intruder came in."

"Would the man you hire need be present during the night hours? Must he sleep among the faded tartans?"

"He would be more comfortable on the brocades, I should think," she answered. "But, in truth, I had not considered it. There is a small attic flat, but I fancy I might use it as a study and spend some evening hours here."

"I see. Would that not defeat your plan of hiring someone to guard against intruders? Though I imagine you, yourself, would present a formidable defense."

She blushed again. "You hardly know me, Mr. Endicott. There is nothing at all formidable about me."

"Then I suppose there is much we shall learn about each other."

Francesca had never hired anyone, but she lived in a house full of servants, and she knew who ought to dictate the rules of employment. The man was making assumptions, which he should not. On the other hand, his assumptions were absolutely correct.

"Would you accept the attic flat in lieu of part of your wages?" she asked, impulsively. Her dream of a little office started to blur around its edges. But then, it was quickly replaced by something more provocative and infinitely more appealing.

"Is there a small stove for heat? Adequate furnishings?" he asked, returning her to practical considerations.

"Yes, I believe there are. We shall have to remove some old trunks and hat boxes."

"Then I am sure it will be suitable. I do not require elegant quarters. Shall I start tomorrow?" Now he spoke a bit too quickly, perhaps as impulsive as she.

"Mr. Endicott, I have not yet hired you," she reminded him.

"This is true." He smiled at her, and she was suddenly lost to all reason. He could be a murderer, for all she cared at the moment.

"Mr. Endicott," she said formally, after clearing her throat. "I hereby offer you the position of assistant at FW Wadsworth, Bookseller and Antiquarian."

"And I accept," he said. "When should I begin?"

"Will tomorrow do?"

****

She was a lady who needed protection. He could be a murderer, for all she knew. He could be intent on doing her harm, robbing her business. He could make off with Madame Cristobel in the middle of a dark night, and no one would be the wiser.

Well, perhaps he assumed too much. Her blasted Lord Anthony would immediately jump to the correct conclusion and tell Miss Wadsworth he distrusted her shop assistant's motives the moment he walked into the shop and into her life. The cheerful cheesemonger would bemoan that he had ever sent the mysterious Mr. Endicott her way and comfort her with a Dutch gouda wheel. And Miss Wadsworth, sadder but wiser, would forever regret not asking for references or for more information about his history. That is, assuming he was not a murderer.

In fact, he was not.

Nathaniel paused amidst the throng of Londoners making their way along King Street, each man or woman to his or her business. Any one of them could have wandered into her shop on a sunny morning and inquired about a position that was not even posted in the window. Miss Wadsworth could have hired anyone.

In fact, she had not.

She'd hired him, and he was a very wise choice. She just didn't know it yet.

There was that business about the attic room, though. It offered him the very opportunities he wanted to make himself free in the shop, but he hadn't even seen the place yet. He recalled the attic rooms at Watch Hill, tucked neatly beneath the old castle's crenellations, and hoped he could stand upright without smacking his head in his new lodgings.

For reasons he didn't care to examine, he imagined a scenario in which he did hit his head most painfully and called out for Miss Wadsworth, who would come running up the flight of stairs. She would ease him onto a bed—had she not said there was one?—and try to stop the flow of his blood with her dainty lace handkerchief. It would be utterly ruined, of course, and when he recovered from his injury he would purchase her a new one at the lacemaker. No matter the course of their life, she would always have this small memento of his gratitude.

Nathaniel stopped short, and the man just behind him uttered a curse as he dodged around him.

What nonsense was he thinking? He was not a writer of tuppenny novels; there was not the slightest bit of romance in his nature. He was a man of mechanical skill, devoted to the art of making things work. Clocks, chimes, music boxes…here was his love. He had been tempted by only a few women in his life, and none of them worked out very well.

And yet, he was charmed by the fact that Miss FW Wadsworth, bookseller, was utterly unexpected. If he had imagined her a woman in the first place, she would have been older, somewhat stubborn in her ways, confident that every decision she made was inviolate. He envisioned gray hair tucked under a cotton cap, protecting her from dust and grease. Her gown would be plain and tidy, just like those of the schoolmistress in Cornwall.

In fact, he recalled Miss Wadsworth's gown actually was plain and tidy, an indifferent shade of blue. But no schoolmistress in Cornwall ever looked quite like her.

Chapter 2

Francesca reported for work, so to speak, several hours before her usual arrival at the shop. The sun was already bright on the eastern horizon, and it looked to be the start of another beautiful day. She really ought to put her little bookstand out on the street this morning, to attract bibliophiles as they passed by. It had not been moved outdoors in a long time, for after a wheel broke on the cart, she only infrequently made the effort to drag it outside and prop it up with a brick. But today, it might be done with an utter lack of her own effort because she did not have to manage it at all.

She only needed to ask her new employee to bring it out to the wide doorstep. With a sudden thrill of delight, she realized she could ask him to do anything at all. But when she started to imagine all sorts of entertaining possibilities, she caught herself up short. She was being absurd, of course. She could ask him to do anything at all, but only pertaining to his work responsibilities, of course.

She waved her hand, fanning her warm cheeks. The sun really was too bright, even at this early hour.

But she came early this morning, before Mr. Endicott arrived, because she first needed to do something for him.

She had sold him on the position because of the prospect of the attic rooms; of that she was fairly certain. He seemed merely curious about the shop and his responsibilities the day before, but as soon as she suggested he might spend his nights on the premises, she sensed he was truly engaged. It was certainly convenient, and he would have his privacy. But now that it was promised, she really ought to be certain that the place was habitable. It might already be occupied by a den of wild dogs, for all she knew.

Francesca paused at the door to the shop, her key in hand, gazing through the window. This morning everything looked at rights again. The drapery was as she'd left it; the bookshelf in the window sturdily upright. She put her ear to the glass and heard nothing, not even wild dogs above. And so she turned the key in the padlock and stepped within.

Pausing for a moment so that her eyes could adjust to the darkness, she breathed in deeply and confirmed all was well. The day before, she had been so distracted by the visual evidence of the robbery, she had not stopped to consider the scent of something in the air that was just as incriminating. But she thought about it afterward: the odor of grease, perhaps. The vague mustiness of damp wool. Something else she could not readily identify but made her think of the docks down by the river.

But none of it lingered this day. Today, she could only identify the more familiar scents of dust, yellowing paper, and candlewax that made the shop recognizable as her beloved home. That she did not sleep here was no consequence; she spent many more hours living here than in the Wadsworth townhouse on Edgware Road.

And now she was committed to sharing her

precious space with someone who would bring his own distinct sounds and scents to the shop. Mr. Endicott had thus far not distinguished himself with his own imprint—he had hardly had the time to do so—but she imagined she would soon recognize him anywhere.

Francesca glanced at the large regulator clock on the wall before locking the door behind her. She had less than an hour before he would arrive and much to do. He hadn't been very precise in revealing his plans, and for all she knew, he might arrive with a cart of his possessions, ready to move into the attic.

She ran up the creaky stairs, which had been constructed with a turn every fifteen steps or so, in order to fit concisely into the narrow space in the back of the shop. At each landing it was necessary to climb over something—a pile of books or a box of clay pottery—that she'd quite forgot was there. This did not bode well for what she might find in the attic itself.

In this, she was not disappointed; the three small rooms looked like they had last been sorted through in the age of Elizabeth. The dust was thick enough to batt a quilt. A water stain on the ceiling looked very much like the map of India and not nearly as inviting. And there was evidence of mice everywhere.

What had she been thinking? And why had her new tenant not bothered to see the place before he agreed to accept it as part of their arrangement? Indeed, it was all his fault! No sensible man would have made a blind decision; Mr. Endicott surely would demand to examine an apple before buying it at the greengrocer, yet why would he do less for a place where he would live?

Francesca ran a finger over the Delft tiles around the small fireplace and was surprised to see the grime came off quite easily, revealing the milky hue and deep blue of the glaze. Someone, perhaps her widowed grandfather, had once lived here and cared enough to decorate the place and make it comfortable. She looked around the crowded rooms and thought they would clean up rather nicely, if she applied herself to the task. From the window, she looked down at a small park, having forgotten it was there behind the row of buildings that fronted King Street. A few trees stretched their branches up to the height of the attic, and their shade would afford Mr. Endicott some degree of privacy. Some steps from the window, directly above the stove in the back of the shop, were the remnants of the small kitchen, where a few copper pots still hung on pegs along the wall. And just beyond was the bedroom, where a sagging mattress was neatly covered with a Holland cloth tucked at the corners. The mice clearly had enough to occupy themselves elsewhere and mercifully left this bed alone.

The stale scent of lavender was most noticeable in this last room, perhaps explaining why the wildlife had stayed away.

Having assessed the landscape, it was time to get down to business. Francesca decided to start on the wooden boxes, prying the lid off each crate with a knife she found on a wooden cutting board. Within were books and letters, and framed prints. She pulled out a collection of tiny drawings written by a neat hand, providing a little homily for each day of the week. The drawings were lovely and the accompanying text very fine. Surely they were the work of a lady.

Francesca sat on the bed to study them more closely, and a cloud of dust rose up around her. She sneezed so loudly, she wasn't sure if she heard some sound from the shop below. Absolutely still, her hand still holding one of the prints, she listened more astutely. And indeed, someone was banging on glass.

Dear God, whomever it was would surely break down the door.

Francesca abandoned her cache of ephemera, and raced down the stairs, only just concentrating on not killing herself in the process. Arriving at the bottom step, she heard a deep voice calling her, and already recognized whom it was demanding her attention.

"You will awaken the entire neighborhood," she chided him when she unlocked the door and bade him enter.

"You must be mistaken about the hour, Miss Wadsworth," Nathaniel answered softly, trying to calm her. "I daresay I could hardly be heard over the din of the street." He studied her for a few moments, and wondered if he had been mistaken about the color of her hair for it now looked rather gray. Indeed, everything she wore seemed to match. A bit of cobweb dangled from her ear and he reached out to remove it before thinking better of it.

She frowned and took a step back. "How did you know I was here?" she asked accusingly. "It is somewhat earlier than I usually arrive."

"I thought you would expect your newly hired assistant to arrive promptly for his first day on the job, lest you decide against him even before he begins work." He smiled, wondering why she was so indignant.

"But how did you know I was here?" she repeated, insistently.

He held out his hands in a gesture of supplication and nodded toward the counter, where her satchel and a wicker basket were in clear view of anyone standing at the door.

"It was just a good guess," he said.

She said nothing for a few moments, and then surprised him by laughing out loud. He had not imagined himself such a wit, but then, he was not sure he had ever had such a clever audience.

In any case, it was as if a barrier had just fallen down between them and nothing now stood in their way.

"I should have been more attentive to the hour," she admitted.

"Were you engaged in some work? Preparing the inventory perhaps, and thus leaving me with nothing to do?"

She laughed again. Indeed, this was very encouraging. "I daresay there is more here than anyone can manage in a lifetime."

"That is very good news, then," he said. She looked puzzled. "If that is so, then I shall not be let go for my inability to accomplish much. You appear to have low expectations."

"You are mistaken, Mr. Endicott. I have very high expectations."

Whatever she meant by that comment, it did not seem to have been uttered quite the way she intended, for she blushed and looked away to the table where Madame Cristobel gazed unblinkingly at them.

He ought to be paying attention to the lovely Miss Wadsworth, but Madame Cristobel claimed him just then. He wondered if the automaton's eyelids could be made to move, along with her lips. Surely the mechanism was interconnected, so both functions would perform in synchronization. Her head undoubtedly nodded up and down as they did so for he could just make out the seam on her neck, beneath her lace collar.

"Then I will endeavor to fulfill them," Nathaniel said, a bit distractedly. He was behaving in a boorish manner, entirely undeserved by a kind lady who offered him a job and a home. She would not have deserved it, even if she offered him nothing at all.

He put all temptation of one sort out of his mind and risked temptation of another sort. Miss Wadsworth met his eyes, and he knew himself a fool. The automaton was a bit of mechanical cleverness. Miss Wadsworth was beautifully clever. And beautiful, as well.

She put her hands flat against her cheeks and breathed out a long, low sigh. On her middle finger, she wore a small cameo ring, and he wondered if it was a gift from a gentleman.

"I didn't hear you because I was in the attic, the rooms you shall soon inhabit," she murmured.

"Oh, indeed," he said cheerfully, having momentarily forgotten that. "Well, I have very high expectations for my new lodgings, you realize. I expect they're elegantly furnished with all the requisites for a gentleman boarder?"

She must have known he was teasing, but she shook her head sadly. "I'm afraid it's an unholy mess. I was trying to make some order out of it."

"And decided to wear some of what you found there?" he asked.

She looked confused. Indeed, this was certainly the type of reception to which he was more accustomed from ladies, for they never seemed to know what to make of him. To be fair, he had only just met her. She could not know what he meant.

"The dust and the cobwebs," he explained. "They don't suit you at all, Miss Wadsworth."

He watched a smile spread across her face, as she gradually understood him. Thus encouraged, he was again tempted, and gently touched her, brushing the cobweb away from her ear. Miss Wadsworth's smile seemed frozen on her lips, and he carefully avoided looking directly into her eyes.

"Are you two already hard at work?" Will's cheerful voice called out behind them. Nathaniel heard no footsteps and had no idea the man stood there, watching them. He quickly dropped his hand and turned to face his other employer.

"Nathaniel, I hope you can give me some time this afternoon?" Will said, coming closer, looking back and forth at each of them, as if he watched a tennis match. "I am expecting a shipment from France and will need someone to go down to the docks and sign for it."

Nathaniel nodded his assent, grateful for the interruption. He had come to London with purpose and determination, but things seemed to be moving too quickly, even for him. "If Miss Wadsworth can spare me," he said.

Again, Will looked from one to the other, and Nathaniel knew what he was thinking. It was absurd, because Nathaniel wasn't certain what he himself was thinking.

"Of course. That is our arrangement, is it not?"

Miss Wadsworth said softly, and paused for several moments. "I am only uncertain when you would wish to move into the flat, Mr. Endicott. It is not possible for both of us to clean out the rooms at the same time, for one of us must be down here in the shop during business hours."

"I am prepared to move in with my few possessions this very day, Miss Wadsworth," he said. "But I am also prepared to clean out the quarters myself, perhaps each evening when the shop is closed."

She hesitated, and he wondered what she had found up there. Perhaps there were treasures that she didn't want him to see. Possibly some he would very much want to see.

"I would be a very poor landlady if I allowed my tenant to sleep among the ruins."

"It is that bad?" he asked, hoping she hadn't changed her mind. He looked up at the ceiling, not so much in an attempt to imagine the rooms he had not yet seen, but rather envisioning how far he would fall if the attic floor collapsed under his weight.

"There are several large crates," she said thoughtfully. "And furnishings that are not likely to be of interest to a gentleman. I do not know if you intend to prepare your own meals, Mr. Endicott, but I believe the small kitchen can be made functional. In retrospect, I believe I may have somewhat exaggerated. The place is not so much a ruin as a dustbin."

"And you are wearing some evidence of that," Will said cheerfully and swept some dust off the coronet of her braids. She did not seem to be at all bothered by his familiarity. "This is how gentlemen of old powdered their hair, I believe."

"If their budget did not allow them a pot of talc," Nathaniel added, getting into the same spirit. "They only needed to rub their wigs against the drapery."

Miss Wadsworth shook her head, loosening her carefully pinned up braids. She could not know what effect such an action, dust and all, could have on two healthy bachelors. Nathaniel suddenly wondered about Will, but the cheesemonger grinned at him and winked.

"Oh, for heaven's sake!" the lady said, throwing up her hands. "You may go to your attic, Mr. Endicott. And you to your cheese shop, Will. It is not yet ten in the morning, and I am already tired of this day."

Nathaniel started to murmur something of reassurance; he wasn't even sure what would come from his lips. But his new employer stalked off in the direction of the back room, a slim string of cobwebs dangling from the hem of her gown. The door closed behind her.

"And I am not yet here a day," Nathaniel said, picking up a delicate ivory comb. He wondered if Miss Wadsworth required it for her toilette.

"Take heart, old man. She has devoted herself to her father's business and is accustomed to a succession of oddities, both in her merchandise, and the people she regularly encounters."

"And what of the people she regularly employs?"

Will frowned and shook his head. "I am not aware of any employees and certainly not regular ones. But she will not fire you until a full week has passed, surely." He took the comb from Nathaniel's fingers and studied it for a moment. "I have not seen this before. Perhaps it was among the attic's furnishings, and she thought you would have no use for it."

"Did you send me to her because you knew she would be indifferent to my company?"

Will strummed his finger over the tines of the comb. "Oddly enough, I sent you to her because I thought she would not be. Indifferent, that is. If ever there was a woman who could quite manage on her own, it is she. And yet, I sense she is lonely. Even Victoria needed her Albert."

Nathaniel doubted he was anyone's Albert, for all he was attracted to the lady. But he still awaited Will's answer. "And what of you?"

Will's smile returned. "I am interested in good cheese, fine wine, sweet preserves, and amusing company. I am not in the market for a woman."

It was as Nathaniel suspected but dared not speak directly. Will made his preferences clear, however.

"And what of her friend Lord Anthony?" Nathaniel asked. "When I found him here yesterday, he looked like he would throw me out into the gutter."

"I have no doubt he thought of it. He is exceedingly territorial, as if he does not already own several fine properties, though most are blonde. He comes here often enough, to protect his interests in his one brunette."

This was also as Nathaniel suspected, blast the man. "He is pursuing Miss Wadsworth, then," he said glumly.

"It is odd, but I do not think so," Will said, and shrugged. "Oh, he flirts and threatens her other customers if they dare to come too near her. He brings her small gifts and makes the occasional purchase. But I honestly do not think he is as interested in her as he is with some of the merchandise in the shop."

"Is he mad?" Nathaniel mused.

"Do you mean, because he repeats the same thing day after day?"

"Most people do," Nathaniel pointed out. "No, I mean because he is more interested in old books than in a young lady."

Will looked at him consideringly, and Nathaniel wondered if he spoke out of turn. After all, Will had just confessed his own lack of interest. But it appeared that while Will did not desire the lady, he nevertheless cared about her welfare.

"Are you?" he asked.

"I…I have only just met her," Nathaniel stammered.

"But you will get to know her well," Will said. "Especially as you will be sleeping on the premises."

Nathaniel drew himself up, though he was still not quite as tall as the cheesemonger. "I can assure you that she will be safe with me here."

Will put up his hands, as if to protest. "Yes, yes. That was just the point. Even so, one never knows what shall happen."

Nathaniel grunted. "Would you feel better if I brought another lady up to the attic rooms?"

"Surely you don't intend…"

Nathaniel put up his hands, mimicking Will's gesture. "Rest easy, sir. I am thinking of Madame Cristobel. She surely will be very good company, will she not?"

A short time later, Francesca regained possession of her little shop. She had listened at the keyhole of the door of the back room, until the doorbell signaled someone had passed through the entrance and she assumed Will finally left. A few moments later, she heard the bell again, and a woman's soft voice, and Mr. Endicott answering her. Footsteps approached, but then stopped in the vicinity of her glass-enclosed case of Asian pottery, just outside the door. Mr. Endicott said something, paused, and finished his sentence. The woman laughed.

Francesca opened the door.

"Oh, good morning, Mrs. Montague," she said, as if surprised to find them there, so close to her refuge. "I must apologize for not greeting you in person. But I see you have already…"

"Oh, yes," the woman said, sounding utterly delighted. "I have already met your Mr. Endicott, who has been so helpful."

Francesca glanced at her new assistant and thought he blushed. She had never seen a man blush before, unless one counted the times she watched her brother at sporting events on a hot day.

"I am so glad to hear that, Mrs. Montague," Francesca said. "For Mr. Endicott has only just started working at my establishment and does not yet know the order of things."

"And yet he manages very well, Miss Wadsworth. You have a most able shop assistant." Mrs. Montague sighed, and gave a lopsided smile.

"Are you interested in our Cantonese vase?" Francesca asked.

The woman looked down at her hands, as if she forgot she held a piece of expensive porcelain.

"I did not know I wanted it until Mr. Endicott brought me to this cabinet," the woman explained. "He is very persuasive, Miss Wadsworth."

"Apparently so, Mrs. Montague." Francesca looked at Mr. Endicott, now thinking his reddened cheeks might have been a trick of the early light. "But I believe he has work to accomplish upstairs this day. Mr. Endicott, am I correct?"

He and Mrs. Montague started to speak at once, but he politely deferred to her.

"Thank you, sir. But now I am quite curious: shall you open a new shop floor with merchandise? Perhaps filled with rare finds that are too precious to relegate to the street level?"

"That may indeed be Miss Wadsworth's intent."

"Somewhat like the secret cabinet that contains the treasures of Pompeii?" Mrs. Montague asked. Francesca wondered how the woman knew about the erotica that had been stowed away in Naples, hidden from the ladies.

"I assure you, all the secrets shall be revealed," Mr. Endicott said, glancing at Francesca. She felt suddenly lightheaded, and it had nothing to do with the erotica of the old Romans.

"Thank you, Mr. Endicott," she said tightly. "I will assist Mrs. Montague."

"Certainly, Miss Wadsworth," he said, and grinned. In this light, his hair seemed nearly chestnut, with pale streaks running through. It reminded Francesca of fine-grained dark wood.

The two women stood silently, listening to his steps retreating up the narrow stairs. A creaky door opened, then closed.

"Where did you find him, my dear Francesca?" Sally Montague murmured.

Francesca pried the precious vase from her

customer's hands. "Mrs. Montague, one doesn't go out searching auction houses and crumbling estates to find a gentleman. My mother and father are even now on an acquisitions trip in Asia, and I doubt they will return with a man to attract new customers into the shop."

"But why would they?" the woman asked, quite missing the point. "You already have one."

"Mrs. Montague, Mr. Endicott is not mine. I simply hired him to set this place to rights, to prepare an inventory, try his hand at repairing some of my ancient clocks. He is not a bit of statuary; he is a man."

"Yes, he certainly is," Sally Montague said, and sighed. "Well, whatever the case, I shall certainly return regularly to admire the merchandise. And if you would be so kind as to wrap up that vase, I shall take it with me."

This was an excellent turn of conversation. Francesca had sold absolutely nothing the day before, in the aftermath of the break-in. And she reminded herself that her beloved parents were probably acquiring enough merchandise on their journey to fill the rotunda of the British Museum. Sally Montague's new purchase had remained on that shelf for as long as Francesca could remember and seemed a permanent fixture. But when one was in business, nothing ought to be considered permanent. Everything had a price, sentimentality be damned.

"I shall take it, Francesca," Sally Montague repeated.

"Yes, indeed, Mrs. Montague. Are you walking? I shall put it in cotton wool, to keep it safe."

"You do that, my dear. And some day, if you visit my home, you will remember that it is the first thing that Mr. Endicott sold in your shop."

Francesca thought about the events of the day before, when she was confronted with so many changes, she could barely think straight. Suddenly, there was Mr. Endicott, sent over by Will and quite ready to move in with hardly a thought about it. It was fair to say that the first thing Mr. Endicott sold in her shop was himself.

She wondered if he might have a permanent place among the treasures, and in her life.

What a fool she was!

Quietly, efficiently, she went about her business, wiping off the vase with a soft cloth before wrapping it. Mrs. Montague asked about the price of a small ivory comb that somehow showed up on the counter and purchased that as well. By the time she walked out the door, Francesca had come to think that this promised to be a very fine day.

And then her new employee came down the stairs, blindly feeling his way from behind a wooden chest.

"Mr. Endicott! What are you doing?"

"Stand back, Miss Wadsworth! I can manage it."

Francesca bit down on her fist as she watched the unwieldy chest crash against the banister and then the wall. She ran forward to clear a space at the bottom of the stairs, hoping the chest wouldn't crash into her as well. But Mr. Endicott was stronger than he looked, and stood still for several moments at the base of the stairs until she assured him that he could just let it down.

"What does it contain?" she asked, when it landed with a thud.

He moved his shoulders back and forth, as if testing that everything still worked. They seemed to work admirably. "I have no idea. Is it not yours?"

"Well, yes, of course. But I don't know what it contains. That is why I hired you, if you recall. To provide an inventory of all the goods herein."

He gave her a look of exasperation and tugged on the lock. "It's rusted solid. Have you tools about the place?"

"My father keeps his tools in a drawer behind the counter." She walked toward a large cabinet, wondering which drawer might contain what she needed. She was immediately correct, on her third guess, and pulled out several small metal implements, the functions of which she did not know. "How are these?"

At least, Mr. Endicott did not reveal his exasperation a second time. He spoke very politely, as if talking to an idiot. "They would be very fine if I intended to build a birdhouse. Have you nothing larger? A mallet, perhaps?"

By the time Francesca found a hammer, she was tempted to hit him over his head.

But when he smiled and said it was perfect, she forgave him. How could she not? He only wished to help her, at a time when she felt she had precious few people who would so offer.

On the other hand, she had already struck a bargain for that help. It was like paying someone to be one's companion, a position that defied all the rules of friendship.

"Oh dear. It looks like a collection of old junk," she said, when he broke open the lock. "I am sorry you bothered with it, Mr. Endicott. And you have injured your hand, which is even more regrettable."

He said nothing for several moments, ignoring the

blood pooling on his white shirtsleeve as he sifted through the yellowing papers, bits of wood, and broken porcelain. Uncovering a pale painted face, he stared at it as Hamlet once contemplated poor Yorick.

The bell at the door jingled.

"I must help a customer," Francesca whispered, pulling herself away. Mr. Endicott did not answer, but studied that small disconnected face as if it were, indeed, an old friend, long lost.

****

"Lord Anthony, you must not worry so," Francesca murmured. "Mr. Endicott is quite industrious. Why, he has already sorted through several crates for me."

"But you know nothing about him, and I do," her friend argued. "I do not trust the fellow. How do you know he will not steal your coins and make off with a rare codex or Napoleon's death mask?"

"Do you have reason to believe he will do so?" When he did not answer, Francesca handed him a second cup of tea. "And that is not a mask of Napoleon. Just some poor soul who died in his bed, no doubt."

"I did not even realize you sold such a morbid things." Lord Anthony frowned in distaste and waved off her offer of a third cube of sugar. "No matter, it could be Napoleon. Where is he, by the way?"

"In Des Invalides, I believe," she murmured.

"Not Napoleon, Endicott."

"He is down at the docks. Will sent him to retrieve a delivery from France." Francesca picked up one of the pastries Lord Anthony brought for them to share. He was a most pleasant guest, and they frequently shared quiet moments together. But today he seemed agitated and even disagreeable. "Why do you distrust him so?"

"My dear Miss Wadsworth—Francesca." He looked at her, as if testing her response.

She was wise not to make any assumptions. A gentleman who uses a woman's name with such familiarity should only have one sort of declaration in mind. And she knew him well enough to know that was absolutely out of the question. He had obligations.

"Miss Wadsworth," he repeated, in a tone which would have brought her down to earth, if she had only left it. "I worry about you."

"That is most kind of you, Lord Anthony, for I daresay no one else does. Will, perhaps. But my parents are off in the South Seas, with not a thought of returning to London until they have purchased every carved artifact for sale in every port. My sister is happily engaged in celebratory work in Philadelphia. And my brother is with Mr. Darwin on the *Beagle*, hoping the captain can chart a course far away from our parents. I believe the Pacific Ocean is very vast, and he is likely to succeed."

"It is very vast," he agreed. He was a very pleasant sort, but Francesca often had the feeling he did not quite understand her. Certainly, he did not understand sarcasm.

Perhaps it was a good thing he had obligations, for she could not abide being bound to a man who lacked wit.

She soldiered on. "So, you see, even those closely related to me do not seem to be very worried about my welfare. They have abandoned me with the expectation that I can manage for myself."

"But they do not understand, Miss Wadsworth," he insisted. "They do not know about the break-in, or that you have hired a strange man who will live here with you, or…is that blood on the cloth?"

Francesca followed his gaze to the counter.

"Oh, it is, indeed. I quite forgot it was there. I am well," she said, holding up her hand. "It is Mr. Endicott's blood, spilled when he was opening a rusted lock. And I do not live here, Lord Anthony."

"You might as well!" he persisted. "You are here all the time. And now that rogue will be here as well!"

Lord Anthony's appetite must have returned, for he swallowed a pastry in one bite.

"If I only had somewhere else to go, I would get out more. But unlike yourself, I am not invited to the theater, or balls, or dinner with the queen. And why do you believe he is a rogue?"

"He has left behind a bloody cloth, for one thing."

"Yes, and you shall probably leave behind dirty dishes and a napkin," Francesca pointed out. "What? Did you intend to rinse them at the sink?"

"One cannot equate cake crumbs with a bloodsoaked rag."

"As I am the one to clean up afterward, I should be the one to make the distinction."

"You know much about me, and nothing about him."

"Yes, that is true. But I might know a good deal more in a week's time."

Lord Anthony muttered something and put down his fork with more force than was necessary. "Would you like to attend the theater with me on Friday?"

Francesca's own fork clattered to the marble tabletop. "I would, indeed."

He stood and brushed off his jacket. "It is settled,

then. It is to be a comedy, and my carriage will pick you up at your home on Edgware Road. You see, I know very well that you do not live here."

Francesca crossed her arms over her breast and smiled up at him. "I was not inviting myself for a night at the theater, you understand."

"I would not ask you unless I wished it."

"It is very kind of you, but it does seem a rather extreme way to keep me away from Mr. Endicott."

"Not extreme enough," he said, or she thought he did. A customer entered the shop just as he spoke and provided the neatest excuse for Lord Anthony to escape. He bowed politely and retrieved his hat before navigating the labyrinth to the front door. As the bell jingled again, she welcomed her customer.

And quickly gathered up the soiled plates and tableware and tossed them beneath the counter.

****

Nathaniel dashed across King Street, hoping he had not missed Miss Wadsworth. But then the door to her shop opened slowly as she ushered out a customer, whose arms were laden with a large package. A statue, by the look of it.

"Good day to you, Lord Craymore," she said. "I hope the duchess enjoys her Venus. Oh, and here is Mr. Endicott, just in time to help you."

The man nodded briefly in his direction but waved him off. "My carriage is just yonder, and I have a man waiting. You need not bother."

Nathaniel stood next to Miss Wadsworth as they watched the gentleman walk past several storefronts and knock on the closed door of his carriage, where his driver apparently slept within.

"Poor fellow. It cannot be too comfortable," Nathaniel murmured.

"The statue is not too heavy, for I wrapped it myself. And Lord Craymore is not averse to doing some things for himself, for he was not in expectation of a title until it came to him a few years ago. It doesn't only happen in novels, you know."

Nathaniel glanced down at her, wondering how she somehow knew what she could not.

"How fortunate for him, but I meant the fellow sleeping in the carriage. It must be cramped, by the look of it." A red-jacketed man jumped from the vehicle, avoiding the step, and stretched his arms before he accepted the parcel from Lord Craymore. "My quarters upstairs, by contrast, are as spacious as Kensington Palace."

"You have not slept there yet," Miss Wadsworth reminded him. "You may have a different opinion when I see you tomorrow morning."

"That is true. Are you on your way out?" he asked, remembering the package he held.

"I have left you several sheets and blankets. I trust you know how to make up your bed?"

"I do. Nothing more is required," Nathaniel said, disappointed. "But I rather hoped you could stay."

"Mr. Endicott," she said slowly. "You do know I have a home not far from here?"

"But you do have to eat, do you not?"

"My cook is undoubtedly poised at the window, ready to spring into action the moment I appear. It is a most agreeable situation, even though the dear woman has been preparing the same meals since before I was born."

"I may tempt you, then," he said hopefully. And by the look of curiosity on her face, he might just do so. "Our friend Will has sent me home with cheese and sweetbreads and a baker's loaf. What say you to that?"

"Would you not prefer to have it all to yourself? You have had a busy day and must have an appetite."

"I have, Miss Wadsworth, but there is far too much for even a hungry man. I think Will imagined I might be able to persuade you to join me."

"Dear Will," she said on a note of sarcasm.

"Miss Wadsworth, I believe he cares very much for you." She nodded and smiled, as if he just demonstrated something by his words. Encouraged, he continued. "Did he not send me to you in the first place, so you would have the assistance you require? And now he is worried that you are not eating well."

"Well, yes. He is like an older brother, always checking in on me, sending over packages of freshly prepared foods." She nodded as she looked up at him. Her eyes were very bright, their pupils overly large in the shadowy light of the late afternoon. "As he sent me you."

Nathaniel's tense shoulders relaxed as he placed the package down on the counter. Miss Wadsworth shared Will's understanding of their relationship, thus confirming they were not interested in each other beyond a close friendship. Will had other inclinations, wise not to make public, and Miss Wadsworth clearly accepted that.

"Lord Anthony was here this afternoon. He looks after me as well." She started to unwrap the package and exclaimed over something that looked like dried fruit. She pointed to a little hutch where fine china was displayed, though he had guessed it was for sale and not for a simple meal at the counter.

"How so?" he asked as he withdrew a few plates and a small bowl.

She waited to answer until he brought them to the table, and she studied him again, her eyes narrowing. Momentarily distracted by the intensity of her gaze, Nathaniel put the dishes down before he dropped them on the floor.

"Mr. Endicott, do you believe I am a woman who needs looking after?"

"No. No, I do not. But please appreciate that most gentlemen would consider it a pleasure and a privilege to look after you." He looked briefly away, hoping that he had the right answer. He had the sense he was negotiating a treaty or something of that sort.

"But you do not," she said. He did not think that would be part of the answer.

"I don't?"

"Of course not, Mr. Endicott," she said dismissively, and waved him off. "I am compensating you for the pleasure of my company. It is quite a different thing, altogether."

"But it is indeed a pleasure, no matter the circumstance," he said, feeling rather gallant. "Just now, I cannot think of a better dinner companion."

She pulled up two chairs that were already set near the counter, and tested one of them. "This one is a bit rickety and may need to be glued."

Nathaniel rocked it back and forth and felt one leg separate from the seat. "I believe I can repair it easily enough. Did a customer ask about it?"

"A customer, yes, though he did not come to buy

anything today. Lord Anthony sat on it as we enjoyed tea together."

He came to buy something, Nathaniel thought, irritably.

"Did you say something, Mr. Endicott?" She set the plates on the table and walked to the wash basin, where she retrieved serving utensils. "And we are going to the theater next Friday."

"Thank you for letting me know," he said hesitantly. He sliced off a wedge of the hard cheese and sampled it.

She looked over her shoulder, and smiled. "Lord Anthony is to be my escort."

The damned cheese tasted sour. "I am sure he is very good company," he said when she returned to the table.

"Yes, he is. He also tempts me with many gifts, though never has he delivered such a cornucopia of delights." Miss Wadsworth pulled out her own chair and sat down, spreading a fresh linen across her lap, motioning that he do the same.

Nathaniel sat, watched her slice the several colorful varieties of cheese, and set about the fruits and breads and meats in a neat spiral, as she might display porcelain or clocks in the shop. Her delicate hands made quick work of it, but she seemed bothered by something.

"I believe I have a bottle of port in the cabinet," she murmured, and gestured for him to remain seated, while she stood to retrieve it. He watched her walk away, fascinated by the gentle sway of her gait, her hair loosening over her ears. He knew so little about her, every moment they spent together revealed some new morsel of knowledge.

"Are you a drinker, Mr. Endicott?" she asked upon returning.

"I am not a Quaker, if that is what you are asking," he said, taking the bottle from her hands. The glass was warm where she'd held it. "I know my vintages."

They clicked their goblets together in a celebratory manner, though there was nothing to celebrate but the pleasures of companionship. And Miss Wadsworth proved herself an excellent companion, conversational about the items on display in the shop, the news of the busy neighborhood, and places where she had not been but was nevertheless familiar with. She was a great reader, which ought not be a surprise to anyone entering the shop.

After she spooned a rich pudding onto his now-empty plate, she sighed contentedly.

"I also know Lord Anthony," he said, as if she might have forgotten that.

"Of course," she asked, sitting forward. "You must have played together as children."

He hesitated, thinking that what they did as children could not be construed as child's play. Was there such a term as "child's warfare"? Indeed, he was lucky that Tony hadn't drowned him in the lake for catching the larger fish. "Yes, we did. But we have not corresponded in many years, nor has he had much to do with the Earl d'Arcques. This shop might be the very last place I would have expected to find him."

"Do you not think there is anything here that might tempt him?" she asked.

From another woman, he would have expected such a blatant appeal to flattery, but Francesca was cut from different cloth. She munched on a slice of melon, looking thoughtfully up at a high shelf, where the automaton sat. He wondered if Tony ever asked her about it.

"Lord Anthony presumes he is the heir to the earl, the current master of Watch Hill. He feels he has much at stake there."

She coughed delicately as she chewed the cantaloupe melon, which was as soft as fresh cream. "And so do you, I suppose."

Nathaniel hesitated, not knowing what she had already been told. "It is where I was brought up, where my father is still the earl's personal secretary. Your friend has been gone from Watch Hill for many years, and we have heard so little of him, I scarcely expected to finally meet him in a small shop far from home."

"What an extraordinary coincidence," she murmured, in a tone suggesting that nothing was less so. "He never mentioned anything to me, for all the time I have known him."

Nathaniel rather thought he would not, but he was not being entirely honest to Miss Wadsworth either. Indeed, it was not a coincidence that he and Tony should meet in this place, as he had already spent some time engaging in discreet enquiries before walking through the door of FW Wadsworth, Bookseller and Antiquarian. And when he did so, he was not so much surprised to see Lord Anthony, but to see that FW Wadsworth was a beautiful young woman, and not a bewhiskered octogenarian.

"I realize you and he are friends, but does a young gentleman usually discuss his prospects with a lady to whom he is not betrothed or otherwise related?" He finished his goblet and reached for the decanter of her very fine port.

"It is clear you are not a Londoner, Mr. Endicott, for here one speaks about such things all the time. In conversations I have overheard between these bookcases, I could probably write a full genealogy of half the titled gentlemen with whom I have only the briefest acquaintance."

She held out her goblet, so he could refill hers as well. He made a mental note to replenish her stock, and perhaps encourage more such conversations.

"What are your prospects, Mr. Endicott? If they are promising enough, I shall have to include you in my genealogy."

She had him there.

He shrugged, as if nothing could be of less consequence. "I have no certain prospects, Miss Wadsworth. I am a secretary's son, who was afforded a very fine education because he worked hard and endeavored to please the Earl d'Arcques. The good gentleman went so far as to send me on a tour of the continent, where I spent some time in Trieste, learning clockmaking in the studio of the late Peter Kinzing."

"That is an unusual skill to acquire, Mr. Endicott. I believe most young men favor oil painting."

"But clockmaking is far more practical, and my great-great-grandfather was a rather noted craftsman in his time. He studied with Kinzing himself and had much to do with the famous lady with a dulcimer."

She frowned. "He had an affair with the lady?"

He smiled. "He created the lady. She was an automaton, given to Marie Antoinette, and copied by craftsmen through all of Europe."

"He must have been very skilled," she said thoughtfully. "Do you share his talent, Mr. Endicott?"

"Not nearly so. But sufficient to imagine that therein lie my prospects."

They sat for several minutes in silence, applying themselves to the pudding and the port. Nathaniel sliced several portions of cheese and offered the plate to Miss Wadsworth. She seemed to be contemplating all they had discussed.

"I have an automaton," she said unnecessarily, glancing up at the shelf.

"I know," he said quietly, as if it could not matter. "I met Madame Cristobel only yesterday, though she seemed a bit sad. But did I not already say that I would attempt to restore her mechanical works?"

"Why, so you did, Mr. Endicott. I did not think you were quite serious."

"Oh, I am quite serious, Miss Wadsworth." He settled back into his chair, and heard it groan in protest. Before anything else, he should repair her chairs, before one of them collapsed under him and he cracked his skull on the floor. "Did I not already say that therein lie my prospects?"

Chapter 3

On Friday afternoon, Francesca left Mr. Endicott in the company of a few late-hour customers, as well as Madame Cristobel, who stared forlornly at Francesca as she walked out the door. Mr. Endicott, true to his word, had already removed the wooden lady from her glass case and pried open the lid of her tiny writing desk, revealing the springs and levers within. There was also a good deal of dust and debris, the detritus of many years of inactivity. Mr. Endicott recovered several coins, a brass button, a minute sugar spoon, and set them down carefully on a glass tray.

Though Francesca had longed for the rare pleasure of attending the theater, she now realized she would have enjoyed nothing more than standing at Mr. Endicott's shoulder, watching him work. His hands were as lean as his figure and were capable of both strength and delicacy. He found his way around the aged clockworks with assuredness, for all she doubted he had ever quite handled someone like Madame Cristobel before.

"Something," she corrected herself out loud.

"Do you require something, Miss Wadsworth?" Mr. Endicott asked, without looking up.

"Only your reassurance that you will be able to tear yourself away from my automaton and care for the customers, Mr. Endicott," she said.

He glanced at an elderly gent who was engrossed in an atlas and then at a lady who seemed more interested in him than in the merchandise.

"You have my reassurance," he said. She thought he winked at the lady.

"Then I shall be off. Do enjoy your evening with Madame Cristobel," Francesca said a bit too quickly. And then, as she walked past the young woman who was more intent on Mr. Endicott than anything in the shop, Francesca did some reassuring of her own. "Madame Cristobel is an automaton," she whispered.

"What is an automaton?" asked the lady, as if she didn't know precisely what Francesca meant.

"Miss Wadsworth refers to the famous lady before me," Mr. Endicott quickly explained and abandoned his tools. "These rare and splendid mechanical figures are…"

Francesca used the opportunity to escape from the shop before she changed her mind. The best she could hope is that her employee would simply bore the lady until she could withstand no more and cry off.

For just a moment, Nathaniel hoped that Miss Wadsworth would think better of her planned evening at the theater and decide to stay at his side while he examined the wreckage of Madame Cristobel's clockworks. He was fully aware, for all the while he worked, of her closeness, brushing against his shoulder, sighing as she watched. She clicked her tongue impatiently as he removed little wads of yellowed paper and bits of metal, when he found nothing of any value, and as she held her breath while he determined what was to be done. In each of her soft utterances, he read a question, but she otherwise remained as silent as a congregant at a holy ceremony.

And then she abruptly abandoned him, more or less thrusting him into conversation with a young customer who edged closer and closer as they spoke. Though she asked several questions about the automaton, she did nothing to disguise her interest in him. He ought to be flattered.

But somehow, her overtures neither gave him pleasure nor appealed to his vanity. This had something to do with Miss Wadsworth, surely. But that lady already made it clear she was interested in Lord Anthony and would rather spend an evening in his company than with her employee. What sensible woman would do otherwise?

Nathaniel knew he had no reason to complain, for he knew better than most the importance of status and one's place in society. It was the story of his whole life, and the reason he sought to learn a trade in Europe, and come to London, in pursuit of a mere dream of his future.

After all, it was not Fate that had brought him to Miss Wadsworth's crowded shop of curiosities. He had something to accomplish while here. It was simply fortuitous that an opportunity presented itself so soon after he started his employment.

"I do not understand why you simply cannot purchase another automaton or ask Miss Wadsworth to do the same," said the lady, interrupting his thoughts. She truly was becoming a bit of a nuisance.

"Madam," Nathaniel said politely, rising from his work bench. "Would you like to see our collection of gold watches? Just now, they are the closest we come to providing automatons for purchase. Indeed, one might call them the cousins of mechanical dolls."

"How very clever of you, Mr. Endicott," the woman grinned. "Perhaps I shall wait until you have one available. I shall leave you with my address, in case you need to call on me."

Nathaniel had lost the thread of this conversation, more intent on reading words on a little scrap of paper that he found wrapped about a spring. "Is reformed...heaven over hell." Some words of Martin Luther, perhaps.

"There are many more to be had on the continent, my dear lady. The name of Peter Kinzing is there revered for his workmanship. You may have overheard me tell Miss Wadsworth that he was an Austrian gentleman who crafted a lady playing a dulcimer for Marie Antionette. No one has ever surpassed him in the art."

The bell at the door jingled, and heavy footsteps trod on the wooden floor. Nathaniel caught a glance of neatly brushed blond hair visible above the row of bookcases and recognized the gentleman he met on the street not many days ago.

"Mr. Dickens," the lady murmured.

The footsteps halted.

"And to whom do I owe the pleasure, madam?" the gentleman asked.

She blushed, and looked away.

"Can I help you, sir?" Nathaniel asked. "Is there something that interests you?"

The man was as affable as he was when they first met. "I am only interested in seeing how my new friend is making out. I just purchased some excellent cheese down the street, and Mr. Picardy told me that you were now gainfully employed and had found permanent quarters as well. As I suggested, you did not need that flimsy map at all; you are perfectly situated."

Nathaniel grinned, and said, "Indeed, everything was settled within an hour or so after we met. I have no experience in such things and yet seem to be managing it to everyone's satisfaction."

He suddenly remembered that they had an audience. "Would you like to see the watches, madam?"

"Oh, no, no," she demurred. "I will return at a more convenient time." She held up her hand to silence him when he protested.

"At your pleasure, madam."

She smiled rather grandly at Mr. Dickens, even more so to Nathaniel, and swept out of the shop.

"You need not be so modest, sir," Mr. Dickens observed. "One could think you have been doing this all your life."

"I feel like I have," Nathaniel groaned. "I have never faced such a barrage of interruptions in a day's work. It's nearly impossible to get anything done."

"You can start by telling me your name."

Nathaniel laughed and did so. "And, of course, I now know yours."

"Yes, yes," Dickens said impatiently, and waved him off. "Everyone does, though it is for my father's fame and not my own. But it is one of the reasons I enjoy losing myself in the shop, usually reading some dusty tome. No one bothers me here, though I confess I like to flirt with the beautiful Miss Wadsworth."

Nathaniel had no business being bothered by this confession, and yet he was.

"Where is the lovely lady, by the way?"

"Miss Wadsworth is at the theater," Nathaniel said. "Do you wish to leave her a message?"

"Not at all, Mr. Endicott. Did I not say I was here to see you?" Mr. Dickens tapped his foot against the wooden floor. "I am curious, for this seems to be a most unlikely situation for a gentleman such as yourself. Are you here because of the lady?"

Nathaniel caught himself before answering in the easy manner in which he and Mr. Dickens had initiated their friendship. He came to London holding his secrets close to his chest, and the last thing he desired was for his story to appear in a book by a prolific novelist.

"I am here because of a lady, though not the one you mean. There she is, watching us from the table. I know something of clockworks and automatons, and Madame Cristobel intrigues me." There, he already said too much.

"I prefer Miss Wadsworth, myself."

Nathaniel did, as well, but he had so little to offer her except for himself. It was the automaton that held tight to her own secrets and might be persuaded to reveal his. But his real fear was that he chased a dream. It looked and felt real enough, but when he reached out to grab it, he awoke in his shabby rooms. While Tony, the man who stood in the way of those dreams, was with Francesca at the theater and undoubtedly trying to seduce her.

"Nathaniel?"

He blinked, and was back in the shop, in the present, with a man who wanted to know his story.

"It is a muddle" was all he said.

Mr. Dickens rose to his feet and gathered up his

purchase from the cheese shop. "I enjoy nothing so much as a muddle, for there is true satisfaction with figuring it all out. Whatever your story, do not be discouraged. You seem the sort of man who would be willing to fight for what is yours. Did we not agree that London is a battlefield?"

"So we did," Nathaniel said, and smiled.

"I will return from time to time, not just to peruse the books, but to see how your story is coming along."

****

Francesca wished she had spent some time and money to purchase a new dress for occasions such as this. Of course, she could scarcely remember when she had an occasion such as this, but that was of no consolation as she rummaged through the outmoded offerings in her wardrobe. Everything she owned looked as shopworn as her shop: gray and blue and utterly practical designs that were perfectly acceptable behind a counter, but rather boring for a young lady being escorted to the theater. Inasmuch as the Theatre Royal was in Covent Garden, patrons might assume Lord Anthony was accompanied by a fruit seller.

He must have known she would appear somewhat less than acceptable, especially in the company he usually kept. But then, perhaps he hoped to impress his friends, who might assume that he was doing charity work and taking an unfortunate dowd for an unexpected treat.

Francesca pulled a soft blue wool dress from her sad collection and recalled when she wore this once-fashionable garment at a cousin's wedding service. It was years ago, and she wasn't sure it would still suit her, but she had very few options. It seemed to have resisted menacing moths, and perhaps it would also resist critical comments. She held her breath and pulled it over her plain cotton shift.

By the time she heard a knock at her door, she was somewhat satisfied with the results. The gown was a bit more snug than it had been when she was twenty-one or so, but the effect was rather flattering. She unearthed a blue Wedgwood brooch that would keep a knitted white shawl in its place, providing the solution to a revealing neckline. And she twisted her long brown hair into a flattering chignon.

"Yes?" she called out, though she knew who would have knocked at her door.

"A gentleman's here for ye," said Margaret, her housekeeper's niece. Or cousin. Or cousin's niece. Francesca wasn't quite sure of the particulars but knew what the girl would say.

"Oh, you look very grand, Miss Wadsworth."

Francesca met Margaret's eyes in the mirror's reflection and believed there was no flattery there, just an honest appraisal. It was all Francesca really needed for the confidence to get her through the night.

"Are you going to a ball? Will the queen be there?" Margaret asked. Perhaps her judgement was not to be credited after all.

"Oh, dear heavens, Margaret," Francesca said kindly. "One doesn't wear a long-sleeved gown such as this to a ball. A grand affair is for sleeveless gowns and off-the-shoulder necklines and rubies and emeralds."

Margaret knew perfectly well that Francesca owned nothing of the sort. A few strands of pearls borrowed from her mother and a delicate cameo ring that her grandmother bequeathed to her was about the extent of her fine jewels. The Wedgwood brooch was pretty but just a small gift from Mr. Charles Darwin, a Wedgwood family relation, twice over.

"Someday, perhaps, you'll help me dress for an elegant ball. I would then require assistance with my hair and my jewels, of course." Francesca sighed. She might as well talk about attending the queen, for all this was likely.

"I would not know what to do," Margaret whispered.

Francesca did not have the heart to say that she did not know either. "I will teach you. Your aunt surely has some experience in the matter."

The maid nodded, both agreeing with her and confirming her relationship with Mrs. Belleron, the housekeeper.

"And now, shall I be off? I expect to return late in the evening but will tell you all about it tomorrow morning, over breakfast." The household was so small, that Francesca was accustomed to sharing her meals with the staff.

"The gentleman is waiting in the parlor. His carriage is just out the door."

"Then I ought to join him before we are late for the play," Francesca said. "Gentlemen do not like to be kept waiting."

But when she descended the stairs, she found Lord Anthony happily engaged with Mrs. Belleron's noisy parrot, exchanging greetings with each other. He looked up when she cleared her throat and spared only the briefest glance for her gown.

"Here's a clever fellow," he said.

The parrot said the same thing.

"Very clever!" Lord Anthony laughed.

"I believe he says the same thing to the sweeps, so don't let it get to your head," Francesca said tartly.

"You're right. The only compliments I desire this evening must come from you," he said.

Francesca smiled, and waited for him to offer the first compliment, on her hair, perhaps, or her brooch. When he remained silent, she considered herself a fool. Whatever his reasons for escorting her to the theater this evening, this was not a prelude to a courtship.

"Thank you, Lord Anthony. I am very much looking forward to seeing the play."

"It is not a farce," he reminded her.

Did he think her so simple she could only appreciate absurd comedy? "I should think not, for most people are familiar with *Coriolanus*."

By his expression, Francesca guessed that he was not.

"Come then," she said. "Let us see the play and discuss its comedic effects afterward." Truly, she did not believe there were any in this most solemn play by Mr. Shakespeare.

And so, with Margaret hanging on every word, and the parrot mimicking most of them, they were off.

It had been years since she had been to the theater; it was even worse than what Francesca had already admitted to Lord Anthony. Her parents had taken her and her brother to a performance when they were little more than children, but because their baby sister was ill at home with their nurse, they left after the first act. Her mother was simply too distracted to enjoy herself.

Much had changed through the years. Not only was she not a child who hadn't understood why her good time was spoiled because her sister sniffled a bit, but her parents were now perfectly happy to leave London for long lengths of time, with scarcely a look back. Their daughter could be dying of consumption or suffering from chilblains or, at the very least, consorting with a murderer, and they would not know.

"We must ascend this stairway to get to our seats," Lord Anthony said, guiding her by the elbow.

Francesca was sorry to leave the lively crush in the lobby, though Lord Anthony led her up the dark stairs with the air of taking her to a secret place. But it proved to be a secret shared by others, for once they broke through the heavy drapery at the top of the stairs, many voices filled the void.

"My mother has been a patron for years, and this is her private box," he murmured, as Francesca sat on a softly cushioned chair. Once she was settled, he pulled up another chair and sat close to the edge of the railing. He waved to someone seated below.

Francesca looked around them, noting three additional seats in the box. "Is she expected this evening?" she asked, thinking that this would be as miserable an evening at the theater, as was the last. Lady Maitland was an unpleasant prig, who would have pushed a young lady through a window if she thought she was getting too close to her precious son. Francesca spared a glance over the edge of the balcony, wondering if an unwelcome lady ever fell to her death from this height.

But Lord Anthony looked at her in amusement. "Surely you don't imagine I would bring the two of you in close vicinity?"

Of course she did not, but then she did not imagine

that Lord Anthony would escort her to the theater.

"Am I so very impossible?" she asked, knowing the inevitable answer.

They studied each other for several moments in the dim light, and she already knew the answer. She had always known the answer. But for a moment, she glimpsed what might have been regret in his eyes, and the slightest bit of longing.

"My dear mother has never allowed herself to forget that her grandfather was a tailor, who was lucky enough to marry the wealthy widow of a gentleman for whom he had just sewn a death suit. I am certain it was a job with very little opportunity for elevation, but a man does what he needs to do. Family legend would have it that my grandmother was particularly impressed by his suggestion that he need only sew the front of the suit, the part that would be visible from the top of the coffin."

Francesca giggled. "How very clever of him."

"And how very thrifty of her. I have been told it was a perfect match…"

Francesca looked at his eyes. "You seem to doubt it."

"No, the only thing is how embarrassed my mother has always been by the circumstances, though the tailor's children married well, and so have his children's children, thus far."

"But you are not yet married," she said, blushing the next moment, realizing how inappropriate it was to discuss such things with him.

"And that is why this—our—situation is impossible," he said forlornly.

He said nothing that she did already know, except

for some of the particulars, and yet she was suddenly hit with a jolt of anger. How dare he trifle with her, treating her like his supplicant? A man who would escort a lady to the theater without any intention of furthering their relationship was a man who had neither courage nor conviction. The Wadsworths were utterly respectable, for all they owned a shop. They lived in modern times, when such things were commonplace.

Or, at least, Francesca preferred to believe it was so.

"You do not seem to mind being seen with a shopgirl," she said tartly.

He smiled, and took her hand. "Mind?" he asked. "Indeed, I am honored."

Francesca sat back in her seat, somewhat confused, but certainly not mollified.

Chapter 4

Nathaniel stood outside the shop watching a light flicker on and off within, illuminating bits of porcelain and the edges of books. He was mesmerized by the show, recalling the tiny glowbugs of Scandinavia, dancing in fields and gardens on the warmest days of summer, occasionally glancing on one's shoulder or hand.

But this was no delightful spark of nature; there was someone walking about the shop with a candle. And the only thing natural about it is that someone might very well wish to rob a shop of its treasures. Not this one, and not this night, though. Nathaniel had been hired to protect it.

For a man of his accustomed equanimity, he was uncommonly angry. He thought not so much of himself, but of Miss Wadsworth, who might have been alone, even sleeping at her desk, if she had not ceded him the evening hours. The door, not surprisingly, was unlocked, and he entered.

"Who goes there?" he called into the silence and picked up a vase, which he somehow imagined he might use as a weapon. "Show yourself."

Belatedly, he realized it might very well be Miss Wadsworth herself who wandered about the shop; that moment of hesitation cost him dearly. Someone, larger than himself, jumped at him in the darkness and thrust him against a bookcase, which promptly toppled, burying him in a pile of heavy volumes. The intruder moved quickly, jumping onto the books and Nathaniel beneath them, as he ran out the door.

The only sound was that of Nathaniel's own labored breathing, and he supposed he ought to be grateful for that. But it was small consolation, for he had utterly failed at the one thing for which he was responsible—keeping the shop safe and secure. He couldn't even keep himself safe.

He tried to stand and realized he was still holding the vase. Somehow, it survived intact. So there was that, at least.

He shifted position and shed books from his shoulders and arms. Something blurred his vision, and when he raised a hand to brush away whatever it was, he came away with something wet and warm and sticky. Damn. He was bleeding all over the damned books. He finally stood, for all he was lightheaded, stumbled to the door and closed it before another rogue came through the threshold.

Or, more likely, a curious passerby, innocently inquiring about evening hours. It took only days for him to already understand that a private shop was a source of great expectation for the public, for people who had nothing to do but spend idle hours browsing for something they did not know they needed. But the man who was here was no curious passerby, for he knew what he wanted and had no intention of purchasing it.

Nathaniel placed the vase on a small table and pushed the books gently out of his path. There would be time enough to restore them to their shelves in the morning, in the early hours before Miss Wadsworth returned to open the shop for the new day. Perhaps she would give him a small respite of time, if she was out late with Lord Anthony.

The thought did not make him feel better as he stumbled up the stairs. Nor did examining himself in the small mirror that hung on the wall of his attic room.

He was still bleeding, and rather profusely, as was common in head injuries. There was blood on his collar and shirt, and it continued to run in rivulets down his forehead and cheeks. He reached for a linen, grateful Miss Wadsworth had provided him with clean requisites, and dampened it before wiping his face. Before the bleeding continued, he wrapped it snugly around his head.

He was tired, dizzy, and in pain. There was nothing to be done but pull off his garments and fall into the narrow bed.

****

Francesca awakened at dawn, as was her habit, and decided to pull her quilt over her head and try to return to sleep. She was not much of a drinker but recognized the symptoms of a hangover, and knew she was in no condition to face the new day.

But even though she wished for the return of sleep, it did not come readily. Instead, she could not help but think of the events of the night before, the lovely theater, the excellent performances, the many people to whom she was introduced. Indeed, Lord Anthony seemed to have no desire to whisk her away after the final curtain—as she thought he might—and instead they spent an hour or so sipping sherry in the theater's lounge. He made no advances, offered no promises, and yet she sensed he did not wish the evening to end. And so she indulged him, to this next day's detriment.

A hot cup of tea was probably what she needed, if she were to accomplish anything this day. After sitting up in bed, she reckoned that the mere act of dressing herself was going to be an accomplishment. And so, stubbornly determined to give Mr. Endicott no reason to wonder as to what went on the night before, she finally arose, and urged her fingers to button, hook, and tie. She thought she looked somewhat presentable at the breakfast table, though Mrs. Belleron wordlessly redid some of the buttons and hooks. Young Margaret stared at her for a few moments as if she never noticed her before.

Once Francesca stepped out onto the street, the cool morning air offered a bit of a respite, removing the cobwebs from her brain and lightening her step. She looked forward to seeing Mr. Endicott this day, grateful that he would be there to manage things, particularly if she desired to take a quick nap on the chaise longue in the back of the shop. Truly, she already desired it, and it was not yet eight o'clock.

The first thing she noticed when she unlocked the door to the shop was that Mr. Endicott must have already been hard at work, for the bookcase at the front of the shop had been reorganized, the shelves filled with books arranged by size, with occasional breaks for small statuary or bowls. The pottery vase in which she usually kept keys and military medals was now on display on a small table at the door. She decided to move it, for Mr. Endicott might not have realized how vulnerable it was there, as customers often came into the shop with umbrellas and canes.

She paused to examine some coloring on the vase

she had never noticed before. Indeed, it did not seem consistent with the raised relief figures on the piece, as it looked as if someone went over it with a rough brush. If she did not know better, she might have thought it was blood.

"Oh, good heavens," she said, as Mr. Endicott came into view. "It is blood."

He put a hand to the bandage he wore around his forehead, paused to examine his hand, and then looked questioningly at her. "Has it started again? I thought I had quite exhausted the supply of blood in my body."

"I am glad you find it amusing. Did your head come into violent contact with my Etruscan vase?" She studied him, considering that he looked rather dashing with his bandage. "There seems to be blood upon it."

"Yes, that is it," he said a bit too quickly.

"Do you intend to spend this day in the shop with that rag wrapped around your head?" she asked, recalling that she hoped to leave him in charge this day, so she could rest. But perhaps his well-being was somewhat more in jeopardy than hers. "It is dramatic-looking, I admit."

"Perhaps it will improve the value of the vase," he mused.

"Do you mean because of the blood?"

"I shall wash it before we open. But I meant because it is such a solid piece," he said smiling and then grimaced.

"Ought I look at your wound before you start bleeding again? I think I can patch you up more neatly, so you won't look as if you have just come off the battlefield," Francesca said, though she had no more experience with injuries and bandages than any other

London gentlewoman. But like everyone else, she had read of the heroism of Miss Florence Nightingale and thought she might be able to take a cue from that lady.

"I…" Mr. Endicott began, and then thought better of whatever protestation he seemed to have. "Yes, I suppose that would be fine."

"You do not seem to have much confidence in my ability," she countered. "But sit in the chair just yonder, and I will have a look."

As Francesca gathered up more linens, a small vial of cottonseed oil, and a bowl of water, she realized that her hangover was quite gone, cured by necessity, she supposed.

She started to pull away the bandage, pausing to dampen the wound when the bandage stuck to dried blood, and then raised a candle to have a better look.

"Are you certain you know what you are about, Miss Wadsworth?" he asked, with more concern than reproof. "You look like you are about to faint away."

Francesca shook her head slightly, as if to bring his injury into better focus. She did feel like she might faint.

"It looks dreadful," she said, before she could stop herself.

"Leave it then. It's just fine, really. It felt a lot worse last night," he said.

"No, I only require a drink of water, and will be fine."

He laughed. "Perhaps you require a glass of port."

"I have had quite enough of that, sir," she said tartly. She pressed cool fingers against his hot forehead.

He squirmed, but only slightly. "Had a good time last night, did you?"

"I did. I think I would like to attend the theater more often. After all, it is one of the reasons one lives in London, is it not?"

"I had not thought of it as a recommendation, but I suppose you are quite right."

"You mentioned it as one of the reasons you came to town in the first place, Mr. Endicott," she said distractedly. His injury had left a jagged wound on his forehead, and he was likely to wear the reminder of his accident for the rest of his life, even with the application of the cottonseed oil.

"Hmmm, I suppose I did," he said. "Well, I am certain Lord Anthony would be happy to oblige you, especially since you appear to have had such an excellent time together."

Francesca let that comment pass. Instead, she was considering the rough state of the wound, glancing back and forth between his forehead and the simple vase that stood at the gateway to the shop.

"Now, Mr. Endicott, will you tell me what really happened last night?"

Nathaniel let out a long breath. He was tempted to say that he would not ask about her night, if she did not ask about his, but this was her shop and her business. Whereas, what happened between her and blasted Lord Anthony was definitely not his.

"Why do you think it was anything other than what I have said?"

"You are not a very good liar, sir," she said, though he rather thought he was good at it, and getting better every day. "You did not injure yourself on a vase. It looks like you were cut with something rough. A blunt knife perhaps, or a board."

He thought it might have been a board, though he could not account for it in the shop.

"It is nothing, really."

"It is something, Nathaniel," she said quietly.

It was not her tone, but the use of his name that disarmed him.

"There was someone in the shop last night," he admitted.

"With you?" she asked.

Fair enough. "I was not here but out with a friend."

"The friend with whom you planned to stay when you arrived in London?"

He glanced up at her, carefully avoiding that which was directly in his line of vision. "You do not forget much, do you? Yes, indeed, I had dinner with my friend at a pub in Piccadilly. You can ask the regulars there, if you require substantiation."

"I believe you," she said, but without any conviction. "Then what happened?"

"I returned late in the evening, at an hour when some men's—or women's—business is finished for the day and others are awakening for the next. There was a light blinking from within, and I thought it might be you, checking on one thing or another."

"It was not me," she said.

"I know that now. The intruder looked nothing like you, to my regret. He was fairly substantial in size and strong enough to pull down the bookcase before stomping on me as he ran out the door."

"The bookcase, of course!" she said, and quickly walked away from him, toward the front of the shop.

He had no idea what she was thinking, until she returned a few minutes later. "There is a broken shelf at the very top, hastily nailed together by Will a few months ago. He is a handy fellow to have as a friend, but his carpentry skills may not be the best."

"Well, neither are mine," Nathaniel admitted. "I suppose my skills as a defender of your property may not be outstanding either."

"You may have other talents," she said. He looked up at her again, but she was determinedly avoiding his eyes. "Why did you say you regretted the intruder did not look like me?"

He paused, trying to recall his own words of a few moments before. The words had just escaped him, and he supposed he was rather thinking that a small woman such as herself would not have been able to inflict much damage. But he glanced up at her profile, admiring the gentle slope of her nose, her long dark lashes, and the pink bud of her pursed lips, and knew those were not the words she wished to hear. Nor were they the ones he wished to say.

"Because such beauty is rarely seen, even in the presence of treasures in a shop on King Street."

Francesca turned to him, her lips slightly parted, and there was nothing to be done but kiss her.

He rose slowly, somewhat awkwardly, and did not surprise her as much as he ought to have done. She hesitated just a moment before pulling him up to stand above her and leaned into his body. His arms held her close, as he anticipated the moment when she would pull away, realizing that they had just crossed a line of propriety. But she did not pull away. She murmured something against his lips, which might have been a rebuff, but her actions did not suggest that it was so. Rather, they seemed engaged in the art of discovery, so that a kiss between them was as sweet as learning each other's story, or one's preference in teas.

Her fingers gently explored his face, running over the lines of his nose and finally coming to rest between their lips. He opened his eyes and looked into hers, wondering at her perfect composure.

"If such is my reward for tending to your injury, I shall insist on examining every scratch and paper cut," she said and smiled.

What a stupid, ungenerous thing to say! Mr. Endicott risked great harm by confronting their intruder. He might have been killed. And now, not only did she make an inappropriate comment about his body, but he might believe that she hoped he would suffer further injury. Indeed, she was so flippant, he might think that she would conspire with those who would do him harm.

She looked into his dark eyes, smiling a bit woodenly, as her thoughts were all in turmoil. Her tongue still savored the taste of him, sweet with the flavor of coffee and sugar, and slightly metallic with the taste of blood. Indeed, a thin trickle of blood was running from his forehead, and she was probably marked with it on her skin.

But he was a man she hardly knew, a stranger, and she had let him kiss her. What if someone had walked in on them, the respectable Miss Wadsworth and her new assistant? What gossip would ensue! She would gain a reputation that could cause damage to her business. Her father would never forgive her, for somehow, sometime, word would reach him in the South Seas.

"Then perhaps I should arrange for intruders to

come in more often," Mr. Endicott said softly, "and chance the consequences."

Her eyes widened with new understanding. She may have misled him into thinking she could have some purpose in bringing in an intruder to cause havoc in her own shop.

But what if it were he who had such a purpose? Where was he last night, when he should have been protecting the premises? She only had his word that another man was here, but what if there was no one else? He could have pulled down the bookcase himself, hit himself on the head with just about anything.

"Are you quite well?" he asked. "You appear to be in some pain. I assure you, I am only teasing that I would invite rogues and thieves into the shop."

But what if he were not? After all, the shop had remained unmolested for all the years she could remember, save for someone slipping an ink pot into one's pocket, or something of that sort. Then, only a few weeks ago, an intruder wrecked the place, and the very same day, Mr. Endicott presented himself. And immediately gained unlimited access to the shop.

Of course, that was her fault, her own stupid, impulsive self.

"I promise, I won't let it happen again," Mr. Endicott said, his voice still barely above a whisper.

"I don't believe it is your fault if someone intends to burgle the place," she said, though she was not sure she still believed that.

"I meant, kissing you," he said, rubbing his forehead.

"Oh, that."

"I seem to have made quite an impression on you,

Miss Wadsworth. It is quite a blow to my manhood."

"Oh, it was a lovely kiss," she said, and when he rolled his eyes, she realized it was absolutely the wrong thing to say. She caught herself quickly. "It is the blow to your forehead that concerns me. It is bleeding again, you know."

He stopped rubbing his forehead. "I fear I may have rubbed some off on your cheek."

"Then please sit down again. Let's try to make you presentable before our first customers come in."

And somehow, the very act of returning to what they were doing only moments before, brought their relationship back to where it was before. It was almost as if their brief moments of intimacy had not happened. Except, now Francesca had reason to doubt the man she was prepared to trust.

"Did you enjoy yourself last night?" he asked, as she pulled away the newly stained bandage. She recalled that patients often distracted themselves from pain or discomfort by speaking of things that really did not matter, that required no particular thought.

"I did, indeed. The play was very well performed, and our seats were excellent."

"You were in a private box, I suppose." He raised one hand, as if to touch his open wound, but then thought better of it and dropped his hand. "I would expect nothing less of Tony."

Tony, indeed. It was easy to forget these two men knew each other for so many years. Though they professed indifference to each other, it was additionally curious that her shop would be compromised twice in the short amount of time since they'd reunited in London. Was it possible their indifference was just a bit of artifice, and they were somehow working together? And for what?

"Yes, Nathaniel," she said, emphasizing his name. "He is a man who likes to be seen. The wonder of it is that he wishes to be seen with me."

"No wonder, Miss Wadsworth. Any gentleman would be honored to be seen with you."

One had to admit the man was a good liar, waxing eloquently and flattering where nothing was to be gained. Unless something was to be gained, and it was all part of a plan.

"This will have to do," she said after several moments. "Please remember that you are not to rub your fingers against your forehead. And for heaven's sake, do not bang into walls or bookcases."

He looked speculatively around the shop. "It is nearly impossible to avoid them."

"Indeed, I bear some scars myself."

"A greater pity, then. I shudder to think of anything that would mar your beauty."

It was very hard to remain suspicious of his motives when he flattered her into blissful distraction.

Chapter 5

"Do you not need to spend some hours with Will this afternoon?" Miss Wadsworth asked some time later.

A group of American visitors had monopolized their time for nearly forty-five minutes but purchased a good deal, as Americans usually did. Miss Wadsworth explained this to him the very first day he worked in the shop; the Colonials were impressed with antiquity, having very little of their own. Therefore, by emphasizing the age of an item, their New York and Boston customers, especially, found such items irresistible.

And so, Nathaniel loaded up several crates with Old World treasures destined for the New World and helped the Americans' driver load it into their carriage. And only hit his forehead once in the process.

"If I am done here, I shall go try my luck with Will. He undoubtedly needs help wheeling in a great circle of gouda or something of that sort." He showed off his growing strength by flexing his arm muscles, watching her watching him. "Do you still need me for anything?"

The look Miss Wadsworth gave him was unsettling, tempting him to pull her close and kiss her again.

"I shall endure the deprivation," she said softly.

She handed him his jacket, which he had shed before carrying the crates outside, and brushed some sawdust off his lapel.

But when he walked out the door a few minutes later, his concern was not for an opportunity lost, but rather that someone else was looking for an opportunity of another sort, watching the shop and looking for something valuable and elusive. As he made his way through the crowd on King Street, he studied the faces of men who stood leaning against lampposts or closed doors, wondering who was furtively observing him, and who might spring to make another move. He paused, tempted to return to the shop, knowing that if Francesca was accosted as he was last night, he would never forgive himself. There was nothing more valuable—and vulnerable—in the shop than its owner.

But he went on as the crowd pushed him forward, deciding that the intruder was a coward who wouldn't show himself in daylight and might very well have already found what he was looking for. And they might never know what it was. Or who he was.

When Nathaniel entered Will's shop, his friend was holding court, as usual. The man had an opinion on everything, from the aging of cheddar to Benjamin Disraeli's Public Health Act. But while many shopkeepers were happy to pontificate and bore customers until they finally made a purchase just to escape the place, Will actually attracted an audience of admirers. They did not have to agree with him, they only had to engage with him. Chimney sweeps had just as much to say as Members of Parliament, and all had equal opportunity to debate the matters of current concern in the gastronomical forum.

It was good for business.

"Well, what happened to you, old man?" Will called out when Nathaniel entered the shop. All heads turned to the door.

"A small accident, nothing more," Nathaniel said, brushing off his concern. "I came up against an opposing force."

Will's customers launched into a discussion of the hazards of walking the streets of London, the careless speed of livery drivers, the ungainly peddler wagons that often blocked the streets. Nathaniel navigated a path around the several men and two women, unbuttoning his jacket once again. On a hook near the cutlery was a clean white apron which he quickly exchanged for his wool garment. Clothes did indeed make the man, for he was immediately transformed from a gentleman to a laborer. Smiling at the irony, he looked up as he tied the apron's cord behind him and met Will's eyes.

Nathaniel shook his head and selected a sharp steel knife as he came to the cutting block. Truly, here was a greater danger to him than meeting a footpad on King Street; a miscalculation of an inch or so could mark the end of his watchmaking skills, for it was a craft that required all ten fingers. A great wheel of gouda already awaited him, and so he went about his business, trying not to be distracted by the voices raised about him. He had much to think about that did not require the opinion of anyone else.

"Have a care with my prized aged gouda, Nathaniel, lest it become food for the street cats," Will said.

Nathaniel looked up, suddenly aware that the shop

was uncharacteristically quiet. The two of them were quite alone.

"There are dancing bears in the square, or something of that sort," Will explained before Nathaniel could ask about the customers, and shrugged. "I cannot imagine why anyone thinks that's more interesting than a discussion of the queen's puppy."

"Bears dance, for one thing. A performance always attracts a crowd. Though why anyone would want to watch the poor beasts being tortured is beyond me."

"I believe your own performance is calculated to attract as little attention as possible."

Did Will already know why he was in London, what information he sought? Did he know who he was? Aside from his willingness to fix his location on King Street, was there anything that had given him away?

"You are too careful and alert to come up against an opposing force, unless that force was determined to collide with you," said Will. "What was it, Francesca's shop door? Did she turn you out, poor fellow?"

Nathaniel felt his shoulders relax. Will imagined a performance that had nothing to do with the Earl D'Arcques or Tony. "Nothing so domestic, Will. I was out last night with a friend and returned to the shop to find someone was there before me."

For all that he felt more at ease, he saw Will grow tense. "And it was not Francesca, for she was at the theater," he said.

"Of course. And even if it were, I announced my presence when I opened the door. And was attacked by a falling bookcase. To add further injury, the intruder ran over the pile of books that buried me and out the door before I could see much of anything, other than he was a large brute."

"And he stepped on your forehead?"

"No, I owe that injury to you. Miss Wadsworth told me that you had hammered together a few boards to repair the bookcase, and perhaps neglected to finish off the project."

"I am not very good at handcrafts," Will defended himself.

"And I am not very good at accosting intruders, it seems."

"Does Francesca know?"

Nathaniel shrugged. "How could she not? I left a trail of blood all over the damned place. And it took her all of five seconds to see that the bookcase had been moved and its contents reshelved."

"Yes, she would notice that at once, for all her inventory seems to be a general hodgepodge." Will folded his arms over his chest. "She probably bandaged you up, as well. Her Florence Nightingale tendencies are rather keen."

"They are," Nathaniel said. Will seemed to be waiting for more of the story. "I confess that is the only comfort in this whole affair."

Will laughed. "And you are a hero, besides. That should be a comfort to her."

"But I'm not. I have done nothing to protect her or her property. I have started the inventory, but that only means that one day she will be able to figure out what the intruder is after, not what is missing after the fact."

"What do you think the intruder is after?"

"Gold, silver, the usual stuff."

"You don't believe that, and neither do I. The thief would have found all that on the first break-in and would not have risked a second shot at it. He is looking for something most specific, a treasure map perhaps, or a rare gold sovereign, or Prince Albert's marriage certificate to a German wench."

Nathaniel was surprised. "Was there such a person?"

"I have no idea, old man. I was only speaking generally. Albert was a bit of a stick and was more likely to have been interested in your mechanical lady than a buxom fräulein."

"Madame Cristobel," Nathaniel murmured. "If she could be repaired and set to rights, she would be one of the most uniquely valuable items for sale. Perhaps we could present her to the queen."

"And see if the intruder tries to break into the palace?" Will said quickly, but his thoughts already seemed to be leading to another conclusion. "What if the shop became the most popular venue on King Street, attracting more than the occasional bibliophile or someone in the quest for a Chinese vase? Would it be easier to flush out the miscreant then?"

Nathaniel placed the sharp knife carefully on the cutting board. "I do not follow. The intruder comes in the dead of night; he is surely not interested in mingling with the hoi polloi."

"I have not heard that expression in years. You must have had an old-fashioned mother."

Nathaniel felt his shoulders stiffen again. What was this about?

"I do not remember her," he said tersely.

"I'm sorry to hear that," Will said, sounding most sincere. "If the intruder has no luck larking about in the darkness in the middle of the night, he may wish to be more direct and approach Miss Wadsworth or you, as a customer. He is looking for something most particular. But if he is the only customer in the shop, he would be rather vulnerable. What if you can fill the shop with customers as I do here?"

"Provide some sort of entertainment, you suggest. One that is likely to compete with dancing bears."

"Precisely. But I was thinking of you."

"Think harder. My dancing skills do not exceed a rather stiff waltz, though I have some skill at the piano."

"And you are a watchmaker, capable of bringing Madame Cristobel back to life."

"I may not be capable of any such thing. Besides, there is nothing particularly entertaining in that," Nathaniel argued.

"Not to you, perhaps. But people are fascinated with the workings of things, of engines, of pulleys and levers, of locks and printing machines. And how can those things compare to our Madame Cristobel? It is one thing to animate bits of metal and wheels, but you would be animating a real woman."

Nathaniel held up his hand. This discussion was not going well at all. "A wooden woman, who is no more real than a gas lamp or music box. Let me remind you that this animation business did not go at all well for Dr. Frankenstein."

Will dismissed the words with a casual wave. "Think about it, Nathaniel. You can set up a workbench in the shop window and just go about your tedious but fascinating business. People stop and watch for a few moments. Then they come in to bother you with questions and look over the merchandise and purchase things. Our intruder will feel emboldened and slip through the door and do the same. Sooner or later, he will reveal himself, without wrecking the place or doing harm to Francesca or you."

"No, and no, and no," Nathaniel said, his upraised hand emphasizing each point. "I was not hired to be on public display, like a sideshow geek."

Will's enthusiasm would not be deflated. "No, but you were hired to assist Francesca, and you would be doing just that. She asked you, most specifically, to see if you could repair Madame Cristobel, and you can keep your promise. Even better, you would no longer have to rely on gaslight to ply your craft. Seated in the window, you have all the benefits of natural light, such as it is. In any case, you will not go blind."

Nathaniel put down his hand. Will would not be deterred, and he was not in an excellent position to argue with him. He could resign from his posts, of course, and simply return to his quiet life at Watch Hill. Quiet, but not untroubled. He had come to London to find something, discover several truths, reclaim what was his.

In that way, he was not unlike the very person they sought to unmask. Something was hidden. And for reasons he could only begin to understand, his own quest nearly perfectly coincided with that of the intruder. But in some ways, the other man gave Nathaniel the opportunity he needed. Perhaps there was sound justice in giving the intruder the chance to expose himself.

And yet, it was absurd. The idea, for all Will's enthusiasm, did not even make sense.

"No," he said again.

"Well, think upon it," Will said, with an air of triumph that might not have been entirely unfounded. "Ah, and here are some customers, American by the look of them. Why not give them a show with your cutlery skills? Everyone loves a good show."

Nathaniel looked to the door and recognized the four men and women who delighted in their purchases at the antiquarian shop only a short time before. They noticed him, too, but clearly did not know why he was familiar. He supposed it was not so much his cunning disguise of a white apron, but rather the change in venue. They were confused, and Nathaniel was disgruntled, but Will was quite right.

They were entertained by his newfound skills in cutting up great wheels of cheese and rewarded him by buying enough gouda to put the American farmers in Vermont out of business.

****

Francesca looked up as Mr. Endicott came through the door. He looked rather rakish with his bandaged forehead but otherwise subdued and thoughtful. She did not really understand him or why employment at an old curiosity shop would satisfy him. His story about desiring employment did not hold water, as he did not seem to be a man without means. In addition, he had a rare skill and could do a lot better for himself. He could open his own shop, perhaps become clockmaker to the queen.

And yet, he wished to be here, dealing with tourists and local customers who bought nothing. That would be discouraging enough, but he remained at risk of injury—or worse—by a mysterious intruder.

Some part of the puzzle remained missing, which

added to her suspicions that the break-ins occurred not because of random chance but precisely because he was here. Did she really believe he was with a friend in Piccadilly while she was at the theater with Lord Anthony? What if he never left the shop all the while?

"Tuppence for your thoughts," he said into the quiet afternoon. He glanced around, approached the table where she sat watching him, an array of brooches laid out before her.

"My thoughts may not even be worth tuppence," she said. "I suppose I am just bothered by this whole business of the break-ins, not knowing when the intruder will make another attempt."

He sat down heavily, as if he bore some of her burden. Inasmuch as he suffered a real injury, perhaps he genuinely did.

"Are you in much pain?" she asked, feeling guilty that it was not the first thing she said when he entered. Whatever his motives for being here, his injury was real enough. She ought to have given him the day to rest, rather than simply patch him up and send him out to deal with her demanding customers.

He put his hand up to his forehead, and frowned. "I almost forgot about it."

"Has no one asked what happened?" she said, now full of indignation.

"If they had, it would not have felt any better than when you bandaged me up," he said leaning forward. But she did not look at the white linen, now slightly stained with his blood. Instead she looked into his dark eyes.

"What is he looking for?" she asked, enunciating each word clearly and slowly.

He didn't pretend to misunderstand what she meant. "I do not know, but he appears to be missing the one thing worth looking for among the shelves and cabinets of FW Wadsworth, Bookseller and Antiquarian."

Francesca felt her cheeks grow warm. She couldn't pretend to misunderstand him either.

"Mr. Endicott, you really do not know me. But even if you did, you would have to admit that anyone in this vast city could find me at any time in the same place where I've been for nearly all my life."

He quickly straightened and, as if to put a finer point on it, leaned back on his chair, so that the front legs were off the ground. His next question surprised her.

"Have you never traveled? Do thoughts of long journeys and discoveries tempt you?"

"They do. They always have. But somehow, I am the one who remains at home. My sister lives in America, my brother sails with Darwin. And I do not know when I will see my parents again, for they seem to be having an excellent adventure." How pathetic she must seem to him, he who traveled much himself and had lived in other countries. "Someone must stay behind, minding the shop."

"But why must it be you? You do not have to abandon all that you know and love. You need only hire someone trustworthy and knowledgeable." He paused for several moments. "After all, you hired me."

"Mr. Endicott," she began, somewhat flirtatiously. "Are you trying to get me to leave on a journey just so you can assume management of the shop?"

The front legs of the chair dropped onto the

ground, allowing him to lean in again. "Not at all. I hope to accompany you some day on all those journeys."

"You are being ridiculous," she said, waving him off. At his crestfallen look, she added: "Or you are light-headed. Your forehead is bleeding again, you know."

"I had a rough few hours at the cheesemonger. Though come to think of it, I have a rougher time here."

There was something in the way he phrased it that made it seem very personal. For all someone tried to kill him the night before, he might have been referring to her putting off his advances.

"Will can be a rigorous taskmaster, I understand. Over the years, he has hired any number of workers, but none seem to live up to his expectations. He hasn't had a bad word to say about you, however."

"I have not been there very long," Mr. Endicott pointed out. "But I have a feeling he may be pushing me away so I may spend more time with you. In the shop, of course."

"Of course," she said slowly. Increasingly, she had the feeling her friends were conspiring against her. "It may only be temporary, for he tends to be very busy in the weeks before Christmas. People do give gifts of viands, you know."

"I suppose that is so, though I'd rather have a book." He glanced at the bookcases that sheltered them. "They offer greater sustenance."

"And yet, you must eat to survive. I also find sustenance of another sort. I have not traveled as you have, Mr. Endicott. But I feel as if I have gazed upon many landscapes in the pages I have read. Sometimes I do that even as I am eating, accomplishing both things at once."

"You are a very efficient woman," he said.

She laughed, tickled by the compliment that was so far from the truth. "And yet, you know better than most how very much I need your assistance."

He nodded, though he didn't look all that convinced of it. He looked again at the bookcases but then focused on the very front of the shop, where the steady river of London's population passed by the large window.

"And thus we are back to our friend Will," Mr. Endicott said. "He has plans for us, you know."

It was just as she imagined, but it would not do to duck the matter.

"I hardly know you, Mr. Endicott. And I am not looking for a husband, no matter what Will has in mind." She stood up and brushed crumbs off her gown. When he didn't answer, she watched him as he rose from his seat. "He could marry you himself, if he so desires."

Oh, dear heavens, had she really said that? Will would probably like nothing more.

Now it was Mr. Endicott's turn to laugh, and to make light of her words. "As to that, he has not proposed marriage. He has something else in mind, however."

"I can hardly wait to hear this," Francesca said, a bit impatient. She put her hands on her hips.

"Will suggests we bring in the crowds on King Street by providing some entertainment in the shop," he explained.

"Theater, perhaps? I did enjoy myself at

Coriolanus, despite the bleakness of the plot."

"Nothing so dramatic. Just Madame Cristobel, and me, trying to set her to rights."

For once, Francesca had nothing to say. She wasn't sure what he was talking about. But if, indeed, she understood what he was saying, she ought to consider the possibility that her two friends had gone mad.

"Madame Cristobel?" She looked to where the lonely lady sat on the counter, and repeated, "Madame Cristobel?"

"To the best of my knowledge, there is only one of her," he said, softly. And then, after a few moments. "That is just the point, you see. She is unique. Few people have ever seen anything like her."

"Anyone," Francesca corrected, though she, herself, had reversed herself on that point of grammar not so long ago. Nathaniel picked up on it at once.

"But that's just the point, Francesca," he said.

She glanced up when he uttered her name and could not look away. She faltered for just a moment. "What is the point?"

"She's just a block of wood, cunningly dressed, with a well-wrought mechanism capable of giving her the illusion of life. And yet, she has an enchanting quality, to which we ascribe a certain humanity."

"She can't do a thing anymore."

"But she might again. Isn't that why you hired me?"

She didn't answer, considering how she might have hired him for all the wrong reasons. She had been perfectly satisfied with her life, until he walked through the door, prepared to rescue her from her predicament. At the time, she assumed her predicament was restoring order to her shop. Now, she wasn't so sure.

He rose from his seat, saying nothing until he stood behind the automaton and raised one of Madame Cristobel's wooden arms.

"Hello, Miss Wadsworth," he said in a falsetto voice. "Please help me."

Francesca laughed, dismissing her troubled thoughts, realizing she had brought this man into her life for all the right reasons.

"What do you wish, little lady?" she asked.

"I wish to be seen and admired and..." Nathaniel paused and cleared his throat. When he spoke again, it was in his deep, familiar voice. "I wish to be in the window and become the most famous lady in London."

"Dear, dear. We don't want the queen to hear that, do we?"

"Perhaps we do. And then she might be curious enough to grace us with a visit."

Francesca laughed and said, "What are you talking about?" And then, when she saw the expression on his face, "You are quite serious, aren't you? What do you propose?"

"I was skeptical myself, at first," he admitted. "But it's easy to catch Will's enthusiasm."

She looked at him, waiting to hear the grand scheme they had concocted. It was her shop, to be sure, and yet she already sensed that these two men were quite capable of overruling her.

"I shall set up a workshop in the window, on the wood platform that's holding up the bookcases. The light is excellent in the morning, and Madame Cristobel will be shown to best advantage."

"So shall you," she pointed out. She wasn't sure

she wanted him in the window, where he was likely to be admired by every woman and girl passing by. There was something vulgar about the notion. "Every time you scratch your nose, you will have an audience."

He looked pensive. "Do I scratch my nose that often?" he asked, scratching his nose.

"I don't know. I scarcely observe you through the day," she lied. "But others certainly will."

"More likely, they'll be observing Madame Cristobel and be witness to her restoration. She is irresistible."

Francesca rather thought the same of him. "And other than creating a crush on the street, what is the point of this little charade?"

"Not a charade, my dear Francesca. I will truly be working on repairing her."

"And when will that project be completed?"

"It may never be completed, truly. But Will's plan is to attract more people to the shop, who will come in to examine the merchandise before moving on along King Street."

"So, this is a business plan? It sounds a bit unseemly."

"Unseemly to attract customers? Does anyone think it is unseemly for Will to host political discussions in his shop? Or for Fortnum and Mason to set out tables in an effort to encourage picnics?" He rubbed his fingers over the fabric of Madame Cristobel's gown, examining a small tear. "But there is more."

Francesca waited, wondering what on earth was coming.

"Will is confident we will catch a thief. The

intruder who appears to have had no luck in the evening hours may be willing to enter the shop when he is in a crowd and not call particular attention to himself. A solitary customer will be engaged in conversation and thus be remembered. But one among many can browse about, ask a few questions, and look through the merchandise without attracting much notice."

"And that is it? That is the great plan? Do you suppose this man will wave a red flag so we might recognize him when he shows up?"

"We lose nothing by trying. I confess, I am not altogether convinced of the value of this scheme, but I am willing to play my part."

"To allow yourself to be part of the furnishings?"

"To give life to Madame Cristobel," he said. "Won't that be enough?"

Chapter 6

It was a stupid idea. Why had he ever agreed to such nonsense? He had not the slightest drop of showmanship in his blood; he preferred nothing more than sitting with a book in a quiet corner, where no one was likely to come upon him. In Joseph Kinzing's clockmaking shop, he was bothered by nothing more than the occasional mouse and the ringing of all the clocks every half hour. Though as to that, he had grown so accustomed to the cacophony, he hardly noticed it at all.

But after a week in the front window of FW Wadsworth, Bookseller and Antiquarian, he noticed everything. Only one thing eluded him.

The number of passersby who thought they were being congenial by tapping on the window to get his attention remained profoundly annoying. Those who entered the shop to discuss the particulars of clockmaking with him, with no more experience than having once owned a pocket watch, provided nothing more useful than the opportunity for him to remove his spectacles and rest his eyes. Ladies came through the door to advise him of suitable dressmakers who would be delighted to garb Madame Cristobel in the latest fashion, for what the automaton wore was, apparently, woefully out of date. And then there were the ladies who simply smiled at him through the window, and those more bold, who came into the shop to flirt.

They might have served a useful purpose, if Francesca Wadsworth had revealed even a flicker of jealousy, but she was far too busy with the rush of customers to worry about women who were leaving their calling cards on his workbench.

Will's prediction was absolutely correct. Word spread throughout London about the show to be seen in the window of one of the oldest shops on King Street; there had even been a small article in *The Times*. The constabulary advised Francesca to place a sign in the window, reminding people not to loiter, but no one seemed to care, including the police themselves. And the shop was full of people, from the moment she unlocked the front door in the morning, to closing time, when it became necessary to guide people out the door because they seemed to have forgotten their way.

Sales were brisk. Francesca asked Nathaniel to pull several trunks from the cellar and from beneath the tables so she could comb the contents for inventory and expressed some concern that she could not keep up with demand for cameos, porcelain vases, and landscape paintings. There was great desire for automatons, but she could only find a singing bird in a small cage. The poor creature appeared to have been visited by moths but sold within a half hour of being placed on the sales floor.

And yet, the one thing that remained elusive and troubling was that thus far, no one revealed himself as a criminal. Indeed, everyone was astoundingly congenial, as if they felt blessed to have been allowed to enter the premises. When a lady knocked over a washstand, she insisted her husband pay Francesca for the loss. That was a very good thing because Nathaniel doubted that the dreadful stand would have sold under any other circumstances. And people seemed pleased to buy merchandise for no reason other than to claim ownership, like the gentleman who bought a book in a language he apparently did not understand.

But no one revealed himself as a criminal.

When he wasn't acknowledging ladies in the window or answering questions about clock mechanisms, Nathaniel attempted to study the customers in the shop, looking for those who made themselves a little too free with the merchandise that was set aside or asking too many questions about the provenance of various items. He was not very experienced in the trade but did not think anything amiss, as he might have done the same thing himself. By definition, a curiosity shop was in business for the curious.

"You're not going to get much done if you keep daydreaming about the divine Miss Wadsworth," a man chastened him. Nathaniel turned in his seat to face Tony. Though he should not have. "Aren't you being paid to devote all your attention to Madame Cristobel?"

He was being paid to swallow his pride, which was one of the reasons he had been happy to forget about Lord Anthony Maitland.

"You forget, Tony," Nathaniel reminded him. "I am being paid to assist Miss Wadsworth and protect her. So perhaps I wasn't daydreaming at all but performing my duty. A very pleasant one at that."

"Yes, I suppose so," Tony acceded, and quickly changed the topic. "Business seems to be very brisk. I hope Miss Wadsworth will be able to indulge me some

103

hours of her time."

Nathaniel watched as the man made his way through several groups of people, chatting them up and admiring their choices. He seemed particularly interested in a small model of a country church and tinkered with the steeple bell until it jingled. But after he examined it for several moments, he handed it back to the customer, who promptly brought it over to Francesca for purchase. While she was wrapping it in newsprint, she looked over the man's shoulder and said a few words to Tony. When the customer left, she stepped closer and engaged him in conversation.

Nathaniel focused his attention on the tiny gear in Madame Cristobel's arm, cleaning away the dust and lint that prevented it from moving freely, and doing his best to ignore everything going on around him, both in and out of the shop.

"You are entitled to step away from the workbench, you know," Francesca said softly.

Nathaniel looked up, surprised and bit embarrassed to realize that he had been so preoccupied, he'd neglected to notice they were now quite alone in the shop. The sun was low in the sky, casting its light in bright shafts over the rooftops, but soon it would be too dark to accomplish anything.

"Lord Anthony says I work you too hard," she said and held out her hand so he might grasp it as he came down the wobbly stairs. "He fears you will grow frustrated and leave me just when I need you the most."

"Does he indeed?" Nathaniel asked, slightly dazed by the very touch of her hand. "What does he know of frustration?"

Francesca gave him a strange look and held tight.

"He does not believe you can repair Madame Cristobel, even suggesting he might take a look at her himself."

This was an odd offer. "Indeed. And what does he know of automatons?"

"I do not know," she sighed, "but he suggested he might have better luck with her."

"Does he fancy being on display in the window? Is he jealous of the attention I am getting from the ladies?" Nathaniel asked, bitterly.

"He harbors no jealousy. Indeed, he offered his mother's theater box to us, so you might have a bit of a respite. Lady Maitland remembers you and your father quite well and is prepared to be generous. It is she who suggested that he might be helpful in restoring Madame Cristobel. Lord Anthony seems above reproach."

Nathaniel somehow doubted that, for this was an even odder offer than the first.

"A jealous man would hardly make such an offer," she added.

"I am quite capable of taking a lady to the theater without his or his mother's gift of tickets. There is something else at work here, and you are quite right that it isn't jealousy."

"I know nothing about that, but Lord Anthony is not the one who is jealous. I am," she said.

Why on earth did she say that? Was it because she watched him for hours, flirting and smiling at all the ladies who stopped by to curry his attention? Was it because his graceful and clever hands caressed a wooden lady, and he devoted hours to her care? Or was it because he only touched her, a living, feeling lady, when she made an offer, reaching out to him to help him do something he was perfectly able to accomplish on his own?

She was dull and uninteresting. She was a mouse in a curiosity shop, the least curious thing in the place. While other ladies flaunted their new bonnets and stylish day dresses, she appeared every morning at the door in a dull wool gown, her hair pleated in a neat coronet. If she didn't call out as she entered each morning, he might not even notice she was there.

"You are jealous?" Nathaniel asked softly and pulled her hand to his heart. "Of what does a clever and beautiful woman have to be jealous? Surely not of frivolous ladies who have nothing to do to occupy their days?"

She stepped back, but he pulled her close.

"I think it must be very pleasant to occasionally have nothing to do," she said wistfully. "Or be considered frivolous. Just once in a while."

He nodded thoughtfully as he reached around her with his free hand and turned the small door sign to "Closed."

"I hope there's no one still about?" he asked, coming close.

She shook her head. The last customer left nearly half an hour before.

"Good," he said and pulled her into his arms and kissed her.

"Nathaniel," she murmured when she was able to breathe again. She clung to him, looking at his lips, willing him to kiss her again. "Nathaniel."

"No one else," he said softly.

"Or everyone else," she said. "We may have an audience, peering in through the window."

"Would that be very bad for business?" he asked,

looking amused.

"It would be very bad for my reputation," she said and nestled closely against him. To hell with her reputation.

"I suspect your reputation is secure, my dear. If anything, there are many who hope to see you happy, knowing how much you have given to your father's legacy. Several people have told me how pleased they are that I am here with you."

"That sounds like Will. As to the others, they may be happy because two of us can provide better service than one."

He frowned, and she wondered if he was put off by her cynicism. But then, something else occurred to her.

"Do they insult your manhood, because you are employed by a woman?" she asked softly.

"Do they insult your womanhood, suggesting that you need a proper man in your life? Nay. They are only those who love you and are worried about your future."

"What? Have they confided such things to you, a veritable stranger?" Francesca argued, feeling a growing indignation. But such emotion could only go so far, for she sometimes worried about the same thing, herself. Especially on a winter night, when her only comfort was a fire in the grate.

Nathaniel put his forefinger beneath her chin and studied her face. She was grateful the light was dim, for she was all too familiar with the creases in her brow and the shadows beneath her eyes. But he must have liked what he saw, for he smiled.

"But what if I am that proper man?" he asked.

"Are you?" She knew her lips moved, but she wasn't quite sure she said anything. And yet, he knew what to answer.

"I'm not that proper," he admitted and lifted her onto the table behind her.

He was quite right, she thought in the few seconds before she lost all sense. For his kiss was not the kiss of a gentleman. He pressed against her, his legs enveloped by the folds of her skirt, and cupped her shoulders with each hand so that it was impossible to shy away. His lips were on hers, her nose and cheeks and eyes, before they assaulted her neck and moved down the length of her throat to the uppermost button on her blouse. Somehow that became undone. No, he was not that proper.

He was wonderful. It was just as it was often written: she fancied she heard fireworks crackling in the night sky.

Suddenly, he became quite still. Had she uttered such romantic nonsense out loud?

"Nathaniel? What is it?"

"I think it is the tea service from Waterford. An Irish lady asked to see it not an hour ago."

"What?"

His hands slipped down from her shoulders, over her upper arms, her elbows. She still wore her long-sleeved gown, and still she shivered. When his hands reached hers, he did not let go but raised her arms as he looked down on the floor. She shifted to the edge of the table, and her gaze followed his.

"Oh, dear heavens," she said, and sighed when she saw the shattered glass sparkling in the dim light. "That was a beautiful set. I even thought to save it for myself."

"In that case, I should like to buy you another, if

you promise not to sell it," he said. The grand moment was gone, as they were back to practical things. Though perhaps not quite. "It could be my first gift for you, the first of many, I hope."

He released her hands, and she eased herself off the edge of the table, right up against his body. She slipped her arms around him and held him closer.

"You do not have to offer me presents of such worth, for I am already convinced of your worth, Mr. Endicott," she said in a teasing tone. But she was quite serious.

She felt the sound of his laughter vibrate against her ear. They stood silently, in each other's embrace, surrounded by the wreckage of their moments of passion. Outside, the hooves of horses clopped in the road, and people called out to each other. But in this sanctuary, there was peace.

"There is much you don't know about me," he said suddenly into the still air.

"And yet I feel as if I've come to know you very well. I know more and more about you every day. But now that you have kissed me, I believe it is your cue to reveal some dark secret. Perhaps you are a prince in disguise or, at the very least, the heir to a gentleman of great wealth. I have a great deal of time to read lady's novels, you see." His silence seemed ominous, and she rushed into the next impossibility. "Or you might be a murderer, of course."

"There is that," he murmured against her hair. "What if I prove to be the mysterious intruder?"

She was disconcerted by his apparent sincerity. "Why, then. I suppose we are safe for now. I hardly think you would use this opportunity to ransack the place." Her first instinct was to take it in good humor, but the question bothered her. "Besides, it's hard to imagine you would knock a bookcase down upon yourself, or do yourself an injury."

"It would be the perfect deceit, would it not?"

"Perhaps, but I would not believe it. You see, I am already gambling on how well I know your character."

Again, he kissed her hair. "Then you may rest easy, for I am not a murderer. Or your damned intruder."

"Then why would you say such a thing? I shall never get a good night's sleep again," she said accusingly.

"It's my job to stay awake during the night, guarding the fortress. But I am coming to think the villain is hiding in plain sight. Why do we assume the intruder is mysterious? He or she could be someone you know very well, someone who is here every day."

"Surely not Will!" The words were out before she could stop herself.

He shook his head. "Perhaps the elderly gent with the patched jacket? Miss Bartleby and her caged dove?" He chuckled, but he may have been thinking of the whole collection of eccentrics who came through the door every day. "Lord Anthony?"

"Certainly not Lord Anthony!" she protested.

"Why not?"

Francesca pushed away but did not have much room to distance herself. Nathaniel dropped his arms and took a few steps back.

"Well, for one, I've known him for several years. I even know his mother, though claim no advantage through that familiarity. But after all, Lord Anthony is heir to the estate in Cornwall, which probably has treasures far surpassing anything that can be found here." She studied him for several minutes, wondering if it was the relationship between Nathaniel and Lord Anthony that remained elusive, and what he knew that she did not. "But you are already familiar with his prospects."

"All too well," he said and drew in a deep breath before he continued. "I wonder he has even spoken of it, for he has not been there since he was old enough to mount his horse and ride away from Watch Hill. I do not think there has been any correspondence between him and the Earl d'Arcques in all the while. But why go to the bother? He has every reason to feel secure in his future, and the value of the property. There are copper mines, you see."

Francesca studied his face, trying to understand what he was saying and—even more—what he was not. But he gave little away, his expression as impassive as when he studied the mechanisms of Lady Cristobel.

"When you first came here, was it with the intent of seeking him out?"

Here his expression did change, and she knew he had been genuinely surprised. "No, I was looking for someone else. I knew Anthony was in London, of course—he leaves a trail of debts wherever he goes—but I did not expect to see him standing here between the bookshelves."

"He is a frequent visitor," Francesca reminded him. "I hardly think he waited to break into the shop when he could walk in at any time. Or, even more implausibly, wait until your arrival in town so he might attack you in the dark of night. Couldn't he have just thrown you off a cliff in Cornwall?"

111

"You have a vivid imagination, my dear," he said, pulling her close again. "But do you not believe I could best him in a wrestling match and throw him over instead?" He flexed his right arm.

"I believe you have been building your muscles by lugging round all the crates in the shop," she said, running her hand over his sleeve. "Whereas Lord Anthony manages to do as little physical labor as possible. He rarely walks out of here with anything heavier than a couple of books."

"Perhaps he isn't interested in anything else."

She raised her brows.

"Very well. He is interested in you. But then, so is every other man, young and old, who comes through the door."

She doubted it but accepted his flattery. "Is that why you decided to stay?"

He grinned and leaned forward to kiss her again. He didn't stop his gentle assault until she was absolutely breathless. "Of course. I am a man who appreciates having a vision of beauty greeting me every morning."

Francesca considered his words, at once so light spirited, and yet hinting at something far more serious.

****

Nathaniel leapt out of bed, wondering how he overslept, when he hadn't done so in years. His habits were embarrassingly regular: up with the sun, reading the newspaper in the late afternoon, retiring a few hours after dinner. He had been warned that life in London would disrupt his lifestyle, and indeed it had.

He simply did not expect how it would or why he would spend half the night in a half-dream state, thinking, imagining, re-envisioning his future. He promised Francesca that he would remain vigilant, listening for an intruder. But that was not the reason he remained awake; it was the thoughts of the lady herself. No woman ever had quite this effect on him.

He paused in the process of pulling on his shirt, knowing that he did look a good deal more muscular than any watchmaker had the right to be. He would allow Francesca to believe it had something to do with his manual work, but more likely his early years helping in the mines had something to do it, as well. He doubted there were any active mines in Piccadilly, but it was not London that had this unaccustomed effect on him. It was a lady who had disrupted his lifestyle.

As he fastened his shirt, he realized how pleased he was that he was not a murderer.

Indeed, it was the first thing she said to him upon greeting him downstairs.

"You're not a murderer," she said. It was a little earlier than she customarily arrived at the shop, but perhaps she considered that she had this bit of unfinished business between them.

"I am much relieved you think so. You should be relieved, as well," he said, knotting his cravat without the advantage of a mirror. It would have to do for now; perhaps, if things did not work out so well in London, he might hire himself out as a valet some day.

"But it cannot be Lord Anthony, either," she pointed out. Perhaps this was her unfinished business. "He was with me when the intruder returned and attacked you. He never left my side, all night."

"I wish that could make me feel better or safer," Nathaniel said. "I suppose that means you're not a murderer either?"

He intended to amuse her, but he saw that he only caused her greater consternation.

"But no one has been murdered, Nathaniel. The events of recent weeks could all be coincidence, the attack on you the act of a desperate man," she argued, and added, "Or woman."

He wanted to say she was undoubtedly right, but by now he was convinced someone was determined to get something he sought. And that her loyal Lord Anthony was as likely a suspect as anyone else, excepting himself. But he could already hear the sounds of activity on the street beyond the door, and there would be time enough later to speak of such things.

"Come, let us see to business," he reminded her. "We should discuss this later."

He walked through the shop just as the great long clock chimed the hour, soon accompanied by a chorus of higher-pitched bells and Nathaniel was somewhat satisfied to realize he was precisely on time to open the door to the waiting public.

Indeed, the public was already waiting. He greeted their customers cheerfully as a flood of people poured into the shop. Several asked why he wasn't already sitting in his seat of honor in the window, but most brushed right past him and scattered down the aisles, each with some specific objective in mind.

He supposed this was when he should be on alert, if Will's theory was to be tested and proved. Someone among them ought to be their intruder, silently searching through the pages of every book or shaking every jar. Of course, it would help to know for what they searched.

And then Lord Anthony, looking very fresh and neat, came through the door.

"Tony," Nathaniel said curtly, pulling his jacket a little closer over his wrinkled shirt. "A pleasure to see you again. And so soon after your last visit."

"You needn't do that act with me, my good man. You never seemed that pleased to see me in our life." Tony lifted his chin and sniffed the air, as if something was stale. If anything, it was his welcome.

"And where is our lady this morning?" he asked.

"I would not call her our lady, for she would not appreciate the possessive," Nathaniel said, even as he hoped she would allow him the privilege of using it. "She is at her desk, reading through several sheaves of papers."

"Then perhaps she would like me to join her, for I am very fond of reading papers," Anthony said.

Here was an unexpected admission.

"That's interesting," Nathaniel remarked. "I never knew you to read at all. Indeed, I recall you teased me mercilessly for my love of it."

"Ah, you misunderstand me, my good man. I don't care for books, with their confusing plots and implausible romances. But give me a few good epistles, some letters from a soldier or young man on his world tour, or even a good will. There I can find just the nugget I need to find myself thoroughly engaged."

"I see," Nathaniel said and rather thought he did. He wondered if his old acquaintance had read any good wills recently.

"Now that we are clear on that, allow me to go to the rear and assist Miss Wadsworth."

Nathaniel stepped in front of him, blocking his

path. "She does not wish to have company."

"Perhaps she does not wish for your company, my good man, but she would welcome mine."

If Tony called him "my good man" one more time, he would throw him out on the street. Or, at the very least, muss his perfectly styled hair.

"I have already said she does not wish to have company just now. Any company. I am happy to give her a message, or you could wait here. Perhaps you could try reading a book: that would be a true curiosity." Nathaniel crossed his arms over his chest.

Tony backed off, and with a rush of pleasure, Nathaniel thought about his boast to Francesca. Perhaps it was not entirely unfounded, for he suddenly felt confident he could best his old adversary in fisticuffs, if it came to it. However, he sincerely hoped it would not come to it.

"Don't mind me," Tony said. "I can take care of myself. You can retreat to your little window and smile at the passersby, like the queen's darling mother once did."

Nathaniel tried to think of some retort, hoping to have the last word. But then he heard Francesca's sweet voice and vowed he would have the last word after all, even if he said nothing.

In the meanwhile, there were customers, a surprising number of them. In this, he had to accede that Will was absolutely correct in the power of entertainment to bring in the curious, the lonely, and those who seemed determined to buy something every day, whether they needed it or not.

"I see all is going well, my good man," said a familiar voice.

Nathaniel turned to face his other employer, who had gladly given him several days off, in anticipation of the many customers coming into FW Wadsworth.

"I was just thinking of you, Will. But please don't call me that. I've heard enough of it from Lord Anthony this morning." He nodded in the direction of Tony's retreating back, following the siren call of Francesca's voice.

"He already stopped by my shop, apparently to question me about why you weren't yet open," Will said, and shrugged. "I told him you were probably otherwise engaged."

"Which led him to speculate about things that are none of his business," muttered Nathaniel. "But have a heart; I opened not five minutes later than I usually do."

"But you have been known to open earlier when a crowd is already forming on the street. What did he speculate about, by the way?"

"I don't see that it's any business of yours either," Nathaniel said, smiling.

Francesca approached them, and Nathaniel looked over her shoulder to see Tony holding an oil lamp, apparently perplexed. Will chuckled, sounding very satisfied with himself.

"Don't make any assumptions, Will," Nathaniel said, and then, "Yet."

"Good morning, Francesca," Will said. "I hope you do not plan to do much bookkeeping on a day such as today."

She blushed, and the word "radiant" came to mind. Nathaniel imagined it had something to do with himself.

"Oh, it is a glorious day, that is true," she said. "On

a day like this, I very much regret not being able to walk along the Birdcage or through Hyde Park."

"I rather meant the climate here in the shop. I hardly have any business at all just now. Everyone is here." Will gestured to the customers milling about, clearly satisfied with himself.

"Shall I send some people your way?" Francesca said, looking concerned.

"Oh, I am confident they will return when they are hungry for other things. One must eat, you know."

Tony emerged from between two bookcases, still holding the oil lamp, shrugging his shoulders. "I confess, I do not see much value in this, Miss Wadsworth. Perhaps you ought to save it for a special occasion."

Francesca took it from him and set it upon a table. "And yet, it feels just like a special occasion today. Like Boxing Day, or the queen's birthday." She was practically glowing.

The two men turned from her to Nathaniel, and he was afraid he might have glowed a bit, as well.

"Every moment in your presence is a special occasion, Miss Wadsworth," Tony said graciously.

She smiled at him, as if he were Paris, and she received his judgement and the apple. Nathaniel scowled.

"Miss Wadsworth," an older lady interrupted. "I am sorry to break up your conversation, but I believe I have an appointment with you."

"Why, you must be Mrs. Blanchard, Lady Sedgeworth's acquaintance," Francesca said, and turned away from all three of them. Nathaniel was curious, but Tony was not ready to let her go, now that he had the apparent advantage.

"My mother is also a friend of Lady Sedgeworth," he said. "Perhaps you know her as well."

Mrs. Blanchard gave him a questioning look.

"Lady Maitland, of Hampstead," he answered, preening a bit.

Mrs. Blanchard shook her head. "I do not know her, my lord. And, in any case, I cannot call Lady Sedgworth my friend. I am her dressmaker, and we have known each other for many, many years. I have made gowns for her since she was a child, and many more for her wonderful collection of dolls."

"That is how I know Lady Sedgeworth, of course," Francesca added. "She has purchased several unusual dolls from me and has expressed interest in Madame Cristobel." She glanced at him and shook her head, just slightly. "I told her that the automaton is not for sale, but she was rather more interested in giving Madame Cristobel a proper wardrobe."

Nathaniel relaxed, though wondered why she had not thought to mention all this to him. Perhaps a few kisses, no matter how passionate, were not enough to ensure the sharing of everything in one's life. He certainly couldn't blame her; he had shared almost none of his life's story, and nothing that was of great importance.

"It is not for me to make suggestions, but perhaps if you have me make several new gowns for you, Miss Wadsworth, I shall create miniature versions of each for Madame Cristobel."

"Of course you must make suggestions, Mrs. Blanchard! For it has been years since I've had new gowns made and have no idea what might be done for my miniature associate. It sounds very clever."

"It sounds like an excellent bit of publicity," Will joined in, as he would. "I think a blue satin gown would be quite flattering, perhaps with a matching fan. Mrs. Blanchard, are you able to fashion a little fan for the Madame?" He gestured toward the window.

"Of course, sir," the dressmaker said, enthusiastically. "I have millinery skills as well. In fact, I recommend…"

Whatever it was Mrs. Blanchard recommended was not of immediate concern to Nathaniel, and he imagined he would hear more about it, in any case. He bowed and stepped away from the little circle, eliciting a look of envy from Tony, and offered to help a gentleman who wished to look at an old atlas. Occasionally, he looked over at the others and saw that Tony looked as bored as Nathaniel knew he would have been. Will, of course, had a lot to say on sarcenet, moiré, and toile. At least, that's what he thought he heard.

But Nathaniel sold the atlas, which was a much better use of his time.

When the first rush of customers finally left, some with and some without purchases, and Mrs. Blanchard set off on her mission to procure all sorts of fabrics, there was a respite from the public life of running a business. Francesca approached him, a bit cautiously, he thought, and was then reassured when he opened his arms to her.

"We are not alone," she warned him, and he promptly dropped his arms.

"More's the pity," he said. "How many hours until we could close up for the night?"

"Much too long," she said softly. "But this is proving to be a very good day. Perhaps I can now afford to order the gowns that Mrs. Blanchard suggests. She will make Madame Cristobel's gowns at no cost, if we advertise her little shop in the window."

"That sounds fair enough," Nathaniel said. "I shall have to discuss this with Mrs. Blanchard before she starts taking measurements, for Madame Cristobel's arms do not move in the usual way. She will need extra room at the elbows and shoulders. I am not certain that she can manage a fan, however much it might complement her blue satin gown. You will probably fare a good deal better."

"You know a lot about this, do you not?" she asked, laughing.

"Not as much as I wish. I am still studying the female form," he said seriously.

She swatted him with a pamphlet she held, probably one given to her by the dressmaker. "We are not alone," she said again.

Chapter 7

For the first time in her adult life, Francesca was impatient, and even resentful, of the little antiquarian shop in which her father and grandfather had labored for so many years. As a child, she sometimes decried her father's inattentiveness, as he turned from her and her siblings to a new shipment of foreign books or a carved coat rack. The dusty and fragile items that consumed his time did not seem at all interesting to her.

But then she grew older, and her brother and sister set off on their own adventures, and her prospects seemed very limited in scope or possibility. And then her own parents went off, to explore the world that they had only experienced through the artifacts they collected, and she was left alone to make a go of the venerable old business. It was a respectable trade, and one that necessitated social interaction and keeping herself in the public eye. She accepted her position with grace and always felt comfortable and safe.

Until the day someone entered her store and destroyed her sense of security. Everything changed that day, for those circumstances also brought Nathaniel into her life.

Whatever happened, whatever future they may or may not have together, she imagined she would always cherish the pleasures of these days, when she flirted with respectability, when every part of her being was acutely aware of the presence of another person, and when she dared to imagine a different narrative to her story.

As a result, Francesca was now impatient with her shop, the customers, and all the treasures within, for she longed to be with Nathaniel and forget about all else.

Throughout the day, she watched him, occasionally meeting his eye. When he thought no one was around, he seized the moment and her and reminded her that it all was real. He made her believe that he might like to forget about everything else as well.

Instead of thinking about all the work that needed to be done, she thought about him and everything they had done and said. How easily they slipped into small endearments and intimacies. How free they had been with their words and deeds. She reimagined it all, recalling everything he had said about intruders and murderers, the estate on which he grew up, his arrival in London.

And yet there was something that remained unsaid, and she wondered how she might reclaim the moment just before they were distracted and that "something" slipped between them.

Francesca glanced around the shop, noting a gentleman perusing the shelves, and another examining the cameo brooches. They were among the regulars, so she doubted they needed help making a decision on items they had looked at for weeks. And Nathaniel was in the window, his hands still, his eyes gazing at Madame Cristobel.

"Mr. Endicott," she said formally, in case her customers listened.

"Hmmm?" he murmured, his eyes still on the

automaton.

She walked to the window, which provided some privacy, for all that hundreds of people walked in the street. "Last night you said something that you did not explain."

Now she had his attention. He turned to her and gestured to the customers, as if she did not know they were there. "And what is that, Miss Wadsworth?"

Now that she thought of it, it sounded a little silly. "You said that you came to London looking for someone, but it was not Lord Anthony."

"Did I say that?" he asked, sounding perplexed.

"Yes, Mr. Endicott, I believe you did. Whom do you seek?"

"Would you believe me if I say it is you?"

"That is very romantic," she said, dropping her voice. "But you did not even know I existed. You thought FW Wadsworth was a man."

"You can forgive me that misunderstanding," he said.

"Were you looking for my father?"

He leaned back so far on his chair, she was afraid it would slip out from beneath him and he would crash through the window.

"I was looking for this lady right here, Madame Cristobel," he confessed and sounded as if he meant it.

"Do I have reason to be jealous of a wooden lady in shabby dress?" she asked skeptically.

"Perhaps you do," he said and again sounded very serious. His chair dropped to all four legs, and he put up a finger, gesturing her to come closer. Surely he didn't intend to kiss her in front of everyone walking by on King Street?

He didn't. Instead, his fingers wrapped around the tiny inkwell that was affixed to Madame Cristobel's small desk, and turned it ever so slightly clockwise. Francesca heard the slightest sigh, like a groan, and then the automaton's delicate arms started to move over the surface of her desk.

All other thoughts passed from her head. She could not look away. Madame Cristobel's arms danced a slow ballet, but one in which she was not quite sure of the steps. Her tiny fingers twitched in the air, almost too impatient for the slow pace of her arms, looking as if they would knead a loaf of bread. Francesca marveled at the show, her thoughts racing from the sublime to the mundane.

"You've done it," Francesca whispered. She was aware that a small group of people had gathered in the street, calling over others. The two gentlemen in the shop came up behind her.

"I have not," Nathaniel confessed. "I have only set her in motion, but she is not capable of delivering any messages. Or rather, I am not sure I am capable of going any further."

Impossible though it was to imagine Nathaniel incapable of anything, she seized on several words. "Delivering messages?"

"Yes. She is not simply a music box dancer, you realize. When she was new, she was capable of scripting several messages, and even drawing a few landscapes. Those are modest accomplishments for a lady of her advanced age but rather extraordinary for an automaton."

Francesca realized his earlier words were, indeed, seriously said. He had come for Madame Cristobel; it was what brought him into the shop on that unsettling day. He'd known about her all the while.

"How do you know all this, sir?" said one of the gentlemen behind Francesca, surprising her, for she had been thinking the very thing herself.

"Why, I know the lady very well, sir. Or, at least, I know something about her. My great-grandfather created her in the early years of this century, and in letters to his family in England, he always wrote wistfully of her, as if she were his lost love." Nathaniel answered the gentleman, but his eyes were on Francesca alone. "He apprenticed at Peter Kinzing's workshop in Trieste."

"I know the name, for it is long associated with such work," the gentleman said. "I recall there was some connection with the French revolution, undoubtedly not a pleasant one."

"You have it right. Joseph Mollinger is most famous for having crafted the lady with a dulcimer over a hundred years ago. Several similar musical ladies were created in his workshop. Kinzing, his student, made a nearly identical one for Marie Antoinette, and no one knows what became of it. It is rumored that it is in a private collection in Vienna, though that has not been substantiated."

There was silence for a few moments, as everyone undoubtedly recollected what became of the unfortunate queen, and how Versailles and the other royal estates were plundered of all their treasures.

"A branch of the Kinzing family lives not very far from here, in Mayfair," Nathaniel added unnecessarily.

"How came Madame Cristobel to London?" the other gentleman asked. "With that Kinzing relative?"

"I don't believe so," Nathaniel said, thoughtfully. "For that, I must refer you to Miss Wadsworth, as she is the proprietor of the shop. I am only her shop assistant."

Everyone's eyes were now upon her, and she shrugged as if it could not matter.

"I have no idea," she admitted. "The automaton has been here for many years but has never before been capable of any movement. She has just been one of our curiosities and an object of great speculation."

"And you have brought her back to life, sir. Well done!" said one of the gentlemen. Several people cheered.

"Not nearly so, I regret to say. Completing the work may be beyond my capabilities," repeated Nathaniel, sharing none of their triumph. Indeed, it was quite the opposite; it was if he pulled a plug from a balloon.

The cheering suddenly stopped, and a few men shrugged as they wandered back to the four corners of the shop.

"You shall have to remind me to never invite you to a dinner party, Nathaniel," Francesca said. "You certainly know how to deflate high spirits."

"Would you be lonely without me there at your dinner party?" he asked. "I seem to be able to attract a good crowd, for all that I am compelled to always tell you and others the truth."

She scoffed at the idea. "Certainly, telling the truth is no one's idea of a popular party amusement. I shudder to think of you telling women how they look in their baggy gown, or commenting on the ill-prepared food."

"I think I've already demonstrated that I know

when silence is in order," he said, and turned to look back at Madame Cristobel, still holding silent on whatever messages her creator wished for her to share. He turned the inkwell, and her movements ceased. "I would have better luck with her, however. I am able to turn her on and off as I wish. You see the mechanism here."

"What would you like her to tell you?" Francesca asked, wondering how important this was to him. His obvious disappointment did not simply seem to be a matter of his lack of skill at watchmaking.

"The truth," he said, and Francesca wasn't sure if he was merely playing on their words.

"Who knows what she might reveal?" Francesca mused. "And, indeed, I now appreciate that you were telling me the truth when you said that you came to London just in search of her."

For all she valued the truth, it did not give her much comfort just now.

"I did not lie," he conceded. "But it now seems that I have found a good deal more than a wooden automaton." His voice dropped to a whisper.

"Will you stay?" she asked, so lost in their own world she did not realize a customer approached.

Nathaniel's eyes glanced meaningfully to the left. "I can stay for a bit longer, but then must go on to the cheese shop. Will has something that demands my attention."

That was not what she had in mind.

Once he started to talk to the customer, explaining something of automatons, from their earliest incarnations to the possibilities of human-sized machines, Francesca escaped back into their own world, though without him. That was the problem, she realized. Knowing what it was to be with him, she did not want to ever be without him. Will would understand. He'd practically forced them to come together in the first place. And he could find another man to cut up large blocks of cheese; anyone could do that.

Nathaniel was an artist, after all. What if he sliced off a finger wielding that huge knife? Then, he would never be able to do the meticulous, laborious work of a craftsman. No, he didn't belong in a cheese shop. He belonged here, with her.

Satisfied with her own argument, she smiled to another customer, and proceeded to show the lady every scrap of brocade she had in the shop, none of which were to the lady's satisfaction.

Francesca, herself, was not anywhere as fussy. When Mrs. Blanchard arrived at the shop several days later, at an appointed time, with the most glorious array of fabrics, ribbons, buttons, and beads, Francesca felt like a girl again. She was so unaccustomed to frivolity, such a stranger to vanity, she scarcely recognized herself. She fancied the thought that once she had some new gowns made just for her, others might not recognize her either, least of all her parents. If they ever returned to London.

"You are far too beautiful to settle for something made for another," Mrs. Blanchard pointed out, as she bustled about. They had retreated to a tiny room in the back of the shop, no bigger than a closet. She paused to study Francesca's form with critical eye, and Francesca hoped more flattery might follow. But instead, the woman looked exasperated.

"Have you never thought about wearing light and airy colors, in bombazine or lace overlay?"

No, of course she did not.

"I've never really needed anything special in my wardrobe, Mrs. Blanchard. Practical and warm garments that do not show stains or dust are perfectly suited to my work here in the shop."

Mrs. Blanchard drew in a deep breath. The exasperation, as it turned out, was only partly for Francesca's lack of self-indulgence.

"And do you spend all your hours here, Miss Wadsworth? There is not nearly enough room in this place for you to model and for me to drape and pin," said Mrs. Blanchard, impatiently pushing away a small cabinet.

Francesca's pleasure now abated, for she had spent the better part of the morning arranging this private fitting space for their use.

"There is my home, of course. It is not very distant, and there is far more room than I know what to do with, for I live quite alone. But I thought having you come here would be more efficient, in case my advice is needed in matters of the business. My assistant is only newly hired, you realize, and not certain about all the particulars."

"If you refer to Mr. Endicott, I am of the opinion that he is familiar with the particulars, and a good deal else, besides. He also seems to be quite capable with his hands."

Francesca could hardly miss the dressmaker's implication, especially as the women's hands hovered about her shoulders.

"And besides," Francesca added quickly, "did you

not say you would create a matching gown for Madame Cristobel?"

Mrs. Blanchard waved dismissively. "Madame Cristobel's gown will be made from the trimmings of the fabric we use for yours. You may believe that she's the star attraction of your shop, but she is nothing more than a doll, a wooden accessory." She mumbled something under her breath. "Do turn around, Miss Wadsworth. I wish to see how well this blue superfine complements your lovely eyes."

They continued in silence for several minutes, each to her own thoughts. While Mrs. Blanchard pinned and pleated, ruffled and flattened, Francesca fancied being the star attraction of her own shop. She supposed it would hardly make a difference to even her most loyal customers, for they surely saw her as no more than a part of the furnishings. But what would Nathaniel say? Would he notice?

"Your young man will be dazzled, I daresay," said Mrs. Blanchard, reading her thoughts. Was she that transparent? "It would do him well to look away from that wooden doll. She doesn't even look like a lady."

"I am sure when you are done dressing her up, she will be the belle of the curiosity shop."

Mrs. Blanchard looked like she swallowed one of her straight pins.

"Perhaps I did not make myself clear, Miss Wadsworth. My intent is that you shall be the belle." She continued quite determinedly, gathering up fabric, and draping it about Francesca's body. "And I mean what I say about that poppet in the window. Whoever carved her knew nothing about a woman's form, for she has neither a waist nor anything resembling a bosom.

She is no lady."

****

Nathaniel looked up from cleaning up the shards of a small vase broken by a most apologetic woman who demonstrated her regrets by neither offering to pay for it, nor helping him gather up the pieces. Not for the first time, he questioned the wisdom of having so much merchandise available for people to handle, or mishandle. But Francesca insisted that customers could not know what they truly wanted until they made a visceral connection with something unfamiliar and exotic.

And now that he watched her slowly approach him, he understood the value of that philosophy, though not in the way she intended. While he had admired her beauty and intelligence from the moment he stepped into the shop all those weeks ago, touching her, holding her, brought him to a wholly different state of awareness. As customers knew what they wanted after handling an item, so he now knew he must have her.

He took a step forward, unable to resist temptation, before remembering that the shop was full of customers, some waiting for him to resume his place in the window with Madame Cristobel. But both the customers and the automaton would have to wait.

Francesca looked flushed, radiant, really. Her hair was in some disarray, and a few stray threads clung to her wool dress. The top three buttons at her neckline were undone, revealing more than she usually allowed customers to see.

He dreamed how much beauty could yet be revealed.

"Mrs. Blanchard seems to have worked wonders,"

he said when she came close.

She misunderstood him, intentionally, he thought. "Oh, the gowns will not be ready for some weeks. And poor Madame Cristobel will have to be patient until we see how much fabric and trim is left over from the cuttings."

"Poor indeed," he said grinning. "I am sure there are many who would be honored to receive the bounty of your leftovers."

"Oh, really, Nathaniel," she demurred. "I have had leftovers all my life and have now decided that new things are infinitely preferable. Certainly, Mrs. Blanchard assures me it is so."

"Yes, I suppose she would. Where is she by the way?"

"Already at work, pinning up the shape of the gowns. She will join us shortly." She glanced about the shop. "Have I missed much?"

"Some breakage, some interest in the Italian statuary, the sale of an enameled snuff box. Oh, yes, and an eccentric old gentleman who had something important to say about Madame Cristobel but could not quite remember what it was."

"Who is he?" She spoke slowly, her eyes never leaving his.

"He told me his name was Greeves, or Greeveson, perhaps. There was something about a son. He came in with his dog, who was well behaved enough, but whose wagging tail threatened everything on the low tables and worried the old man. Oh, and he wished to know if I found the parts of another automaton that was broken, but Madame's mate."

"Well, have you?" She sounded perplexed but did

not deny such parts existed. They might prove quite useful to him now.

"You know I have not," he said, wondering what she kept from him. Odds were about even, he supposed. "I know of no such thing."

Mrs. Blanchard chose that moment to come through the office door. She sneezed rather dramatically and immediately attracted an audience.

"It is no wonder your automaton's gown is falling apart," she said. "Dust has that effect on fabric. And on one's lungs, of course. Miss Wadsworth, you really must get out more once you have your new gowns. It would do them well and wouldn't hurt you either, I believe." The woman glanced from Francesca to him and squinted. "It would do you both well."

"Thank you for your good advice," Francesca said graciously. The dressmaker made a sound of impatience and brushed past them. They watched as her rolls of fabric knocked against fragile figures and several fossils from East Lyme, until an incoming customer held the door open for her.

"She does have a point," Nathaniel said. "While you promenade along King Street in your new garments, you might hand out business cards along the way."

She gave him a bemused look. "I don't think she is thinking of my business success as much as my social success. Why else would she suggest you accompany me?"

"I would very much like to escort you, of course," he said, wistfully. "But Mrs. Blanchard cannot know how busy we are in the store. Perhaps you should hire a shop assistant for your shop assistant?"

"I hope your assistant would not be invited to move into the attic rooms. It would be a bit crowded up there."

He held her gaze. "On the other hand, I am doing so well, it might be time for me to rent my own rooms, or perhaps a modest townhouse."

"I cannot make you out sometimes, Nathaniel. You would have me believe you are in need of employment and could scarcely afford rooms for yourself. Are you in expectation of a modest inheritance?"

Here was a moment of truth, he realized, and cleared his throat.

But Francesca looked away as if she already knew his answer and smiled at an expectant customer. Nathaniel wasn't sure if the man grinned because he overheard their conversation or if he was just pleased to be the object of her attention.

Briefly, Nathaniel envied the fellow. After all, it did not take him long to understand that it was a mixed blessing being close to her all day, every day. On the one hand, she was his to admire and respect. On the other, he could only rarely claim her full attention, unless he pulled her up to his attic rooms.

And yet, he thought it would be as close to heaven as he would likely get.

Considering her present circumstances, Francesca could not remember feeling as satisfied as she was at this moment. But, indeed, it was because her present circumstances were so unexpected and so gratifying that she was in a place of joy. Only weeks before, losing the sanctuary that her shop always afforded left her bereft and despairing. And then Will pushed Nathaniel through her door, and suddenly they came to an amicable agreement, and now the shop was full of interested customers, and she was to wear new gowns, and Madame Cristobel was getting the attention she deserved, and she herself spent hours of each day with a man she was coming to love.

She dared to imagine Nathaniel might spend his life in her shop and with her, and they should never get tired of it or each other. It was a bit of a fool's dream, of course, for they scarcely knew each other. And yet, the thought kept intruding into her practical and sensible thoughts.

"Miss Wadsworth, I don't believe you've heard a word I've said," said Miss Tupper.

Francesca blinked at the familiar customer who stood before her, wondering how she came to be standing there, and what on earth she said.

"I apologize, Miss Tupper. My thoughts were on...ah...the arrival of a new shipment of goods arriving from China."

"Your father always gave me his full attention," Miss Tupper grumbled. "And would hold rare porcelain pieces for me to see if I approved. I expect there are some pieces that might interest me, arriving in that shipment."

Francesca considered that there might indeed be, if such a shipment actually existed.

"I shall send a note to you as soon as I receive it, and Mr. Endicott would be happy to unpack it all for your perusal."

"I should enjoy being present for that, while I peruse him."

Francesca blinked, not sure she heard the lady, always so proper, say such a thing.

"Are you aware I own the Pipedown Music Hall?"

This was rather unexpected. Whatever she expected to be the source of Miss Tupper's income, it was not the popular and somewhat bawdy theater.

"Yes, indeed," Miss Tupper said without waiting for an answer. "It was my father's, and now it is mine."

"How very fortunate for you," Francesca said. "I have something of the same circumstance, myself, though my father was alive and well as of a letter I received two months ago."

"Yes, we live in modern times. When I was a child, there was no talk of a woman running a business, though it was not impossible. Only a bit disreputable."

Francesca reflected that one's reputation would suffer a good deal more if one owned a music hall than if one owned a shop but decided not to point that out.

Miss Tupper continued. "Indeed, times have changed. One is likely to see just about anyone in attendance, all the best people. So your presence would scarcely be noticed."

Francesca wondered if that was a compliment, sort of.

"I should like you to come as my guest, with your young man. I daresay he would not be above himself, either." And then, for the first time in all the while Francesca knew Miss Tupper, the woman smiled.

Now there was no doubt whom she meant. Was it possible that everyone in London was trying to make a match between her and Nathaniel?

"That is very generous of you, Miss Tupper. I haven't ever been to a performance, though I have heard that both European and American singers grace the stage. Did not Lillie Langtry appear only recently, as her welcome to a new life in London?"

"Yes, yes. It's not only Punch and Judy reviews, you know. The quality will only come for quality."

"Yes, I do know that," Francesca reflected, thinking of her own customers. They only wanted the best. Those who were just now clustered about Nathaniel's workbench knew Madame Cristobel was a rare commodity. They might also think the same of the watchmaker.

"I hope Tuesday next will suit you and Mr. Endicott. When you come, please give the attendant my name, and he will direct you to my private box."

"Thank you, Miss Tupper," Francesca said, too surprised at the invitation to decline or demur. And then, after a few moments, "I am sure we will enjoy it. And will you be there?"

Miss Tupper gave her a disparaging look, and answered, "I do not usually mingle with the masses. But I shall be off to Paris on the next day and will leave instructions for my manager."

"That sounds lovely, Miss Tupper. I have never been to Paris. Will you be there on an extended stay?"

"Not at all, for I can scarcely abide the place. I intend to watch a performance of the Songbird of the Seine. A rather elegant chanteuse, though there are rumors that she hails from Manchester. I, of course, shall find out the truth of the matter."

"Does it truly matter if she is as good as people say?"

"Does it truly matter if one buys an Etruscan vase from FW Wadsworth, Bookseller and Antiquarian and later determines it was made in the potteries?"

"Yes, I see your point. One wants to get one's

money's worth."

"I always do," Miss Tupper said and sniffed. Francesca decided that meant there was nothing that overly impressed her in the shop. Miss Tupper started to walk off but then reconsidered. "When Mr. Endicott has his automaton moving about, I should like to purchase her. I believe she would make an excellent entertainment in the Pipedown lobby. And she would be likely to bring in new customers, as I suspect she has done here."

"I am not sure Madame Cristobel will be for sale, Miss Tupper."

Again, that rare smile. "Of course she shall be, my dear Miss Wadsworth. Does not everything have a price?"

Francesca was wholly disconcerted by this conversation and found herself distracted throughout the rest of the day. And yet, what did Miss Tupper say that wasn't true? As businesswomen, they both knew that it was possible to buy nearly everything, including merchandise, staff, good service, loyalty. And for all that Francesca ran an honest enterprise and was able to afford a few fine gowns, she would never be a lady. Concerns for her reputation were irrelevant, for she scarcely had a reputation to risk.

Nathaniel Endicott was a man who could not be bought. She might have thought so, on the day he showed up at her door, but she did not doubt he would be perfectly able to manage without her attic rooms, the small salary she paid him, and, indeed, herself, whenever he accomplished what he wished in London.

She needed to talk to him, to settle her unrest. She wanted to discuss the matter of attending a music hall review, though she suspected he was already familiar with such things from his travels to Paris, and Trieste, and Amsterdam. She wanted his approval of receiving their tickets as gifts, inasmuch as he seemed offended when Lord Anthony offered to send them to the theater. And she wished to discuss Madame Cristobel's future. Had he already hinted to customers that she might be available for sale? Were both she and Madame Cristobel getting new gowns made so they could be better displayed in the marketplace?

She finally caught Nathaniel's eye and watched him stand and stretch his arms. Several women gazing through the window noticed that, too. But instead of coming to the back of the shop, where she was fixed at the counter, he gave her a little wave and pointed down the street to Will's shop. In a moment, he was out the door, making his way through his delighted audience.

Must she always share his attention?

After several customers left, she walked through the shop, straightening the shelves as she moved. Why was no one capable of putting an object back where he found it? Most Londoners seemed to have no more interest in order than the intruder who wreaked havoc all those weeks ago.

And where was he, anyway? The stupid scheme that Will and Nathaniel concocted did nothing more than make Nathaniel and Madame Cristobel minor celebrities. A few more people came by to shop, to be sure, but many more stayed outside, watching the show in the window. And she was no closer to solving the mystery of what the intruder wanted. No one who visited the shop was particularly odd or asked too many questions or pocketed silver spoons. Or more than usual.

An elderly man stood outside the door, admonishing a large dog. A few moments later, he entered the shop, quite alone, and Francesca recognized him as someone she had seen before.

"Are you Mrs. Wadsworth?" he asked, removing his hat. Yes, he had been here only a day or so ago.

"I am Miss Wadsworth," she explained. "Francis Wadsworth is my father."

The man tapped his bald head. "Of course. I am living in the past. You are far too young to be Mrs. Wadsworth. I thought you might be Charity, for so she looked when last I saw her."

Francesca drew a long breath.

"You knew my mother?" Her mother so rarely spoke of her own family, but that she lost her own mother and sisters to smallpox when she was a little girl. Her father survived with several facial scars, but young Charity Williams somehow escaped unscathed. That is, if losing most of your family could be considered unscathed. "And to whom do I have the honor of speaking?"

"I am Horace Graves," he said and stiffly bowed. "I was the driver who brought your mother to London when she was a young girl. To her aunt, Lady Everly."

"Yes, I have heard much about Lady Everly." There was another sad consequence of her mother losing the other women in her family, for she always insisted that the less said about her aunt, the better for them all. "My grandfather sent my mother to his sister so she could improve her situation in society."

"Your grandfather sent your mother to London so she could share the company of women, if you don't mind my saying. He was a kind and gentle man, but he had no idea how to raise a daughter. I believe he hoped to marry again but died himself some years later."

"Do sit down, Mr. Graves. You seem to know a great deal about my family."

"They were almost like my own," he said, grasping the back of the chair so tightly, his knuckles whitened. He sat down heavily. "I remember your mother sobbing nearly all the way to London, and me not knowing what to do to comfort her."

"How awful for you," Francesca murmured. "What did you do?"

"I sang to her, trying to cheer her up."

Francesca thought about a young girl leaving her home and father to be thrust into a strange new life in a big city.

"Over the hills, over the rivers, on roads the old Romans trod…" she started to sing, a bit unsteadily.

"You know it, do you?" Mr. Graves looked at her, clearly pleased.

Francesca nodded. "It was the lullaby she sang to her children when we were babies. Perhaps it reminded her of home and was the only thing she brought with her on her journey."

"What makes you say that?" Mr. Graves said, surprised. "Mr. Williams sent nearly everything that reminded him of his wife and the other girls, along with her. Clothes, books, ribbons, shoes, dolls, watercolors of puppies and horses. I thought the wagon would collapse under the weight of everything that came with her, though she was no more than a mite herself."

Francesca shook with the certainty that she already knew something she just never thought much about before. "What else came with her to London?"

"Why, I wanted to tell that young man who works in your window all about it. I thought he would be the one. But he is just a craftsman and may not know much of the history."

Nathaniel was more than a craftsman and knew a great deal, but Francesca was reluctant to reveal her hand. Or Nathaniel's.

"What else came with her to London?" she repeated.

"Now that I think on it, it wasn't all girly things. Her father sent her with crates and crates of treasures, most of which had been in Charity's family for years. I recall Mr. Williams telling me there was silver and Roman vases, and I should keep an eye on the stable yard when we went inside a posting house to eat. He didn't want anything stolen, you see. There were clay animals from Egypt, though I don't know what anyone would do with that nonsense. And the lady in the window, of course." He glanced in the direction of the worktable, where Madame Cristobel slumped facedown at her desk. "Your grandfather said, aside from your mother, that was the most precious thing to be delivered to Lady Everly. 'Christ's Bell,' he called her. I thought she was intended for the belfry of a church."

"That's a natural enough suggestion, Mr. Graves. But I would have thought whatever came with her was intended to pay for her expenses. The family was not wealthy." Francesca was suddenly reminded of all her parents' stories, told over many years. "As it is, young Charity Williams married the one man who would appreciate both her and her family treasures. My father already possessed this small business and, with his marriage, gained a partner and inventory to sustain him for the rest of his life."

"Little Charity married well. I am glad to hear of it."

Francesca wondered if she already said too much. "Is that why you come to visit, Mr. Graves? To hear how a little girl's life turned out?"

Mr. Graves looked perplexed. "Yes, there is that, of course. I am happy for her. But there is more."

"Yes?" Francesca vaguely wondered if he was requesting recompense for his information.

"I happened to walk down King Street while in town to visit my son and his family, and heard about the automaton in the window of a shop. This one in fact."

"Of course," Francesca said impatiently.

"And I wondered what became of the man," he said.

"My father? He is traveling with my mother."

"No, the other," Mr. Graves said, nodding his head. "Your Madame Christ's Bell did not come alone. There was another, a man, wrapped in linen like some Egyptian mummy at The British Museum, who came with her, in a crate full of papers and books, and tools covered with oil. To protect them from rust, you know."

"No, I did not know," she said, but her thoughts were not on tools undoubtedly better preserved than herself. She thought of the crates so long abandoned in the attic, and the sheafs of papers that she only occasionally bothered perusing. "I did not know."

"He was in parts, all broken up. Mr. Williams said that someone took a mallet to him, looking for a treasure inside and leaving him all to pieces. I don't know if the bloke found anything, but Mr. Williams gave me some more parts after I returned from London. I still have them, never knew what to do with them." He shrugged. "You can have them. They are rightfully yours, I suspect."

"Thank you, Mr. Graves. I will look for the other pieces, and if I find them, we can attempt to put the automaton together or at least, give him a proper funeral."

He shrugged again and left her alone in the shop, intrigued and certainly confused.

Chapter 8

When Nathaniel returned from the cheesemonger, he said something quite unexpected. "Would you like to go for a stroll with me?"

Francesca eyed him somewhat suspiciously. "And what is our destination?"

"Do we require a destination?"

No, she supposed they did not, though it had been some time since she walked through the streets of London for the simple purpose of taking the air.

"One usually knows where one is going, Nathaniel," she pointed out.

"Is it not a bit of an adventure to set out, and not know where the path might lead? It could be compared to starting a new friendship; one doesn't know where one might end up." His smile was a little lopsided, as if he couldn't decide if that was amusing or not. "Let that be our destination, then. You and I shall set forth and see where it goes."

There was no point in arguing with him, mostly because she couldn't think of anything more pleasurable than to walk around town with her arm through his. Wordlessly, she went to the back of the shop and retrieved her bonnet and a blue knitted shawl, in case they remained outdoors in the cooler evening hours.

"What if the intruder comes by when we're gone?"

she asked when she returned to his side.

"Are we destined to never be outdoors at the same time? What will happen when we go to Miss Tupper's bawdy review in a few days' time?" She laughed at his assessment. "Yes, she told me all about it. Besides, I asked Will to have a look every so often. He approves of my plan to whisk you away for a bit and was happy to oblige."

She stopped laughing but accepted his arm as they walked out the door, locking it behind them.

"I forget sometimes you are a London lady. Country folk think nothing of walking about, through the meadows, up hills and down to the beach, observing the clouds rolling in. In fact, I find it clears my thoughts of all that bothers me." He led her down King Street toward St. James. "Indeed, we do not lock our doors, either."

She suddenly remembered Mr. Graves and her mother's lullaby.

"I entertained a very interesting man this afternoon, who told me of another I should meet," she said.

She felt his muscle tighten. "I suppose it's your blasted Lord Anthony."

"No, not at all. In fact, I think you already met him. Mr. Greeves? His name is Mr. Graves, who knew my mother when she was a girl. He was very charming."

"Richard the Third was said to be very charming as well," he said under his breath. "And yet you trusted this Mr. Graves? He could be our thief, for all we know."

"I suppose he could be, but he knew things that I doubt anyone else would know," she said. "I do trust him."

"That could be his perfect ploy to make himself free in the shop. And with you. I don't like this at all." He stopped, and turned to face her. "And he spoke of another man? Do not allow them into the shop if I am not there with you."

"I suspect the other man is probably already in the shop."

He looked away, so she wouldn't hear him swear. But she did and was more amused than offended. Turning back, he asked, "Does the blighter refer to me?"

She patted his arm, gently, and was tempted to do even more to reassure him. But they were on the street, surrounded by half of London.

"Apparently, Madame Cristobel has a brother. Perhaps a husband," she said. "Mr. Graves told me that he delivered my mother to the home of her aunt, along with Madame Cristobel and the parts of a gentleman automaton, as well as all sorts of treasures to serve as a dowry when my mother was ready to marry."

"The parts of a gentleman automaton, you say?"

Francesca heard the relief in his words. He took her arm under her elbow, and they resumed their stroll.

"Mr. Graves says so. I know nothing more about it, or him," Francesca said.

"I believe I do. Do you not recall? I may have uncovered parts of him when we looked through some of the trunks that were in the attic. Though as to that, at the time I thought I was looking at the painted face of a woman. She certainly appeared more feminine than Madame Cristobel, whose features are a bit hard." He touched his own aquiline nose and nodded. "But your parents stored him for all these years, whatever his sad condition."

"You do not know my parents, but you do know the shop. Does it look like my parents ever discarded a single thing they possessed?" She laughed again, thinking of the great volume of merchandise he had yet to uncover and inventory. And therefore stay with her.

"Well, we should be grateful for that. Monsieur Cristobel could have been tossed onto the junk heap years ago or made into a table lamp. Or a door stop."

"But there you found him, most likely still packed away in the trunk he arrived in. There are so many crates and boxes full of things I haven't even seen. But someday we shall have a full inventory and perhaps find many other surprises as well."

"I have been in the cellar, you know, and am already familiar with the contents of the attic. There aren't that many things that look like they've been untouched for so many years."

"Oh, Nathaniel, you don't know half of it!" she said, and he glanced down at her, surprised. "You have never seen my parents' home here in town. There's scarcely enough room to place a pocket watch on the shelves in the parlor or the library. Or the bedrooms, for that matter. Now that I think of it, Mr. Graves spoke of Egyptian artifacts, and I'm almost certain they are in the dining room. I suppose the rest of Monsieur Cristobel could be tucked away in a cabinet or closet."

"I suppose we might not be the only ones looking for him, either," he said, and they continued in silence, each to his or her own thoughts.

"Where are we?" Francesca asked, suddenly.

Nathaniel looked around and realized they had gone some way, though he scarcely remembered how they came to be in this place. His distracted state proved his own words about losing oneself in the journey.

"Why, the Inns of Court are just yonder. This is the Temple Church before us," he said.

"Dear heavens, you have just demonstrated how much of a recluse I've become. I scarcely recognize the place, and you know it immediately, though a stranger to London."

"But not a stranger to books and maps, my dear. Even in far-off Cornwall, we know about the Temple Church, built by the Knights Templar to remind them of their Eastern conquests. There's nothing else quite like it on our busy island. Samuel Johnson thought so too; I believe he lived not far from here." He paused, thinking he was indulging in showing off his new knowledge of the town. "Besides, I am down here often, on my way to the docks."

"Oh, yes. Of course. Perhaps I should get out more often."

"Perhaps we will," he said, hoping she noticed his small amendment. "Are you hungry? We have come a long way."

"I find that I am. But I do not know of any dining establishments in the area."

"I do," he said, and winked at her.

He thought about several places he had frequented in the past weeks, with their customary boisterous conversations fueled by men who drank too much and worked too hard. He had learned a lot about their lives, their politics, and their expectations. As for the latter, they were fairly modest, as few expected to accomplish much more than their fathers before them. About this, he was noticeably silent in their company, though no one seemed to notice.

He glanced down at the lady at his side, for she was a lady, for all she kept a shop and eschewed balls and dinner parties. He wasn't entirely sure what she thought of his place in society, though she already accepted him as at least her equal and possibly more than that.

"I know a quiet place where the food is quite good, and we're more likely to find those employed at the Inns of Court than dockworkers." At her sigh of pleasure, he added, "Are you too tired to walk there? It is fairly close by."

"If I were too tired, would you carry me all the way?" she asked.

He hoped she was teasing, and yet somehow her question seemed like a test.

"No, I would hire a hackney cab," he said. "Shall I do so?"

She met his eyes and he tried to see himself as she saw him, if she already guessed at his life and politics and expectations. He already told her as much as he ought and was truthful—or nearly so—in all. But the time would come, perhaps very soon, when all would need to be laid out on the table.

"I suspect I can manage it so long as I have the support of your sturdy arm. But I believe it is important to assess the situation before one encounters the absolute necessity of acting or relying on one for assistance. One never knows."

Still looking at her, he said quietly, "So it was a test. Did I pass?"

She did not look away. "Did I not already make

that clear, Nathaniel?"

He turned, thinking about the direction they ought to go, to the dining room and to all other things. "I am not sure it counts unless one knows one is being tested. But now that I do, I shall proceed more cautiously. Have a care for that tree root, my dear."

He felt her body press against his as she came closer to avoid tripping over the bricks raised by the growth of the tree. He looked up at its spreading branches and marveled that such natural beauty could thrive in such a place as London. But then, there was Francesca.

"Have you always lived in London?" he asked her as they walked along.

"Oh, yes, of course. My parents had no desire to leave their shop, never really trusting it to anyone else, and we rarely ventured much farther than Windsor. It is why my brother and sister both escaped, you see. And now my parents seem to be making up for lost time."

"And what of you?" he asked. The bright red shutters of the dining room were already in view. "Do you trust me enough with your shop so you might take off for distant shores, perhaps Margate or the Norfolk Broads?"

"So far as that?" she laughed. "Miss Tupper has already teased me with thoughts of Paris. But there is more to travel than walking along the sand or admiring famous landscapes. One ought to have a traveling companion, one to share it all with."

By that, he hoped she meant him. It seemed that their whole conversation this afternoon was replete with trapdoors and smoke and mirrors.

"Let us take the first step by sharing a good

dinner," he said, and opened the door before her, ushering her within.

He had chosen wisely, Francesca reflected, admiring the simple decor of the dining room, its watercolors of the ships docked at Greenwich, and shelves of books along the walls, inviting quiet contemplation rather than rowdy arguments. A low hum of voices vibrated in the room, and there were several couples, such as themselves, enjoying dinner.

Well, perhaps no one was quite like them, but no one would know that they were employer and employee.

"Are you the oldest child in your family? The one who would naturally take up the mantle of your parents' business when they decided to travel?" Nathaniel asked, his fork poised in the air and punctuating his words.

"I am, and responsibility has always fallen on my shoulders. When I was scarcely more than a child myself, I entertained the younger two, while our parents were occupied with all their other treasures. But now my little sister is already married and making a life for herself in America. And my brother yearns for the adventure of the sea, without actually being in the navy. He is the resident naturalist on a small ship. I daresay he is learning how to sail and tie all sorts of knots, for there must be many hours when there are no rare birds or iguana to be seen."

"And so you are an accidental shopkeeper of a curiosity shop, which I suppose is a curiosity in itself. What would you have preferred to do?"

"It hardly matters now, but I suppose I would have married and filled our nursery. I would have been introduced to many eligible bachelors and even attended a few balls. My great aunt might have arranged for such things, as she did for my mother. But she was not altogether pleased with the results, hoping for, at least, a minor lord. So here I am, on the shelf. Just like Madame Cristobel, poor thing."

He put down his fork and leaned closer. She noted the fine line of his lips and how they were reddened by the port they were drinking.

"That is what was expected of you. It may still be expected of you. But what do you dream about? If there were no family obligations or expectations, what would you have done instead?"

The temptation was too great. She met him halfway over their narrow table, and kissed him on the lips, savoring the taste of the port, and of him.

For a moment, she thought the whole room was silenced by the boldness of her action. But then she realized everything else was drowned out by the thrumming of her pulse in her ears. She sat back, and everything was as it had been.

Except, it wasn't. She had the audacity to kiss a man—on the lips!—in a public room. Anyone could have seen them, and everyone probably did. But she felt elated by her boldness, and strengthened by his very touch.

"Is that what you would have done?" he asked lightly, as if it were the most natural thing in the world that she should do this. "I must say, I heartily approve."

"I thought you might, but I did not plan it at all. I suppose that's the answer to your question: I would have acted on impulse, done what I pleased, seen where my imagination might take me. I might have written a book."

He nodded. "Yes, that seems to be the inclination for adventurous ladies, whether or not they publish their narratives in their own name. You have a step up there, my dear."

"What on earth do you mean? I haven't written anything but bills of sales for several years."

"I refer to your name, not your manuscripts. You have already assumed the mantle of FW Wadsworth."

"But it is quite true," Francesca argued. "It is my name, too."

"Then I admire your parents for their foresight. They must have known how useful it would be."

They continued their dinner in silence, during which Francesca wondered if her parents actually devoted much thought to what she was doing, what she hoped to do, what she dreamed about. She thought Nathaniel might be the first to ask her about her feelings about her own life. He could be acting selfishly, trying to assess her relationship with Lord Anthony. Or wondering about his own future with her.

But she rather thought that he wished to know because he cared about her and perhaps was a man stalled in his own destiny and looked for insight from others.

"Have you had enough to eat?" he asked, intruding on her thoughts.

She looked down at her empty plate and the few forkfuls of meat remaining on the serving dish.

"You must have thought me a starving woman, Nathaniel. I will savor the walk back to the shop, for I have supped enough to carry me for miles."

"Then let us be off, then. But not to King Street. At

least, I shall not deliver you to the shop. I will escort you to your home."

"But what if someone is lying in wait at the shop?"

"I will be prepared to fight him off this time. If not, kindly call the doctor when you come to the door tomorrow morning." He dropped several coins on the table and reached for her hand as he stood.

"Come and give me courage for battle as we walk off our dinner."

The evening was still warm when they stepped outside. Barristers working late hours brushed past them, and flower sellers coaxed them into buying bright blooms to appease their waiting wives.

"Would you like flowers?" Nathaniel asked. "They're very pretty."

"I have already cost you a pretty penny this evening, sir. I don't pay you that much."

Her words abruptly reminded him of their formal relationship. And yet, when she leaned over to kiss him in the dining room, he never felt so much at home. They could have been an old married couple enjoying a special evening on the town. More likely, a young married couple, so much in love, they didn't care who witnessed them showing their affection for each other. Indeed, that felt about right.

"Let us walk along the river," he said. "It is a bit out of our way but much more picturesque."

"Unless the tide is out, and the riverbed stinks like a slaughterhouse," she said. "You surely are a newcomer to these parts if you do not know that."

"Well, let's chance it, then," he said ruefully and led her past Soames' famous home with its collection of art and artifacts, the Inns of Court, and the Temple

Church, looking like a holy vision in the setting sun.

"Something is amiss," she said suddenly, as men rushed past them, toward the embankment.

"They're fishing a man out of the river," a woman said, beside them. She stood leaning against a lamp post, looking grim.

"I wonder if they need help," he murmured and dropped Francesca's arm.

"That is very noble of you, Nathaniel, but these men know what they are doing," she said. "I am sure they pull people out every day, dead or alive."

"Do Londoners not know how to swim?" He was no more than a boy when his father threw him into a lake and taught him how to swim to the bank. "Though I suppose the current is very swift and likely to defeat the best of us."

"Or a person is already dead when he or she is thrown off a bridge or passing boat," she pointed out, and then, at the look on his face, "What? It is an ugly fact of life here. But the river usually gives up its secrets."

They stared at the drama unfolding before them, at the men who plunged into the water fully dressed, and the bundle of wet cloth that was revealed to be a man's burial shroud. Nearby, a dog barked plaintively.

"Good God," Nathaniel said, genuinely appalled. "Come, let us away.

He reclaimed her arm and led her up the stairs, through the crowd of curious bystanders. When a man tipped his hat at Francesca, Nathaniel looked down to see that she nodded briefly.

"Did you know that man?" he asked, mildly curious.

"Hardly," she responded. "I do not know his name, for I don't believe he has ever purchased anything at the shop. But I have seen him there once or twice."

"Funny that he should be here."

Francesca made a sweeping gesture with her free arm. "Look around you, Nathaniel. It seems that half of London is here, watching the show."

"I would rather be at the Music Hall," he grumbled.

"And so you shall be, in only a matter of days. I take it you have no objections to attending, so long as anyone but Lord Anthony has provided the tickets?"

****

"You are cordially invited to my home for dinner this evening," Francesca said, on the day of their attendance at the Music Hall. She attempted a formal bow. A Spanish comb tucked loosely into her hair dropped to the floor. But she didn't have to worry that the awkwardness took anything away from her intent. Or Nathaniel's response.

"You don't owe me a meal just because I took you to a dining room," Nathaniel answered, without looking up from his work. He was intent on brushing oil on Madame Cristobel's joints. After their lengthy walk the other evening, Francesca felt she required some oiling herself.

"Can I not invite a friend to my home, without keeping a tally?"

"A friend?" he asked, and finally looked at her. From his seated position in the window, he still bested her in height.

"Perhaps more than that," she dared to say.

"And friend, as well," he repeated. "I imagine it is the best of all situations, and one ought to settle for nothing less."

"You speak as if you know," she said. "Then let me say my housekeeper is rather anxious to meet my new friend. And I have already told her that she need add another place setting at the table. Will that do? I suggest you arrive at five o' the clock, and we put a sign in the shop window that we shall be closing early."

"Shall we not leave together?" He was right to question the logistics, for their relationship was fraught with various challenges.

"It would appear too familiar, I daresay. No, I intend to leave soon, as I have much to do to prepare for tonight. Mrs. Blanchard has not yet finished my new gowns, so I shall have to consider my sorry wardrobe and how I might shine in the luminous company of the Music Hall regulars. I would not want to embarrass Miss Tupper, you understand."

"Oh, yes, as she is the very epitome of good fashion," he said, bemused. "Dinner and music and thou. It sounds like a lovely evening. Especially the 'thou.' "

Francesca didn't know quite how to answer this newly emerging Nathaniel Endicott, so much more lighthearted and winning than he was when he first came to her two months ago. She was about to answer when she caught sight of a face in the window, first looking at Nathaniel's workmanship and then glancing furtively about the shop itself. He looked like a man who did not wish to be seen, and yet he was clearly visible to every passerby on King Street. She did not think she recognized him and certainly not on King Street.

But when his face turned toward the sun, Francesca

realized she saw him only recently, on the stone steps of the embankment several nights before, when the drowned man was pulled from the river.

"Francesca?" Nathaniel asked softly. She vaguely considered that he surely wished for some affirmation of his words. But she was preoccupied and not with thoughts of flirtation.

The stranger nodded to no one in particular and walked to the door, turning the knob.

"We have a visitor," she said to Nathaniel. And quickly turned to the opening door. "Good day, sir. May I be of assistance?"

"Yes," the stranger said quickly glancing around him. "I was recommended to your shop by an old acquaintance."

"How nice. And whom might that be?" Francesca asked politely, though there was something about the fellow that put her on edge. She glanced at Nathaniel and saw that he had gone back to his work on Madame Cristobel's arm. Here could be their intruder, and her protector was more interested in a spot of oil on the table.

"I'm not rightly sure," the man said. "He was a brown-haired man, about yea high, with a red nose."

"Did he have a mustache?" Francesca asked.

"Yes, yes that's him. Did you know him?"

"He sounds like nearly every gentleman who comes through the door. A little like yourself, in fact."

"It wasn't me," the man protested. "I do not have a mustache."

"So I see," she said, thinking it really was time to leave. "But the man of whom I'm thinking has a mustache."

"He must have one, then."

Really, this was getting ridiculous. "And I noted you spoke of him in the past tense, sir. Is he no longer with us?"

"In the past what?"

This was enough. "I shall have to leave you now, for I have a very important commitment. But I shall trust you to my assistant Mr. Endicott. Mr. Endicott?" Francesca spoke a little too loudly, but she managed to get Nathaniel's attention. "As we already discussed, I am off. But this customer may require your help."

"I am happy to assist in any way, madame." Nathaniel stood, nearly bumping his head on the embossed metal ceiling. As he stepped down, a shadow fell upon him, and Francesca looked out of the window.

"Oh, shall I ever leave?" she sighed.

It was Lord Anthony who had splayed himself across the glass and, satisfied that he saw what he wanted, chose that moment to enter.

Francesca sensed, rather than saw, the man beside her stiffen. Lord Anthony frowned, just perceptively, before launching into his customary greeting.

"Ah, you are a sight for my weary eyes, Miss Wadsworth. And you here, too, Endicott?" he added as Nathaniel stepped down just between them. To the stranger, he said nothing.

"Welcome, Lord Anthony. Alas, I shall have to leave you to Mr. Endicott's company, as I am just departing."

"Just departing? I have never known you to step out in the middle of the afternoon."

"I imagine there are other things you don't know about me. But as if happens, I have an engagement tonight. I have tickets to the Music Hall."

Lord Anthony laughed. "The Music Hall? That hardly counts as an engagement. But I hope you are not attending alone? It is not the thing to do."

"Then you'll be happy to know she is going with me," Nathaniel said rather gruffly.

"Ah, well. That makes perfect sense. Your taste was never very fine, was it, Endicott?"

Nathaniel narrowed his eyes. "If you are suggesting that the lady is not up to your lofty standards of good taste, then I demand you give her an immediate apology."

Lord Anthony stepped back, momentarily confused. Francesca pitied him because his wit was no match for Nathaniel's, as she suspected it was also no match for his mother's tart tongue.

"That is not what I meant, as I am sure you know."

"He's a good man," the stranger said suddenly.

"Oh, you know each other, then?" Nathaniel asked.

"No, not truly," Lord Anthony clarified. "Perhaps we saw each other in Piccadilly? At the newsstand?"

The man began to protest, but Lord Anthony raised his hand to silence him. "Yes, I am quite sure that was it."

"And I am quite sure that I must leave, in order to be ready for tonight," Francesca said, and nearly stumbled in her haste to get out the door.

Nathaniel caught her arm before she could injure herself and set her upright. He could hardly blame her for rushing to get out the shop and lamented the fact that he could not follow.

Instead he was obliged to stand between one of his least-favorite people and another man who must be as confused as he. And yet he was curious, for the two of them seemed to know each other.

"Is there any way I can be of assistance, sir?" he asked the stranger, not entirely sure if Francesca had already offered as much. He hadn't been paying much attention to their interchange.

But if the man had already spoken of his interests to Francesca, he seemed to have forgotten it now. He shrugged and glanced at Tony, as if he could provide the answer to the most obvious of questions.

Tony blinked twice, which, as a signal, was as stupid as Nathaniel thinking that it was a signal. Tony probably had a spot of dust in his eye.

But, in any case, the man seemed to come to his senses. "I would like to see a book, sir. Yes, that's it. A book that has maps in it. Maybe one of the Americas. I'd like to get a look at Lisbon." The man nodded, pleased with his rambling story.

Nathaniel reflected that the man was as poor an actor as he was ever likely to meet, with the possible exception of some of the cast of this night's Music Hall performance. "Then you are looking for Iberia, sir. I believe I have a volume that might interest you."

Tony cleared his throat.

"And you, Lord Anthony? Is there something I can bring you? An atlas, perhaps? While my customer looks at his map of Portugal, might you be interested in a historical atlas of the Cornish coast? I believe there is some property there that particularly interests you."

Tony scowled. "I know that property as well as do you, but the more luck mine that I shall own it someday. It will be most unfortunate for you, for you and your father shall never walk its park again. As to this shop for which you now seem to be the gatekeeper, I believe there is nothing here that interests me at this moment. There is one thing that continually beckons me, but it appears to be temporarily off the shelf."

Nathaniel reminded himself to behave. And yet, it was nearly impossible to resist demonstrating how possessive he might also be, for what he desired. "Yes, I believe the treasure to which you refer is already spoken for. As a frequent visitor to FW Wadsworth, Bookseller and Antiquarian, you must already know that one must be prepared to act quickly on an acquisition, to guarantee possession."

Tony said nothing, and Nathaniel wondered what his real interest was in Francesca. Aside from the obvious. But a man asserting some claim to a woman's attentions ought to be prepared to make good on his intentions. It had not taken himself long to know how he felt about Francesca and convince her to chance the consequences of a relationship. But Tony knew her a good deal longer and seemed prepared to do nothing for or with her. The excuse of his mother's disapproval hardly withstood close scrutiny.

Though, as to that, Lady Maitland would probably make his life miserable if he ever dared to do anything to cross her. Nathaniel remembered how she made a play for his own widowed father and, unable to make a conquest, attempted to sabotage his relationship with the earl. That she was unsuccessful did nothing to allay any fears that she could be a threat at any time.

"As a frequent visitor, I also know that customers change their mind about their possessions and sometimes return them to the shop," Tony said, nastily, and returning Nathaniel to the present.

For once, Nathaniel had to agree with him, not for the sentiment, but for the general nastiness of the conversation and the metaphor they were employing. If Francesca heard them speaking of her thus, she would have kicked them both out in the street, sprawled in the filth left behind by too many people and too many horses.

"Let me find that volume on Iberia, sir," Nathaniel said, cutting off all further conversation with Tony. "I am sorry that I have made you wait while Lord Anthony and I had our little talk on shopkeeping."

This scene was getting worse and worse.

"What's Hiberia?" the man said.

Nathaniel rubbed his aching forehead, wishing himself along the waveswept beaches of Europe's southernmost shores. But anywhere would suffice if he could avoid the absurdities with which he was presently confronted.

He smiled, knowing it was as good as pasted across his lips. "Iberia refers to the great peninsula of Spain and Portugal. I shall show you a map, as you desire, and that should clear it all up. You may choose to visit Iberia when our London weather turns wet and cold."

"Mayhaps I will," the man said.

"Mayhaps I won't," echoed Anthony, though no one had asked him.

Nathaniel had already turned his back on him but pivoted slowly where he stood. " 'Tis a pity then. I undoubtedly speak for others when I say that it would give some people great joy were you to travel a great deal farther."

It was a good exit line, and Nathaniel took advantage of it. And yet, when he heard the two men talking, he all but forgot his mission and instead slipped behind a bookcase, struggling to hear what was being said.

****

Francesca stood anxiously at the parlor window, watching for Nathaniel's arrival. He would surely walk and thus would appear on the right, from the direction of King Street. On the other hand, if he stopped at the haberdashery to have his boots shined, or his hat moistened and shaped, he might come from the left, where the sun hung low in the sky. She blinked, momentarily blinded by the light.

"Step away from the window, Miss Francesca," Mrs. Belleron admonished her. "Men are quick to take advantage when they know you are anxious to see them."

"But he won't see me, Mrs. Belleron. I'm sure I'm well hidden behind the curtains."

"That will be the first place he'll look, and he'll see the lace dance in the soft breeze when you dash away."

"And what if he does, Mrs. Belleron? Of course he'll know I'm anxious. I invited him to escort me to the theater, for goodness sakes. And here to dinner, as well."

"Poor little chick," the housekeeper said, and made a noise like a broody hen. "One doesn't do such things, you know."

Francesca, already agitated, became exasperated. "How would I know?" she countered. "My whole social life revolves around a dusty old shop, and the people who read books while standing up, so they don't actually have to buy the volume. If I didn't ask Mr. Endicott to join me tonight, I would have dined quite alone and given up the Music Hall tickets to you and Mr. Gleason."

"As if I would go anywhere with that old fool." The housekeeper took the edge of her apron and wiped off an imaginary spot from the well-polished desk. "But still, it would have been quite merry."

"It is not too late. You may still go if you wish."

"Oh, but what would you and your young man do here if I do not chaperone?" And then, in thinking about it, Mrs. Belleron added, "Oh, no. You may not know to keep away from the window, but you're not such a child to not know about…other things."

"No matter," Francesca said, laughing. "For here he comes now. In a carriage, of all things!"

"I doubt he would come astride a white horse and carry you off," Mrs. Belleron said brusquely. "But away with you! Go to the top of the stairs, and I shall call you down, as is proper! And do something about that errant curl over your ear. The man will think you were outside, cleaning the windows!"

Francesca raced up the stairs, just as she heard the knocker announcing Nathaniel's arrival. And then again; Mrs. Belleron must be standing just inside the door, rubbing her hands in glee, making him wait.

Francesca used the respite to look at her reflection in the mirror, for the millionth time in the past hour. Actually, she liked that curl, which was not quite errant. She had twisted it around her finger not more than ten minutes ago and saw how it bounced around her face. She looked like a woman who was tidy, but not too fastidious. Clever, but possessed of enough wit to enjoy the frivolities of a music hall.

In short, she looked like a woman who was

prepared to thoroughly enjoy herself in the company of a very fine gentleman, at a place as far removed in spirit from their usual haunts, as it was possible to imagine. A music hall was a place of reckless joy and good spirits.

And yet, her small shop had somehow already provided the same.

She listened to the murmur of conversation below and Mrs. Belleron laughing in a manner that made Francesca wonder if it had been bottled up for years. Certainly, she had never heard it before. She was so distracted that she nearly missed the gentle call that floated up the stairs, announcing that a guest had arrived.

"Miss Wadsworth? My dear, Mr. Endicott has arrived to dine with you." Mrs. Belleron, who had been born in the East End somehow managed to sound like the queen, herself.

Francesca descended the stars on cue, feeling a bit like one of the royal princesses, though one wearing a dress that had belonged to her younger sister. She briefly wondered how many older sisters were the recipients of worn and outgrown garments.

But no matter if they were, for the expression on Nathaniel's face as he looked up at her made her forget where they were, and what she wore, and that they had a very avid audience of one.

He had the grace to look not altogether surprised but admiring and appreciative. He might have been as distracted as she was, for he held out a small bouquet of flowers before she even arrived on the landing. And because the blossoms were in her path, she stepped right into them, releasing the glorious scent of lilies and roses.

"How lovely, Mr. Endicott," she said softly. "You must already know how very much I enjoy flowers. Mrs. Belleron, would you kindly place them in a vase? They might be a lovely addition to the dinner table."

"Oh, certainly, Miss Francesca," Mrs. Belleron said, with a touch of the East End returning. She briefly dipped and practically skipped from the foyer.

"She seemed very glad to see me," Nathaniel said. "And yet she must do this all the time."

"Sound like Queen Victoria bestowing a knighthood? No, she doesn't do this, as you say. She mostly makes sure I eat properly and remembers to shut the flue. I'm afraid I bore her to tears, as evidenced by her excitement when I told her you were coming for dinner."

"If she is at all like the housekeeper at Watch Hill, she is hopeful that you will marry."

"I daresay she has given up on me, but she does enjoy cooking and baking, and I hardly give her the opportunity to exercise her skills." She tried to remember the schedule she had rehearsed with Mrs. Belleron and realized it was time to invite him into the parlor. "Come, let's sit while she puts the final touches on our dinner."

Francesca walked through the door and was at the other side of the room when she realized Nathaniel was not at her heels. Instead, he stood at the entrance, systematically looking from floor to ceiling, assessing the entire room. She should have thought of this; a man so interested in art and artifacts would think himself in paradise.

She sat down on a rigid armchair, fixing her skirt about her.

"Understand that my parents never sell their very favorite pieces but have always brought them home instead. These things were the childhood friends of my brother, sister and me. We especially liked the clocks."

"So do I," he said, predictably. "I have never seen anything quite like this."

He studied the year-going regulator clock, crafted in Vienna more than fifty years ago. Her father had brought it home for Mrs. Belleron's convenience; once wound, it would go continuously for a year.

"It seems to have the Graham escapement." Nathaniel sighed in reverence. "It's beautiful."

She supposed she ought to feel even a bit slighted, inasmuch as he seemed to have forgotten she was there. But there was some pleasure in amazing a gentleman, even if it was not with one's errant curls and slightly-tight-in-the-bosom gown.

As if he knew what she was thinking, he looked across the room, to where she sat.

"And I have never known anyone quite like you," he added.

"That's much better, Nathaniel. I hope it's because of my own assets and not my father's. Why not sit with me, while we wait on Mrs. Belleron's word? I can try to tell you about everything you see in his collection."

He made his way to her slowly, pausing to pick up one thing and then another. She was tempted to throw something at him, to get him to only notice her. But then he hastened his step and came to her, bent at the waist and kissed her boldly on the lips.

He tasted of mint and coffee, and his cheek was rough where he rubbed against hers. His fingers came up to entwine themselves in that little curl, and her arms went around his shoulders, bringing him close. Gone was her impatience and anxiousness, her uncertainty and doubt. She thought of nothing but how much she should enjoy doing this every day of her life.

Outside, in the hall, Mrs. Belleron rattled the china dishes a bit loudly, though she was a woman who was always overly cautious about the care of the antique Wadsworth dinnerware. Nathaniel was upright in an instant, licking his lips in satisfaction.

"I heartily appreciate your assets, my dear," he said.

She grinned like a self-satisfied fool.

"But I also like your family's other treasures."

"Dinner is served," Mrs. Belleron called from the door. "I hope everything is to your satisfaction."

Nathaniel took Francesca's arm, and as he escorted her from the room, they walked right by the housekeeper.

"Oh, it is, Mrs. Belleron. It truly is."

Chapter 9

Nathaniel realized he was homesick. Not for the great estate at Watch Hill, where he had spent most of his life. Or for the low-ceilinged flat in Trieste where he learned much of his craft. And certainly not for the drafty attic rooms above the shop. No, indeed; he was homesick for family and for dinners in a small dining room and conversations in an overly furnished parlor. Perhaps it had to do with the comfortable home, much loved by the Wadsworths. But more likely, it had to do with Francesca Wadsworth, much loved by him.

That was it, of course. He never felt such a rush of warmth as when he greeted her after an absence of a day or even an hour. He never knew a woman to be so undemanding of his time, while somehow commanding all of it, at any moment. And this night, sitting across from her in her family's dining room, enjoying Mrs. Belleron's hearty stew and roasted potatoes, he felt like he was truly home.

Now, walking into the music hall, he realized how much he resented sharing her attention, for she seemed to know a good many more people than she had led him to believe.

"Come here often, do you?" he asked under his breath.

She turned on him with a broad smile. "I've told you: I have never been in this place before and know not what to expect. But I suppose I shouldn't be surprised to see some of our customers and other tradespeople from King Street. There is Mr. Marley, the shoemaker. And Mr. Denison, whose bespoke shirts are made for the prince himself."

He wasn't sure he recognized anyone, until Miss Tupper herself came toward them, her arms outspread. The crowd parted before her, and people followed her in curiosity. They must have thought the Lord Mayor had arrived, at the very least.

"I am so honored to have you here," she said to them, though her attention was all for Francesca. "Please follow me to my box, so you will be settled before everyone else enters."

"Thank you, Miss Tupper. It is a remarkable crowd," Francesca noted. "It is we who are honored, for did you not tell me you did not make a habit of mingling with your patrons and that you would be in Paris?"

"I am already back from that wretched place and saw all I needed of that overrated showgirl," she said, and shook her head sadly. "I needed to be here, though for a tragic reason. There is a pall over the mood tonight."

Nathaniel thought the pall was enough to wake the dead. "What has happened?"

"One of our own has lost his father. I have employed Mr. Graves for ten years as our stage manager, and his father is no stranger to us. He was here for several days and helped us as he could. It is a great loss."

"Mr. Graves!" Francesca nudged him with her elbow. "And is it the father or son who died?

"I am sorry to hear it," Nathaniel said sympathetically, determined not to reveal anything. He nudged Francesca back. Nearby, a chorus of boisterous men broke out in song.

Francesca took the hint and said nothing more.

Miss Tupper led them up a spiral staircase and to the front of the theater. "It is where my father always presided over the audience, and how he ducked out quickly if the ticketholders were displeased with the show." She sighed. "It is difficult, you understand, to find entertainers who are always on their game, always funny or always on key. It is why I should like to purchase your Madame Cristobel, once she is fixed, of course. I imagine she will always repeat her performance to perfection."

"I am not sure I shall ever part with her, Miss Tupper. Please do not get your hopes up," Francesca said gently. "And in any case, she may prove very temperamental and not do well as a performer at all."

"I know, dear," Miss Tupper said. "It was just what I was saying to Mr. Graves the other evening, after a particularly dreadful show. It happens, of course. His father heard part of our conversation and seemed very curious about your automaton. He is from the country, you understand, and does not usually see such exotic things." She paused and then corrected herself. "He was from the country."

"Did he find our city so disagreeable?" Nathaniel asked, thinking it more likely that someone found the old man disagreeable.

Miss Tupper appeared to consider this. "You might say that. He somehow fell into the river and drowned. The current is often strong, but his son asserts he was a strong swimmer all his life. One must assume the cause was something else; perhaps he had a weak heart or fell and hit his head."

"How sad," Francesca murmured. "As we all know, the river is full of hazards."

Nathaniel tried to catch her eye, but she studiously watched her step as she mounted the stairs.

"And here we are," announced their hostess. "I have asked for tea and biscuits to be brought up to you, and you shall be quite comfortable here."

"That is just lovely of you, Miss Tupper," said Francesca. "And so generous. Will you not join us, even for a short while?"

Nathaniel hoped she would not, for all her kindness.

"Oh, dear, no. Mr. Graves is not himself, of course. I cannot ask him to manage the stage and performers this night. They will have to listen to me, instead."

"I am certain they will, Miss Tupper. Everyone here must respect your authority," Nathaniel said.

The woman shook her head. "It does not matter that I am the proprietor; unless she is the queen, a woman does not receive the respect as does a man in the same profession. Miss Wadsworth knows of what I speak."

Nathaniel glanced down at Francesca and saw her nod sagely. He wondered if the two women had spoken of this before, as they seemed in perfect accord. And yet, he was not surprised, for she had welcomed him into the shop, believing that she needed protection from an unknown threat.

"I shall leave you now. Please do not hesitate to ask the ushers for anything you might need. And I do hope you enjoy the show. There is to be a parody of *The Winter's Tale*."

"That certainly sounds like fun," he said. "And will there be a bear, to terrify all the audience?"

"To eat the audience, more like. But we live in an enlightened age, Mr. Endicott, and I do not wish to torment a wild animal."

"That is most progressive of you," he said.

"And economical, of course. Why hire out a bear when we can have my own terrier for free?" Miss Tupper pointed out. "But little Barkis can be quite a terror as well."

"Is that not a character in one of Mr. Dickens' books?" Francesca asked.

"Quite good, Miss Wadsworth. But it seemed a perfect name for my little beast. You shall hear him shortly, and I believe will agree with me that he has earned his name. Poor Mr. Graves brought his own dog with him to town, and Barkis tormented the poor animal."

With that, she smiled and bowed and left them quite alone. The other ticketholders were filing in to their seats, beneath them. Nathaniel held out a chair for Francesca and settled himself beside her before either of them spoke.

"Mr. Graves is the man who drowned the night we walked along the embankment," he said with certainty.

Francesca looked at him as if she had quite forgotten he was there. "You are new to this city, Nathaniel. People drown in the Thames every day. My father's sister died when she was a child, and their boat overturned."

She was being sensible, of course. She was always

sensible, but for the day she hired him on the acquaintance of a half hour.

"This music hall is not that far from the river. A man wishing for a short diversion might very well have walked along the embankment and fallen in. I suspect they are one and the same," he said.

"And is that all? Did you not hear that he was interested in the talk about the automaton?" she asked sharply.

"He is the old man who came to the shop," he said slowly, trying to understand where Mr. Graves fit into the puzzle.

"Of course. He is the very same man who came to the shop a few days ago and told me about bringing my mother to London, along with Madame Cristobel."

"Yes, but why now, and why was he murdered?"

"It must have been an accident. Who would want him dead?" she said quickly. "But just the same, I regret that I didn't pay more attention to him. I would not make a very good police detective, you see, for I would ignore all the best clues."

He studied her for several moments, though not actually seeing her. He felt that things were beginning to fall into place. "Sometimes, the most important clues are right in front of our eyes. That is the very point of Mr. Poe's 'The Purloined Letter.' "

He knew her well enough to know that she was perplexed but would get the reference. But he went on, for this was not the time for a literary review.

"And Miss Tupper has just told us that he was interested in her idea of procuring an automaton for the music hall," he repeated her words.

Francesca looked like she might jump out of her

seat. "And that man on the embankment, who tipped his hat at me. I knew I had seen him before, and I believe he has been in the shop! Friday last, when Lord Anthony came by."

"Are you certain of that?" Now he was as agitated as she. What if this hat-tipper overheard some bit of conversation? What if he pushed the old man into the water? What if he was interested in the automaton for his own purposes—or someone else's?

Her lips parted, as if she would speak, but she thought better of it. Several minutes passed, and he didn't press her, instead looking down at the crowd, looking for a familiar face. From this vantage point, the view was mostly of derby hats and a few hair ornaments.

"I saw his face in the window," she said at last. "He was watching you working at the table. No, he was looking past you, into the shop. I would have walked outside to invite him within, but I was talking to Lord Anthony at the time."

Nathaniel recalled Tony's visit of a few days before, but he didn't remember a man at the window, looking at him or anything else. No wonder though...his attention was all for Tony's conversation with Francesca. Now he had to consider that the two men were somewhat connected.

"I will not believe that Lord Anthony has anything to do with all this," she said suddenly.

He looked at her, surprised. "I did not say so."

"But you were thinking it," she responded.

Damn, but she was good.

"He is not the sort of man who would consort with murderers," she went on. "I will not believe it."

But Nathaniel remembered the boy who had grown into the man. Murder might not have been in his repertoire, but larceny and lying and cruelty to animals certainly were. Cruelty to other small boys, as well. Mean-spiritedness was so much Tony's stock in trade, Nathaniel had wondered if he had mistaken his identity when he met up with him in Francesca's shop weeks ago.

"Nathaniel?" Francesca asked.

"Hmm?" Nathaniel asked, before recollecting where he was, and with whom. He patted her hand until she pulled it away. "Let us enjoy this evening my dear. Your Lord Anthony has done enough harm to me in his life; I will not have him spoil another evening. Look: it is soon to begin."

****

The music was loud, and the crowd boisterous. Barkis proved to be more amusing than a bear, especially when he leapt from the stage onto a man's lap. But it would not have much bothered Mr. Shakespeare, for he would not have recognized the performance as a parody of his play. A woman with two of her attributes on show sang a ditty in such an odd, strained voice that Francesca considered that if not for those very attributes, she might have guessed the performer to be a man. Indeed, that conceit might have been more Shakespearean than the night's play itself.

A magician appeared but briefly, and quickly left the stage when his rabbit failed to materialize. And a man banged away at a piano with the finesse of a cow. Francesca had never heard a cow play the piano but imagined it must sound something like this.

In any case, she appreciated that Madame

Cristobel, poor broken thing that she was, might yet perform better than anything or anyone they saw on the stage this night, Perhaps she ought to sell the automaton to Miss Tupper, out of pity.

And yet, the rest of the audience seemed to love it all. More than that, they stood and applauded every dreadful bit. She watched Nathaniel out of the corner of her eye, and he did little more than politely applaud the conclusion of each act, and once did so before the act had actually concluded. Instead he was clearly distracted, lost in thought, here, and yet not here.

"Is it done?" he asked at one point.

She didn't think so. "I have no idea. I have never done this sort of thing before."

"I suppose we must thank Miss Tupper, for we would not wish to lose her as a customer. And yet, please don't encourage her, for she may decide to give us tickets on a regular basis."

"Well, if you will not attend with me, perhaps I should bring Lord Anthony."

That finally got a rise out of him. "No, you will not do that, under any circumstances," he said, rather forcibly.

"You cannot tell me what to do, Nathaniel. Please recall that I managed very well for all these years." She folded her hands in her lap, lest he dare pat her again, like a puppy. Barkis would not stand for it, and neither would she. "You do not have a claim on me." She spoke so softly, she wasn't sure he even heard her.

But he did and nodded thoughtfully.

"Perhaps I shall, some day. And when such a day comes, so would you have a claim on me," he said, lifting her hand from her lap, and kissing her palm.

In her whole life, not even when her parents set off for their travels, did she have such an aching sense of longing. But she knew too well about hopes and expectations, and the despair of disappointment.

"Would the claim be so strong that you would remain in London with me?" she asked, her voice cracking. "Your home is at Watch Hill, where your father awaits your return. And I must remain here. You grew up on the rugged cliffs above the sea, and I grew up on the rugged streets near Mayfair, where the roughest waters are the Serpentine, on a windy day."

"Must you remain here forever?"

"I am the only one left in my family, through no fault of my own. The responsibility is mine, but I have no reason to complain. After all, look who walked through my door." She met his eyes and saw the creases that appeared whenever he smiled. Since she knew he was not much more than thirty years of age, she supposed that was a consequence of too much sunshine. One did not suffer the same consequences along Rotten Row.

"There are many people who walk through your door, and they do not all treat you as well as you deserve."

"I suppose you mean Lord Anthony," she said.

"I was rather thinking of the unknown fellow who ransacked the place," he said tartly. "But Tony is not the best of fellows either."

"And yet your acquaintance, as sour as it is, was fostered in Cornwall. London does not enjoy a monopoly on bad behavior."

"Bad or good: you are likely to find someone to run the shop, as easily as you found me."

"It was not so easy," she whispered.

"I did not hear you," he said and leaned so close, his breath ruffled her hair.

"I have been waiting for you to come through that door for years," she admitted.

He said nothing for several moments, and Francesca realized they were nearly alone in the seats, as everyone else had filed out.

"Then I will stay. I would not want you to say such things to the next man who came through your door."

Francesca opened her lips to speak, when they were interrupted by a fellow with a broom.

"The party's over," he said and sneered, though she doubted he witnessed anything more than Nathaniel holding her hand.

"You are wrong, sir," Nathaniel said. "I have just received reassurance that it is just beginning."

****

"I imagine it isn't suitable for me to invite you back to the shop," he said, once their carriage had started off down the street.

"Because it is my shop?" Francesca asked. "It is your flat, however, and you may invite anyone you wish to join you there."

He glanced down at her and was certain that she was thinking of what might happen if he offered an invitation, and if she accepted.

"You are a very generous landlady, but I believe you have prior obligations."

"What on earth do you mean?" she asked, indignantly. Well, she had every right to be so, for he had worded it very poorly.

"It is just that you seemed to suggest that you lived

quite independently on Edgware Road."

"I do," she reminded him.

"Mrs. Belleron would have something to say about that. I suspect she was deputized by your mother to keep a watchful eye on you. I fear that if I had been presumptuous enough to arrive on foot, like a pushcart peddler, she would have booted me out the door, without announcing me."

She laughed, which confirmed his assessment. "I see your point, and it is probably quite accurate. I just never thought about it before."

"Because she trusted everyone else you invited for dinner?"

Francesca sobered at once. "Not at all, Nathaniel. It is because I don't believe I ever invited anyone other than my cousin's widow before. He is one of my father's business associates, and the dear man must be past eighty."

"I see. So, age makes all the difference."

"I think you make all the difference, which is why you are quite right. I must be returned home promptly, with the lace on my bodice quite intact."

"If that is the only guidance you can offer, I think I can manage to leave the lace as it is."

And then he pulled her into his arms and left everything but the damned lace quite awry and rumpled.

****

He wished he hadn't been so disgustingly honorable, because the hardest thing he ever had to do was to deliver her to the door on Edgware Road. She did not possess her own key, apparently, but Mrs. Belleron had undoubtedly been watching at the window, for she opened the door before they could arrive at the top step.

"Did you enjoy the show, my dears?" she asked, straightening Francesca's bonnet.

"No," Francesca said, at the same moment he said, "Yes."

"Well, each to his own opinion, I always say," she said. "Will you be coming in for a cup of tea or hot chocolate, Mr. Endicott? Though the hour is rather late."

Francesca glanced up at him and smiled. "Thank you for your suggestion," she answered for them both. "It is late, and Mr. Endicott must be returning to the shop."

Mrs. Belleron seemed relieved but would not let him go without an inquisition. "And you manage well, there, if I might inquire? How do you do for meals?"

"Why, thank you for asking, Mrs. Belleron," he said and bowed lightly. "I have been in the habit of making do for myself for years. And when I find myself quite exhausted by all that I must accomplish during the day, I just walk down the street to the cheesemonger, and enjoy some of his viands." Francesca murmured something about the fact that he doesn't work all that hard, but he chose to ignore her, for once. "But do I take it that you're inviting me to join Miss Wadsworth again for dinner?"

"That would be lovely, Mr. Endicott," answered Mrs. Belleron. "Please do."

With an exaggerated sigh, Francesca walked between them into the house, her hand waving into the air.

"Well, I never," said Mrs. Belleron. "Off she goes

without a 'pleasant evening,' or a 'thank you.' "

"No matter," he said. "She must be rather tired herself. She worries overmuch about her responsibilities."

"Would that her parents worried a little more about their responsibilities to her!"

"I am sure they do," he said. "But fear not. I shall keep an eye on her whenever she is in the shop. I have vowed to protect her."

Mrs. Belleron gave him such a smile, he thought she could light up the whole street. He was quite right about the housekeeper, of course. She took responsibility for Francesca when she was at home, as he would when she was at the shop. It was reassuring.

But Francesca was right about one thing as well. Mrs. Belleron had been fully prepared to be rather critical of him, and he was confident he passed her test.

As the hired carriage rumbled down the quiet London streets, traversing the short distance between Edgware Road and King Street, Nathaniel was lulled into a state that was neither dream nor reality, neither anxious nor not quite at rest. His life had taken an unexpected turn. Several, in fact. His journey had been somewhat prescribed for him since he was a child at Watch Hill. His father had done what his own father had done before him, and his father before that. The Endicotts were relations to the Earl D'Arcques, and the vagueness of the particulars was never too closely examined because the men in both families were like brothers to each other, and it had been so for each generation. Nathaniel had every expectation of inheriting a position on the estate, and no expectation of inheriting anything else.

That changed when he went off to the Continent and secured an apprenticeship in the Kinzing workshop. He supposed that most young men, given the opportunity of a grand tour, would acquire paintings and sculpture, archeological artifacts and natural specimens. Gambling debts, no doubt. And women.

But he was not most men and, doubting he would ever own a grand home of his own, was inclined to collect rare watchworks and mechanical creations. More important, he learned how to repair and tune them to perfection, making him dependent on no one else to maintain his collection.

He did not gamble; he was not rich enough to risk his security. And he did not meet many women; he was not tempted enough to risk his sanity.

And now he was here in London, gambling on an obscure hope presented to him in an honest conversation with the earl and tempted by a woman for whom he would risk anything.

He glanced out the window when the carriage slowed and recognized the small shops and townhouses that lined the usually busy street. The moon was nearly full and cast a gentle illumination on the scene, reflecting in the wide-paned glass windows of each business. Nathaniel saw the neatly stacked jars of jam in Will's window and the elegantly feathered hats of the milliner's shop next door. A familiar mongrel paused in front of FW Wadsworth and barked. The dog was accustomed to receiving Nathaniel's leftover meats and probably was hungry.

But no. The reflection of his wagging tail appeared in the window, and there was other movement, perhaps that of a person, patting him on the head. The image was not yet clear.

Nathaniel tapped the roof of the carriage with his cane, and the driver came to a halt. He was down the steps before the driver could assist him, and Nathaniel paid him generously, for it was good to have a reliable driver when one did not have the convenience of one's own carriage. The driver was clearly grateful and began to thank him, but Nathaniel waved him off. Left in the dust kicked up by the wheels, Nathaniel studied the scene across the street.

There was a man, patting the dog with one hand and reaching into his breast pocket with the other. Nathaniel tensed, fearing that the stranger would harm the dog, but soon realized that what he held was a meat patty or something of that sort, for the dog was happy. More to the point, he stopped barking. That clearly made the man happy.

Turning away, he stood with his back to Nathaniel, gazing into the shop window, rocking from side to side. Suddenly, he stopped, seemed fixed by something within, and edged sideways to the door. He turned the knob, first one way and then the other. Using his shoulder, he pushed against the frame.

That was enough. Feeling in his pockets for something that might be used as a weapon, and finding nothing other than a small pocketknife that would hardly be sufficient to core an apple, Nathaniel quickly set out across the street.

The dog saw him first and wagged his tail, perhaps hoping for another patty. Nathaniel scratched him behind his ear as he said, "We do not keep such late hours, sir. Please come back when we are open for business."

The man jumped about a foot, startling the dog. "I am only looking for something," he said quickly.

Nathaniel crossed his arms over his chest, rubbing the edge of the knife against his thumb. "Well, then, may I help you? What is it you hope to find?"

"A book," he said quickly and stepped forward, so he came into the moonlight.

Nathaniel recognized him at once, for this was the man who took up far too much of his time only this afternoon, as he groped for some location, some reason, why he should wish to own an atlas. What did he want?

"Are you back for that atlas, then?" he asked.

The man squinted into the dim light. "It is you, then? The shopkeeper? I hardly recognized you in that get up."

"Yes, it is I. You may have heard that clothes make the man," Nathaniel said, a bit put out that dressing like a gentleman would provide such an excellent disguise. "You must have a desperate need to rediscover Iberia, to arrive so late, and hope to find us still open for business?" Nathaniel continued. "Perhaps you found yourself quite alone on a sleepless night, with a great desire to calculate the distance between Lisbon and Evora? You wish to explore the Roman ruins?"

"Yes, that is it," the man answered, and glanced behind him.

"I will help you, then. Though not in time for this night. I shall pull it from the shelves and put it aside for you." Nathaniel wondered if the man knew that he knew this was all nonsense. "Come back first thing in the morning, and you shall have it."

The man nodded, took another glance behind him and ran like a thief down the street. He might very well have been a thief but did not have the opportunity to display his talents. If that was the case, Nathaniel suspected those talents would be very poor, indeed. He glanced down at the dog, as if seeking an explanation, but the beast only studied his empty hands.

"I would be very much surprised if he ever came back," Nathaniel said, and the dog met his gaze. He was struck by a remembrance of the dogs he knew as a child and young man, and what good companions they were; one could confide anything and know his secret was safe. "Will you guard the door, in case he does so?"

The dog continued to gaze up at him as he unlocked the door, which was why he should not have been surprised when the little fellow followed him into the shop and promptly settled down for the night, under a chair.

"Let me know if we have any more unexpected guests," Nathaniel said and wearily made his way up the stairs to his attic.

****

Francesca noticed something unusual in the window when she entered the shop the next morning.

"Are you aware there's a dog sleeping under Madame Cristobel's table?" she said to Nathaniel when he emerged from behind a cabinet.

"Is there, now?" he asked. "No, I hadn't noticed."

She looked sternly at him.

"Well, yes. But didn't you warn me about the dogs when I first came into the shop?"

Still, she said nothing.

"But you needn't worry about this fellow. He's quite agreeable and in good health. I haven't even found a flea on him. I decided to call him Pip, Philip

Pirrup to new acquaintances. Barkis was already taken, you see."

Finally, she relented. "I suppose Pip has the qualities of loyalty and goodness and would make for a good watchdog?"

Nathaniel nodded. "Yes, there is that. Unless, of course, someone offers him a pork patty."

"This shop is getting rather crowded," she said, as she rubbed Pip's silky ears. She should have thought of getting a watchdog weeks ago, rather than just pretending she kept a team in the back room. But then, she would not have met Nathaniel, and the shop would not have been nearly so crowded now. Some days she felt as if he completely filled the empty spaces in her life.

"There will be one less customer, I fear," he said. "A bloke who didn't seem to know which end was up in an atlas but nevertheless seemed rather desirous of acquiring one."

"He doesn't seem like a very good customer," she murmured. "Was he afraid of Pip?"

"No. Actually, he seemed to know him well. Actually, I think you may know him as well."

She dropped her hand. "He is Pip's owner, I suppose? Someone must have taught the fellow how to behave."

"I am not sure about that. He was fidgeting with the knob on the front door when I arrived here last night."

"I was talking about the dog of course."

"I know."

"Well, then, who is this odd man?" She honestly didn't know whom he meant. Not Lord Anthony, surely? For all Nathaniel did think him odd. But she recalled Lord Anthony did not like dogs overmuch.

"I believe he may be the man who tipped his hat to you at the river, the same man who has idled his way here in the shop some afternoons. Lord Anthony is already acquainted with him."

"Perhaps he recommended our services?"

"Perhaps Tony is paying for his services. That seems as plausible as anything else."

For all Nathaniel suggested, for all the two men so obviously disliked each other, she still found it impossible to believe ill of Lord Anthony. Had he not been her friend for so many years? Had she not attended the theater with him? If Anthony wanted anything more of her, or her shop, he would have already taken it. Or, at the very least, asked for it.

She nodded, hoping that would be enough answer for now, and walked past man and dog to the counter, where she was delighted to see croissants and honey waiting for her. No matter that she already had breakfast at home; walking through the streets to her shop had already given her a renewed appetite. Nathaniel anticipated this, as he already understood what would give her pleasure, what she would hunger for. She scarcely understood it herself. But since his arrival, she suddenly longed for things she barely tasted before and now savored some hitherto unknown delights.

She glanced at Nathaniel, but he was already stepping up into the window, with Pip at his heels.

Chapter 10

Nathaniel paused in his work, holding Madame Cristobel's amputated right arm in the palm of his hand. For all his success at finally giving her movement, he was dismayed at the erratic rhythm of her arms' elevation. The poor thing behaved like a nervous matron, which might be the case for anyone enclosed in glass for fifty or more years. But just now, being enclosed in an airtight box seemed very desirable, as a dreadful odor pervaded the shop.

He glanced at Pip, sleeping beneath his workbench, but his companion was at rest, sensing nothing amiss.

Nathaniel held his breath and met the watery eyes of a man, a stranger, whose garments immediately revealed the source of the stench. Nathaniel was an accomplished swimmer, but even he could not hold his breath that long. He ran his hand slowly before his nose before he drew in the fouled air in the shop and coughed.

"And who might you be, sir?" he asked, ignoring the polite conversation that had become his habit while he was in the shop. This was not the moment for "How do you do?" and "How might I help you?" He just wanted the man to leave.

"Jimmy Witt, sir," the man answered and bowed. "At your service."

"I am glad to hear it. But I don't believe Miss Wadsworth has advertised for assistance."

"No, indeed, I have come of my own free will." Witt straightened up, as if to emphasize his status. "I have acquired things that might be of interest."

Nathaniel heard rustling in the back of the shop and sensed Francesca approaching.

"Miss Wadsworth is the one you wish to see if you have something to sell, for she is the proprietor." Nathaniel felt a bit guilty, as he would wish to protect Francesca from any sort of invasion, including those to her senses.

"No, sir, what I have is for you." Witt pulled something wrapped in a filthy rag from his jacket. He glanced about, and thinking better of putting it up on the workbench, laid it at Nathaniel's feet, on the elevated platform. Pip approached it cautiously, sniffed, and gave a whining sound. Nathaniel was tempted to do the same but then caught his breath. And not because of the odor.

Stained and water-damaged was a tiny arm, articulated at the elbow, and still attached to a spring that popped from the shoulder joint like a muddy sprout in the early spring. And there was more: a bit of something glinting in the sun, a metal box that could fit into the palm of one's hand, shards of blue willow porcelain.

"You see," Witt said, "the arm is very like the one you have there, on the table. Mayhaps, it is its match."

"I have both arms here on the table, but you are quite right that it is very like." Nathaniel prodded the sodden pile with his shoe and decided there was no hope for it but that he sacrifice his finger to the mess. He bent down, aware that Francesca was now quite close.

"And where did you acquire this merchandise, Mr. Witt," he asked, trying not to sound disparaging or even ironic. He guessed that the man, despite his name, would not be appreciative of irony. "Locally, I daresay?"

Witt laughed. "As local as you get!"

Nathaniel guessed he meant the sewer.

"I spend my hours on the bankside waiting for the low tide that comes twice a day, to shovel through the mud. It's thick with riches."

"I do see a coin here, gold by the look of it," Nathaniel pointed out. "Do you make a living by this?"

It was an absurd question, for whatever the man fished out of the Thames could hardly be a living. But Witt had a ready answer.

"It's honest work," he said, defensively. "For us mudlarks."

Nathaniel straightened, and looked directly at the man. Was he mad? Did he think he was a bird? He had never heard of such a thing but remembered a nanny who thought she was the reincarnate of Marie Antoinette, so he supposed such a thing was possible.

"A mudlark is a person who mines the river's waters, who speculates on a great find every day of his life. Men such as he have found Roman swords, ship cargoes, pottery, old clasps and buttons," Francesca explained to him. And then, to their guest. "You must forgive Mr. Endicott, as he is new to town."

Witt tipped his hat to Nathaniel's ignorance.

"But why have I never seen you before?" she asked him. "Surely you have found things before today."

"Oh, certainly ma'am," Witt said glibly, clearly more at ease now that he found an appreciative audience. "I most often bring my finds to a couple of shops on the East End. But one of my mates told me about this place, and the doll in the window. That one, over there. So he thought I could get a bit more for the arm here."

"You must thank him for me," Francesca said, most graciously. Nathaniel wondered if she was suffering from a cold and could not smell the stink that probably already pervaded every surface of the shop. She appeared unflappable. "And while Mr. Endicott is quite right that I am responsible for the purchases, I believe your items are his specialty."

She nodded at Nathaniel, awaiting his next deed. It looked like he was going to have to touch the stuff after all. He took a small scrap of rag from the workbench and reached for the filthy little arm.

The mud and dirt came off easily, almost too easily. There was no evidence of longtime deterioration, and the spring was free of rust. He laid it next to Madame Cristobel's dismembered arm, and it was as close a match as could be imagined. What was this? How likely was it that one should find a part of a rare automaton in the silt of a churning river? Were they once manufactured like the bowls of the potteries?

"This piece hasn't been in the water very long," he reflected.

Witt became a bit defensive. "I came by it fairly, in this morning's low tide."

"I do not doubt it, Mr. Witt. If anything, it is somewhat more useful to me." Nathaniel said the words before he thought much about it. He supposed he wasn't a very good businessman, for he ought to be dismissive, pointing out its utter lack of value. He looked at Francesca, but she was more interested in what remained in the cloth.

"And what is that box?" she asked, though Nathaniel noticed she did not make a move to touch it. He supposed that was what she was paying him to do.

"I don't rightly know," Witt said, and shrugged. "The spring from the arm was attached to it, so I dredged it up together."

Once Witt described the find, Nathaniel knew what it was, without even looking too closely. And yet, his audience was watching and waiting, so he supposed he ought to take his cue. He retrieved it from the floor, and wiped it off. Then, as a tiny latch materialized, he picked up a screwdriver, and pried it open. The box revealed what he knew it would.

"It's a mechanism, of the sort one would find in a music box," he announced. Witt sighed in disappointment, but Nathaniel could sense Francesca's excitement.

"I think we shall purchase your day's find, Mr. Witt," she said quickly. "Come to my desk with it, and we shall negotiate a price." She spared a glance for Nathaniel, and raised her brows.

Yes, she knew that they had something here but probably had no more understanding than he of how such parts had washed up on the banks of the Thames.

****

"I must go home to change my gown, Nathaniel," Francesca said, as soon as she let Mr. Witt out of the shop. "Perhaps even bathe."

He looked at her from his seat in the window, and smiled. "You look perfectly lovely, my dear."

She was not in the mood for flattery, not now. "How nice of you to say so, but have you noticed the whole shop reeks of Mr. Witt's presence? I am going to be ill. We must open the doors, and I must have Mrs. Belleron clean my garments or consign them to the rag heap." She walked to the door, propped it open with a heavy book, and gasped for air.

Nathaniel appeared behind her and clasped her shoulders. He must have taken her quite at her word.

"That is the price of doing business, I suppose. I don't think anyone has ever been asked to leave a shop because they smelled like a sewer, but I imagine Will might do so if Mr. Witt stepped into his establishment. However, I doubt Mr. Witt shops for continental cheeses and specially commissioned jams."

Francesca turned in his arms, oblivious to anyone walking along the street. "After what I paid him, he might very well show up at Fortnum and Mason and order a banquet."

"He did that well, did he?" Nathaniel mused.

"Well, what did you expect? I saw that look you gave me. You wanted that poor arm, and that water-filled box."

He nodded and drew her into the shop. "Yes, I did."

"Oh, I cannot remain here, Nathaniel. I feel like I'm going to faint. We must do something."

"Let us close for an hour or so and take a walk in the park. Pip needs to get out, in any case. Right, old boy?"

The dog barked in agreement. Francesca considered that Nathaniel was not only able to work his charm on spinsters and cheesemongers and housekeepers but on stray dogs as well. Possibly on anyone and anything excepting Lord Anthony.

It was a glorious day, so warm and sunny that

Francesca might have deemed it worthwhile to spend an hour or so in the park, even if her shop didn't smell like trash left out in the rain. Pip seemed to be in his element, running ahead of them, waiting for them to catch up, sniffing packages and items left on the side of the road.

"Come, boy. Come with us!" Nathaniel called out, and three urchins turned to face him. He waved them off, but Pip was at his side in a moment, as if the two of them were simpatico for years and not just for a matter of hours.

"He seems to have adjusted to your commands, as if he has heard them since he was a puppy. It's easy to wonder…" she began.

"I know what you are about to say, and I would think the same thing had I witnessed it. In fact, last night I thought he might have already been familiar with the shop, as he seemed to guard the door, and then made himself quite at ease when I let him enter."

"You were taking a chance with that," she said, and Pip excitedly rubbed his nose against her closed hand. She opened it, regretting that she had nothing for him.

"Do you mean, he might have run roughshod over the china and crystal? Chewed up some old family bibles?"

Francesca was surprised she hadn't thought of this, for these were the things that were supposed to be most precious to her. She glanced up at Nathaniel, realizing that was no longer the case.

"Were you not worried he would bite you in your sleep? Attack you so he might plunder whatever you have in your cupboard?"

Pip ran between them, jostling Francesca aside, and

wagged his tail as they came to the gutter.

"Yes, he seems very fearsome, indeed." Nathaniel laughed. "But you are quite right that he could have posed a danger. And yet his behavior, and that he is clean and well-fed, suggests to me that he has become separated from his rightful owner. Someone has cared for him, trained him, even loved him."

"Poor fellow," Francesca murmured. And then, at the look on Nathaniel's face, said, "I do mean his owner, of course. Pip seems quite content. But somewhere in London there's a man or even a whole family, missing him. What if someone comes forward here on the street, or recognizes him when we get to the park?"

"I have thought of that. With only a few hours acquaintance, I can hardly lay claim to Pip as my own, for all I named him." Pip saw the green expanse of Hyde Park spread out before him and dashed ahead, just avoiding getting clipped by a passing carriage. Francesca caught her breath. "I must be prepared for someone to come forward to call him home."

"How would you feel?" she asked, thinking there were precious few people who ever asked her how she felt about anything.

The look Nathaniel gave her suggested that he was unaccustomed to it as well. "I shall be sorry, of course, though happy for what would surely be a grateful reunion. And then, with the permission of my landlord, I may seek to bring home another street dog. I have nearly forgotten how much companionship a little dog might provide. Perhaps I'll find a puppy, ready to be trained."

They crossed the street more cautiously than Pip

and followed him into the park, where he was chasing down a squirrel.

"Puppies are quite difficult to have about, I believe. We might have to hide away the crystal and china, after all."

"I have thought about that. My window looks down upon a little courtyard, a secret garden. That is, if one can call an overgrown tangle of weeds a garden."

"I nearly forgot about it, until I went up in the attic to see if all was suitable for your residency," she admitted. "There is a door to it in the back of the shop, behind the shelves of Roman statuary. I don't think it's been opened for years, perhaps not in my lifetime."

"I thought I might spend some time unsealing it, if you and Madame Cristobel will allow me the opportunity. I'll move the antiquities, pull out the shelves, and open the lock if we can't find the key."

"You can do that?" she asked, genuinely curious.

He gave her a look suggesting it ought to be self-evident. "Then I'll clean up the plot, get rid of the vines and weeds, build a little shelter for my pup. At night, and in cold weather, he can come up to the attic with me."

They started down the lane toward the Serpentine, drawn by the sound of children calling and ducks squawking. Pip forgot about the poor squirrel and flirted with a little terrier.

"You have been thinking through this to the last detail," she said admiringly.

"I have been thinking about a lot of things," Nathaniel acknowledged. "Most of them more complicated than how to keep a dog away from the merchandise."

She had also been thinking and dreaming about some of them as well. But she doubted this was the moment for Nathaniel to make a romantic overture. Instead, she anticipated what he might say.

"You are wondering how Mr. Witt came upon automaton parts just at the moment you are actually restoring an automaton."

"Yes, there is that. But it's possible pieces of Madame Cristobel's cousins have been washing up for years and no one happened to think they were of value until now. Witt would have tossed them back in the river, if not for someone telling him I might find them of interest."

"But did you not assess the parts and find them reasonably undamaged? That they might not have been in the water for very long?"

"Yes, and that is what started my train of thoughts. Perhaps they only recently spilled into the river and did not travel very far along the current because someone had them on his person when he, himself, spilled into the river?" His voice, usually so steady, rose to a question at the end of the sentence.

"Good God. Do you mean poor Mr. Graves?" Francesca felt guilty that she had nearly forgotten about the kind old man. "And he knew about my mother, and the things that accompanied her to London. Did he not say he had some parts from a male automaton?"

"Of course. And then there is the man we saw at the river when Mr. Graves' body was found. The bloke who was trying to get into the shop just last night and who has made up some ridiculous stories about things he wanted to buy. I doubt he's interested in buying anything."

"Certainly, some customers spend a lot of time deciding what they'd like to buy," Francesca reminded him. He looked at her, raising his brow. "Of course, that man has no idea what he might buy and may not be prepared to spend tuppence in the shop."

Nathaniel nodded. "He might, however, be prepared to steal something. Though he doesn't seem interested in the things that usually can turn a quick profit, like the silver. He wants something else and not necessarily for himself."

"Do you mean, he is working for someone?"

"That's an odd way to put it, but you may be right," Nathaniel said, pulling her over to a park bench. Pip studied them for a moment, perhaps waiting for a picnic lunch to materialize, and decided he might have better luck splashing about in the pond to the delight of several children. And the chagrin of their nannies.

"He seems to know Lord Anthony." It was time to admit that Anthony seemed to have some connection to this mystery, for she resisted it long enough. She still resisted it. "But I have known him for years, and nothing ever seemed amiss before."

"Nothing?" he asked. "No curiosity about your maps, your cameos, your collection of hair pins?"

"He never seemed interested in anything, before you arrived." She thought about that for a few moments, watching Pip making a dog's fool of himself. "Everything started just when you arrived."

They stared into each other's eyes, looking for all the world like two lovers on an afternoon outing. But Francesca knew that Nathaniel was trying to read the truth in her eyes, as she was in his. What did he have to do with all this?

"Everything started just when I arrived in London," he repeated. "That is right. But you are wrong about one thing. Your Lord Anthony most certainly was interested in something in the shop, and that had nothing to do with my arrival."

He loved to make her blush, but there was no art to it. It was too easy, even for a fellow like himself, unaccustomed to arts of flirtation or flattery. In fact, this was another consequence of his intersection with Tony; for all he spent a good part of his life competing with Tony on horseback, on the sea, in the library, and in the gaming room, they never before competed for the affections of a woman. And yet, as soon as Tony entered the shop and Nathaniel saw the response that the man elicited from Francesca, he knew that he wanted what his old nemesis wanted. Right now, looking at the pink stain on Francesca's cheeks and neck, he vowed that he would gladly give up all claims to Watch Hill, if he could only have her.

"It is not a coincidence," he said at last, unable to tease her just for his own pleasure. "I would not have come to King Street if I did not have a purpose and a plan. Between you and Will, you made it irresistible to stay"—her blush returned, but he was being practical here, not flirtatious—"for otherwise I might have deemed it necessary to stay in those rented rooms on High Street and come around to the shop every few days. I would have been your most annoying customer, rather than your most annoying assistant."

"You are never annoying, Nathaniel," she murmured. "But I am not as certain about having a large dog underfoot."

Nathaniel glanced at Pip, galloping through the

water, and thought the poor ducks would have a harder time of it than either of them.

"Pip will be most annoying to anyone trying to break into the shop, so I could give him a bye on that score." Pip, hearing his new name, paused in the water and raised his ears. The ducks flew off, perhaps looking to set up new quarters in Regent's Park. "There were two things that surprised me when I first came to the shop that morning."

"So you mentioned. That I am not my father is one. But what of the other?"

"That Tony was already firmly entrenched in the shop and in your favor." That is the part that still intrigued him, for how could Tony have known that there was something of value, of personal gain, for him, amongst the shelves and cases. If, as he suspected, Tony was the one who hired Witt to case the place and commit theft, why did the attempted robbery occur just as he, himself, arrived in London? Who would have alerted Tony to his quest?

"But I have known Lord Anthony for many years. He is several years older than I am, as I suspect you are as well, and when he was a boy, he would come to the shop with his mother. Lady Maitland always made such a point of explaining how difficult it was to give up any of her treasures for sale and would tell Lord Anthony that his father never cared for such things, in any case. But now that I think about it, she must have been trying to justify her actions to him and to my father." She pressed her fingers to her forehead. "She just needed the money."

Nathaniel nodded. "Your father must be accustomed to such sentiments. No lady would want it known that she was strapped for cash."

"Yes, that must have been it," Francesca agreed. "It's nearly impossible to feel any sympathy for her, but Lord Tristan must have left her in a difficult knot. Lord Anthony has always been in expectation of an inheritance however."

"Yes, I know all about that," Nathaniel said and cleared his throat. It was time to tell her everything, or nearly everything. "When he comes to the shop, does he purchase the things his mother sold to your father?"

She looked at him in surprise. "No, he rarely buys anything. I have flattered myself into thinking he is coming to see me, for all his mother has made it clear that I shouldn't harbor any hopes in that area."

"Her hopes lie elsewhere. In Cornwall," he said tersely.

"With the Earl D'Arcques, I suppose."

"Yes, you could say that."

She turned on the bench, and her knee touched his thigh. "How strange it is to think that while you and he were friends in Cornwall, he and I were friends right here in London."

"I wouldn't say we were friends and doubt it will ever be so."

"Are you not going to tell me what it is between you?" she asked softly.

He said nothing for some minutes, allowing the sounds of the park to fill the space between them.

"What is your story, Nathaniel?" she continued. "Why are you here? Why would someone with your advantages take up residence in an attic and agree to modest employment? And what do you want of me?"

He returned her gaze, though knowing full well she

did not quite mean what she said. Her familiar blush spread across her face—he was happily quite accustomed to this—but now he felt that he, himself, would incinerate just by staring into her eyes. He knew damned well what he wanted of her but was startled to see that she also wanted it of him. It was possible to hope that, regardless what came of his avowed purpose for coming to London, he would succeed far beyond his rather mundane expectations. What are a title and small fortune next to the possibility of love?

"I have come to claim my legacy, to stand in line for an inheritance that is not yet mine," he said, realizing that he just made his mission as succinct and straightforward for himself, as for anyone else.

"Do you mean, because you lack proof?"

"That is true, though in this case, there is no claim because the benefactor is very much alive."

"He is the Earl D'Arcques, of course. The issue of his health was the first confrontation I witnessed between you and Lord Anthony." Her voice ended in a squeak when Pip came galloping up and shook himself out a few feet away from him. "Oh, good heavens, Nathaniel. Look what your enthusiastic friend has done to us. You shall have no problem with your launderer, of course, but I shall have to answer to Mrs. Belleron for this."

"He has made quite a mess," Nathaniel agreed, though saw no reason to admonish a dog who was simply doing what dogs do.

"Something like your own situation?"

He was surprised she jumped to this conclusion. "No, not at all. Like an act five thespian waiting in the wings, I came quite late to the action, arriving just in time to attempt to change the course of the play. But the narrative was set in motion long before I was born."

"Given your recent reluctance to go to the theater with me, I am astonished you are so familiar with stagecraft," she said a bit loftily. Pip sat down in front of her and put his large head in her lap. Instead of brushing him off, she rubbed him between his ears.

"The problems began because of the theater," he said. "Have you ever heard of Christian Oliver Bell?"

Her hand froze, and she turned to him again. "Everyone has heard of him, for his exploits are legendary. The great Lord of Disguise, the mere actor who traveled to Paris on the eve of the French Revolution and impersonated King Louis, so that the real king could escape."

"So, you know about that?"

"Of course," she said and went on to prove it. "The story about the Englishman who risked his life to save the French king? And how the ruse was discovered before the king could get away, and…"

"…and Christian Bell was executed by guillotine?" he asked.

She nodded sadly, her enthusiasm deflated. She knew the story as well as anyone, he supposed. As well as he did himself, until only a few months ago.

"Except, he was not," he said quietly.

"No, Nathaniel, I am sure you are wrong. I read a book about it; we have it among the biographies in the shop. I think it's entitled: *The True Story of the Great Christian Bell.*"

"The Great Christian Bell is also one of my personal greats, you see. He was my twice-great-grandfather."

He had never said it aloud, nor was it ever discussed.

He looked out on the prospect before them while he let her digest these tidbits of information. They sat on their bench, close to the footbridge, at a low point in the landscape, where the opposite bank rose at a gentle slope to a broad field. Children tumbled about, ignoring the calls of their nannies and the occasional parent, and beneath a tree were several large dogs harnessed to small wagons. Nathaniel imagined the well-bred beasts envied the freedom of Pip, who splashed about in the water and retrieved small balls, delivering them to laughing children. Nathaniel felt a pang of regret, guessing that Pip's owner might very well pass through this company and recognize his missing pet. But that was precisely as it should be; someone had trained Pip and fed him and raised him from a pup. Whoever it was deserved to have him returned and welcomed back into the shelter of his family. From Pip's tolerant behavior, Nathaniel was sure there were children in that home.

Someone would recognize his dog. His. He reminded himself not to make any assumptions.

"He did not die," Francesca murmured. She put her hand on his thigh, where her knee had touched him minutes before.

He tried to keep his mind on their discussion. "Apparently not. That book was written by his son, also Christian Oliver Bell, who perpetuated the rather more gallant legend that his father was executed by the angry revolutionaries."

"Rather more gallant than what?"

"The truth, of course. I have only recently discovered that the lord of disguise made his way to

Trieste, dressed like a lady's maid and accompanied by one of Marie Antoinette's companions."

"That must have been rather intimate," Francesca said.

He wondered why that was the first thing that came to her mind. "I assume it was. He married her, you see, and she became my twice-great-grandmother, Rosemarie. I never before knew her name or identity."

"She was a maid, but maid to a queen. She must have come from an excellent family and might have escaped execution as well."

"In any case, she married a titled gentleman. The ridiculous name of the Lord of Disguise was not simply for the stage. His father was an earl, who was descended from the ancient *comptes* D'Arcques. Christian was his oldest son and inherited the title while he was still in France." He looked down and put his hand over hers.

"Then it must be settled? If you can establish lineage, what more do you seek?" Francesca asked. "Must you present proof to the current earl, at Watch Hill?"

She understood the matter, perhaps better than anyone. And the story of his quest was unlikely to interest any other woman of his acquaintance. He dared to think she already understood how this was her quest, as well, how it could have consequences for her own story.

"Not yet," he said tersely. "There is more to the history, for having escaped death once, Christian Oliver Bell was not likely to risk it again. He slipped into anonymity in Trieste, found employment in the workshop of Kinzing, with whom he was already somewhat acquainted. His son couldn't mention that in the book, of course, because the Lord of Disguise was supposedly already dead. But he does devote several pages to his father's fascination with Marie Antoinette's lady with a dulcimer, the famous automaton. You see, it all connects."

"I do not see," she said, finally sounding exasperated with his narrative. He kept his hand on hers. "What does Lord Anthony have to do with this?"

He was a little put off by her concern for Tony, but he couldn't ignore the connection. There would be time for details when, and if, more information was brought to light.

"When Christian was declared dead, his younger brother Anthony inherited the title. He was Tony's twice-great-grandfather. There was also a half brother, James Endicott. Years later, he went to find the older brother in Trieste, but Christian refused to return to England. Endicott did not come back empty-handed, however. He brought his young nephew, grandson of one Christian and son of the other, whom he soon adopted. There is where the family names converge. But he also brought various gifts from the continent, to grace the halls of Watch Hill. I found the old inventory several months ago, along with the documents on which I base my current understanding, and it includes several paintings looted from Versailles, some Roman statuary, and two automatons."

"Then you and Lord Anthony are distant cousins?"

How interesting that she should tease out that fact and not say anything about the automatons. "I'm afraid so," he admitted. "Did you not immediately see the family resemblance?"

"I never knew two men more unlike each other," she said quickly.

This, at least, cheered his soul.

"But why are you telling me all this?" she asked, which had the effect of deflating that bubble of good cheer.

He caught her hand and brought it to his lips. She turned to face him, her own lips parted.

"Can you not guess?" he asked.

"Is it to impress me with the fact that my shop assistant is actually a lord in disguise?" she said, looking into his eyes. She lowered her lids to ward off the sunlight, and he imagined she must look like this upon awakening.

"It is not that, for I know you well enough to understand you would not think it very important," he admitted. "What is important is that I love you."

"Oh, yes," was all she said, but her words promised everything at once.

"I did not expect it, for it is something I never felt before. But I now believe I have loved you since our first discussion in the shop, when you trusted me enough to hire me on the spot."

She recalled that day, which wasn't so long ago but seemed a lifetime away, and how she regretted her decision almost immediately, thinking he might be a murderer. Or at the very least, the intruder of the night before. But she thought she might have begun to love him that day, as well, for her emotions were dashing far ahead of her reason. There was something he brought into her life, that she had not been aware she lacked. And now, she couldn't imagine living without it, without him.

She blinked into the sunlight and realized he now stood above her, his hand reaching down to her. That such a moment should occur in a public park, surrounded by laughing children and one enthusiastic dog, seemed somehow appropriate, for they were so rarely had time for just the two of them. She took his hand and rose.

"Have I shocked you, Francesca?" he asked, as they started down the crowded path.

She hadn't said anything since her simple affirmation. And she was shocked, more at the knowledge that she felt quite the same way than that he should risk it all by saying it out loud. The poets wrote longingly of unrequited love, and she knew several ladies who knew something about that. But that her own unbidden feelings were, in fact, requited was the most surprising thing of all.

"If I am shocked, it is to find myself in a state of such joy, that I can barely find the words to answer. But you deserve an answer, do you not?" she asked.

"Save your words for another time, my dear. You have already given me the answer I wished for."

And so they walked along in silence, through a thinning crowd. Behind them, Pip barked and rushed up to walk alongside them. Francesca felt a rush of guilt for she had quite forgotten about him. And now, oddly enough, she and Nathaniel were no longer simply a couple, they were now a family.

"Good boy," she murmured. And at Nathaniel's curious glance, added, "Both of you."

Nathaniel laughed out loud, when a man interrupted him.

"Good day, sir. Madam," he said. He was neatly

dressed and wore spectacles but was not otherwise distinct from the throngs of men who walked through Hyde Park this day.

"It is a very good day," Nathaniel said, still smiling. "And how may I help you?"

"I was only wondering about your dog," the stranger answered. He reached into his pocket and produced something wrapped in waxed paper, opened it, and offered it to Pip. "Yes, this is he. Not many dogs have a taste for eel, you know."

Pip gobbled it up and then gazed beseechingly at the man's hand. Francesca felt a pang of regret, for she knew how much Nathaniel would be pained to give him up.

"Is he yours, sir?" Nathaniel asked, quietly. Francesca heard the disappointment in his voice.

"No, but I know the old fellow who owns him. I haven't seen them for a week, at least, and hoped nothing was wrong. The weather has been grand, and I would have expected to see them here, together, as usual. Though as to that, they were just visiting from the country and might have returned."

"Do you know the fellow's name?" Francesca asked, guessing Nathaniel would not have the heart to ask or learn the answer.

The man looked perplexed and put his hands in his pockets as he meditated on the matter. Pip took the liberty of sticking his nose in one of those pockets, presumably the one that had contained the cooked eel. But the man didn't seem to mind and gently eased him out. "This cheerful beast is called Bertie, like one of the queen's boys. That much I remember."

"Bertie," Nathaniel repeated. "And his master?"

The man shook his head. "That I cannot recall. He is gray-haired, a bit bent over, with great calloused hands; he is a working man, I'd wager. Sounds a bit like a Cornishman, as you do, sir."

Now Francesca was a bit perplexed, for she somehow never considered Nathaniel's dialect before, nor did she ever pause on his pronunciation.

"A bit like this?" he asked, cheerfully.

She turned to stare at him, realizing how readily he was capable of turning it on.

"Right you are, sir!" said the man.

"Well, then," Nathaniel said, continuing in the same way. "If you run into him again, please let him know Bertie is quite safe and taken care of. He can claim him at FW Wadsworth Bookseller and Antiquarian on King Street. Do you know the place?"

"No, but I wager he does. He once told me he was interested in odd bits of junk. The sort of thing the mudlarks find along the river."

"How lucky you found us, sir. Do stop by whenever you are in the neighborhood, and particularly if you have some leftover eel sandwich. Bertie would be delighted to see you again, as would we," Francesca said. "And your name?"

"Haworth. James Haworth." Mr. Haworth bowed just slightly, patted Pip's head, and started on his way. She watched him walk away, as did Nathaniel; though as to that, Nathaniel might have been more concerned about Pip running off with him. Satisfied that Pip was remaining with them, and Mr. Haworth was not turning back, they now looked at each other, surely knowing what the other was thinking.

"It's Mr. Graves," they said, almost at once. Pip

nuzzled between them.

"Poor Pip. He must have come to the shop with him, and came back to find to find him," she said.

"Or lost him at the river, recognized us when we came to the bankside, and followed us home."

Francesca smiled, thinking how easily he could speak of home, when it was no more than a suite of tiny rooms where he lived quite alone.

"We ought to let Mr. Graves at the Music Hall know we have his father's dog," Nathaniel said. "It may give him comfort to know his father's companion is safe. He may wish to claim him."

Francesca glanced up at him. "How would you feel about that?"

"Oh, I imagine I shall be able to come and visit every so often. Perhaps I'll walk over with a new dog of my own. London does not seem to lack for dogs that need good homes."

"One might say the same for street children, but one does what one can."

For now, Pip was his, or theirs. He danced alongside them as they walked through the park, toward Kensington Palace, and stopped several times as he seemed to listen to something in the wind.

"Why, it's music," Francesca said as they came to a rise in a stand of trees. "I believe it's coming from the band shell."

As they came down the slope, they saw a crowd had gathered, most sitting on the grass, and some dancing on the lawn, enjoying an afternoon concert. The abandon with which small children enjoyed the Serpentine was replicated here in the spirit of adults.

"Shall we dance, Miss Wadsworth?" Nathaniel

asked, leaning close, so she could hear him over the noise. Even so, she wasn't entirely sure she heard him correctly.

"Do you mean, you wish to celebrate?"

"Celebrate, indeed," he said and nodded. "Does it matter that much to you that I might someday be an earl?"

She stepped back, so she could look directly at him. "That means nothing to me. Surely you already know that?"

"I do. It is one of the reasons why I love you." A couple sashayed past them, laughing as their hair caught the breeze. "And I may never establish a valid claim, in any case. We may be no better off than we are right now."

"Is that so very bad? You still have excellent prospects."

"I have an assured position as secretary to the Earl D'Arcques. If Tony inherits, he would be my employer, and I daresay he would keep me on, just to rub it in. Though as to that, I doubt he will spend much time at Watch Hill."

"You would hate being under Lord Anthony's thumb, no matter how long his reach. Why not instead consider your prospects as a partner in FW Wadsworth? Unless you prefer to remain with Will?"

"I prefer to remain with you," he said, taking her shoulders. "Come, let us dance before Pip jumps up on the stage and starts begging the musicians for eel sandwiches."

She laughed, knowing that whatever happened, he was hers. He was clever and witty, well-intentioned, kind, and honorable. He was good-looking and always looked good to her. And, as she discovered within minutes, and despite the irregular surface on which they moved, a rather excellent dancer.

Chapter 11

Several days later, they were apart, though not for very long, or for any lack of desire. It was simply that Mrs. Blanchard completed Francesca's new gowns and refused to allow her to be fitted in the tight confines of the shop. Nathaniel knew little about ladies' fashion but looked forward to seeing Francesca in the tight confines of her new garments. The very fact that she argued that she was quite content with her customary sturdy wool garments was reason enough to believe that Mrs. Blanchard's creations were going to cover less and promise more. He imagined that the next time they danced, he would be envied for partnering the most beautiful woman in London, hitherto hidden in plain sight in a shop on King Street.

She was beautiful. He did not have to be in love to recognize that, for it was the first thing he'd thought when he first saw her. And she, all distraught and confused after the suspected robbery, could hardly have been at her best. And yet she was. She didn't break down and sob, as most people were apt to do in a crisis, and she had the good sense to hire him. He had expected to find her father but immediately felt amply compensated for his error.

"What are you mooning about?" Will said, startling him. He had quite forgotten where he was, and there were customers about. Will, however, was not a customer, not in the usual sense. He could come in for a bowl or a platter and repay Francesca with food and drink. All in all, Nathaniel thought Francesca got the better end of the bargain. "Are you dreaming about our darling Miss Wadsworth?"

"As a matter of fact, I am," Nathaniel admitted. Will probably understood this before he or Francesca did. "Do you have a problem with that?"

Will said nothing for a few minutes, as Nathaniel wondered if this was the moment his friend would confess to what was already apparent to those who knew him best. That Will's preferences were illegal was of no matter to Nathaniel, for he could not understand why their government thought they could legislate human behavior, beyond murder and thievery.

"Yes, I do," Will said at last. "For I stand to lose you, do I not? The future Mrs. Endicott would not wish Mr. Endicott to come to her bed smelling like cheese."

Nathaniel gave a sigh of relief; for just one moment he wondered precisely what Will meant about losing him. But now his friend's intention was clear, and he continued as though they were on a shared mission. "What do you know of her parents? How do you suggest I get her father's approval."

"Ah, are we up to that, already? Congratulations, you lucky man."

A gentleman glanced up from his book and smiled.

Nathaniel held up his hand. "No, we are not quite up to that, for we have done nothing more than dance together in the park and attend a performance at the Pipedown Music Hall. The latter could hardly be an inducement for romance, for the performances were quite dreadful. Oh," Nathaniel added, suddenly remembering. "And I did dine at her home."

"Did you, now?" Will gave a low whistle. "Well, that's remarkable in itself. Mrs. Belleron is quite a Valkyrie and would have kicked you out on your arse if she did not approve."

"Would I sound uncommonly immodest if I say I believe she liked me?" Nathaniel asked.

"I would call it the ninth wonder itself." Will looked very satisfied. "If that is so, you need not fear Francesca's parents. Mrs. Belleron rules that household, and the Wadsworths would trust her in this, as in everything else."

Nathaniel mused about this. "You do not think they prefer a gentlemen or someone with great expectations?"

Will looked at him in surprise. "Are we discussing the same Wadsworths? I am thinking of a couple, perfectly reasonable and charming, who have set off on a grand adventure without a thought to their daughter's own desires or prospects. Besides, I thought you were a gentleman."

"I am a watchmaker, employed part time at a cheese shop," Nathaniel said, his eyes never leaving Will's.

"True. I don't know how or why I didn't already know that."

"What is it you don't know?" asked Francesca, coming through the door. They both turned to look at her, and Nathaniel wondered if Will saw as much as he did. Probably more.

Her face was pink, as if she had been running, and she was already pulling off her cotton shawl. She stamped her boots on the straw mat, and Nathaniel reflected that she did even this simple action with grace.

"I merely wanted to know why Mr. Endicott wasn't already in the window, entertaining the customers with his crafty handiwork. The wastrel has spent at least ten minutes debating the price of cheddar cheese." Will managed to sound exasperated and cheerful all at once.

"I hired Mr. Endicott to serve my customers," she said, coming between them. "Even those who come into the shop for an idle chat or wonder if I am about so they could speak to me."

Will leaned closer to Francesca and Nathaniel thought he said, "What if the chat is not idle at all, but is about you?"

Francesca's eyes widened, and she looked at one of them to the other. "Well, do not let me interfere with gossip. In case the two of you are terribly curious about the matter, yes, I have my new gowns, and yes, Mrs. Blanchard will be stopping by tomorrow with fabric and lace to outfit Madame Cristobel in the manner to which she once was accustomed. As to that, my automaton will be more expensively dressed than many women who live in London."

"Perhaps you can send the fabric to the women's home, to provide for the poor?" Will suggested.

She shook her head and raised her eyes to heaven. "Even the poorest women would have garments that cover all their body parts, and there is not enough fabric for that. Madame Cristobel can make do with far less." She put a hand on each of their shoulders and passed between them before making her way to the rear of the shop.

"What made you say that?" Nathaniel asked.

"That she provide for the poor? Francesca is a

benefactor of several organizations, mostly providing for the education of the illiterate."

"No. I mean, why did you tell her we were talking about her? She would see that as very rude."

"My dear fellow, do you possibly imagine she didn't already know what engaged us? Whatever else do we have to talk about of any import?"

"I can think of a few things." Nathaniel said. "But do you think she will have me?"

Will smiled. "So, you see? We have nothing else to discuss, of any import at all." He raised his hand. "If she doesn't have you, she is a fool. And Francesca is nobody's fool."

He started toward the door, pausing once to study an oval plate.

"Take it, for the cheddar," Nathaniel said.

"Of course. Why not, for the cheddar? Tell Francesca I shall send over some brambleberry jam, though she must be careful not to spill it on her new gowns."

And with that, he tucked the platter under his arm and joined the flow of pedestrian traffic on King Street.

Francesca wasn't sure if she should be flattered or dismayed that two handsome bachelors were talking about her. Of course, Will was more like a brother, certainly a friend, who always looked out for her welfare. And Nathaniel was something else.

A friend certainly, but nothing like a brother.

What were they talking about?

She busied herself with a customer, who decided to purchase a painting by Turner. Granted, it was a very small Turner, but the sale was sufficient to pay for her new gowns. Her father would have been delighted to know of the transaction or would have once been delighted. Now, Francesca wasn't sure if it mattered to him at all. Indeed, would it matter to him to learn that Madame Cristobel might be on the verge of writing script in her neat little hand again? Would it matter to him to find out that his daughter was thinking of marriage? Almost immediately, she dismissed those ungenerous thoughts. After all, her father provided for her in the way he knew best, by ceding her his business, the work of his whole life. That he was now reaping the reward of his business by traveling throughout the world was a well-earned privilege. That she was also reaping rewards of that business was not necessarily well earned but was a delightful privilege.

Smiling, altogether content, she sent the customer and the Turner on their way, and as her gaze followed them to the door, she caught Nathaniel's eye. He looked solemn, as if he worried about something. She hoped it wasn't her.

"I have just sold the little Turner landscape," she said to him, coming closer, hoping to cheer him up or, at least, get him out of his reverie. "Are you not pleased?"

"I am sorry to hear it, for it reminded me of the hills of Cornwall, and I thought to purchase it myself. I am always sorry when something I desire gets away from me."

Perhaps she was right in thinking he was worried about her.

"I am not leaving," she said softly, not at all sure this is what he wished to hear. "Indeed, I am in no hurry to return home this evening, for Mrs. Belleron has just announced that she must go to Surrey, to see to an aunt who is quite ill."

"Ah well," he said, brightening. "I am sorry to hear it, but perhaps I can persuade you to take a walk with me when we close the shop. We can dine together, though it will be a bit of a challenge with Pip accompanying us."

"Must we take Pip? We can walk him before we go out and leave him to guard the shop."

"Ah, but Pip is the very point of the afternoon journey. As much as I hate to see him go to another, I would like to take him to Mr. Graves at the Music Hall, to see if he went astray when the elder Mr. Graves met his unfortunate end."

"I see." Perhaps it was the possible loss of Pip that put him in a solemn mood. So much for her own vanity. "The dog would provide some consolation, perhaps. You've grown very fond of him, but your—our sacrifice—is nothing to Mr. Graves' loss. As you see, I've grown rather fond of him, as well."

As if he understood what they were about and how he might lose the cozy companionship of two people who provided for him, Pip spent the rest of the day ingratiating himself to them. He stood guard at the door, wagging his tail at each entering customer. He asked only once to go outside to take care of his own business, and this by a gentle nudge at Francesca's leg. He did tricks for a little boy and, by doing so, entertained the child so that the father could peruse several books without interruption.

When, at last, the remaining customers left the shop, laden with purchases. Pip started to bark excitedly.

"Give me just a moment, old boy," Nathaniel said,

loosening his cravat and pulling it from his collar. Suddenly aware that Francesca watched him, he stopped. "I will go upstairs and change my shirt before we go. I'll be down soon."

She continued to watch him as he went up the stairs but did not close the attic door behind him.

This is what he does when I leave each afternoon, she realized. The shop becomes his domain, his own estate, with no one to witness his state of undress, or his private moments. The ache in her chest was so palpable, she thought she'd stopped breathing. But she knew she wasn't ill—quite the opposite. She knew how much she wanted to be alive and share such moments. Not necessarily in an attic room, though she imagined wherever he was would be home for her.

When he came down the stairs, she was just where she stood when he left her.

He paused on a step.

"Is everything all right?" He touched his cravat, his brown tweed lapels, his hair, as if wondering if he forgot something.

"I have been thinking about something, nearly forgotten. You spoke of Christian Bell's book about his father, and I mentioned we had a copy here. I've looked for it this afternoon, and it is nowhere to be found. But on the day I met you, Will helped me gather up the books that had been thrown around the place and mentioned the curious fact that the authors of the displaced books all had names that started with B. Could the intruder have been looking for Bell's history?"

She was sorry she said anything, for he now looked troubled, and they had been looking forward to a pleasant evening.

"Aside from that, everything is perfect," she said, and it was. He looked somewhat distrustful, nevertheless.

But he knew her habits, even if she was just getting to know his. He paused at the coat tree, where her black velvet jacket had been hanging all day, and shook it out a bit before bringing it to her. She, accustomed to the dust in the shop, always shook it out as well. But she always put it on herself.

Not today. Nathaniel stood behind her, holding out the garment and easing her arms into the sleeves. Smoothing down her embroidered collar, his fingers were cool against her neck. She thought he kissed her hair.

If he suggested she return with him to the attic, she would have raced him up the stairs. She started to lean back, against his chest.

"Well, we're all set now," he said, returning to business. Or nearly. His voice was hoarse, and he cleared his throat.

"I am ready to face the world," she said, boldly.

"Miss Wadsworth," he said formally, and he offered his elbow. "I suspect you are always ready to face the world."

As they pressed close to each other to get through the doorway, she said. "I believe that is true, or at least, I am very good at presenting the illusion that it is so. But it is ever so much better to face the world with someone at one's side." Pip barked as he ran ahead of them. "And a dog to lead the way."

"This may be the last time we'll step out with him," he said.

Francesca was now convinced this thought had been bothering him all day. She loved him all the more for his compassion for an animal who might have had to make his way on the rough streets of London, but for having been taken into a home.

"But we don't know if he truly belonged to Mr. Graves, and we certainly won't leave him at the Pipedown Music Hall if he won't be welcome there. Or if we doubt he'll be treated kindly."

"If he did belong to Mr. Graves, his son will surely want him."

"If his son already has five sheep dogs, ten cats, and twelve children, he will be happy to pat Pip on the head and bid you take him," Francesca shot back. For some, a dog is a companion, and for others, just another mouth to feed.

"You really are ready to face the world, my dear. All practical and common sense," Nathaniel said.

Francesca wasn't sure she liked that very much. Perhaps it was the effect of having those lovely new gowns. She certainly would not feel very practical or commonsensical in those. Though truly, she thought as she glanced up at him, she wasn't feeling that sensical at the moment either, though in her plain wool dress and worn velvet jacket.

They walked toward the Pipedown, pausing to return greetings with people along the way. Francesca would have thought that she was fairly recognizable to people in the area, but it was Nathaniel people greeted, and with no more provocation than that they knew him from his work in her shop window. At the fifth such encounter, he murmured to her, "We shall have to tell Will of his success."

"I am sure he already knows all about it," she answered. "But look, is it possible the Pipedown is closed?"

"It is far too early for crowds to gather for a show," Nathaniel said, as if he knew. A young boy stood in front of the theater, handing out broadsides advertising the evening performance.

"Why, look here. It's Bertie," he said as they drew close. Pip greeted him by licking his face clean.

"Your guess appears to be accurate," Francesca said to Nathaniel, knowing he would wish it to be otherwise.

"Is Mr. Graves within, lad?" he asked the boy.

"Just saw him, sir. Go up this alley, and knock on the side door." He studied Francesca for a moment. "I'm not sure a lady would be welcomed, though."

"Whyever not?" Francesca whispered. "But I shall stay at the door, just the same."

"The entertainers are undoubtedly getting into their costumes and may not be entirely respectable," Nathaniel answered as they started down the narrow alley.

"You seem to know a lot about this place."

"Not this one, no. But I've had my share of music halls."

"There's a lot about you I don't know, Nathaniel."

"We'll have to rectify that," he said, when they stopped at the closed door. "Let's have Pip stay with you, while I seek out Mr. Graves. Goodbye, boy."

Francesca didn't mistake the resignation in his voice, or the finality in his valediction. But she was distracted by the other thing he'd said, about getting to know him better.

In the end, Nathaniel regretted that he had ruined a perfectly wonderful day by anticipating the loss of his four-legged companion. He couldn't remember when he had been in such a sulk and was quite ready to turn back several times while they walked to the Pipedown. But Francesca had seen things a bit differently, and she was absolutely right.

Mr. Graves accompanied him to the door and stood for several minutes, gazing down at Pip. Pip showed no sign of recognition and certainly nothing of enthusiasm. He just stood in Francesca's shadow, watching the progress of a beetle making its way across the bricks.

"Yes, that's my dad's dog," said Mr. Graves. "You're welcome to him. I never cared for him, and all I'd do is feed him all day."

"Are you quite certain, Mr. Graves? He must have been with your father when he drowned," Nathaniel said gently and caught Francesca's look of irritation. Indeed, she was probably right. He was sinking his own boat, after managing to get it seaworthy.

"Well, it's not like the dog can tell me what happened or what the old man said. Some nonsense probably, about things that happened forty years ago. Take Bertie. He's all yours. If he eats too much, you can let him go on the street. I'm sure he'll find someone else to take him in." He squinted up at the sun, low in the sky. "Well, I best be back to the stage. Something's amiss with the curtain."

When the door closed behind him, Nathaniel realized he was grinning like a fool.

"Come, let us go before he changes his mind," Francesca said hurriedly. "I know all about such things, what with people coming back the next day to buy something that has already gone out the door with another customer. Pip is yours. I don't like the name 'Bertie' in any case."

"But Bertie is a prince, and Pip is just a farmer's brother-in-law with great expectations."

"I shall take my chances with the one who has great expectations," she said, which made him smile all the more.

He knew of a cheerful and reasonably clean pub, not far from King Street, and they made it their destination after returning Pip to the shop. He was immediately recognized by the proprietor, who led them to a table near the window, away from the crowd, in which some might recognize him as well. He came here often enough, by himself or with Will. But never with a lady, which would surely lead to some good-natured ribbing.

He was all for the ribbing, even welcomed it. But he did not know if Francesca would be so amused, particularly as nothing was settled, other than that they imagined they loved each other. He wasn't a hundred percent sure he knew what that meant, but with each hour he spent with her, he had a keener understanding. It was as if in getting to know her better, he understood himself better as well.

It was a bit like his appreciation of Madame Cristobel, the other lady in his life. In trying to bring her out of rusty inactivity, he was closer to the truth about himself.

He sat up straighter in his seat. He hadn't thought about the automaton in hours, so preoccupied had he been with Pip's future.

"What is it, Nathaniel?" Francesca asked. "Surely,

you are no longer concerned with Pip's welfare? He will be fine at the shop, with his food and water. As we shall be with ours." She picked up her glass of ale and sniffed it suspiciously.

"The ale is well brewed here," he reassured her, though it lacked the strength of Cornish ale, which could knock one off one's chair. "I am thinking of something else that happened before you came to the shop today. I quite forgot about it."

Francesca studied him as she sampled the ale with her tongue and replaced her glass on the worn wooden table.

"It is Madame Cristobel," he went on. "I would like for you to see her, for I managed to further clean up her clockworks. But it can wait for the morning, as she is not going anywhere. I hope."

She looked down at the table, and he thought she was contemplating the blasted ale. He would order tea for her if she disliked it so much. But then her eyes were on him, and he knew that whatever she now said was of more serious import than a beverage.

"I do not have to return to Edgware Road this night. There is no one at home."

And in that moment, Nathaniel knew that he understood everything that truly mattered.

Francesca knew the full implications of her simple statement, and as Nathaniel did not say anything more about it, she knew he was aware of them as well. She knew what she desired, what she wished for, what she ached for, but did not know how to state it more clearly than she already did. She, who bargained with men about costs and provenance, was nevertheless ill prepared to bargain over the matter of her own self. But she was not merchandise to be bought and sold, and what she gave, she would offer most willingly.

After dinner, they walked silently through the streets, pausing to admire the setting of the sun between the buildings or a new store display. They walked past town houses, where one could gaze upon families dining in well-lit rooms, and modest homes, where the sounds of children could be heard through unshuttered windows. The fog coming off the river settled on the landscape like a blanket, quieting the sounds of the street. And cinders from nearby furnaces fell from the sky like blackened snow. This was London, where she had lived her entire life.

And yet tonight, she imagined she was setting off on a voyage of discovery.

"The place looks quiet," Nathaniel said as they approached the shop. "Pip must be doing his job."

"Either that, or he is sound asleep, and our intruder has made off with the cash box."

Though they both had the key to the shop, Nathaniel waited for her to unlock the door. It was natural enough, for she was the proprietor, but Francesca imagined he was letting her know she was still very much in charge. The door opened to familiar smells and everything as it ought to be.

Nathaniel stepped up into the window and carefully retrieved Madame Cristobel.

"Could we not leave her where she is?" Francesca asked, slipping off her velvet jacket. "Surely it would be safer?"

As he walked past her, holding the automaton, he said, "Safer, as we would not risk her falling to the floor, but less safe if someone happens to observe us through the window."

Pip suddenly appeared at his side, pushing against his leg.

"Here, Pip," Francesca said, and tugged him away. Pip watched Nathaniel anxiously, waiting for the very moment he could be greeted in the manner to which he had become accustomed. When Nathaniel settled the automaton on the wide work table in the center of the shop, woman and dog approached. He spent a few moments looking at Madame Cristobel, turned the knob that was a miniature ink well, and stepped back.

Music filled their small space, tinny and beset with pauses, but clear enough to be identified as Rossini's *Thieving Magpie*. This would be extraordinary enough, but suddenly Madame Cristobel came to life, as well. Her frail arms, which had already demonstrated their strength in the twitchy movements Nathaniel had exacted before, now moved through the air in graceful sweeps.

"She is conducting the music," Francesca murmured, altogether fascinated by the performance. "She should be holding a little baton in her hand. Do you see how her hand seems to be grasping something?"

Somehow, she had never noticed that before and felt a bit embarrassed that she paid so little attention to anything other than the automaton's face.

"That is an interesting thought, but I believe she should be holding a graphite pencil, and drawing pictures of gardens and flowers."

"But her arms are in the air, Nathaniel."

He nodded. "That is my next challenge. It took me this long to control her movements, so she doesn't look like she's running from a fire. And now I must bring her down to her desk, and provide her with paper."

"How did you manage it?"

"Oddly enough, by replacing her works with the mechanical box Mr. Witt provided. Though rusty and frozen, the gears were pretty much intact and merely required lubrication. But even if the final result is not to our satisfaction, I believe I can cannibalize the mechanism for most of what is required, and find the rest with what we have here, among the watches."

"You have a rare talent," Francesca said softly.

"No. I merely know how things work," he said and put his hand on her waist.

Francesca looked up, parting her lips, but realized he did not have conversation in mind. At least, not at the moment. Instead, he started to lead her in a waltz, circling around between the bookcases and cabinets, the statuary and easels of landscape paintings, as if they did this all the time. She wondered if he had this in mind when he pulled Madame Cristobel from the window, away from the public eye.

When she was well and fully breathless, he stopped behind a cabinet and kissed her, undoubtedly knowing she wouldn't and couldn't protest. Behind them, Madame Cristobel's music box played on.

"I believe you do have a rare talent, as well as knowing how things work. That should get you far, Mr. Endicott," she said against his chest. A button on his jacket pressed into her chin.

"Will it get us as far as my attic?"

"Surely you don't doubt that," she said, and it was not a question.

"I doubt you intended it to be a trysting spot, when

you offered it to me months ago."

"But I did not know you then, Nathaniel," she said and blew out the candle that burned on the work table. "But I did wonder, though briefly, if you would entertain other ladies in its palatial splendor."

"There are no other ladies," he said and caught her hand, kissing each finger in turn. "And it is indeed a palace, if one is with the right person."

Pip looked disappointed when Nathaniel motioned that he must stay behind, and so they left their dog in the company of Madame Cristobel and her tinny orchestration.

"Come," he said and led her up the narrow stairs. After so many years, they had finally been cleared of all the boxes and broken statuary and papers that had been set aside and otherwise forgotten and blocked the way.

And now, Francesca mused, all the impediments were gone. She had been imagining this moment far longer than it had become a reality to consider.

The door was open at the top of the stairs, but he closed it behind them.

"It is indeed a palace, is it not?" he asked and laughed as he dropped her hand. He gestured about the tiny place. "And here is where I dine, and here is where I read. And just here, in this sturdy chair is where I do my best thinking."

She laughed and put one unsteady hand to her forehead. "It is such a modest place. I'm now ashamed I offered it to you in the first place. Your best thinking is surely worth a good deal more."

"One can be a genius in a prison cell, Francesca. It's possible to imagine a whole world here." He reiterated his earlier assurances by adding, "As long as you are here with me."

But this was no longer the prelude to a seduction; it was the seduction. She discarded her last shreds of propriety as Nathaniel pulled off his wool jacket and his already-loosened cravat. This landed on the wooden floor, but he didn't seem to notice. His eyes never left her face.

"Are you sure about this? You need only say 'no' and make your escape," he said. "After all, you hardly know me."

As an argument, it was merely a polite offer, for they were past dancing about the matter.

"But of course I do, Nathaniel," she said. "How can you imagine otherwise? When you think of how many hours we have already spent together, it would practically add up to a lifetime for anyone else. Besides, I have been dreaming about this since the day you walked into the shop."

He took a step closer and put his hands along the length of her back, patting her. "I must be mistaken about something," he said, and frowned.

Francesca was confused. "No, you aren't. I want this, I want you."

He grinned and kissed her on the forehead. "I am glad for that. But I don't know what to do about this dress."

Francesca had no idea what he meant, until she focused on the shell buttons on his shirt. She removed her hands from his waist and turned just enough so he could see the line of buttons that ran up the side of her gown.

"You are accustomed to fine ladies, I daresay. Those who have maids to dress them in the morning and remove their garments at night. But I have only Mrs. Belleron and her niece, who are occupied with a good many things other than seeing me fastened into my dress. My dresses are made so I can manage to dress myself." She held her hands aloft as she turned in a small circle. "Unless I happen to have someone to help me, of course."

"You have me," he murmured. And then, more clearly, "And if you only say the word, you will have me to help you every day and every night."

Slowly, tantalizingly, he undressed her, until she stepped out of the pool of her gown wearing only her shift. The little room still retained the heat of the afternoon sun, but she shivered.

"Come, come here," he said, pulling her to the narrow bed. "It's not the best mattress, but you must appeal to the landlady if you have any complaints."

They sat on the edge, and the mattress sagged beneath them.

"Why did you not tell her it was so uncomfortable?" she asked.

"It's not, truly."

He stretched out along the counterpane and drew her down on top of him. Pressed against him, she felt every line of the body she had only wondered about for all these weeks. Her imagination did not do him justice.

His fingers retraced the path down her back, and his lips caressed her nose, cheeks, and lips. His legs entrapped hers and brought her even closer. She murmured some nonsense that he seemed to understand, for in one deft moment, he turned her over and was suddenly upon her. If the mattress was uncomfortable, she was blissfully unaware of it. She only felt him, the weight of his body, and the roughness of a long day's growth of his beard.

With his free hand, he pulled up her shift and cast it aside. That such thin fabric should have so separated them was scarcely worth contemplating, for she now reveled in the feel of his body through his linen shirt. She had never experienced anything like this, and yet it felt both familiar and achingly divine.

And then he left her, as his lips made their way down her body, tasting and testing.

"Oh, goodness," she moaned, and squirmed beneath him. "Oh, Nathaniel. Please come back to me."

He was back upon her in one graceful push.

"Hush," he said and covered her lips with his. "I have never left."

And then he was pressing against her, and just when she thought she would die for wanting him, he was within her.

"Oh, dear heavens," she said, and it was the only sensible thing either of them said for some time.

****

At last she was utterly sated and couldn't think or do anything but to lie languidly in their narrow bed, warmed and loved. She closed her eyes, surprised and a bit guilty when she woke up some time later, Nathaniel still covered her with his body. Satisfied with herself, and even more so with him, she listened to the sounds of the chimes downstairs and the occasional carriage clattering down King Street. A window rattled, and the branches of the tree in the tiny back garden rustled against the glass panes. All that she had known for years, she now greeted with the air of discovery. This truly was a brave new world, to which she belonged and now Nathaniel belonged here as well.

"Whatever are we to do?" she asked the cracked ceiling.

He stirred but only to move his face from the hollow of her shoulder.

"Again?" he asked. "Shall we do it again? I think you're going to kill me."

But it would be such a lovely way to die, halfway to heaven.

"Yes, if you're up to it," she said, recognizing something in herself she never knew existed. She was neither reckless nor wanton, but a woman who knew what she wanted and how to ask for it. And how to embrace it when it came.

Their lovemaking was even better the second time, and the third, until Francesca imagined she and Nathaniel would only improve with age and experience, like one of the fine wines Will sold in his shop.

Will. What on earth would he say when he realized—which he surely would—what happened? He'd thrust them together, after all. How quickly all that had happened, in a matter of hours on a day already fraught with uncertainty. And how quickly things had escalated last night. This night.

"What shall we do now?" she asked again, smiling.

"Sleep, I hope," Nathaniel said, lifting his head from the rock-hard pillow to rest on her breast. "We still have a few hours before we open the shop."

She kissed his hair and shifted, hoping to make them both more comfortable. The bed really was dreadful. It was a wonder either of them were able to sleep.

"I meant about you and me, this room, your work,

my shop, your future. There is so much to think about."

"Our future," he corrected her. "Whatever happens, we will face it together. And I should like very much to make it official and introduce you as Mrs. Endicott to all the fellows who come to the shop for no other reason but to gaze longingly at you and pray for the sight of a bit of ankle." He sat up and pulled the counterpane out from under them, to spread it carefully over their naked bodies. She was now thoroughly embraced in his scent. "I much prefer to keep that bit of ankle, as well as everything else, for myself."

Francesca thought very much the same thing, but it was his chest, his shoulders, his strong hands she savored.

"What do you say?" he asked.

"I love you," she said.

She couldn't see his face but felt his heart beating against her cheek. "I mean about getting married."

"But you haven't asked me yet," she said, and quickly relented. "You must know I should adore being married to you, but there is time enough. I am rather enjoying these stolen, somewhat illicit, moments. I have been the good girl all my life, and where has it gotten me?"

She felt him laugh. "To a night of pleasure in a garret?"

"With you," she added.

"Well, then, Miss Francesca Wadsworth, would you do me the honor of becoming my wife?" he asked. "I hope you will forgive me not going down on one knee, but I'm likely to pick up a splinter from this rough floor."

She laughed with him, even on this most solemn of

occasions. And yet, it was hard to be entirely solemn when one was naked and entangled with someone else's arms and legs on a sagging mattress. But so, she guessed it would always be with him, through years that would include beauty and splinters, joy and sorrow. Had she not seen it with her own parents?

"It shall be a story to tell our children one day," she said.

He was so still, she thought he had gone back to sleep.

"No, I rather think not," he said.

She could not help but laugh again. She thought she had never felt such joy in her life.

Chapter 12

"I cannot go through this day, greeting customers, looking like this," Francesca said, staring at herself in a long mirror. The morning chimes were ringing in the shop, the daily cacophony nearly perfectly timed. It was the second thing Nathaniel noticed about the shop months ago, for it required a talented clockmaster synchronize so many movements.

But on that day he first noticed Francesca. He perfectly recalled the day; the syncopated chimes, Will's conversation, the hum of other customers were background noise to her very presence.

"I think you look just splendid," he said and meant it.

She turned from the mirror, though she could see him very well within it. "But only you could think it, my dear. All the more because you look like a suitable mate for me this morning."

"I think that's quite appropriate," he said.

"Of course, but no one else knows that yet," she pointed out, correctly. "I doubt anyone would think something amiss if your jacket looks a bit wrinkled and your cravat askew."

He looked past her to see his image in the mirror. He rather thought he did a good job on his cravat. He had practiced the art for years, as did any man who hadn't the advantage of a valet to do it for him.

"But surely someone will notice that my hair looks like I weathered a cyclone, and that I may have slept in my dress," Francesca said, interrupting his thoughts.

"But you did not," he answered, stating the obvious. Truly, he grasped at straws. He couldn't explain it, even to himself, but he didn't want her to leave to go home and repair her image. Not now, or ever.

Even in the early morning light, he could see that she blushed bright red. It wasn't very gentlemanly of him to remind her that what little sleep she had last night was while she had nothing on at all.

"Nor did I place it on a hanger and smooth out the creases. I suppose I had other things on my mind," she said matter-of-factly and then smiled, looking quite satisfied with herself. With him too, he hoped. "Still, I shall return to Edgware Road to see to my ablutions and return within a couple of hours. You will hardly notice my absence at all."

She was wrong, of course. But he could hardly keep her captive in her own shop.

"Did you not say no one is home?"

"Which is all the more reason to see to deliveries and if anything arrived in the post, and that all else is well. I do know how to dress myself." She started toward him. "You may recall, we discussed this last night."

Nathaniel didn't actually remember what they spoke about but doubted there was much sense in it.

"And, as it turns out, I also know how to tie a man's cravat. It is a skill I learned over many years while working with my father." She came close and put her arms around his neck. "He would often loosen his

243

cravat while working, and then need to straighten it up in anticipation of an important customer."

She pulled him closer and kissed him, reassuring him at once.

"And that is a skill I learned only recently, while being in the shop with you," she whispered in his ear.

"I think we require more practice," he said.

"I think you would prefer to put up the Closed sign on the door," she said, tugging at his cravat and looking at it with a critical eye. "But Madame Cristobel is watching us, Pip is awaiting his breakfast, and customers are surely on their way. If Mr. Blackford comes by, tell him that I am firm on the price of that mantel clock. Though truly, it's an ugly piece and I'm not sure who else would want it in his house."

She was back to business, then. Well, so would he be. "Then why not let him have it as a better price, just to get rid of it?"

"Nathaniel," she said patiently and backed away. Yes, she was back to business, and not their business. "If Mr. Blackford wants it, it is only because he wishes to turn a profit. I don't care if he makes a small fortune on it, but I do wish to recoup what my father paid for it. I checked the ledger soon after he left yesterday."

"Clever businesswoman," he said and bowed, just slightly.

"Yes, I am. And that is why I must go home, so I will look like one." She walked past him to the door, stopping at the coat tree to retrieve her bonnet, and waved briefly over her shoulder as she walked out into the sunlight.

Pip looked up at him, beseechingly.

"Don't worry. She'll come back. We're just here to

do her bidding," Nathaniel said, and patted his dog's head. Indeed, Pip was his. Francesca was his, too. As he was theirs. "Come, let's find a good bone for your breakfast. And some porridge, too."

After years of living a fairly liberated life on the continent, as a bachelor in Trieste and traveling from one inn to the next, he now felt uncommonly domesticated. Here he was, feeding his pet, waiting for his lady to bathe and dress, taking care of the family business. His reasons for coming to London gave him not the slightest premonition of such things to come. His life was so unfettered that laying claim to an inheritance that included the only real home he ever knew was all he'd had in mind then.

Startled by a rap on the window, he looked up to see Mr. Dickens waving at him through the glass. How different it might have turned out if he hadn't been encouraged by the man's belief in the ability of a perfect stranger to fight for what he desired. The joy of last night might never have happened. Though as to that, things might very well have turned out the same at the end, but the joy might have come on a slower, more circuitous route.

Mr. Dickens came through the door and spent a few moments glancing about the shop, taking in the scents and sights.

"I envy you this place, you know," he said. "Each night, when I'm sitting at home, looking at the wearisome use of gold leaf and tassels, I envy you these dusty books and odd pieces of Roman statuary."

"They are all available for sale, my good man. Is there anything particular I might show you?"

"Yes, indeed. Perhaps you have a young lady

available, with dark hair and light eyes. Slight of form, except where it matters. I envy you close proximity to her, as well."

Mr. Dickens was only teasing, of course, and yet, for the first time, Nathaniel resented the utter familiarity of the comment, and the idea that Francesca was something to be had.

"Why, what has happened?" Mr. Dickens asked a bit anxiously, sensing Nathaniel's displeasure. But then he guessed what was the matter, even before Nathaniel could say a word. "Oh, yes. I see. I suppose congratulations are in order."

Nathaniel purposefully misunderstood him. "No, I'm not much closer to uncovering the truth about certain things."

"That is not what I speak of, as well you know." Mr. Dickens came closer and flicked Nathaniel's cravat. "No man, master or valet, would knot his cravat in such a manner. This was tied by a lady."

"You cannot know that," Nathaniel protested. He never heard of such a thing.

"But I know it now, for you have given yourself away," Mr. Dickens said, and chucked him under his chin. "So, congratulations are in order. Where is the lady?"

"Madame Cristobel is in her place in the window," Nathaniel said, waving him off.

"And the other? Whatever you have accomplished with the automaton, I am certain you have not managed to get her to tie your cravat."

Nathaniel did not intend to reveal more than was necessary. "She had several errands to run about the neighborhood and will return soon."

"Shall I congratulate her as well?"

"No," Nathaniel said quickly. "Things are not yet settled, though I am optimistic they will be shortly."

"Better and better," said Mr. Dickens. "This sounds like a mystery. And does it involve the automaton, as well?"

Nathaniel wondered how or why his friend guessed this was a possibility and hesitated to say anything at all. Then, as if on cue, there was a tap on the window.

"Ah, here is my neighbor Will Picardy, who is known to you as well."

"Even better," said Mr. Dickens. "If he brings toast and jam, we could have a bit of a party."

But Will came through, empty-handed. He looked from one to the other and asked, "Am I interrupting anything?"

Mr. Dickens laughed. "I hoped to enjoy myself perusing a new book, and perhaps partaking in a small feast, but as it seems I am mistaken, I will get back to my pen and paper."

"Do stay for the company?" Nathaniel asked.

"Another time, gentlemen," he said lightly and walked to the door. Turning back, he added, "I do like the name of your lively dog, Nathaniel."

After the door closed behind him, Will said, "He is a strange fellow, you know."

"I know, but I am indebted to him. After all, he sent me to you almost as soon as I arrived in London."

"That reminds me; my mother regrets that she has not invited you to dine at our home, so that she might welcome you to London, as well. Are you available Friday next? She has been anxious to have a suitable lady for you to meet, and I suggested she include

Francesca in her invitation."

"She knows Francesca, of course."

"Of course. Our parents have known each other for years, and I suspect they always hoped she and I would bring both families together. And that is yet another reason why they are disappointed in me."

There was no need for an explanation. "I shall ask Francesca if she is available next Friday and let you know her answer."

"And if it just you?" Will asked. "What shall I tell my mother?"

"I will wait on Francesca's answer. But if it turns out that she urges me to attend without her, please advise your mother that she does not need to invite a young lady simply for my amusement at the dinner table. I shall come for the conversation and the food."

"Both promise to be excellent." Will tapped a silver fork against a crystal vase, listening to its perfect tone. "There is something else you may find excellent, that I may have neglected to mention. My parents have a small collection of clocks and timepieces. I have a bit of interest in them, as well."

"This is news, certainly. Why have you never told me?"

"I admit to a bit of interest but have no particular talent. Nevertheless there are some simple tasks with which I might assist you. Oiling the clockworks, perhaps. If I take care of that, you would have more time to devote to Madame Cristobel. I know that is of upmost importance to you. Or perhaps, once was?" Will smiled as he picked up a porcelain box, from which a few musical notes escaped. "I am capable of changing springs in overwound music boxes. Why else do people discard them, but for the fact they can't get them to play a little piece by Mozart? I can also help you with your naked lady."

"I beg your pardon?"

Will grinned. "Cristobel, of course. The poor darling must be embarrassed to be undressed for all of King Street to see. Though, as to that, she doesn't have much to reveal."

"The automaton," Nathaniel covered his error quickly, embarrassed himself for what he let his friend see. "In fact, perhaps you can help me with it. I came upon some spare parts, remarkably similar to Madame Cristobel's inner works. I cleaned them up and have been very happy with the results. Come, let me show you."

Will and Nathaniel stood shoulder to shoulder in silence, studying Nathaniel's handiwork.

"And how did you come upon these parts?" Will asked.

"A mudlark came in, recommended by another antiquarian. He, Mr. Witt, pulled these parts from the river," Nathaniel said, knowing how ridiculous it sounded.

"Do you know how long and deep that channel of water runs? You could sooner find a button you lost years ago somewhere on the Matterhorn."

"I did not say it was likely, only that it happened," Nathaniel said and turned Madame Cristobel's inkwell, so she might conduct her invisible orchestra. "Though there is a bit of a connection in the narrative, making it only slightly less a coincidence."

"I should like to hear this work of fiction."

"No, it has truly happened, however unlikely." And

so Nathaniel launched into the story of how Mr. Graves visited Francesca at the shop and told her about her mother's arrival in London, along with boxes of treasures acquired by her father. How he and Francesca unwittingly witnessed the elderly man's body recovered from the unforgiving river. And how, so soon afterward, they learned his identity when they went to the Pipedown Music Hall.

"And so you believe such things were in his possession when he splashed into the Thames?" Will asked, his disbelief evident in his tone. "And that, after being found, they were brought to the only person in London who might have some interest in them?"

"I have no other explanation for it," Nathaniel said and shrugged.

"I always thought you were a man of logic and reason."

"I always prided myself on the same, and yet, there it is." Nathaniel also considered his own behavior of the night before and how quickly reason had abandoned him then.

"Why, here's a good fellow. He has a good home here," Will said as Pip sashayed toward them, wagging his tail. The dog thrust his head right into Will's hand, waiting to be patted.

"He is my new guard dog, as you can plainly see," Nathaniel said ruefully, for Pip would happily lead a thief right to the cache of Roman coins Francesca kept buried somewhere in the shop. "I now believe he came here looking for his lost master, who, as it turns out was Mr. Graves."

"The man who drowned?" Will asked in disbelief.

"I know. It all comes back to the elderly man and

his drowning. I did the right thing and brought Pip to the music hall, though it grieved me to do so. But the younger Mr. Graves had no interest in keeping him. And so, I now have myself a fine pet. Francesca is fond of him, too."

Will studied him and smiled.

"Francesca, indeed," he mused.

"She is Francesca to me," Nathaniel said, feeling the pride that came with that announcement. "At last."

"It has not been very long. But I suppose it is inevitable," Will said agreeably. "But she is still your employer, is she not?"

Nathaniel nodded, knowing how differently their relationship would be perceived if their roles were reversed and he were her employer.

"Do you not see how poor Mr. Graves is just incidental to this story? It does not come back to him, but rather to her, your Francesca." Will looked to him for confirmation, and went on. "Her store, more likely. After all, would you have arrived on the scene if the Earl D'Arcques had not given you the name of this place, remembering that young Charity Williams was sent to London with all her father's treasures, and eventually married Frank Wadsworth?"

Nathaniel thought it now seemed part of another life. But it was his life, and now his future. And that meant it was Francesca's, as well.

"And Charity's father was also known as an antiquarian, collecting all the detritus no one else in the neighborhood wanted. His second wife did not want it either," Will said. "As I say, my family has long known the Wadsworth family."

"I assume she did not want Charity either,"

Nathaniel said, remembering what Mr. Graves told Francesca when they were alone in the shop. "And that's when Mr. Graves comes into the story,"

"Because he drowned and had a dog?"

Here is the point where they began, and the story still seemed to turn on an extraordinary coincidence.

"Because he was the driver who brought Charity to London."

Will let out a long breath and looked like he often did when reasoning with a difficult customer.

"Come, have a look at our automaton and how far I've come with her," Nathaniel invited him, and bid him step up into the window. "Next to the story of how we all came to be in London with an interest in this shop and the contents therein, figuring out her mechanisms should be easy as sin."

Will, always more of a showman than Nathaniel, bowed to the window shoppers and removed his jacket with a flourish, before sitting down. He turned Madame Cristobel's ink well and surely exaggerated his pleasure at seeing how well she managed to wave her frail arms.

"You needn't go overboard with your response. The shoppers are more interested in you than in our mysterious automaton," Nathaniel said, knowing it all too well, and remembering it was Will's suggestion that it be so.

****

Francesca walked down King Street, absolutely certain that no one particularly noticed her and yet imagining all the while that she commanded everyone's attention. What everyone said was true: clothes make the man or woman. And wearing a smart new dress with hand-wrought applique on the sleeves and collar made her a woman full of confidence and pride.

Mrs. Blanchard had done that for her. And, Francesca supposed, Nathaniel had his part in that as well, and that had nothing to do with the clothes she wore. Or not.

For all she was still haunted by mystery and uncertainty about her business, she felt absolutely glorious. And as she approached the shop and saw a small crowd gathered at the window, her cup of joy truly runneth over, for they were there to admire the man she could now rightly claim as hers. After weeks of harboring some resentment toward those who flirted with him, her self-doubts dissipated with the dawn of this new day.

But just then, Nathaniel came through the door with an elderly gentleman and held up a small stained glass window to the sun for both of them to properly admire.

The group clustered at the window did not seem to notice them. What was this?

She asked the very same question when she joined the crowd.

A lady she did not recognize—and more important, did not recognize her—turned to face her.

"Why, there is a new gentleman in the window, and he is even more admirable than Mr. Endicott."

Francesca followed the lady's pointing finger and saw Will, smiling and waving at everyone. Oh, good heavens.

She skirted the crowd to advance on Nathaniel and their customer, still in the doorway. Nathaniel looked away from the glass, toward her, and squinted. He looked confused. They had been apart for a few hours;

had he quite forgotten who she was?

She paused, not understanding any of this, and cocked her head, impatiently waiting for his recognition.

And in a matter of moments, she saw relief transform his expression, soon replaced by a look of frank admiration. Perhaps too frank.

"Mr. Endicott," she said pointedly, reminding him where they were. "Have you told our customer that this pane of glass was rescued from the Lady Chapel on Grosvenor Square, after the ancient building burned to the ground? It was struck by lightning not five years ago, and much of the beautiful stained glass was destroyed."

"My grandmother lit candles there for nearly all her life," their customer offered. "I thought this bit looked familiar, for I used to accompany her there when I was a child."

"Your recollection must be excellent, sir," Francesca said, more than a little surprised at such an assertion. "I understand there were a great many stained glass windows, and several were quite large. This is but a small sample."

The customer stood his ground. "But a thing of beauty, even in its smallest parts, remains memorable and cherished."

It was a rather poetic pronouncement for a bustling afternoon on King Street, and Nathaniel readily embraced the sentiment.

"Yes," he said solemnly, watching Francesca's face all the while. "I have proof that it is so."

"Well, then, my good man," said their customer. "I shall purchase it at once and admire it for the rest of my life."

"Excellent," Nathaniel said. "I intend to do the same." He bowed and gestured for Francesca to precede them into the shop, and she scowled as she passed him. The sense of joy that kept her buoyant as she walked down the streets of her neighborhood was drowning now in her belief that she did not quite know what was happening.

Will awaited her within and blinked as she approached.

"Yes?" she asked irritably. "First, Nathaniel looks as if he does not know me, and now you are giving me a second look. Have I sprouted wings, or something of that sort?"

"Nothing so mundane, my darling," Will said gallantly, as well as absurdly. "You have abruptly abandoned your schoolmistress mien and have arrived at your kingdom looking like its queen."

So that was it, was it? Well, she could hardly blame them for thinking so, for she felt some of that power herself. But, truly, had she been such a dowd?

"No one ever doubted it," Will quickly added, without her really asking. "But why did you wait so long?"

Francesca glanced toward the back of the shop where Nathaniel was carefully wrapping the stained glass in newsprint. He looked up at her and seemed frozen in place.

"Perhaps, Will, perhaps I wished to impress people with my business acumen, my practical and efficient manner, my good sense. People trust their schoolmistresses, do they not? I am not so sure they implicitly trust ladies with lacy bonnets and scalloped hems."

"Ah, Nathaniel," he said. "Perhaps you will join our conversation. Our Miss Wadsworth is a bit bothered by our reception of her sudden transformation."

"And that is quite another thing," Francesca argued, not quite willing to let it go. "It is not sudden, by any means. I had to choose fabrics, buttons, trims. Mrs. Blanchard had to make muslin gowns for fittings and spent weeks sewing everything together. This has been going on forever, it seems."

"But not that anyone would know," Nathaniel said sensibly. "One has no idea what goes on in a lady's private life." He looked at her in a way to let her know that his good sense was easily abandoned.

She knew she blushed like a fool and quickly turned away. There wasn't much remaining of her good sense, either.

"I am glad you were able to sell that panel of glass. Surely the gentleman has a remarkable memory to recall where it once was placed, years ago," she said, watching Will at the same desk where she was accustomed to seeing Nathaniel. "And what are you doing there? Do you not have your own shop?"

Will looked up and dropped a small screwdriver on his lap. As he raised a hand to retrieve it, he knocked over a jar of oil.

"I am making myself useful, as you can see. Though I am not certain what it is I'm trying to get out of Madame Cristobel."

Francesca waved her hand dismissively. "Nathaniel believes that Madame Cristobel has some important information bound up in her cogs, waiting to spring loose."

"That is rather apt imagery," Nathaniel said admiringly. "Your excellent friend Lord Anthony probably wants the information, not the automaton. She is just the means to an end. As he may believe that I am the means to reveal the message of the automaton. And you, dear Francesca, are the means by which he may always have access to the shop."

"How flattering you are, Nathaniel."

"And you?" Will asked him.

"I am the impediment to his success. He has ever belittled my abilities, such as they are. Why would he think any different now?"

"Then we should end this charade right now," Will said. "So we don't hasten the process of discovery."

Nathaniel raised his hand. "But I stand to gain a good deal, as well. It may change the course of my life."

"You do not intend to be a shop assistant for the rest of your life? You're very good at it," Will said wryly.

"I haven't heard any complaints," Nathaniel answered and met Francesca's eyes. "But I am quite weary of displaying myself in the window, whereas you seem to be enjoying himself. It is your show. I am content to stay right here."

While his words were simply stated, Francesca preferred to believe deeper meaning there. Would Nathaniel stay here, with her? Would he expect her to leave all this, for the green hills of Cornwall?

"Yes, I see you are," Will said. "But I expect a quiet afternoon with my cheddar and French brie. You can just stay here and gaze upon each other. Miss Wadsworth," he said formally. "My mother requests your presence at a small dinner party in several days' time. She mistakenly addressed it to Mr. Endicott, but you can bring him along, of course."

"Why, I should be delighted, Mr. Picardy. I have just had several dresses made and would enjoy an occasion to wear one of them. Indeed, my dressmaker is now all set to make miniatures of the same dresses for Madame Cristobel."

"Excellent. Perhaps she would therefore be able to come as my partner," he said.

"The dressmaker or the automaton?" Francesca teased.

Francesca glanced at Nathaniel and thought he winked at her.

As Will took his leave, he held the door open for Tony, who sauntered into the shop.

"Why, it's like a family reunion," he said, looking from Francesca to Nathaniel.

"Except we are not a family," Nathaniel said, irritably.

"You surprise me, Nathaniel. Is that not the very point of your quest here in London? Are we not indeed distant cousins?"

"The greater the distance, the better for both of us."

"Lord Anthony, how lovely to see you," Francesca interrupted.

Nathaniel wondered how he could manage to completely cut her off from Tony without causing a great rift in their own relationship. She seemed to enjoy Tony's company, and he wished he knew why. There had to be more than a trip to the theater and the occasional baguette to account for it.

"Miss Wadsworth, you are truly a vision," Tony

said gallantly. "The dress suits you to perfection. Is it new?"

"It is. I thank you for noticing, Lord Anthony, but you are a flatterer. For most of my customers, I am just part of the scenery."

"But I am not a customer."

You're here to buy something, Nathaniel thought and edged closer.

Francesca turned flirtatiously and put up her hands to remove her hat, which she had neglected to remove since she came into the shop. Tony watched her, looking as seriously contemplative as a statue in Trafalgar Square. And yet, Nathaniel doubted the man was as contemplative as Pip.

"We do have much to offer here," Francesca said. "Though I know you are most interested in Madame Cristobel. Would you like to try your luck with her? Mr. Endicott just offered Mr. Picardy the chance."

Francesca was being provocative, unexpectedly bold. But whatever game she played, all suddenly became clear to Nathaniel. They all wanted something in this little shop. But while their interests might have once been identical, that was no longer the case. Nathaniel now knew he only wanted Francesca. And he saw enough to realize that whatever Tony wanted, it was not Francesca.

And, of course, Tony wanted Madame Cristobel, not so much as to possess her, but to possess her secret.

"You may know Miss Tupper, who occasionally visits. She wishes to purchase Madame Cristobel for the lobby of the Pipedown Music Hall," Francesca said.

"I do not know her," Tony said quickly. "Nor does my mother."

Nathaniel wondered why he would bring up that lady, when no one suggested she played any part at all.

He said, slowly, "Perhaps not, but do you know Mr. Graves, her stage manager? The poor man whose father only recently drowned in the Thames."

"I do not believe I have ever met him," Tony said, a bit warily.

"But you have heard about the elder Mr. Graves and his dreadful murder."

Tony stepped back, as if avoiding a trap. But he stumbled right into it. "I had not heard it was a murder, but an accident."

"Oh, but you had heard about it," Francesca said, advancing so closely, she could have been standing on his toes.

"Hasn't everyone? I must have read it in the papers or heard about it at my club," Tony said, his back against a cabinet.

Francesca resumed her expression of sweet innocence. Nathaniel realized that he would need to recognize this if he intended to spend the rest of his life with her, for otherwise he would be hopelessly lost in any argument.

"But only imagine," she mused. "A stranger to town, a man of no consequence, pulled from the river. Why, *The Times* would be full of nothing else if they covered such an unfortunate event each time it occurred."

"I hadn't heard," Tony volunteered, "nor read of it. My mother never said anything of it at the breakfast table and could be appointed to the constabulary, for all she knows everything that happens in this town."

Nathaniel knew he was reading too much into this

conversation, but he would swear that Tony grew a bit desperate at the word "constabulary."

"And then there's the business of the mudlark and the curious things he found," he said, still watching Tony. "But no matter. No one is interested in that."

Tony opened and then, wisely, shut his mouth.

"Well, let us leave it at that," Francesca said, effectively shutting down their conversation.

"That is best," Tony said, seizing an opportunity to escape. "I must leave at once. I have much to do this afternoon."

"I do not doubt it. But what brought you by in the first place? Is there something you wanted?" Nathaniel asked, trying to emulate Francesca in his cheerful and disarming approach.

But she was much better than he and, in any case, had much more practice.

"A friend never needs a reason to come by for a visit," she said. "Please let us know what your mother thinks on this matter, as well as all others."

Francesca was exhausted. The physical aches and weariness that left her acutely aware of last night's passion were only heightened by the mental exhaustion of practicing diplomacy between two warring factions. How simple her life had been when her daily exercise consisted of little more than walking back and forth from home to shop and occasionally sweeping up the shards of a broken vase. Now, she required the strength of Hercules and the wisdom of Solomon just to get through an afternoon.

She glanced at Nathaniel keenly focused on Madame Cristobel, trying to reveal her secrets and yet knowing full well he might be on a fool's errand. She wished it all over, whatever the outcome, a small part of her resentful that she had to share her lover with a wooden mechanical doll.

"Miss Wadsworth!" came a voice at the door.

"Mrs. Blanchard," Francesca called out, a little louder than necessary. The dressmaker wasn't deaf, though it appeared that Nathaniel was. He didn't look up. "Did you leave something behind at my home?"

"Not of which I'm aware," returned Mrs. Blanchard, coming closer. "I must say, the dress thoroughly suits you. I'm so glad you selected this superfine."

The woman was as accomplished a saleswoman as she, for they both were fully aware that Mrs. Blanchard made all the choices. Francesca was simply her willing accomplice, but now a grateful one.

"I have been receiving compliments on it all day, and you may have gained a few new customers, Mrs. Blanchard."

"I am delighted to hear it, but just now I have to satisfy a most demanding lady." She glanced at the window, where Nathaniel still hadn't looked up.

"Surely not Madame Cristobel," Francesca laughed. "I am sure she will understand if you take another before her. I do not find her demanding at all."

"Well, she seems to require the full attention of Mr. Endicott, at present. Do you not think that rude of her, when you are standing here, quite alone? Still, for a dressmaker, there is no one more demanding than a naked woman." Mrs. Blanchard opened her bag and pulled out scraps of fabric, laces, and buttons. "I am prepared to make her undergarments as well and provide cotton wool to stuff her corset. The poor thing is not very well-endowed."

"And yet the gentleman does not seem to notice," Francesca pointed out. "So long as she moves to his will, he is quite happy."

"Now, why wouldn't he be?" Mrs. Blanchard asked and turned toward the window. "Sir, Madame Cristobel and I require some privacy, please."

At last, she had his attention.

"What do you propose to do?" Nathaniel asked, setting down his tools.

"Nothing more than to dress our lady in the manner to which she ought to be accustomed," Francesca chimed in. "In fact, Mrs. Blanchard needs to take some measurements. As you already know, her talents are incomparable."

Mrs. Blanchard was all business. "It is no art, sir, to create beauty when one is already working with beauty. This poor poppet, on the other hand, desperately needs my help."

"She desperately needs my help, as well," Nathaniel added, stepping down. "But you may be up to the task better than I today."

Chapter 13

For the first time in her life, Francesca opened her closet to a wardrobe of gowns and did not have to worry if a garment was too loose in the shoulders or too tight across her breast. She would not have to worry about tripping over the length of the skirt or if the hem revealed too much ankle. These were her gowns, and her only regret was that she had not allowed herself such indulgences years ago. But then, there had never seemed to be a good reason to do so.

Mrs. Belleron, only just returned from her brief journey, seemed just as excited as she. But the dear woman might have just been pleased that Mr. Endicott was escorting Francesca on a second outing. Francesca was pretty certain Mrs. Belleron would not have felt the same way if she knew what else had been going on while she was absent from town.

"You have your heart set on Mr. Endicott, and I can't blame you," Mrs. Belleron said, as she fussed with a bow on Francesca's bodice. "He is a fine figure of a man and clearly has his heart set on you."

"I don't know how you can understand all this, unless you already asked him point blank."

"Questions don't need to be asked when the answer is already so clear," Mrs. Belleron said, as if nothing could be more obvious. "But you haven't settled everything yet, have you?"

"Do you mean, has he asked me to marry him?"

"Or have you asked him to marry you." Mrs. Belleron frowned at the somewhat lopsided bow and did not meet Francesca's eyes. "I wouldn't put it past you, for you always had a will of your own."

"Would you say the same if I were a man? Like Mr. Endicott or Will or Lord Anthony?" Francesca attempted to laugh, though she did not find any of this amusing. "They are the men in my life, who like to tell me what to do with it."

"Certainly not like Lord Anthony," Mrs. Belleron said, frowning. "From what I hear, the young man doesn't do as much as spit on his boots without the permission of Lady Maitland. But it is just as well, for he can offer you little more than Mr. Endicott."

Francesca wondered what else Mrs. Belleron heard from her well-connected sources. "Did you not just compliment Mr. Endicott on his good looks and good taste?"

"I did. But will you be content to work your whole life in a dark little shop, as your mother did with your father? I saw firsthand that it is not always an easy life, and sometimes means sacrificing a good deal. Your great aunt tried to warn your mother of this."

"And is that why she cut her off without offering so much as a wedding breakfast when she married my father? Did she see her own indifference as part of the sacrifice?" Francesca imagined she was above such considerations, that lack of wealth was not an impediment to love. But then, she knew something of which Mrs. Belleron was unaware. Which, of course, might never come to be. "If such things as you imagine come to pass, I am sure Mr. Endicott and I will manage with some success. I suppose you are telling me all this, so I can be prepared if these are the last gowns I shall ever have made for me? Well, that's more than most women can claim."

"No, dear. I was rather thinking that there will be other eligible gentlemen there this evening, no doubt. Even those in trade can have excellent connections, as well you know."

"Oh, no, Mrs. Belleron. I hardly know anyone else who will be there."

"You hardly know Mr. Endicott, either, but that hasn't stopped you."

"I may know more than you realize," Francesca said. And then, at the look in the housekeeper's eyes, "And I believe he's at the door right now. Would you kindly let him in? I should be down in a few moments."

****

"Mrs. Belleron seemed less than happy to see me this evening," Nathaniel said, once they were seated in the carriage. Francesca was pleased to see it was the same vehicle that he rented last time and thought the groom looked familiar as well. "Did I leave footprints on the rug when last I came by?"

"Nothing so trivial, Nathaniel," Francesca confessed. "She is worried about my prospects, primarily because she doesn't think you have any."

"Is that not something I should discuss with your father?"

"I suppose it is, if he ever gives you the chance to do so. I do love my parents, and appreciate how much they have provided for me. But I am coming to think I have lost precious time in their service, while I might have been doing other things. Going out in society, for one. Having new gowns made, so I might do so with some measure of pride." She looked down and saw that his hand rested on her own. She lifted both, and kissed his. "Having a lover," she added.

With his other hand, he caressed her cheek and brought her closer. "No one can see us," he said and kissed her. Within moments, he pulled her onto his lap and brought his arms around her. The bow Mrs. Belleron had fussed with was soon untied, and her neatly curled hair fell about her ears. She was struggling to untie his cravat with her one free hand, when the carriage lurched to a stop; she might have slid off his lap if he had not caught her in time.

"Oh dear," she murmured. "What are we to do?"

"Get married, perhaps?" he said reasonably, brushing his hair off his forehead with his long fingers. "Though if I have to wait for your father, it may be a few years before we can do so."

She smiled, suddenly not caring all that much about her appearance. "I was talking about my hair and gown, but you have touched on the very point. My father and my mother have allowed me to make decisions in all else; I shall decide whom I wish to marry."

"Well, I hope that means me." He hesitated just a moment, catching her mood. "And if I can prove my worth by helping you with your hair and putting your gown to rights, would I improve my case?"

"Very much," she said solemnly, raising her hands to her curls. "I cannot tolerate a man who knows how to take things apart but refuses to put them back together."

"Then you have chosen wisely, my dear. For if I understand anything, it is how to restore things to their proper condition."

"And you have also demonstrated your prowess in deconstruction, much to my satisfaction. Indeed, I think you'll do."

He seemed intent on the buttons on her bodice, and the intricacies of tying the bow. Francesca thought that he had a harder time of it than Mrs. Belleron, for all he said, but they were in a moving carriage.

"But what of Mrs. Belleron?" he asked suddenly. Not for the first time, he seemed to read her thoughts.

"What of her?" Francesca asked, and then recalled they had been speaking of the housekeeper. "Do you still imagine she is against your suit? I think she adores you but is just trying to be judicious. After all, when first you came, she was overly relieved there was someone who might spend an evening with me, perhaps the only one in all London. Now that you've appeared a second time, she feels obligated to be cautious and ask the questions that a father would ask, as you say. That's all it is."

"No, there's something else, Francesca. I don't know of a man who wouldn't want to spend an evening with you. Any man—or woman—would admire your beauty, your wit, your cool self-confidence. You are, in every way, admirable and desirable."

She studied him closely, which wasn't difficult, as the carriage was quite small. She didn't care about any other man—or woman. She only wanted to hear this from him.

"You have it wrong, Nathaniel. It is not so much that no one else would have me, but rather, that there has been no one else whom I would have. That is why dear Mrs. Belleron has been so worried. I believe she thought she would be stuck with me for the rest of her life."

"Worried, is she?" He smiled as he put his arm about her shoulders. "I can't think of anything better than being stuck with you."

****

Nathaniel looked at Francesca's face as they stepped out of the carriage in front of the Picardy town house, wondering why she had said nothing about it.

"I imagine there is none like this in all of London," he said, "and perhaps not in England."

The design and details reminded him of Bavarian cottages, for they were frivolous and intricate. On this stately street, the Picardy home stood out like a swan among the geese. Or a cuckoo, more likely.

A large clock was mounted into the keystone of the arched doorway, framed by two small wooden doors. A window was open to the street, and a violinist's waltz played out onto the otherwise quiet street. Though Nathaniel didn't recognize it, Francesca surely did, for she started humming to it.

"Would you like to dance?" Nathaniel asked. With her hand still on his elbow, he turned in to her and held up his right hand.

"I can't think of anything I would enjoy more, but we must remember that we are standing in the middle of Mayfair and would attract quite an audience. You and Will would probably say that it would make for excellent publicity for the shop, but I rather think all we would accomplish is to embarrass our hostess."

"It would accomplish something else, of course," Nathaniel said and waited for her to meet his eyes. "We would dance again, and once again to the tune of a music box. It seems rather apt."

Her eyes glimmered in the evening light, as if she shed tears. But he only saw joy there. "Do you mean, because that is what brought us together?"

"So it seems," he said, thinking how easily it might have pulled them apart.

She shook her head, just perceptibly, and dropped her hand as she turned to the splendid façade of the townhouse.

"It's extraordinary," she sighed, and he thought she meant the wonder of being in love. But she had quite changed the subject—or returned it to where they started once alighting on the street. "Years ago, I marveled at the perfect symmetry of the two trees growing against the brick walls, but now I appreciate how much time has passed. They are quite large now."

"I envy you and Will knowing each other for so many years."

"Should I also envy you and Lord Anthony?"

Nathaniel hadn't yet responded to that when the great door under the arch opened, and Will stood at the head of the stairs, tapping his foot impatiently.

"Are you intending to spend the evening admiring the brickwork?" he asked. "You must come in to save me. There is hardly anyone younger than sixty within, and I have had my fill of hearing how difficult it is to climb the stairs in Westminster."

"Well, it is," Francesca whispered. "I once went with my father when he was called upon to examine a small clock, and he was exhausted at day's end."

"Are you speaking of the same man who is now climbing volcanoes in the Pacific?"

"Well, there is that." She giggled. "But it is easier

for him to complain to me than to my mother."

"Are the two of you laughing at my misery?" Will asked. He waved them on. "Come, come in, and see if I am not accurate about the drama in the parlor."

Nathaniel, divided between loyalty to his old friend and a great desire to spend the evening on the steps, talking to Francesca, decided he should attempt to do both and move their conversation indoors.

Will wasted no time in making introductions, and Francesca was both surprised and delighted to meet so many people who knew her parents.

"Why, you look just like dear Charity, but a good deal younger," said Mrs. Caswell who, not surprisingly, looked very much like her own daughter.

"As she is my mother, you are right on both counts, Mrs. Caswell," Francesca replied, and heard Miss Caswell laugh behind her.

"But why have we never seen you? Where have you been hiding? Surely you don't live in the shop?" Lady Damison questioned her. "Although, as I recall, your father lived there before he married your mother. There is a flat up in the attic, though most unsuitable for anyone other than a servant."

Francesca caught Nathaniel's eye, and he shook his head, just slightly. Miss Caswell took the opportunity to sidle up to him and demand his attention.

"I am surprised you know of it, Lady Damison, for I had little knowledge of it myself. And yet, when I was up there recently, I saw dishes in a small cupboard, and linens on the bed, even after all these years. They needed to be laundered, of course," Francesca added quickly. "But how did you know?"

"Your mother, of course. It was such a big scandal

at the time." Lady Damison pulled her away from the circle of guests to a dark corner, but that didn't discourage four other women from following them. Dear heavens, was it possible she and Nathaniel were not the first to have a secret affair in the attic? Though it appeared her parents' affair was not much of a secret. Francesca again sought out Nathaniel, but Miss Caswell managed to engage him so that he faced the opposite wall.

"I fear this may be information I have no desire to hear, Lady Damison," Francesca said though she thought she'd die of curiosity. It was simply that she did not want the others to hear whatever it was that tainted her history.

"But that's just the point, Miss Wadsworth," Lady Damison said. Francesca still did not see it. "It was a big scandal then, but would hardly be worth the retelling in today's society. We have become so progressive these days."

The other ladies, perhaps not quite as progressive, leaned in so close they were breathing on Francesca's bare neck.

"Your mother was a Williams, of course. Though her own mother was a schoolmistress in Cornwall, she came from a good family, and a generous one. Years before they adopted a child, I believe, whose own parents had escaped the Terror in Paris." Lady Damison waved her hand dismissively. "But I hardly recall that, so no matter. What does matter is that after Celandine Williams died in an accident of some sort, their daughter was sent to London to live with Celandine's sister, Lady Everly. Lady Everly gave her niece, your mother, every advantage. And then, Charity met your father in his little shop and insisted on marrying him!"

"Was that the scandal?" Francesca asked in a low voice.

"Of course not! He was of a good family, as well! The Wadsworths were booksellers to the king!"

Francesca thought she'd burst with curiosity.

"The matter had to do with the fact that they wished to set up housekeeping in the attic, the better to devote all their hours to the shop. It was impossible! Lady Everly said that she would not permit their marriage until he bought a townhouse, at the very least. A house in Windsor would be preferable, of course. But a townhouse would do."

"And I suppose it did," Francesca said, though still perplexed. Was this the nature of scandal in an earlier time? And what if her father had not the funds for an outright purchase, but only managed to come up with the funds to rent? Would such a failing have ended his hopes, the consequence of which would have been that her brother, sister, and she might never have been born?

Now that was a real scandal.

"Why are you smiling, my dear?" Lady Damison asked, irritably. "Do you not see the impossibility of a niece of Lady Everly living in an attic like a French artist near their red windmill?"

Francesca wondered what they would think of Charity's daughter being seduced in that attic, and by a man to whom she was not yet married.

"The Moulin Rouge. It would have been just dreadful," Francesca conceded, unwilling to start an argument in a house in which she was a guest. "Not at all as romantic as lady novelists would have us believe."

The ladies behind her, clearly all such believers, sighed.

****

Francesca, reacquainting herself with the Picardy home and collections, appreciated the respite from conversation that their fine dinner afforded, when she could say less and observe more. The decor on the façade of the house proved to be no more than a prelude to the glories within, where there were curiosities and marvels on every spare surface. One hardly noticed the damask wall coverings for the shelves of artifacts that ran floor to ceiling.

"The Prince of Wales would think he'd arrived in paradise, if he dined with us this night," Nathaniel, who sat on her right, said to her between courses.

"Do you think he would have enjoyed the consommé? It is rather tasty, and thicker than usually prepared." Francesca set down her spoon. "I wonder if the family has a French cook."

"Not quite. I believe Monsieur Jean is Swiss. But you surprise me. I would have thought you would comment on the Waterford crystal before the soup. Or the rare amphora on the mantel. Nevertheless, I am told the best thing awaits you in the lady's drawing room, on which you'll report to me later."

"Will it be a conversation with Miss Caswell? She seems to know you quite well. Perhaps she will reveal all your flaws to me, in an effort to scare me off."

"She is only trying to make Will jealous. I believe he is the true object of her affections."

"Oh, truly? She manages to hide that very well." She paused, sorry to tease him when he really had done nothing objectionable. The servant's arm momentarily blocked their view of each other and provided a convenient reason to change the subject. "What awaits me in the drawing room? And where will you be, by the way?"

"Ah, you will have to see for yourself. I have been told you will know it as soon as you enter the room." Nathaniel prodded at the sliced beefsteak on his plate. "I will be in the billiards room, no doubt. It is what gentlemen do, when they're not at their place of business."

"My father does not have a billiards room on Edgware Road," Francesca commented.

"Of course not," he said. "From what you tell me, I suppose he was always at his place of business. I don't know how your mother finally dragged him away."

Francesca smothered her laugh into her napkin.

****

"You seem to enjoy Mr. Endicott's company," commented Mrs. Picardy. She took Francesca's arm in hers as they walked down the hall with the other ladies, after dinner. Will's mother was very soft spoken. When Francesca was a child, she attributed it to the fact that she spoke with a slight Continental accent but now appreciated it was simply in accord with her whole manner. Mr. Picardy was a fine match for her, for Francesca could hardly hear his words across the dinner table.

She wondered how they produced such a son as Will, who was flamboyant and dramatic, and incapable of speaking at a whisper. Just now, she could hear Will yelling about something down the hall. Mrs. Picardy must have heard her son, as well.

"My son tells me you have an arrangement with

Mr. Endicott that seems to be working well."

"I find it very agreeable," Francesca said, hesitantly. She wondered what part of their arrangement was part of Will's conversation.

"He is a very agreeable young man and a good friend to Will. I would have enjoyed having him as a guest here, but he seems to prefer taking the rooms in the shop."

"I hope you don't hold that against me, Mrs. Picardy. When Mr. Endicott came onto the scene, my shop had just been broken into, for the first time in my memory. Will thought I might appreciate having someone around to protect the property."

"And protecting you, of course," Mrs. Picardy said and smiled. She turned back to the others. "Mind the step here, ladies."

"I have managed very well by myself all this time. But I confess, I was rattled by the intrusion."

"Most women would adopt a guard dog in such circumstances."

"And I have, since then. Or rather, Mr. Endicott has adopted a pup. He calls him Pip."

"He is a fan of Mr. Dickens, then. I am not surprised." Mrs. Picardy led her through double doors into a large room. Though the evening was warm, there was a fire blazing in the hearth.

"I am also familiar with his books. His son is a regular customer at my shop."

"Is he indeed? When you see him again, do give him my best regards. The poor man had a rather tough time growing up with those parents, the mother always with child, while the father always complaining publicly about her weight gain and fooling around with an actress. He deserved to have all his books tossed into the river."

"I'll be sure to tell his son, when I see him," Francesca said.

Mrs. Picardy laughed. "Yes, do. And now let me introduce you to a friend of mine."

Francesca was surprised when her hostess brought her to the far side of the room, while the other ladies were behind them. Who awaited them while they enjoyed dinner?

And then she saw her. She wore a white lace gown, jacketed in silk and her hands were poised over her instrument. Her hair was piled high on her head, in the style of another century, and her bright eyes were fixed on them as they approached. Reflecting the light of the fire, they looked curious, and very much alive.

"Why, I don't believe I require an introduction," Francesca said softly. "She is the dulcimer player automaton, is she not? But I don't understand. Is she the very same android that was taken from Versailles when it was ransacked by the mob? How did she survive such wanton destruction?"

Mrs. Picardy laughed, clearly delighted by Francesca's knowledge of the player's history. "She is but one of twelve sisters, all closely copied to resemble the original, made by craftsmen in Trieste. I believe this lady was made in 1770, nearly a hundred years ago. Her dress is a bit dated, but her music remains fashionable."

Mrs. Picardy pressed a small button, and the automaton raised her hands and began to play. The other ladies gathered around them, cooing over the automaton as if she were a talented child.

"My son tells me you have given Mr. Endicott the

opportunity to try his hand at repairing an automaton in your possession, Miss Wadsworth. Might she be one of the lost sisters?"

"Perhaps a cousin, though not from the musical side of the family. My lady is of a literary bent, or at least she will be, once she's repaired. Her name is Madame Cristobel."

"Is that not a man's name?" Miss Caswell asked. "As in Mr. Coleridge's poem?"

Francesca opened her hands in supplication. "I suppose so, and indeed, she does look a bit boyish. My dressmaker complains that she lacks the requisites of a woman. But we have always called her Madame Cristobel, and so she remains until we know otherwise."

"She is the one in the window on King Street, is she not?" asked Mrs. Reed. At least, that's what Francesca thought was her name. "No wonder your companion looked familiar to me."

Once again, Francesca considered how all roads seemed to lead back to her automaton. And yet, unlike her relative with the dulcimer, Madame Cristobel still revealed nothing.

"Come, ladies," Mrs. Picardy urged. "Excellent desserts await us, including Sacher tortes, an old Viennese favorite. That is where I was born, Miss Wadsworth," she said in a lower voice to Francesca.

"If I had remembered that, I would have brought you a porcelain plate, a commemoration of the Spanish Riding School. It has been in my shop for a while, just awaiting the interest of one of your countrymen. It is now yours, if you will accept this little gift from me."

"It would be an honor, my dear."

They sat down together. Francesca would have enjoyed spending the rest of the evening with her hostess, but there were others, and they had much to say.

"Do you go out in society much, Miss Wadsworth?" Miss Caswell asked. "I have not seen you around."

"I am not a lady of much leisure, Miss Caswell. My dear parents are off on some adventure and have left me the care of their shop on King Street. It keeps me very busy."

"Oh yes, of course," Miss Caswell said. Francesca felt somewhat guilty about being resentful of the woman. After all, she knew nothing about Nathaniel's relationships with her or anyone else. Of course, she didn't know his relationships with anyone else, either. "And that is where Mr. Endicott lives, I understand."

"And works," Francesca pointed out. Apparently, Miss Caswell knew some things. "He is trying to bring Madame Cristobel back to what she must have been at one time, even if she doesn't play a dulcimer."

"Mr. Endicott," Lady Damison said, in between bites of her torte.

"Do you intend to sell the automaton when he is done with her?" another lady asked.

"Many people have asked about that, and I've had a few offers. But truly, she is part of my family, and I can't imagine parting with her."

"Mr. Endicott," Lady Damison repeated.

"Have you had her for very long?" another lady asked.

"She came with my mother from Cornwall, when she was only a girl. I suspect my father was entranced by both young Charity Williams and Madame Cristobel when he proposed marriage. Lady Damison only just told me about that part of my history."

Lady Damison wiped her lips. "Yes, that is it. When we spoke before dinner, I could not remember the name of the man who traveled to Switzerland and returned to Cornwall with two automatons and a young boy. But I remember now. It is an interesting coincidence, really. His name was Endicott."

****

"I hope you are not bothered by Miss Caswell," said Nathaniel when they were back in his hired carriage. "I rather think Mrs. Picardy intended her for Will, but she seemed to prefer talking about Madame Cristobel."

Francesca smiled, which was somewhat of a relief. She was so pensive, he thought he had done something to offend her.

"Do you really think so? I rather thought she just preferred talking to you. Not that I blame her, of course."

Better and better. He had not thought her at all jealous in nature, but perhaps she understood something of what he felt when Tony came to the shop, reasserting some sort of imagined claim on her attention.

"But Will is an excellent sort," he insisted. "He and I have similar talents, but he has much more reliable expectations and a stable presence in London. Why did she not spend the evening talking to him?"

She sighed in an exaggerated manner. "Sometimes, Nathaniel, I believe you have more experience with Madame Cristobel than you do with real ladies."

"You did not seem to complain a few nights ago.

Or last night, for that matter."

She hit him gently with her fan. "That is not what I mean, and you know it. It is only that ladies know at once if a man is uninterested in her, and I don't think Will even troubles himself to disguise it."

"I saw nothing of the sort," Nathaniel argued.

"Precisely. It was clear to me from the moment he met us outside, on the stairs, that there was nothing within that held his attention. And then, as soon as we entered, there was Miss Caswell. She clearly had followed him to the door, and yet he closed it against her. No wonder she was so happy to see you."

This was not exactly what he expected. What seemed like sincere flattery now had him reduced to a consolation for blighted hopes. For the first time, he wondered how long Tony had led her along.

"But no matter. It seems that wherever we are, or whomever we're with, it is Madame Cristobel who is the center of all attention. If I must be jealous of anyone, it surely is she, that little vixen."

He watched, fascinated, as she did a delicate little act with the same fan that he teased him with a few minutes before. One by one, she spread each section, revealing the printed silk concealed by the whalebone. Where the fabric caught, she repeated the step, until a faded landscape was on full display. She edged closer to him as she raised it to their faces and kissed him behind the little landscape. She was right; he didn't know women that well at all. For she quite amazed him, and deliciously so.

"We have arrived at Edgware Road," he said after an achingly short amount of time. The carriage stopped. She looked up, her reddened lips parted in surprise.

"You know. Your home?"

"My home. I was never so reluctant to enter."

"But you are not alone tonight. Mrs. Belleron has returned and is probably watching us from behind the lace curtains this very minute."

"Yes, I am sure she is, so we ought to give her a bit of a show. But I would rather spend the night with you," she said and kissed him again.

She was right. If she could surprise him twice in a fifteen-minute drive, he really did not know women that well at all.

****

Pip provided some consolation, however, and jumped all over him as soon as he unlocked the door of the shop. The poor fellow dashed out into the night, and Nathaniel reflected that the dog was not accustomed to waiting so long for satisfaction. Nathaniel knew something of it himself. But he locked the door behind them, and they headed off into the night.

They were not alone, for the streets of London were rarely empty of people. But when the shops were closed, and the only customers on King Street were either looking for a stout drink or woman, the scene was dramatically different from that to which most were accustomed. Gas lamps cast a soft glow on the paving stones, providing enough light to allow one to see one's way, but not enough to reveal the filth that lined the gutters. The quick movements of small creatures reminded Nathaniel that rats undoubtedly outnumbered human inhabitants in a city, and theirs was the kingdom each night. Even Pip seemed to understand this, and he left them unmolested as he trotted down the street at Nathaniel's side.

In the distance, a church bell tolled the hour, and Nathaniel was hit with a pang of longing for home and for the small village in which he had grown up. There, he heard the bells toll every hour; it was part of the symphony of life in the countryside. In London, all other church bells deferred to the one at Westminster, known familiarly as Big Ben, as if it were Christ's bell itself.

Something tickled in Nathaniel's memory, something he remembered and was reminded of only recently. He looked down at Pip, who gazed back at him forlornly, as if to remind him that even if he somehow knew what his master was thinking, he could not talk.

"It's a new day, Pip. We have much to do, for it's past time I brought Madame Cristobel back to life. Once we solve her riddle, all else will be resolved." Pip looked like he was perfectly content as they were and vigorously wagged his tail. "Oh, you'll be happier once we return to Watch Hill and you'll have acres to roam about. And we'll bring Francesca back with us, and she'll have a home of her own. And Tony…Tony will finally accept his lot in life and merely be the well-heeled heir to Lord Maitland. He'll finally call off his dogs."

Nathaniel looked down, to Pip's intense gaze. "I do not intend to insult you, Pip. You are the noblest of your species, and they are the lowest of theirs. But you may end your days chasing squirrels and rounding up sheep. It's not a bad lot either."

Apparently satisfied, Pip sauntered off to examine a parcel that looked like it fell off a carriage, Nathaniel walked on, fairly well satisfied with how things were progressing and how one's life could take some unexpected turns.

Another church bell, nearer than the first, chimed, and Nathaniel frowned as he checked his pocket watch in the dim light. It was out of synchrony with Westminster's grand clock by nearly ten minutes. He considered that this might also be said for his own life, until he had arrived at FW Wadsworth, Bookseller and Antiquarian, that is.

He replaced his watch, feeling the slight vibration of its mechanism beating against his hip. Pip returned to his side. And he studied the night sky, for once unobstructed by the customary fog.

Indeed, he believed all the stars were in alignment.

****

Francesca rose early and surprised Mrs. Belleron when she showed up in the breakfast room at least an hour before her accustomed time.

"Miss Francesca!" the housekeeper cried, clutching her heart. "You gave me a fright! I have only just begun to poach the eggs and make toast."

"Don't worry about that. I shall just have some sliced meats and a cup of tea," Francesca reassured her. "It's my own fault for not letting you know to expect me earlier than usual, but then, I hardly knew it myself. I didn't sleep well last night and saw no reason to remain in bed any longer."

Mrs. Belleron paused, holding a silver tray. "Are you well, Miss Francesca?"

"Oh, very well," Francesca said. "Truly, as well as I've ever been in my life."

"Yes, I see that now. I'll start the kettle going." Mrs. Belleron used her shoulder to push open the door.

Francesca watched her and wondered if she, herself, would soon walk out of the housekeeper's life. The thought, somewhat regretful but also buoyed by a sense of adventure, was with her while she enjoyed her simple breakfast and read *The Times* and then left for the shop. It all somehow seemed like a voyage of discovery: her whole day was at once slightly out of alignment and yet perfectly in harmony. It was early enough in the morning that she heard the distant strains of the Westminster clock, but enough past dawn that the gas lamps had already been extinguished. Flower sellers were jockeying for best positions along the street, and for a brief while, she followed a milkman as he delivered tall cans from one house to another.

She would miss this if it came to pass that she would live in Cornwall. But then, she imagined that living with Nathaniel would provide considerable consolations.

She wondered what he was doing now, if he was already awake. Perhaps she would surprise him by joining him in the attic. Perhaps they would open the shop late this morning, or perhaps not at all.

But in less time than usual, it seemed, she was on King Street, and the shop looked like they had forgotten to close it the night before. But they surely had, and nothing was amiss except her fanciful thoughts, for there was Nathaniel, already seated in the window.

"Have you been awake all night?" she asked as she entered the shop. Belatedly, she glanced around to be certain that they were quite alone. Pip appeared from behind an old oak chest and came forward to greet her. But Nathaniel didn't look up from his work on the automaton. She wondered if he thought that if they had spent the night together, she would know perfectly well if he slept.

But that was among the pleasures yet to come.

"As it happens, I didn't sleep," he finally answered, and looked up, as if to confirm who stood there. He nodded briefly and returned to his work. If this was the way he intended to greet her after hours apart, it was just as well they didn't spend the night together.

"Well, I had a lovely night's rest," she said and rifled through the contents of a box that had been delivered the day before. She saw a few interesting items, but her assessment of the rest of the lot would surely disappoint the lady who had looked like she was hopeful for a good price on the collection. "I just thought I might come in early and examine the contents of Mrs. Darnwell's consignment."

"You'll find nothing there, but for a few mosaic pins that were undoubtedly purchased in Florence. They're sold on every street corner, you know, along with the plaster models of Michelangelo's David."

"Yes, of course," she said and tucked the pins back into the box before he could see that she already picked them out. She had no idea what they sold on the streets of Florence. "I just hope I can find something, just to make Mrs. Darnwell happy."

"You have a talent for it, so I'm sure you will. You certainly made everyone happy last night," he said.

"Including you?" she asked, thinking of the brief interlude in the carriage.

"Especially me," he said. "In fact, you made me so happy, I couldn't sleep."

She wasn't quite sure what he meant by that but ventured a fair guess. He studied her, perhaps gauging her reaction, and then went on.

"Pip and I walked through the streets for well over an hour, enjoying having London pretty much to ourselves. The sky was unusually clear, reminding me that there are worlds beyond our own, but we'll never see them. Pip was not so philosophical, I believe, as he thought an empty crate discarded on the side of the street to be infinitely more interesting than anything in the heavens. When I finally wore him out, we returned here so he might rest, but I decided to the spend the rest of the pre-dawn hours with Madame Cristobel."

"Does she make you happy, as well?"

"Not as much as I'm sure she will, once I figure out how to restore her. Mr. Picardy gave me some ideas on that last night."

"Is that what you were talking about in the billiards room? I thought you gentlemen took an inordinate amount of time, leaving the ladies rather bereft in the parlor. We had nothing to do but to talk about gentlemen."

"I do not doubt it, since all gentlemen talk about is ladies."

She could no longer resist him nor keep up this somewhat scolding conversation. She no longer cared why he didn't sleep or what he and Mr. Picardy discussed or what he thought about Florentine mosaic jewelry. She just wanted to be with him.

"Do you need a hand?" He offered his as she stepped up the stairs into the window.

She grasped his strong fingers even as she said, "I am capable of climbing stairs. I have legs under this skirt, you realize."

"I can do better than merely realize," he said and

released her.

She sat on the opposite chair, where Will positioned himself the day before. "Do you truly think you can restore Madame Cristobel?" she asked. It was the first time she'd expressed any doubt.

"Would you be very disappointed if I cannot? I fear it may be true."

"Do not fear anything," she said, "for I do love you so."

They sat in their wooden chairs, not touching but grinning at each other like two thieves who thought they made off with paste diamonds and instead found themselves in possession of the Crown Jewels.

And so they might have remained but for Will tapping on the glass and waving at them before he entered the shop.

"Do take it in the right spirit when I say that the two of you look like idiots who are up to some mischief?" Will said. He looked in Mrs. Darnwell's box, held up one of the brooches, and threw it back in. "Do I need to hire a new shop assistant? I do not seem to be able to keep them for very long, and you have been with me for a matter of a few months. Or do you simply prefer to play with mechanical dolls?"

"I do not consider myself a mechanical doll, Will," Francesca said, assuming an air of indignation.

Nathaniel cleared his throat, but Will laughed at the two of them.

"Nor are you. But I reckon you owe me the services of another assistant. After all, I hired Nathaniel in the first place, and now he only wishes to spend his time here. Not that I blame him."

"I believe Nathaniel intended to come to me in the

first place, Will," Francesca said. "Or, more accurately, to Madame Cristobel."

"Do I have a voice in this?" Nathaniel asked.

"No," said Francesca and Will in unison.

"Very well. Then I will go back to work," Nathaniel said. "At least Madame Cristobel doesn't talk back to me, though I dearly wish she would."

"What do you expect her to say?" Will asked. It was the most obvious of questions, and yet no one ever bothered to ask it.

Francesca waited for Nathaniel to answer, but, as before, he was intent on the workings of the automaton. Will glanced at her, and she shrugged. She could not help but feel that they were irritants, interrupting the work of a master.

"She will not talk, of course," Nathaniel said at last. He paused to flex Madame Cristobel's right wrist. "The music box is the only sound you'll hear, and that is a much simpler mechanism to repair. Usually, a music box requires a new spring because people are apt to overwind it. As you told me, Will, anyone could replace that, even you."

"Thank you very much," Will said. "Why don't you go over to my shop and set out the new delivery of bramble jam? And I'll work my magic with Madame Cristobel."

"I'm beginning to fear magic is what's needed," Nathaniel said solemnly. He turned the inkwell and the lovely Mozart waltz began, a sweet air in the sonorous tones of the clocks that lined the walls. "But the music box is already functioning. It's the other thing that has me perplexed. When the automaton was created, she held a piece of graphite in her right hand and could write on a piece of paper placed on her desk. Do you see this dial here? She is mechanized to write five or six different messages; it's not clear how many."

"Do you mean, something like poetry or passages from the bible?"

Nathaniel nodded. "Something like that. Madame Cristobel was one of two automatons made by Christian Bell, a man who escaped the French Terror and never returned to England or France, though he had holdings in both nations. I have reason to believe he embedded a message in one or the other's clockworks, intended for his descendants.

"How very dramatic," Will said, and waved his own hand in a flourish. "Would it not have been easier to just write a will?"

"Easier, but not necessarily safer. Bell escaped certain death in Paris and feared for his life and those of his family. He must have thought this was a safe ploy but did not count on the automaton coming into the possession of others and having her mechanism in disrepair."

"I hope he was not a relative of either of you, for the man seems possessed of much imagination but little sense," Will said.

Francesca caught Nathaniel's eye and raised an eyebrow, for it was likely Bell was related to both of them.

"If he had any sense, he certainly would not have given his automaton such an obvious name." Will looked from one to the other. "Christian Bell? Cristobel? Surely you saw that at once?"

Francesca would not admit that she had not. And she considered herself a woman of considerable good sense. But it certainly explained why the little madam had a name best known for being a moniker of a man. She blinked and realized Nathaniel was still studying her. *He knew. He knew this from the start.* The information he sought was to come from Christian Bell's namesake, by proxy.

Chapter 14

"When were you going to tell me?"

Francesca had every right to demand this of him, and yet he wasn't yet ready to answer her. He trusted her, and she had been infinitely patient with his preoccupation with repairing the automaton. There was no logical reason to withhold anything from her. And yet, the legacy of several generations was riding on his success, and if he failed in his quest, that part of Endicott history would likely die out. Years ago, her family intersected with his, and if all went as he hoped, their families would again intersect, most intimately, and for years to come.

"Surely you realize that your success or failure in this endeavor has nothing to do with our happiness?" she said, reading his thoughts. "More than anything else, I would just find great pleasure in Madame Cristobel's restoration. It matters little if all she has to write is 'Sing a song of sixpence' or 'Jack Spratt would eat no fat.' Our lives would still go on, would they not?"

"They would, my dear," he said, rising from the chair in the window and stepping down to meet her. Will already left, and the first customers had not yet arrived for the day. "The fact that you have faith in our future, whatever it holds, just confirms why I love you. I certainly need not fear that you are marrying me for my money."

"But will you marry me for mine? Or just to get your hands on strange and useless curiosities?" She spread her arms to suggest the greatness of her holdings.

He caught her around the waist and whirled her in a circle, before kissing her to stem the flood of her teasing. Whatever happened, they would not be poor, either in good humor, love, or financial assets.

A knock on the shop window quickly restored them to business-like solemnity. Nathaniel set her back down on the floor and ran his fingers through his hair before turning to acknowledge their audience.

"It is Mrs. Blanchard," Francesca said, straightening her skirt. "How decent of her to give us warning and not simply come through the door."

"It would have been more decent to just continue walking and not interrupt us at all," Nathaniel said, resolving to rethink that pledge to good humor made only moment before.

Francesca looked over her shoulder as she stepped to the door, silently reminding him that FW Wadsworth was open for business, and not the sort of business he currently had in mind.

"Mrs. Blanchard," she said cheerfully as she flung wide the door, nearly knocking over a potted plant. "How good to see you this morning."

The dressmaker scrutinized her for several moments. "I should like to restitch that neckline, Miss Wadsworth. It seems to be pulling somewhat to the right."

Nathaniel decided it was a good opportunity to retire to his attic, for he had foregone breakfast in his enthusiasm to commence work on Madame Cristobel.

"Do not go far, Mr. Endicott. My business is with you, this day," Mrs. Blanchard called out. "Or rather, with your little poppet."

Nathaniel winced. His automaton deserved more respect than that. Though, as he watched Mrs. Banchard pull something from her carpetbag and recognized it as a miniature of the beautiful dress Francesca wore the night before, he realized this was, indeed, guaranteed to give a naked wooden automaton a modicum of respect. If he only had the ability to make her write again, she would finally have the full measure.

"Oh, how utterly charming," Francesca said and held the tiny gown up to the light coming through the window. "I daresay Madame Cristobel will do it more justice than I do."

Nathaniel joined them. "Though it is only fair to tell Mrs. Blanchard that you did her a great deal of credit when you wore it last night." The woman had already seen them kissing a moment before; she would not be surprised to hear they stepped out together. "I have no practice with such things; would you like to dress the automaton for us, Mrs. Blanchard?"

"To be sure, that is why I am here," she said and took the dress from Francesca's fingers.

It was true that Nathaniel had no practical experience in the art of dressing a wooden figure, but he rather thought it was like dressing a baby. Such things he had witnessed back at Watch Hill and in various boarding houses through Europe. The problem was that neither a baby nor a poppet had any inclination to be helpful, to insert an arm into a sleeve or clench a fist so that fingers did not snag on the tatted lace. The sounds Mrs. Blanchard made suggested it was not going so well for her either, and at one point he heard a little crack and the slide of metal.

"Oh, dear. I might have broken her wrist," the dressmaker said. "I may have to fashion a little sling to match her gown."

Nathaniel glanced at her face and was horrified to realize she was entirely serious. But his interest was not so much in her suggestion but in the fact she might have set back all his hard work. He took the automaton away from her, though gently, and flexed her right wrist forward and back.

"Is she well?" Francesca asked, in the same tone she might have used to inquire about a fevered child.

Nathaniel set Madame Cristobel before her desk to give her the advantage of gravity and straightened out her gown, lest it be a hindrance to her movement. "I think she is quite well, but shall soon see. Mrs. Blanchard, if my guess is correct, you shall be inducted immediately into the guild of clockmakers, for you may have accomplished what my poor efforts could not."

"I didn't mean anything by it," the woman said, mistaking his meaning.

"Are not the best inventions created by fortunate accidents?" He glanced at the window and, happy that for once they did not have an audience, he turned the ink well on Madame Cristobel's desk.

"Oh, my heavens," said Mrs. Blanchard. "She is alive."

Francesca said nothing, just stared at her longtime companion with lips parted in awe.

And indeed, whereas there was much anticipation when Madame Cristobel was capable of fitfully moving her hands in the air, Nathaniel now had to remind himself to breathe as her arms did a balletic dance over a desk that did not yet offer her paper, and with a hand that did not yet hold graphite.

"You have not only clothed the automaton in elegance and decency, Mrs. Blanchard," he pronounced. "You have given her a voice. Whatever it is she has been unable to articulate for so many years will now be revealed through the movement of her articulated wrist."

Mrs. Blanchard, flushed and perhaps embarrassed by such accolades, mumbled something under her breath about the automaton's voice complaining that the garments of a lady were not for him.

"Perhaps he wished to be in disguise, so no one would guess his true identity," said Francesca, artlessly. "And so he has kept his secrets for so many years."

Mrs. Blanchard laughed. "The very idea! That he should have secrets other than this one."

But Nathaniel knew precisely what Francesca was thinking. Christian Bell, whose long-ago ruse to impersonate Louis XIV and thus save him from the guillotine failed; and so he assumed another identity and escaped to Trieste as a woman. He may have created the pair of automatons with clockmakers even while he still hoped for an opportunity to return to France. But whatever he hoped, he certainly was the one who sent them to England with his only son, years later, when his half brother James Endicott adopted young Tristan Bell as his own.

"One never knows, Mrs. Blanchard. But more will surely be revealed in time," Francesca said. "Poor Madame Cristobel has been silently watching over my shop for all these years, so must have overheard a great deal of gossip. Perhaps she was witness to a great love affair or a stealthy theft. She might be a foreign spy. Or even a fortune teller."

That she was a fortune teller was very much the point, or at least, Nathaniel hoped it was so.

"I think I should remove her from the window," he said decisively, ignoring the protests of the ladies. "After all, she might reveal some embarrassing facts, and that would not do at all."

He handled her carefully, as he lifted her glass case and brought her to the cabinet on which he first saw her, many weeks before. Francesca, anticipating his move, cleared the path before him. He did not discourage her; while an accident might have restored the automaton's ability to write at her desk, dropping her now would likely destroy both her and his great expectations.

Several other customers were now in the shop, expressing some disappointment that the automaton was no longer on display in the window. But Mrs. Blanchard handled them, explaining with unsuppressed pride how it was she who managed to finally fix the automaton, as well as dress her in the manner in which she should have been accustomed. She confided to some that Madame Cristobel was somewhat flat chested and required cotton wool to fill out the bodice of her gown, poor dear. And to those who offered even the vaguest interest, she happily offered her business card. Finally, satisfied that her work was done, and that, with great success, she waltzed out into the sunlight of the new morning.

"Has she revealed anything yet?" Francesca asked

impatiently, knowing full well that she wasn't being at all fair to Nathaniel. When he looked across at her with an expression of indignation, she knew it was entirely deserved. After all, she had waited for all these years for Madame Cristobel to do anything but gather dust on the shelf. She, and the automaton, could wait a bit longer. Still, she could not resist saying, "Why not drop her on the floor? If it worked for Mrs. Blanchard, it might work for you, too."

He studied her for a moment before opening his mouth, and Francesca braced for his retort.

But Will returned to the shop just then and interrupted whatever Nathaniel was going to say.

"Will," Francesca said, happy for the reprieve. "I enjoyed myself immensely at your parents' home last night."

"Did you, indeed?" he asked, smiling. "They were delighted that you were able to come. Surely there are too few people who appreciate the cacophony of a dozen clocks chiming at midnight, not to mention neighbors who are willing to tolerate the outside performance. Indeed, my parents have had more neighbors than anyone else in Mayfair, for each family's tenure is of short duration. Somehow, I do wonder why."

Francesca laughed, grateful for his good humor.

"Is our hardworking man-of-all-trades about? Not that I presume it is your business to know his habits, but I assume you'd have seen him if he's about somewhere. I see Madame Cristobel is gone from the window. Have they eloped?"

"I assume the lady would not be able to decide between the two of you, for all the attention she's had."

Francesca waved her hand toward the cabinet in the back of the shop, where Nathaniel watched them impatiently.

"Then let her choose whichever one remains unclaimed, which I presume means me," Will said. "Just as long as she isn't swept off her feet by Lord Anthony, for he would wish to be a suitor, too."

Francesca hadn't even thought about Lord Anthony for some time. For one, any lingering hope she had about their future was dispelled and, happily, forgotten. And, more compelling, there was something about his part in recent events that was not yet revealed.

"If you do happen to see him, do tell him he's too late."

Will joined Nathaniel at the cabinet, pulled up a chair, and leaned in, to watch him work. Watching them, Francesca had a brief recollection of her father, bent over in similar fashion, hard at work repairing a broken vase or dented metal plate. If he should suddenly appear at the door, he would probably walk right past her and sit down with them. He knew little about clocks, but for knowing how to keep them running, but would wish to learn from Nathaniel. And then, quite possibly, he would be willing to take full credit, as Mrs. Blanchard did, only a short time ago.

And then, it was not her father at the door, but Lord Anthony himself.

"Good morning, Miss Wadsworth. You look like you have seen a ghost."

"Not all. It was only that I just thought about you, not a minute ago."

"It is as I hoped. I daresay all your thoughts were encouraging to my suit?" he asked, and handed her a packet. By the look and feel of it, Francesca guessed that he had stopped by Will's shop and brought her bread and sliced Cheshire cheese.

She wondered if she should give it back. "I did not realize you had a suit."

Lord Anthony put his hand to his heart in a gesture of shock. "How could I not have made that clear?"

Francesca would not have reminded him of the many ways he did not, if everything was as it had been weeks before. But she understood now how Lord Anthony had trifled with her affections for his own amusement. And perhaps it was worse than that, and he only used her to gain access to Madame Cristobel.

Wisely, he did not wait for her answer. "I notice the automaton is gone from your window, as is Mr. Endicott."

Yes, it was worse than just trifling with her. But she knew that.

"Has he taken her from you?" he asked, the anxiety clear in his voice. "I know how dear she is to you and how he coveted her. Though I thought he also coveted..." His voice dropped off as he perhaps realized he went too far.

"Would you be surprised if I told you that he has taken her to Watch Hill, to meet the Earl D'Arcques?" She knew she was being daring and certainly reckless. But the look on Lord Anthony's face told her all she needed to know. He knew what damage a working automaton could play on his own life, own expectations. Nathaniel was right to warn her about his intentions.

Just then, Nathaniel and Will gave a cheer of triumph.

"Ah, I see," Lord Anthony said slyly. "I see I need not have worried for you at all. You have not just one gentleman, but two, guarding your interests. Or rather, those of Mr. Endicott."

He sauntered toward the back of the shop, making no secret of his arrival. Nathaniel glanced past him to Francesca, looking concerned.

For once, she let them deal with their own problems. Her destiny was already tied to Nathaniel, no matter what happened. She only prayed they would not hurt each other.

She spent the better part of the next hour sorting through her books, deciding which might be placed on the cart outside the door, where they may be damaged by rain or dust, or stolen. Some of them were acquired by her father years ago, when he must have thought them of some value. But anything that remained on the shelves for more than ten years did not pass the test of time, but rather, of being unsalable. Francesca stopped short of calling any book worthless. But what if no one wanted it? Her father was incapable of throwing anything out onto the curb.

She supposed she was lucky for that, for Madame Cristobel might have otherwise been consigned to the trash heap years ago.

"He is wasting his time," Lord Anthony said behind her. She turned around to face him, and saw a flash of anger in his eyes. "He is wasting your money, as well. If Mr. Endicott is your shop assistant, he should be engaged in doing other things."

"Do you not think Madame Cristobel will command a good price once she is repaired? Miss Tupper has already asked about her, as have several other interested parties."

"But she will not be repaired. He doesn't have the talent to manage it, for all he boasts about apprenticeships in Trieste. He is no more than a dilettante, pretending to have a skill, when all he can do is scratch at the door of respectability."

Francesca's growing loss of faith in anything Lord Anthony proposed to her now descended into a total collapse of trust.

"I am not sure what you mean by that, or why it possibly matters," she said softly.

"My mother is a true arbiter of society and class," he continued. "She has strong opinions about such things, and particularly about Endicott's pretensions."

"I am sure she does," she said. "When did she last meet him?"

When he didn't answer, she went on.

"He is a gentleman. But even if he had not been born so, he would have certainly earned it by hard work and kind behavior. I see nothing in him that is anything less than respectable." She reached for a small plate, tired of him voicing the opinions of his mother. "Will you join me for lunch?" she asked.

"I find I have a pressing engagement," he said, about as convincingly as anything else he said.

"Then, good day to you, Lord Anthony. And thank you for your gift, which we shall enjoy."

"I am sure you shall," he said and marched out the door.

Francesca waited just until the door closed behind him and turned to see what had cheered Nathaniel and Will at the same moment Lord Anthony announced his interfering presence.

She knew what it was even before they spoke. She saw it in their eyes, their smile, their clear anxiety to share something with her. As she approached, she saw Madame Cristobel already held a bit of graphite between her fingers, and its dust was sprinkled across her bodice and skirt. Mrs. Blanchard would require smelling salts if she saw this.

"Yes?" Francesca asked.

"Yes," they said, as one.

"Has…has she revealed all?" she asked, stumbling in her words and in her steps.

Will caught her arm and steadied her. "Let us say, instead, that she has revealed some."

"And yet, she does that with remarkable clarity." Nathaniel's excitement was not to be diminished by his friend's halting praise. "She has already written some fine little sketches and at least two proverbial sayings that even I recognize as biblical. All this would be enough reason for celebration. But there is more." He urged her to step closer and handed her a magnifying glass. "Do you see the dial next to her inkwell? There are six possible patterns for Madame Cristobel to follow, very similar to what others from the same workshop can produce. But then, unmarked, and just slightly to the right of the sixth, is a seventh. This is quite unusual."

"It is not a proverb, then," Francesca said, trying to understand it all.

"Not one with which we are familiar, in any case," Nathaniel said and turned the inkwell to set the automaton in motion.

Nothing happened for a few moments, which felt like an eternity. But then, Madame Cristobel came to life, her head bobbing back and forth as she appeared to peruse the sheet of paper Nathaniel provided for her. Her hands, once those of a musical conductor, gently lowered upon that sheet, her left hand holding it secure, and her right, inscribing something with a great deal of deliberation. Her movement was fluid, elegant, poised. She was a lady, after all.

To escape harm where once was peace

To hide from danger that would not cease

To find joy a lady is transformed

By goodness and beauty a gentleman is reformed

A marriage a home a son a triumph of heaven over hell

For proof of such look to the vestry in ancient Christ's Bell

Francesca squinted at the tiny script and remembered she had been given the magnifying spectacles that Nathaniel usually used when he worked. At once, the words became clearer, as did a dainty border of little flowers she recognized as native to the Alps. The written page, its poem and artwork, were nothing short of a mechanical miracle, and yet somehow Francesca could only focus on the indifferent grammar and poor verse.

"There is no punctuation," she said, for want of truly knowing what to say. Too late, she realized that simple praise was all the two men desired.

"Madame Cristobel did not have the advantage of a tutor, my dear," Nathaniel said patiently, clearly disappointed in her words. Francesca saw Will glance at him.

"And Madame Cristobel is not the sort of thing one would find in a church vestry," Nathaniel continued. "I am not sure Christian Bell would be likely to show up in a vestry either, from the little I know of him. But I think we've been looking in the wrong place. It's not the man that holds the key; it's a church."

"But what if Christian Bell had a particular reason to appear in that church, so similar in name to his own? A funeral, perhaps. A baptism. Or something else. And perhaps this poor bit of poetry does not refer to him or to his automaton," Will murmured. "Madame Cristobel is merely the messenger."

"And an extraordinarily unreliable one, at that. Her message, such as it is, might have been lost to all time." Nathaniel nodded his head in a clear imitation of the movement of the automaton, as if replicating the process of revelation. "It is the church," he said, at last.

"What is the church?" Will asked.

Nathaniel gently pried the paper from beneath Madame Cristobel's dainty hands.

"The church holds the answer I seek; the proof is not in the automaton, but in the church. She only points the way."

Francesca was perplexed. "But which church? There are thousands of churches in England, and surely even more in Italy?"

"But there is a rather unusual one in Trieste, for it is a remnant of pagan times. It reminds one of the Temple Church, which we visited not many weeks ago, for its design and great antiquity. There also is such a church in Bristol, and though it is named Holy Cross Church, everyone refers to it as the Temple Church, with great familiarity. In the same way, I doubt many people recall the original name of the small round church in Trieste, as it is rarely known by it. For when a belfry was built many years ago, perhaps to claim a place on the skyline or to call sleepy parishioners to prayer, it became known as Christ's Bell Church." Nathaniel set down another square of paper and pressed Madame Cristobel in motion once again, watching as she inscribed each word.

"She has nothing more to say on the matter, but I was never more certain of anything as I am of this. I must go to Trieste."

"Allow me to go with you," Will said at once. "I yearn for adventure. I'll close the shop for as long as we're away, unless someone will look after it for me."

"You are both going to Trieste?" Francesca asked softly. She couldn't help but now feel that once Nathaniel found what he sought, she would lose him. It was against all reason, to be sure, but she couldn't help herself.

Whatever Nathaniel heard in her plaintive voice was enough for him to immediately seek to reassure her, though they had an audience in Will and several others who had entered the shop. He took the magnifying glasses from her before drawing her close and kissing her. "I will come back before I am even missed. You will have Madame Cristobel for company and, if you keep her well supplied with paper, can allow her to demonstrate her talents to all our customers. Excepting one."

When Francesca looked up, she saw Will tactfully studying the automaton and not directly observing what they were doing. But he nevertheless was able to discern when they were quite done, perhaps because he could see their reflection in Madame Cristobel's glass case.

"Yes, indeed," he said, turning toward them. "I yearn for an adventure. When do we leave?"

"As soon as we can," Nathaniel said, meeting Francesca's eyes. "The sooner we go, the sooner we return. And I hope we do that with good news."

"Give me but an hour," said Will, unrealistically.

"Give me one last night," Nathaniel said boldly. Francesca blushed like a fool, but Will was unfazed. She wondered how much Nathaniel had already confided to his friend.

"In the morning, then. I will need some time to explain all this to my parents," said Will. "But they will be happy if I promise to bring them back a clock."

"I hope to return with more than that," said Nathaniel and closed Madame Cristobel's case.

****

Francesca walked along King Street, feeling empathy for the ancient soldier who ran the twenty-six miles from Marathon to Athens, knowing he had bad news to deliver at the end of the journey. She tried to recall the pleasure with which she left her home and traveled the same route yesterday and consoled herself that Nathaniel was going off to find justice for him and his family name. But his passionate lovemaking last night was both divine and a bit desperate, so that she couldn't help but feel he intended it as a sort of valediction, something to remember him by if he didn't come back.

Throughout the evening they spent in his narrow bed, he reassured her a thousand times that he would return soon, and they would then be married, and she might find herself Countess D'Arcques, mistress of Watch Hill, at some time in their future. And as she was ever known as a sensible young woman, unaccustomed to histrionics or distressing thoughts, she should have been well satisfied by the late hour when he brought her home to Edgware Road.

But she was nevertheless fully accustomed, perhaps too much so, to those she loved departing from her life. Her sister was the first to go, off to America, and not likely to ever return. Their brother was gone next, anxious to set forth on his own adventures, with scarcely a look behind him. Francesca often told herself that she heard nothing from him because he was so engaged in his seafaring life that he scarcely had time to write, but in her darker moments, she feared another truth.

And then there were their parents, who left behind their business and their daughter with equal regret or possibly no regret at all. Unlike her brother, they did write occasionally, and seemed to be having a grand time. Francesca did not know how long they would be gone but couldn't help but imagine they would be tempted to remain in a warm and sunny place and perhaps open an outpost of FW Wadsworth, Bookseller and Antiquarian on a tropical beach. They certainly had not suggested a date for their return, although Francesca was sure to keep the sterling polished, in case they intended to surprise her one morning at the shop.

Whatever their intentions, they had all left her, and now Nathaniel was leaving, too. It was not so much that she thought he trifled with her, but travel was fraught with hazards, and there were any number of reasons why a person might not arrive at his destination, either going or coming.

"Nathaniel," she said softly, as she entered the

shop.

He stood gazing at Madame Cristobel, and Francesca thought his lips were moving. He was so intent in his quiet conversation that he did not seem to notice she had entered. So she quietly hung up her jacket on the coat tree and glanced at the window, which had now been cleared of all the tools and spare parts that he had used to skillfully restore the automaton to life. They were now replaced by a display of the double photographs intended for use in stereopticons, and several of those viewers as well.

Francesca picked up a photograph she hadn't seen before and read the scrawling text that identified the scene as a view of Trieste. How thoughtful of Nathaniel, she thought wryly. She supposed he intended she would always have this token of their love, to warm her through all the cold winters ahead, if he did not return to do the warming himself.

"I have been waiting for you," said Nathaniel, behind her. "I thought you'd be here earlier."

She jumped about a foot, and the top of her head met his chin. She turned to face him. "I find I am much exhausted from last night's exertions, though you seem to have recovered."

He rubbed his jaw looking as unhappy as she. "I shall sleep in the carriage, as does everyone else. After a while the trees and thatched roofs become less picturesque, and the countryside becomes one boring eternity until one arrives at one's destination."

"But your first destination will be Sheerness, will it not? I imagine the Channel will offer splendid views."

"On a fair day such as this, the waves will be as gentle as a rocking cradle," he said, and finally smiled.

His words had the effect of making her even more unhappy than she already was. She had considered so many things about their relationship, but not yet the possibility that there might be a child. And what, then, if he did not return? She had a fleeting image of her parents returning to not only discover the polished silver, but a squalling infant.

On the other hand, her mother often bemoaned the fact that they would not likely ever see her sister's children, and how much she wished to become a grandmother.

"What is it, Frannie?" he asked.

He surprised her for the second time in a matter of minutes. No one, aside from her parents, ever called her by that name, and she was sure she never spoke of it to him. How did he know? She thought her heart would break, for hearing it from him.

"I will come back to you," he said. "Is that what it is? Do you imagine I will suddenly find what I never managed to discover over the course of years on the Continent, when I have everything I want right here?"

"Nearly everything you want," she dared to suggest to him. "Why else would you leave me now?"

"A man cannot search for something for so long and then abandon his quest when the search is nearly at an end. Would you have me walk away now? And spend the rest of my life wondering what I might have missed?" He paused, perhaps seeing she was not persuaded. "You might wonder as well, for what I seek affects you. And our children."

Her expression turned to one of surprise for she realized that he had been thinking about such things as well.

"There might be dangers," she reminded him, at a loss for words more compelling.

"There might be dangers here," he pointed out. "Don't think I haven't thought about that. But you shall have Pip for protection."

Pip, hearing his name, rose from his favorite sheepskin rug and rubbed his nose in Nathaniel's hand.

"You might drown at sea," Francesca argued, somewhat unreasonably.

"You might have to face an intruder here," Nathaniel shot back, somewhat more reasonably. "Do you forget, it is what brought me to you in the first place?"

Francesca knew she exhausted all excuses and appeals. He would go, without her. He spoke of a quest, and she knew perfectly well that women—with the possible exception of Joan of Arc—did not set forth on great quests. And poor Joan had to do it dressed as a boy.

Something just occurred to her. "Are you descended from Joan of Arc?"

He laughed. "We will soon find out, I hope. But it would not be a very close relationship in any case, for I don't believe she had offspring. I imagine they would have been rather adventurous if she had. The current earl packs a travel bag when he journeys as far as a dinner party in the neighborhood."

Francesca gestured at the photographs now displayed in the window.

"If it is an adventure you want, my love, I promise we shall have adventures all our life. There are places I wish to show you, and many more we shall discover together."

Those words finally dispelled her anxiety and sadness, though she had heard them before and understood that this would be the life they would share. When Nathaniel put his arms around her and pulled her close, she went not with any sense of acquiescence but to gather strength from his love.

"I won't be long," he said into her hair. "I think I know just where to go, and what will be revealed. The real battle will come when I return with proof of what my father and his father long believed, which will surely be challenged by Tony. He is the one who worries me."

"You have already promised me that you will face no danger," she reminded him, whispering in his ear. When he didn't answer, she realized that, for all his reassurances, he still worried that Lord Anthony might act against her. "And I will not face danger either. I have known Lord Anthony for many years, and he will not harm me."

"I will kill him if he does."

"Don't be so dramatic," she said, just before he stopped her with his lips.

And so they might have remained if Pip had not warned them of a visitor.

"Have you had enough time to say your goodbyes?" Will asked cheerfully as he came through the door. "Oh, for goodness' sake, it's not as if we're sailing to the far side of the earth. Make good your promises, and let us leave with enough time to make our Channel crossing to Vlissingen."

"Have you already packed your travel bags?" Francesca asked Nathaniel. "You may not be gone long but must require certain necessities."

He reached into his breast pocket and pulled out a copy of Madame Cristobel's script. "This is all I require but am bringing a few shirts, stockings, shaving kit..."

"Oh, have pity," Will lamented. "You're not even married yet. And have you forgotten Scotch whisky, gaming cards, and blunt for gambling?"

Nathaniel glanced at Francesca. "He is only joking, of course."

"Of course," Will said, somewhat unconvincingly. "But let's be off."

And they soon were, in a flurry of activity and checking pockets and gathering up papers and with one final kiss. From Nathaniel, of course.

"Be safe!" Francesca called as they stumbled out the door. She looked down at Pip, who seemed as forlorn as she.

****

It had been weeks since the shop had been quite so quiet, with the only conversation sustaining her through the day the few words she shared with her customers. Predictably, several regular customers stopped by to see that all was well, and she did commiserate with Pip and Madame Cristobel from time to time, but she missed Nathaniel's presence and the certainty that, if he was not about at any particular moment, he would be soon.

The scheme to have him exhibit his skills in the window once seemed like a stupid idea, like some cheap ploy used by salesmen selling miracle cures on the street. But it had the effect Nathaniel and she desired, in all ways. Customers had flocked to see what progress was being made on the automaton, and the publicity brought in people like Mr. Graves and Mr. Witt, the mudlark, who became part of the story. That the living window display did not yet bring in the intruder was only a minor inconvenience, in light of the fact that Nathaniel was now on his way to recover his family's story.

But if the intruder still intended to make an appearance, Francesca hoped he would wait until Nathaniel returned.

"My dear, you look like you are quite bereft," Lord Anthony called out from the door. "I bring you offerings of my good company as well as a bottle of birch beer and cucumber sandwiches. The cheesemonger has closed his shop, so I had to go farther upstream."

Though Francesca now had several reasons to be distrustful of her visitor, she couldn't help but smile. They had been friends for so many years, and it was always understood that such would be enough to share between them. For as much as she loved Nathaniel, she did sometimes regret that he brought an animosity into the relationship between her and Lord Anthony, such that things could never go back to the way they were. But now, as in everything about the shop, it was as if the intervening weeks had not happened. Francesca was lonely enough to pretend it was so.

"Come, sit at the table, Lord Anthony. It is so nice to have you visit." Francesca cleared some daguerreotypes of the queen from the table and found a few clean serving utensils. From one of the cabinets, she pulled two goblets.

Lord Anthony came down the aisle of the shop, nodding to a few indifferent customers, and pausing for a moment to consider Madame Cristobel atop her cabinet.

"The poor dear has been relegated to the general merchandise, has she?" he said, laughing. "I suppose she remains as silent as ever?"

For all her pleasure in seeing him, she still hesitated to tell the truth. Nathaniel had given her enough reason to distrust him, though she wished she could just forget about that. "She is able to twitch around a bit, and the music box now plays, but nothing more. Perhaps she is fated to be forever mute and just observe everything going on around her, keeping it to herself."

"An admirable trait in a woman," Lord Anthony said, a bit too loudly. Loud enough to elicit laughs from some of the gentlemen in the shop.

But to think such a thing or find humor in it was not an admirable trait in a man, she thought. Had he always been like this? Had she not noticed, while basking in the pleasure of his company?

She sat in her chair, allowing him to unpack his offering. She didn't think he was above serving her.

"Nathaniel is not here, I suppose?" he asked. "Have you fired him from your employ for his inability to do what you hired him to accomplish?"

"He has accomplished a great deal, for I hired him to organize the stock and unpack crates and such. I have no quarrel with his work."

"But he didn't manage to bring the automaton to life. Nor did his friend, who lives in that absurd house." Lord Anthony set the bottle in the middle of the table and looked expectantly at her. She relented and filled both their glasses. "I expect your customers were impatient with their lack of success, so you ousted them from the window. It was very common of them, in any case."

"I am sure your mother would not have approved," Francesca said. "And yet they seemed to be a very popular addition to the commerce on King Street."

"And where are they now?" Lord Anthony asked, not meeting her eyes.

She hesitated, perhaps a moment too long. She did not have any intention of giving him this information, but it would not be too much trouble for him to learn the truth from others.

"They have gone to Trieste."

"And left you quite alone, have they?" He clucked sympathetically.

"I am accustomed to it," she said, and it had the advantage of being the truth.

"They have left you with a broken automaton. It appears my old friend Nathaniel has given up."

"I would not say that. I believe he is very close to repairing Madame Cristobel."

"Is he indeed?" Lord Anthony said thoughtfully. Francesca realized she already said too much. "And he's gone back to Trieste, but perhaps intends to return with spare parts."

"He did not say," Francesca said quickly. "Please pass me the bottle? It is very warm in here."

Lord Anthony looked around the shop until his gaze returned to the automaton. "It is indeed. Would you like to join me tonight at the theater? I know my mother does not intend to use her box."

It would be a mistake, for things seemed to be moving too fast. She should remain at the shop for as long as possible, at least until she could take Pip out for his evening walk. But she was lonely and she did enjoy the theater, and nothing was likely to happen at the shop.

"That sounds lovely. What are we to see?" she asked.

"I do not recall. Something about soldiers returning from war, and sparring lovers and some perfidy." He seemed perfectly uninterested. If Nathaniel spoke like this, she would have been immediately suspicious. But Lord Anthony was not a very good student of the theater. Indeed, she was not sure he was a good student at anything, except possibly navigating his place in society. She was not certain of that either.

"It sounds like *Much Ado About Nothing*," she said. "It is a comedy, and very enjoyable."

"Then we shall go. There is not much ado here, so we can both use a diversion."

She assumed that the only diversion he intended was to attend a performance and be seen in his mother's lofty box. If she was being entirely truthful, she would admit she rather liked it, as well.

"Yes, I should enjoy it. But it is necessary for me to take Pip on his evening walk, before he settles down for the night. Perhaps you can return me to the shop for a brief while after the performance? Or better, I can ask one of my neighbors." Francesca felt her head spinning as she thought of the possibilities.

Lord Anthony looked pensive, as if he hadn't thought about this and wondered what the fuss was about.

"You needn't worry," he said, and paused. The reassurance was spontaneous, but the explanation for it, apparently not. "Oh, yes. Of course. I will have one of my men come over and do the deed, if you just tell me what needs to be done. Will the mongrel obey him?"

Francesca bristled at the use of the word "mongrel," though that was precisely what Pip was. Still, he was such a fine, sweet fellow.

"His name is Pip, and he will obey anyone who treats him kindly. It took only a matter of minutes before this place became home to him, as if he had lived among us all his life."

Lord Anthony nodded. "I had no idea."

Francesca thought this a very strange conversation. "Why would it have mattered, but for this evening's plans? Were you afraid to come by, fearing that he would bite your leg?"

"Is he not a guard dog, here to protect the shop?"

"But not a very good one," Francesca continued. "Besides, I am pretty sure I already know the identity of the perpetrator. I've reported him to the constabulary, and no more mischief has been done."

Lord Anthony seemed to take in this whole interview with an air of befuddlement, and her words only seemed to add to his utter lack of sense as to what was going on.

"That's very good news, of course. And what is his identity? Some guttersnipe, I suppose?"

And this, too, betrayed something of Lord Anthony's persistence in putting himself above others. But then, even Mr. Witt identified himself as a mudlark. And Nathaniel was a watchmaker. And she was a shopkeeper. There was no avoiding it, it seemed. "I am not at liberty to say," she answered.

"Well then, no matter. What time should I tell my man to arrive, and where shall he find the key? How long a walk is the dog accustomed to taking?

"Pip enjoys a walk of about an hour. And the key shall be under the flowerpot," Francesca said and reached for her goblet.

"That should be enough time," Lord Anthony murmured, not looking befuddled at all.

Chapter 15

"You look wonderful tonight, Miss Wadsworth," Lord Anthony said gallantly—or almost gallantly—as he helped her into his carriage. "I have not seen you wearing this gown before, and it is quite flattering."

She rather thought so, too. She recalled the first time he took her to the theater, when she pulled nearly all her gowns from the closet, trying to find one that wasn't worn or too tight or too short in the hem. Purchasing new gowns might have been an indulgence, but it was long overdue. "Thank you very much, Lord Anthony. I have just had some new gowns made for me, and I believe this is my favorite."

He didn't say anything else until he circled the carriage and climbed in on the opposite side. He was not a large man, but the vehicle rocked back and forth on its suspension.

"And yet I believe I've seen it before."

Francesca thought about that for a few moments. "Oh yes, of course. Madame Cristobel has one just like it."

"Of course, I remember now. Though she hardly does the dressmaker justice." He tapped the roof of the carriage with his cane, and they were off at a slow trot through the streets.

"She's a wooden doll, Lord Anthony. I don't think Mrs. Blanchard was inclined to flatter her unnecessarily."

"Whereas when I flatter you, it is quite necessary," he said.

"Do you think I have so little sense of self-worth?" she asked, and it was a real question, devoid of any flirtatiousness.

Lord Anthony either did not wish to answer, or he had no idea what she was talking about. "Oh, look," he said, peering out the window. "There seems to have been an accident."

Francesca followed his gaze, and saw little more than a pushcart had been overturned and its irate owner was screaming like a Valkyrie. She did not appear to be in ill health. It was not much of an accident, which was good, but made for an excellent diversion, which might have been better.

They rode the rest of the way to the Theatre Royal in Covent Garden in silence.

****

The production of *Much Ado About Nothing* was delightful, with Francesca particularly pleased that she recognized the actor playing Dogberry and had sold him a copy of the play not many months ago. He did justice to the absurdity of his lines and played his part with a great deal of pleasure. Once, she thought, he gazed up at the box in which they sat and winked at her.

But, in fact, several people noticed her and, even more, that she had returned with Lord Anthony as her escort. She supposed attending the theater once with a man was merely an item of minor gossip. But twice was already a statement of some intent, and the gossip might be a reasonable topic of discussion in drawing rooms on the day after. Francesca guessed Lord Anthony would not have encouraged such idle conversation, for his mother would certainly be displeased to hear of it. And yet, he seemed to revel in the attention. He was as happy as she had ever seen him.

"You enjoyed the play as much as I did," she said, when they finally escaped the crowd in the lobby. "Some consider it one of Shakespeare's best."

He nodded briefly as he raised his hand to call up his carriage. "It is much better to see such plays in a large crowd so one knows when to laugh. I despised reading them when I was at school."

"Were they not performed by students?" Francesca knew little about it but had heard that at the universities, the plays were presented as they had been at the Globe three hundred years before, with men playing all the roles.

"I suppose, but I was not much interested in them." The carriage pulled up, and the groom jumped down. "Ask your friend Nathaniel, if he ever returns to London. He went in for that kind of thing. We were at Cambridge together, you know."

No, she didn't, though it mattered little. They settled into the carriage for the short ride to her home, and she waved briefly at a few acquaintances still milling about on the street.

"I might not have finished if not for him," Lord Anthony went on. "He got me out of a few scrapes and helped me through my exams."

This did seem to matter, as well as surprise her. She leaned forward in her seat. "So, you were friends? Somehow I thought you cared little for each other, even as boys."

"There is always resentment when one has what

the other desires, I suppose. For my part, I have never desired anything of his. Except, perhaps, the answers to questions on examinations." He settled back in the velvet cushions, effectively ending the discussion.

Such a statement should also end any gossip. Though others might not know it, and Lord Anthony might be oblivious to the effect of his own admission, it was clear she was not worth his resentment. For all he seemed anxious to bring her to the theater this evening, they would just remain friends.

****

Nathaniel stood at the wrought-iron gate that separated Christ's Bell Church from the busy street and wondered that such an ancient building had survived intact for hundreds of years as the city grew up around it. It was not so unusual when one saw great monuments and castles, but this small sanctuary might have gone unnoticed but for its group of parishioners. Built of stone and stucco, it reminded him of an elderly relation in the midst of the gaiety of a family celebration.

Will roamed about the gravestones in the small churchyard, where the stones were so close together, it was necessary to step over them to go from one path to the next. The maritime climate had weathered the monuments so that the names and dates were barely decipherable, and lichen obscured whatever remained. Will ran his fingers over the carvings, relying more on touch than on sight to read what they revealed.

"Do you intend to stand there all day? I think I found him." Will crouched before a modest gravestone.

Indeed, they had a purpose in coming here, and there was some urgency in that. Nathaniel considered he could save such reveries for another day, perhaps when he described to his own children where their thrice-great-grandfather lived and died. He went through the gate.

And there he was: Christian Bell, Earl D'Arcques, born in one century and died in the next. An actor who found favor with two kings and sought sanctuary in a city ruled by neither. He was a man of dualities, complexity, and mystery. Nathaniel wasn't sure if he would feel proud to be related to such a cipher, but he was certainly intrigued by the possibility.

"I don't see anything about his impersonation of a woman," Will said, and moved on to another monument, surely the tallest in the graveyard. In high relief, the portrait of a young woman wearing a coronet was carved; she held an infant who reached for her crown with a weathered hand.

High above them, the hour was struck in the bell tower, tolling the remembrances of loss with which they were surrounded.

"But here's a woman. A lady, in fact." Will brushed aside some dead leaves. "I think it says she was Collette Bell, Countess D'Arcques. There's nothing about the child, though."

"Perhaps that was intentional, if they were hiding the infant's identity from those who would harm them. That there is a child on the gravestone is, in itself, a key to the truth." Nathaniel, who was pensive and solemn only a moment before, shivered with excitement.

"As is the fact she is identified as Bell's countess," Will pointed out.

But Nathaniel held up his hand. "It may have been an honorific. We have no proof they were truly wed, and it would not have mattered to anyone else. And after all these years, who would have come to discover them here?"

Will grinned. "Why you, of course. As you found the automaton and made her speak again, and this forlorn graveyard, where words shall lead to the truth. Why not go in and find them, for it's the hour of your meeting with the curate."

It was the hour of reckoning, to be sure. Nathaniel removed his hat as he walked toward the ancient portal of Christ's Bell Church.

****

Francesca opened the door to the shop, happy to duck out of the steady rain. It was to be another day without Nathaniel, but she was reassured that friends would be near and customers would likely keep her well occupied throughout shop hours. It might be a fine day to sort through the great collection of tableware on display throughout the shop, for Nathaniel's inventory had revealed matching pieces to various sets placed in no particular order. Indeed, it was becoming fashionable to mix and match different patterns, to give dinner guests the illusion that they dined in a pastoral setting. It was quite ridiculous, really. Those who had no recourse but to use mismatched tableware would probably have given anything to own finer things.

But before she took off her jacket and sat down to work, she must take Pip out for his morning walk.

She retrieved the key that Lord Anthony's man had used the night before, and as she opened the door, she automatically knelt down, knowing Pip would be upon her in a second. But instead, she heard him barking, as if from a distance. She followed his desperate sounds to a little-used closet and wrestled with the stuck door. Pip pushed his way out and greeted her in the manner to which she had become accustomed.

"Why, what is this?" she asked, rubbing his head. "How did you lock yourself inside the closet?"

She studied the door and knew it was impossible for him to have wandered in and shut the door behind it. The wood was warped by years of dampness, and the bottom edge scraped on the floor. "You poor boy. Did you spend the whole night there?"

No doubt he did, and she would have to ask someone else for the "why" of it all.

"Come, let's go for a walk and figure this out." The words were enough for Pip to abandon his display of affection—and gratitude, no doubt—and turn toward the front of the shop. His wagging tail whipped across Francesca's face, and she fended him off. "Enough!"

As she rose to follow him, she saw a shard of broken glass on the floor. And then another. And then a small knob, as from a miniature cabinet. She did not have to see more, but was compelled by both despair and confusion. She already knew what had happened sometime in the night but was left to wonder why. Behind the great cabinet in the middle of the shop, Madame Cristobel and her housing lay on the floor, shattered into a hundred pieces.

When Mr. Dickens came upon her, after she had returned with Pip and still had no idea why Madame Cristobel had been so brutally destroyed, he joined a small group of sympathetic customers, who helped her retrieve all the pieces and place them reverently on the cabinet which displayed the automaton the night before.

"It is as if I am at a funeral. It was my fondest hope

to purchase Madame Cristobel to entertain my customers," sobbed Miss Tupper. She then passed out flyers for that night's performance at the Pipedown Music Hall.

"But where is Mr. Endicott in all this? He will be most aggrieved of all," said Mr. Dickens. "All that work, for naught."

"He is away for a few days, on business. But I'm not sure that even Mr. Endicott can repair such damage," Francesca said, knowing it was quite unlikely he could do so.

Miss Tupper knelt beside her, reached under a table, and produced half of a tiny face. "Is Mr. Graves' dog to blame?"

"I don't think so," Francesca said, gesturing toward the sunny window, where Pip slept as if nothing mattered at all. "I was out in the evening, and a friend of a friend was going to take him out for his evening walk. But when I arrived this morning, Pip was locked in a closet. All else is as it should be, but for Madame Cristobel."

"Then it is clear what happened," said a solemn gentleman. "The dog knocked over the automaton, and the man in charge locked him in the closet, so he would do no more damage."

Mr. Dickens reached for Francesca's hand as he rose, and she stood next to him. She saw him nod before she spoke. "I doubt it, for Pip is a very careful little fellow, much more cautious than some of my customers. I believe he was intentionally locked in the closet, and the damage was then done."

Her comment fell upon the group like a heavy horse blanket.

"Was anything else damaged…or taken?" asked Miss Tupper.

"I don't believe so," Francesca said, suddenly tired of answering questions, and saddened by the loss of Madame Cristobel, and yearning for Nathaniel to return from Trieste. It was all too much to take in at once.

"It is a true detective tale, then," said another man, on a gleeful note. "We shall call it murder most grievous, for someone has made sure that Madame Cristobel will never reveal her secrets, such as they are."

But Francesca knew the automaton already revealed her secret, and it might be most consequential.

"She certainly shall never speak to us again," she said, and her audience sighed, as if it were the most eloquent valediction. But for the lack of a church service and a repast, it seemed the saddest of funerals.

"What are you to do?" Mr. Picardy asked, some time later. More than anyone who surrounded her this morning, Will's parents understood her love and fascination with Madame Cristobel.

"I fear there is nothing I can do. This was an intentional act, and certainly not one that can be blamed on Pip. If he had knocked her over, there would have been breakage, of course. But look at this: each piece looks like someone attempted to grind it to dust. After she was thrown to the floor, he stepped on the parts, rendering them all useless and unrecognizable." She held up a fragment of wood that might have been one of the two painted shoes. "But I am still unable to find the clockworks, and I've looked all over."

Mrs. Picardy sat down in the window, her back to the street. "And that is the essence of Madame

Cristobel, for what is she if she cannot move? A poppet to model some garments and a relic of the last century. The poor thing has not weathered it well."

"It was murder, for all the constabulary is perfectly willing to see it as an unfortunate accident. Someone wanted her dead." Francesca joined Will's mother on the window seat, hearing the patter of raindrops on the glass. "I know I sound a fool, but she did have presence, and personality, if not a soul."

"And she did have knowledge, which someone preferred to remain hidden forever. I suspect it is Lord Anthony Maitland, for he is the only one to gain from this." Mrs. Picardy smiled knowingly. "Oh, yes, my son told me all about his interests here. Was he not worried when Mr. Endicott set out to work on her and discouraged you from allowing him to do so? Did he not watch Mr. Endicott's progress every day, though the window and from within?" She took Madame Cristobel's shoe and tapped it gently against the step. "Will suspects he also had a hand in the drowning of Mr. Graves, for the man knew too much. The gentleman was quite right. There was a murder."

"But Lord Anthony was with me last night," Francesca said, still straining to find her old friend innocent. She didn't sound very convincing, even to herself. If her friend was a murderer, she just as easily could have been a victim.

"That was no accident, surely. He saw his opportunity and had to get you out of the way." Mrs. Picardy glanced at her and saw the expression on her face. "I only mean away from the shop. Whatever else he might have done, let us believe his affection for you is sincere. The 'friend of a friend' you so evasively mentioned this morning was his friend, I presume?"

"Yes, of course."

"Then don't protect him anymore. He's not worth it. But he is dangerous, and if he becomes desperate enough, he will go after you or Mr. Endicott, perhaps both. Old Pip is lucky he survived the night, for Lord Anthony sounds stupid enough to think the dog could be a witness to all his misdeeds."

"I don't think him stupid," Francesca said.

"My son tells me otherwise. Perhaps because he didn't claim you when he had the opportunity and no competition. You could have been Lady Maitland if he had a drop of sense in him."

"His mother would never have allowed it," Francesca said, suddenly grateful for that. "But perhaps I am also stupid, for refusing to believe he could be what he is."

"Not stupid. Overly loyal, perhaps. Ever optimistic. Unable to believe ill of anyone. But never stupid."

"But what if I'd married him?"

"Did he ever suggest it?" Mrs. Picardy asked and, when she didn't answer, went on. "If you had, I prefer to believe you would have reformed him, made him better than he is. But if you had, he would have had two women in his possession, not one. He wanted Madame Cristobel. And if he couldn't have her, no one could."

"I daresay he would not have felt the same about me," she said.

"Which demonstrates his stupidity, does it not? We are back to the beginning, then."

"I wonder what will happen when he discovers that his destruction of Madame Cristobel is all in vain?"

They looked at each other, seeing the truth in the

other's face.

"He will come after Nathaniel," they said, as one.

****

Nathaniel shook hands with the curate of Christ's Bell Church, sizing him up, wondering how much he should be told, or warned that there might be others looking for the information Nathaniel sought. Mr. Albani, tall and lean with spectacles of unusual thickness, looked like he both understood the delicacy of the situation while scarcely containing his enthusiasm.

"You have traveled far for this," he said.

"I have made the journey before, for I lived not far from here," Nathaniel explained. "The more frequently the destination is visited, the less onerous the travel."

Mr. Albani removed his glasses, revealing very pale eyes. Though the church was dimly lit, he squinted at Nathaniel, perhaps wondering if they met before. After a while, during which Nathaniel did not know what to say, Mr. Albani cleared his throat.

"I believe I have found precisely what you seek," he said.

****

"We must warn them," Mrs. Picardy said. "Do you know their direction? My son ran out of the house with little more than a wave of farewell."

Francesca felt like a fool. Any woman who sends her lover off on a quest to a foreign country ought to know where he intends to stay. But she was all too accustomed to partings and was often in the netherworld of not knowing where a loved one was, or when he or she would return. And, in any case, she trusted him implicitly.

"They will return," she insisted.

Mrs. Picardy raised a brow. "I do not doubt it, but do we not wish to warn them before they step into a trap?"

"Do you think Lord Anthony would harm them?"

Mrs. Picardy's expression revealed exactly what she was thinking. "I am concerned for both of them, though Mr. Endicott is surely the target. Perhaps they will have an accident. Perhaps they will only be delayed. But I don't feel well about this situation at all."

"You ladies needn't be so dramatic," said Mr. Picardy, speaking up for once. "The boys can take care of themselves."

"They are not boys," his wife reminded him.

"All the better. They can protect themselves."

"But from whom? They will not know if they are dealing with friend or foe," said Francesca.

Mr. Picardy didn't answer but looked like he saw a ghost.

"Lord Anthony Maitland," he said quietly. "I have not seen you in an age. What brings you here?

"I came to visit Miss Wadsworth, as I often do. A rainy day is a fine time to seek refuge among her treasures."

Francesca stood to face him. "It is not such a fine morning for me, I fear. There has been mischief done in the shop."

She paused, waiting for him to say something of his friend, or an excuse for Madame Cristobel's plight, but he gave her nothing.

"Have you spoken to your friend this morning?"

Lord Anthony looked aghast. "Did he not return the key?"

"The key was just where it ought to have been. But Pip was not in his place, and Madame Cristobel was definitely not in hers."

He looked to the window, though Francesca didn't know if that was to check on Pip, or to see if the automaton had mysteriously reappeared.

"Where is the old girl?"

"If you are referring to Madame Cristobel, I am sad to report that she has met with an accident and is deceased." She regretted this admission as soon as she said the words. Lord Anthony smiled, but she didn't know if he was happy to hear it or merely amused by her words. "And Pip was locked in a closet when I arrived this morning. I should like to speak to your friend."

But she had given him too much time to think through this too-subtle accusation.

"I am sorry, but he has left for the countryside this morning. I was happy to secure his services for last night." Lord Anthony looked theatrically rueful.

"And what services were those, my lord?' Mr. Picardy asked.

"I certainly didn't ask him to destroy the automaton, if that's what you're implying, sir."

"I'm not implying anything. In fact, I don't think anything was said of the automaton other than she met with an accident," Mr. Picardy said, rubbing his chin. Francesca thought his son got some of his own theatrical skill from him.

But she was now fearful of another sort of accident.

But Lord Anthony looked more excused than violent.

"Mr. and Mrs. Picardy, would you excuse us for a few moments? I wish to speak to Miss Wadsworth in private about a matter of business."

"What is this about the automaton?" he asked her, when the Picardys removed themselves to the displays of fine silver in the rear of the shop.

"I thought your friend might have told you before he left for the countryside. To Cornwall, perhaps?"

"Cornwall? Why, not at all. He is visiting his elderly grandmother in Surrey." Lord Anthony pulled his collar away from his neck.

Francesca began to think he might have had a reason to go to the theater, other than simple entertainment. Indeed, it was probably intended that he get her away from the shop and give his man the all-clear to accomplish whatever he wished to do. But that was for one evening and probably their last sortie as well. But watching him now made her believe he was honing his skills as an actor.

"I shall have some questions for him upon his return." She waited to see if he would offer up another excuse, but he merely continued to look uncomfortable under her scrutiny. "Madame Cristobel was pushed from her cabinet last night and lay in pieces on the floor when I opened the door this morning. Pip was locked into the closet in the back of the shop."

"Well, that's clear, isn't it? My man came in, found the wreckage obviously caused by the mongrel, and decided it best not to leave him loose in the shop. After all, there's no predicting what a mad dog might do."

"He's hardly a mad dog, Lord Anthony, nor has he damaged anything else in the store, with a few exceptions of some plates being knocked over by an exuberantly wagging tail."

"That's it, then."

"That's not it. I can scarcely lift the automaton myself; she would not have been pushed over the ledge by a dog's tail. Nor would a dog have crushed each splintered piece and made off with the clockworks." She glanced up, giving him one more chance to confess or atone. "I don't profess to have the talents of one of Bobby Peel's men, but I daresay your man—does he have a name?—locked Pip in the closet precisely so he could do the damage and not have to reckon with a dog."

"I cannot explain what my man did, for I only asked him to go for a walk and lock up after himself."

Still, he didn't mention the man's name.

"Perhaps not. But you surely can explain why every path in this mystery, in the things that have happened in the past few months, all lead back to you?"

Lord Anthony loosened his tie. Now he did not look merely bothered by the warm weather; he looked like he was about to choke. "I believe your imagination is running away with you. This is a very unseemly conversation."

"Unseemly. Oh, yes, I understand. Your sensibilities are offended because you are a gentleman."

"You needn't use my position in society as a weapon. I have ever treated you like the lady you are. Have I ever prevailed on you, taken advantage of your gentle nature?"

"Please tell me one thing: when you renewed our childhood acquaintance some years ago, did you already know you were looking for something most specific? And that it was probably hidden in the

335

automaton?"

"I believe I came in looking for a book," he said primly.

"That is what you said. But that is not what I asked." For the first time, she felt as if she had the upper hand in this conversation. "Tell me, Tony."

His eyes widened when she called him by the name Nathaniel used.

"Tell me," she repeated.

"My mother sent me here."

"Oh, dear heavens," she said in disgust. "Did she send you to find a copy of *Jane Eyre* for her? Or a copy of *Debrett's* more likely?"

He leaned, sagged, against the door jamb. He looked utterly defeated, and yet Francesca found no pleasure in that.

"My mother was a dear friend to your mother's aunt, Lady Everly, the one who raised your mother after she was delivered to London. It was no coincidence, for they knew each other as girls back in Cornwall. They each married well, perhaps better than one ought to expect from their modest childhood."

"Even a Cinderella might marry a prince, ever so often," she said.

"Your mother's aunt—your aunt too, I suppose— told my mother about the automatons that came with your mother from Cornwall, not only beautiful and cunning in their design, but also the repository of a family secret. There were always rumors of a marriage, of course, and a child who was adopted by another family. But much of this was simply attributed to the fear of retribution after the French Terror. The Earl D'Arcques was an old French title, of course."

"Of course," she murmured. "And he does not have a son."

"Or any surviving children. When it became likely that he would die without issue, my mother reminded me of the old story, and how it might matter very much in my own life. I am the recognized heir, of course."

"You have mentioned it." Now that she heard this story from several perspectives, it made more sense than from any single point of view. And surely, it was the oldest story in the world: one inheritance, two claimants, revenge and loss. "Jacob and Esau."

"I know not who they are, but it is mine."

For the first time, Francesca felt fear in his presence. It was not so much the words he said, but the way in which he said them, most particularly his almost breathless emphasis on "mine."

With that, he seemed to discard all kindness, all feelings toward others. She did not think she was reading too much into it to imagine he was capable of everything she now suspected him of doing.

"They are men of the Bible, of course," she said.

"And there is a saint named Anthony, but that doesn't change anything."

She had stopped listening to him and wished nothing more than to push him out the door and into the rain. "But that doesn't make you a saint, either." She took a step forward.

"I never claimed to be one," he said and smiled.

She thought they were back on safe ground, when he added, "And now tell me what they discovered and why they have gone off to Trieste. Don't deny that they are there, for I've had men watching the shop, both within and without. And the automaton revealed nothing."

"Then you admit to having a part in her destruction?"

"Do you not already know it? I place little value on playthings."

"What do you value?" she asked, almost afraid to hear his answer.

"On property and status, of course. Who does not?" His face fell into shadow as a carriage passed on the street. "And you."

"I am sorry, then," she said.

"For getting what I want?"

"For not getting what you want," she said, knowing he would not be so desperate if he did not think Nathaniel would succeed in his mission. "And for the loss of our friendship. I very much enjoyed the time we spent together, which had nothing to do with property or status."

"Can we no longer be friends?"

Now she knew he was not only desperate but likely delusional. He scarcely knew what he was saying. For all he hired others to do his bidding and commit murder and destruction, he did not yet understand that she was also a player in these affairs, and her own happiness was very much at stake.

"No, Lord Anthony, we can never again be what we were," she said, glancing back to where Mr. and Mrs. Picardy watched. When she turned back to the open door, Lord Anthony was already gone.

****

The train was going to be late arriving at Charing Cross, which was not a keen advertisement for the rail system. But a herd of sheep had wandered onto the tracks almost as soon as the landscape of a seaside community evolved into farmland, and the engineer apparently valued humanitarian interests over efficiency. And so, while the crew went out to herd the sheep, the passengers settled down with their books or their knitting, to wait out the delay. Will promptly went to sleep.

And though Nathaniel had Henry Thoreau's *Walden* open on his lap, his thoughts were not with life in a small New England town or a simple life on the banks of a placid pond. There, too, train tracks intersected with the natural world, as they did just now in the English countryside.

He and Will had only been gone for two weeks on their quest, staying on after discovering what the Endicotts had always believed and what the Earl D'Arcques had always preferred to believe. In the days after Nathaniel found the proof of his twice-great-grandparents' marriage in the faded registry book in the vestry of Christ's Bell Church, there were letters to be written, legal matters to see to, and testimonials to be drawn up and reviewed. If his world had shifted under his feet the moment Francesca proclaimed her love for him, it now seemed he stood on bedrock, certain in his expectations.

And yet, only two weeks had passed.

He remembered that Thoreau once pointed out to his friend Emerson that he had traveled much in Concord, suggesting that he did not have to venture far to have everything he desired. So it felt to Nathaniel just now, for in the length of a journey to Trieste, he imagined that he, too, had everything he desired.

He closed the book on his lap.

Letters were already sent to his father and to the earl. His father was always content with his situation in life, and often reminded Nathaniel that he had good—if not great—expectations and was free to make the best of his circumstances. But the Earl D'Arcques had been restless about the future once it was clear that he, himself, would never have children, and that Tony was not only his nominal heir but would eventually inherit Watch Hill and take his place as a leader in their small corner of Cornwall.

Nathaniel imagined his father reading his letter, putting the paper on a pile of other missives on his desk, and resuming his bookkeeping for the estate. But the earl would gleefully throw his letter up in the air and call for a glass of port to celebrate the triumph of truth over ignorance. Nathaniel did not think he was being too full of himself to imagine this would be so.

He knew what the others would say and do. Already, in the dim vestry of the church, Will told him that nothing had really changed. And Francesca would remind him that they were already perfectly happy, she a shopkeeper and he a watchmaker, and so they could have lived all their life together.

Then there was Tony. He had been a child who could not walk away from a lost chess match without overturning the board, and he had become a man who would not walk away from property without burning it to the ground. He had already built a network based on revenge and hate and capable of murder, and that was simply to prevent Nathaniel from repairing the automaton and discovering any mysteries she'd kept to herself for over a century.

What was Tony—or his henchmen—likely to do

when he realized all was now revealed? How would his mother egg him on, demanding he prove his manhood and withholding her affections until he did what she wanted?

Lady Maitland. He hadn't really thought much about her in years but suddenly remembered her cold and calculating gaze, her arguments with the earl, her insistence that Nathaniel was the one who let the chickens out of the henhouse, tampered with her son's school exercises, and stole her hatpin. That her own son was later caught using that pin to punch out the eyeballs of the painted ancestors in the portrait gallery, did nothing to make her think otherwise.

For the briefest moment, Nathaniel spared some sympathy for Tony, for he must have been miserable growing up with such a mother. He never quite thought about it that way, for he had not grown up with a mother at all.

But that was in the past, and there was enough to worry about for the present. If Nathaniel was hesitant to leave Francesca unprotected two weeks ago, he suddenly was overwhelmed with a sense of helplessness that there was nothing to do to help her now, if Tony was in a vindictive move. He must get back to London.

He glanced out the window at the baaing sheep and wondered if the crew could use a hand to get the beasts off the track. He didn't know a lot about it himself but was perfectly willing to lift each sheep, one by one, and set it down in the nearby meadow, if it would only get them on their way.

But just as he slipped *Walden* into his bag, the train jerked forward, and they were on their way to London.

****

A late afternoon thunderstorm emptied the shop of a few customers, cleaned the streets of waste, and left the air crackling with unusual energy. Francesca, dismissing any lingering fears she had about Lord Anthony and still not certain when Nathaniel would return, decided she was safe enough remaining at the shop, taking care of a few matters. Lord Anthony had not shown himself for several days, and she decided he knew there was nothing more to be accomplished by distracting her from the business between him and Nathaniel.

Indeed, Nathaniel had made no announcements of his plans to return or if he was successful in Trieste. Over the course of the past few days she wondered if, perhaps, Lord Anthony was right in his insinuation that Nathaniel was only using her to get what he wanted.

In her quiet moments, she wondered if she would ever get what she wanted.

Madame Cristobel was gone. Even if Nathaniel returned to her, to them, she doubted there was anything he could do with the broken pieces of what had once been an extraordinary machine. She felt a little foolish, having swept up every last scrap of fabric and splinter of wood, and placed them in a basket. She wondered if there had ever been a funeral for an automaton, or were they simply consigned to the trash. Or thrown into the river, where bits and pieces were recovered by mudlarks.

A crash of thunder startled her, but not as much as Lord Anthony, who now stood at the door. He removed his dripping hat, and shook his head, in imitation of a wet dog.

Francesca picked up Madame Cristobel's shin bone, broken at a sharp angle, and slid it up the sleeve of her shirt.

"Francesca," Lord Anthony said, urgently. "Are you alone?"

Surely he did not expect her to admit to it?

"I…" she began, but he grabbed her before she could come up with an excuse. She slipped her feeble weapon into her hand and thrust it against his side. He looked down in surprise, and she expected him to laugh at her because the point barely creased the cloth of his jacket. But he didn't laugh.

"I am not the enemy," he said, and almost sounded persuasive.

"You have certainly given a fair imitation of it," she said, pressing the wooden point again him again. It broke off in her hand. "You have done everything possible to implicate yourself in this nasty affair, including using me as a decoy so you can send your thugs in to steal or destroy what is not yours. You are indeed the enemy."

He looked over his shoulder, but there was nothing but the rain and an occasional runner seeking shelter.

"There's no time to explain now. We must go. We must leave here at once." He started to pull her to the door.

"I am certainly not going with you," she insisted, and stood her ground.

"I am trying to save you," he said. "I know you don't believe me, but you must trust me." Nevertheless he released her.

"You have done everything possible to let me know that you are not to be trusted, that you wish to harm Nathaniel and do me harm as well." A sudden thought made her drop her hands in surrender. "What have you done to him? Is he already dead?"

He looked at her, and she saw the utter defeat in his eyes and in the slump of his shoulders. "I have done nothing to him; I only know he and Picardy have already arrived at Charing Cross."

Then he would be safe. Perhaps he and Will would go to the Picardy home first, hear the story from Will's parents, and proceed with some caution.

But just then Nathaniel himself came through the door, dropping his wet bag heavily on the rug. In a repeat of Lord Anthony's actions of a few minutes before, he took off his wet hat and shook the water out of his eyes. Francesca's relief turned to fear, for all that she was grateful he was alive and, apparently, well.

But neither of the men seemed to notice she was there.

"Tony," Nathaniel said, not sounding surprised, but remaining where he was.

"We have to talk, Nathaniel. I have only just discovered something."

Nathaniel nodded. "We do have to talk, for I have discovered something as well."

As he took a step forward, the door swung open again, hitting him in the back. Mr. Witt stood there and removed his wet hat. Francesca's first thought was that this scene looked like a music hall comedy, with two men ready to do battle with each other, and another, completely witless, coming onto the scene. But she was wrong about the two who would do battle, for Mr. Witt pulled a pistol from his jacket and raised it over Nathaniel's head.

"Here's the bloke I've been looking for," he crowed, but his moment of triumph cost him any advantage he might have had.

Nathaniel's arm shot up, and he knocked the gun out of Witt's hand. And right through the window. As shards of glass showered down upon them, he tussled him to the ground, shouting something about Mr. Graves. Lord Anthony cursed colorfully, in a manner quite unprecedented in their friendship, and jumped into the fray—literally, for he was on top of both of them in an instant. Francesca heard someone screaming, and then realized it was she. But her cries were enough to finally arouse Pip, who jumped on the pile of men and embedded his teeth in Lord Anthony's upper arm.

A gentleman walked in with the pistol, asking if it belonged to anyone about, and was kicked in the shin for his trouble. He dropped the weapon and ran back out into King Street, where an enthusiastic crowd had already gathered outside. They cheered when a large table was knocked over, strewing painted figures across the floorboards. They applauded when a vase somehow flew through the broken window.

As Francesca rushed to support a bookcase before it dumped its volumes on top of the men and dog, she yelled for someone to get the constabulary.

"Call off your dog," one of the men shouted in a strangled voice. Francesca got as close as she dared and tried to drag Pip off the tangle of arms and legs, when he repeated, "Call off your dog."

But it wasn't Lord Anthony, speaking of Pip. At once, she recognized the voice as Nathaniel's, and he seemed to be speaking of Mr. Witt. And, entirely without her help, he twisted out from under the heavier man and pulled him to his feet. He slammed him against a high chest, holding him by his neck, as if he had him in shackles. With his free hand, he gestured menacingly to Lord Anthony.

Francesca felt chilled as she recalled his quiet words of a few weeks before, when he challenged her to admit that she didn't think he could beat Lord Anthony in a fight. She thought he was teasing then. Now she knew he was deadly serious. She hadn't reckoned with such a capable protector, even when she hired him to safeguard the shop, for here was a part of him she scarcely recognized.

Nathaniel released Witt, who slipped to the floor, cursing abundantly.

"There's a lady present," Nathaniel growled.

"I doubt I have any remaining sensibilities left to be assaulted," Francesca said tersely and picked up the pistol.

She couldn't tell if Nathaniel grinned or grimaced, as blood streamed from his nose into his mouth. But then he turned to survey the scene still unfolding.

He whistled, a strange high-pitched sound, and Pip abruptly stopped his assault of Lord Anthony. What had this man and dog been doing in all these weeks when the shop was closed? Could they have been preparing for precisely this event? Pip barked once, but Francesca wasn't sure if it was to acknowledge Nathaniel's command or to let Lord Anthony know he wasn't quite through with him. In any case, he trotted amiably over to stand at Francesca's side, sniffing the pistol and perhaps disappointed that it wasn't a baked ham.

Lord Anthony rose slowly, gripping his torn sleeve, and then put his hands up in a sign of surrender.

"It wasn't me," he said weakly. "That's what I had to tell you."

"It bloody well is you," Nathaniel said in a strange voice, taking Lord Anthony's hands in his and dropping them to his sides. The surrender was self-evident, in any case. "You've been planning this all our life."

"It wasn't me, or, at least, I never intended for it to get this far," Lord Anthony said plaintively. "It was my mother."

Nathaniel stepped back and accidently landed on Mr. Witt's hand, which caused the man to renew his stock of expletives. But no one seemed to notice, or care.

"What are you saying?" Nathaniel said slowly, spitting out blood.

"She knew. She knew all the time. From the time we were boys, she constantly reminded me that you were going to take what was rightfully mine, and that any claim you might have was illegitimate. Each time we visited at Watch Hill, she spent the entire journey pushing me, denigrating you, suggesting all sorts of mischief, short of pushing you off a cliff."

"You came damned near close to that, as I recall," Nathaniel said and sat down heavily on a chair. Francesca handed him her handkerchief, which he looked at as if he never saw such a thing before. He put it into his breast pocket. "But I always suspected she had some interest in my father. Did she imagine he would be keen to marry a lady whose son killed his?"

Lord Anthony, astonishingly, smiled. "Your father had the good sense to avoid her like a mouse does a cat. I recall he spent most of his time locked away in his study, always working on the books for the estate."

"He was and is devoted to the estate," Nathaniel acceded.

"But did not want it in the way my mother did. She intended to prevent him from ever finding out the truth, if it were to be found, and believed if they married, she could keep him from it."

"She promised me money," Mr. Witt wailed, from his seat on the floor.

"Shut up," said Lord Anthony, and for some moments, there was silence. The crowd outside had dissipated, as there was nothing particularly entertaining about several bloodied people sitting about, and a young woman holding a pistol.

"I have found it, Tony," said Nathaniel quietly. "I have the papers. Christian Bell married Colette, and their legitimate son was brought back to England, along with the two automatons. Madame Cristobel, who very likely ought to be Monsieur Cristobel, did not reveal the truth; she only revealed where the truth was to be found. I shall have to thank her."

"It's too late for that," Francesca said. They were her first words since all this started. "She was destroyed, utterly destroyed. All your hard work is for nothing."

Witt coughed loudly. "I had a hand in that," he said proudly. "The old lady still owes me money."

"You'll have to take it up with her," Lord Anthony said, though he scarcely spared a glance for him. "That's how I knew the truth of my mother's involvement. She wanted me to get Francesca out of the shop, so Witt could make one last attempt to get what she wanted. I suppose I always knew but could not acknowledge it."

"Or stand up to her," Nathaniel said. It was the final, leveling blow. Lord Anthony's legs seemed to buckle, and he steadied himself on the window ledge.

"Did you send for me, miss?" A constable appeared at the door. He looked around at the scene of destruction and looked sorry that he had somehow missed the show.

"I believe this man," Francesca said and pointed to Mr. Witt, "has much to answer for, possibly including murder. Certainly willful destruction of property. But I believe I can handle the rest."

"Yes, it appears you can, miss," he said, and laughed. "It's not often one sees a lady ready to discharge a firearm."

Francesca looked down, having completely forgotten what she held, and how it came into her possession. "That is true, sir. But a lady cannot always rely on a gentleman to protect her."

****

Some hours later, after a glazier had replaced the shattered window, and the shop had—once again—been swept up of all painful memories, respectability seemed to be restored to FW Wadsworth, Bookseller and Antiquarian.

"Welcome home," Francesca said, as she replaced a bandage on Nathaniel's shoulder, where a sliver of glass from the shattered window had cut through his jacket and pierced his skin.

"Indeed, it does feel very comforting. I believe I should like to stay here, possibly with seasonal visits to Watch Hill," he said, taking the light tone from her. "You are wrong about one thing, though."

"I have been wrong about many things," she

reminded him. "Though Lord Anthony was not quite the complete villain, as you painted him. He really was my friend."

"Some friend," Nathaniel said under his breath. "But you are wrong to say that all my work on Madame Cristobel was in vain. We shall consider that she made a deathbed confession, telling me where to go to reclaim what is mine, and what shall be ours. What shall, some day, be our children's."

"But we have lost her."

"But in my search for her, I have found you. Do you think you can bear to be married to a cousin, however distant? Who would have imagined such joy when I showed up at your door all those weeks ago?"

"Is that all it was?" Francesca asked, and lightly pressed on the bandage, hoping it would remain secure. "It seems a lifetime ago."

Nathaniel pulled her close and kissed her. "No, my dear, the lifetime is yet to come."

Epilogue

On the October day Francesca Wadsworth took the name of her new husband, any lingering regrets she harbored for the absence of her closest family members were happily compensated by the absolute joy with which dear friends shared the celebration. Letters had been sent to all those who customarily would have been witnesses to the ceremony in the small church near the great Marble Arch, but only Nathaniel's father was able to attend, doubly happy for all that had transpired since he last saw his son. The Earl D'Arcques, too frail to travel, presented them with a wedding gift of a honeymoon journey, and the hope that they would conclude their travels at Watch Hill, where he anxiously waited to meet the bride and congratulate his new heir.

Mr. and Mrs. Picardy reminded anyone who would listen that they were somehow responsible for the brilliance of the match, hosted a sumptuous wedding breakfast, and invited everyone Francesca and Nathaniel knew, and a good many others besides.

"Your parents have been most kind and generous," Francesca said to Will, kissing him on the cheek. "And all for the fact that you are Nathaniel's best man."

Will looked over the crowd assembled in his parents' parlor and drawing room. "I rather think it is a gesture of gratitude, for giving me another reason to get out of the house and a place to go during the day. They may be the only parents in Mayfair delighted to have their son working in a shop."

"Are you very certain about this? You may find it very boring to remain among the books and clocks, now that the star attraction is gone," Francesca pointed out.

"It is true. All those gentlemen who would otherwise stop by just to catch a glimpse of you, are going to be horribly disappointed."

She swatted him playfully on his arm. "Flatterer! I meant Madame Cristobel."

"Ah, yes. The late Madame Cristobel, of course." Will sipped champagne and smiled. "But I will have Pip for company and might never give him back to Nathaniel when you return from your journey. He and I intend to become business partners, solving mysteries and apprehending criminals. We are very good at that."

"But not as good as I am," interrupted Nathaniel, raising his glass. "Nor my new wife. We may very well take on some cases ourselves, if we manage to have any leisure time."

Francesca met his eyes and smiled. "Yes, we shall be very busy."

Nathaniel said nothing for several moments, and she knew how perfectly they shared the same hopes and anticipation for their future together. This man, who was not even known to her six months ago, was now everything, everything she ever really wanted. He leaned over and kissed her again, renewing the promise they made only an hour before, in the presence of everyone now surrounding them.

"I'm glad everyone else is so happy," said Will, stepping into their circle. "I am the one suffering here. I have lost the best assistant I ever had. And as all these witnesses here will attest, I was the one who gave away the bride."

Francesca laughed as Nathaniel released her and turned in his arms. She felt embraced by these two men she loved, a dear friend and her cherished husband. For all they teased, this day was not to be reckoned by any losses, for they had gained so much.

Several hours later, Nathaniel helped his new wife into the carriage, for the first step in their journey to Trieste. As she spoke to Mrs. Belleron with last minute instructions and a somewhat teary farewell, Nathaniel helped the driver distribute the load of trunks and cases that would accompany them on their honeymoon. Even though Francesca had warned him, he was still surprised by the amount of baggage filled with his lady's necessities. How had he managed to travel all these years with a single carpetbag?

Mrs. Blanchard had something to do with this, no doubt.

Finally satisfied that the carriage would not tip over at the first turn in the road, he climbed into the carriage and offered his own farewell to Mrs. Belleron. As the carriage started to roll down the street, he and Francesca turned to face each other, alone for the first time on this very busy day.

"And what is this?" Francesca asked, gesturing to a small wooden chest he had placed on the facing seat. "I did not pack so much that we needed to bring our baggage within."

"That is true, but only just," he said, grinning. "But I thought she deserved to travel with us, as we are so indebted to her."

Francesca looked uncertain, and then nodded her understanding. "Of course. Madame Cristobel comes with us to Trieste."

"I have already corresponded with the curate of Christ's Bell Church, and he has agreed to lay her to rest in the churchyard with our ancestors," he said, tapping the box, as if to comfort the parts and pieces of the automaton within.

"Is that not sacrilege?" Francesca asked. "There are poor souls who could not lie in consecrated ground; how is it possible that a curate would allow a mechanical lady to be buried there?"

"Well, you, yourself, have occasionally reminded me to refer to the lady as 'she,' " he pointed out. "And besides, I have pledged to finance the rebuilding of the ancient church belfry, before the salty air of Trieste utterly destroys it."

"You have bribed a man of the church." Francesca sighed. "This does not seem like an auspicious beginning."

He took her hand and removed her silk glove. "Well, I didn't bribe the minister who married us this morning, and that would matter a good deal more. Besides, this is the best of beginnings, for we may put the past to rest before continuing the next chapter in our history."

"Madame Cristobel, having brought us together to deliver her long-hidden message, will finally return to her maker. I am certain that is not what is usually intended by that phrase, but it seems perfectly apt." She reached up to caress his cheek. "I shall miss her."

"As shall I. But she won't be forgotten," he said, putting one hand over hers and pulling her close with the other.

And with the wooden chest containing the remains of the automaton jostling along with them in the close quarters of the carriage, they began the next chapter.

A word about the author...

A writer for most of her life, Sharon Sobel is the author of sixteen published novels, short stories, and many essays. She earned a PhD in English and American Literature from Brandeis University and is currently a professor of English at the University of Connecticut and at Connecticut State College. She was Chapter Liaison and Secretary of the Board of Directors of Romance Writers of America, a founding member of its Connecticut and Lower New York chapter, and was twice president of The Beau Monde, the national chapter devoted to the interests of writers of the Regency period. A native New Yorker, Sharon also lived in Boston and The Hague before moving to an eighteenth-century farm in Connecticut with her husband and family.

Website: www.sharonsobelauthor.com

Thank you for purchasing
this publication of The Wild Rose Press, Inc.

For questions or more information
contact us at
info@thewildrosepress.com.

The Wild Rose Press, Inc.
www.thewildrosepress.com